Also by Doug Richardson

Lucky Dey Thrillers
Blood Money
99 Percent Kill
Reaper
The Night is Never Black
Hip Slick and Dead

Other Fiction
The Safety Expert
Dark Horse
True Believers

Nonfiction
The Smoking Gun: True Stories from Hollywood's Screenwriting Trenches

A LUCKY DEY THRILLER

DOUG RICHARDSON

AMERICAN BANG

los angeles

Velvet Elvis Entertainment
6038 Tampa Avenue
Suite 366
Tarzana, California 91356

Copyright © 2016 by Doug Richardson
Cover design by Karen Richardson
Cover photo: © [lunamarina] / Adobe Stock

More information at www.dougrichardson.com
ISBN: 978-0-9964563-9-5

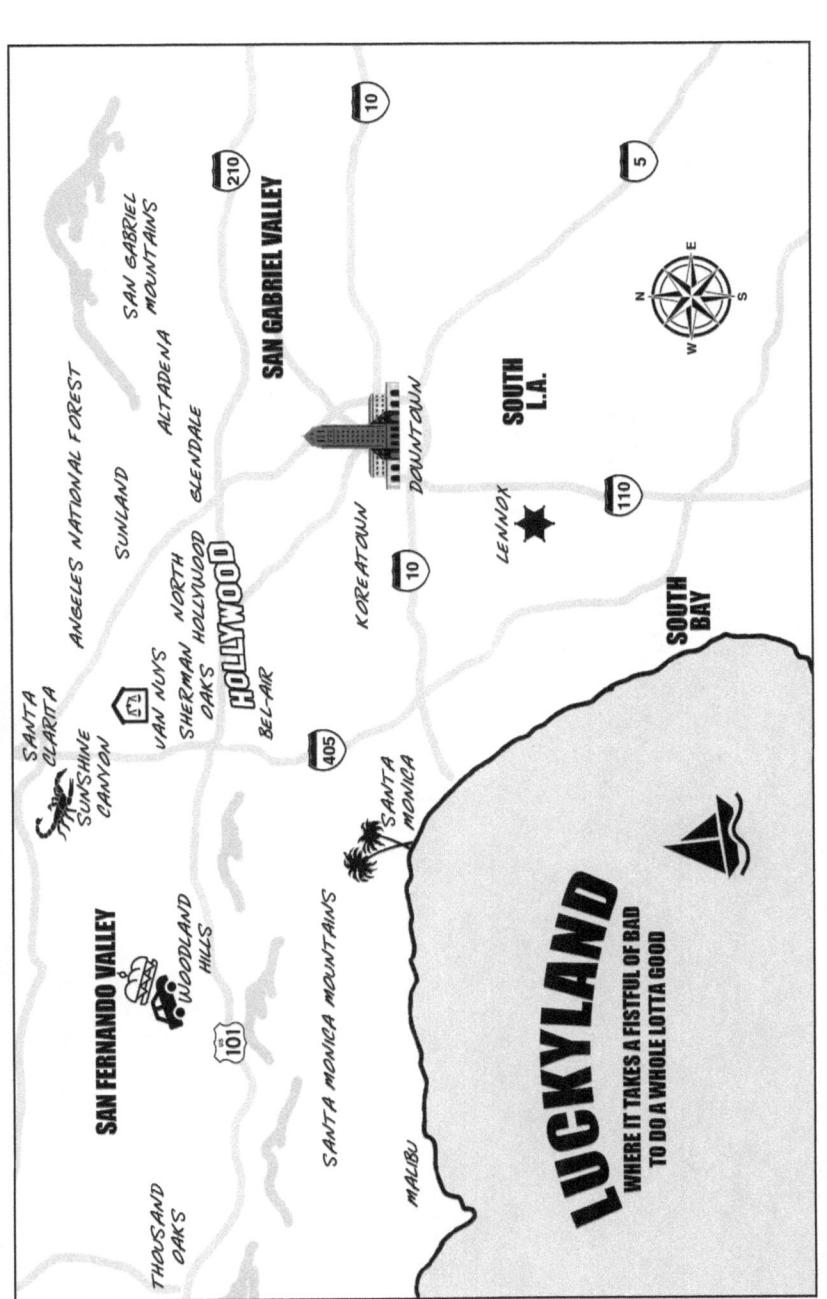

For my father
H. L. "Bill" Richardson

Thursday

1

Woodland Hills, California. 6:30 p.m.

Johnny B. was frustrated.

All he wanted was a Philly steak sandwich with no cheese and a Diet Coke with a slice of lemon to go. As orders went, he thought it was a no-brainer. Even in his stubborn mind, he couldn't imagine how the simple request had turned into a hang-up.

"Thirteen-inch Philly steak," Johnny B. repeated to the Asian woman behind the counter. *Korean Nazi*, the teen complained to himself. For him it was like hitting the reset button on one of his video games. He tried to sound polite, but understood that what felt polite coming out of his mouth sometimes didn't come off that way. "No cheese 'cause I don't like cheese. A large Diet Coke with a slice of lemon. And that's to go, puh-lease."

"I got all that," annoyed the sub shop's co-owner and manager. She was half Johnny Boy's size—barely a hundred pounds under her white shirt and apron. Her face was as wrinkled as a dried fruit. "But I say to you, 'No lemon for Diet Coke.'"

"But the man before—he got a lemon with his iced tea," argued Johnny B. without a tinker's clue concerning the line of diners queuing up behind him. The line was out the door of the tiny takeout shop that was little more than a counter and an old, yellowed backlit menu board hanging over a one-man kitchen.

"I say no lemon for Diet Coke," repeated the old woman.

"If I order iced tea do I get a lemon slice?" clarified Johnny B.

"You want ice tea now? You just say you want Diet Coke."

"I want Diet Coke. Just need a lemon to go with my Diet Coke."

"No lemon for Diet Coke." The old woman punched up the order on the cash register. "Twelve dollar, twenty-six."

"How about I order a small iced tea with a lemon slice? Plus the Diet Coke. Plus the Philly steak."

"You change your order now?"

"If it gets me a lemon slice."

The old woman stiffened, arms akimbo, her sagging skin jiggling where her biceps should've been. Her face was screwed into a churlish question mark.

"Why you like lemon with Diet Coke?" she persisted.

"I dunno," said Johnny B., too tense to shrug. "'Cause it tastes good?"

"Well, that's your mouth!" she accused.

"Philly steak," began Johnny B. again.

"There's a line, you know?" sounded a heavyset voice two customers behind Johnny B.

The eighteen-year-old heard the man, gauged the voice as someone much older, with some authority, and probably unafraid to get physical. Violent, even. Johnny B. hated being touched. Without his special cocktail of psych meds, he might scream out loud if anybody pressed into him for anything longer than a brushed back or an "excuse me" while in line at an amusement park like Six Flags Magic Mountain. But Johnny B. wouldn't— or couldn't—even half turn to acknowledge the impatient people behind him. If he did he might lose his place, or his patience, or his sketchy temper.

"Philly steak," repeated Johnny B., peeling off a twenty-dollar bill from his rubber-banded roll of bills. "Thirteen-inch. No cheese. Small iced tea with a lemon slice. Large Diet Coke."

"I no care no more," mumbled the old woman. She cleared the order, re-added the total, and handed the change to her blockish customer. "Takeout order wait over there, okay?"

"It's 'cause I'm Armenian," stated Johnny Boy. "I'm not stupid. Nobody likes the Armos."

"Next customer, please," ignored the old woman.

Johnny B.—a.k.a. Johnny Boy—or John Bartholomew Kasabian, as it read on his driver's license—sidestepped from the counter and stood uncomfortably against a round metal pillar, holding his receipt in both hands and focusing on his calm place. His face felt hot and flushed. Though that could've been from spending the day at Zuma Beach. He thought perhaps he'd stood out like a sore toe, not having thought to bring beachwear. In his black Wranglers and black T-shirt, Johnny B. was always comfortable. His redundancy in clothing was both his trademark and his armor. His mother called it his daily superhero outfit. On his feet were always a pair of Converse Chuck Taylors and his hair was a monthly Supercuts dark brown spaz of ethnic pride. With that, his stocky build and walk, and the freshly inked Armenian Power cross on his right forearm, anybody who knew Johnny B. could see him coming from a mile.

People know 'n' respect me 'cause I'm known and I'm a certified Armo badass.

From behind the cooktop swerved a Korean man, equally slight as his co-owner wife, only inches taller with a drawn face under a disposable paper chef's cap. He spoke in a foggy whisper while handing Johnny B. the to-go sack.

"Wife not happy since hysterectomy," croaked the old man. "Sorry about lemon slice. I give you extra inside bag."

Nodding an expression-free thanks, Johnny B. accepted the bag and both drink cups before dumping the iced tea into the garbage bin next to the side exit. He was hungry; his stomach had been grumbling since it had long ago digested his usual morning meal of a Starbucks frap and two apple fritters. Passing three more storefronts until he reached the street corner, Johnny B. stood at the stoplight and repeatedly rabbit-punched the crosswalk button. With every strike it beeped for nonexistent blind pedestrians. The Ventura Boulevard traffic washed past, the flow of cars and trucks hustling east and west in an ear-throbbing crush of Los Angeles white noise. For the moment, the ubiquitous sound drowned out his gastric bombast.

The sun had just dropped below the horizon, leaving the boulevard in shadow and the October sky with streaks of pink and vanilla. Opposite Johnny B. was the Walk/Don't Walk display. It appeared permanently stuck on its red-letter denial. On the side street across from the Chevron station waited Johnny B.'s ride, a black Ford Shelby Mustang so damned new it still bore the dealer's stickers.

And this badass can't wait to stink up the new leather with a hot Philly steak.

Johnny B. could smell the sub through both the foil wrap and the bag. His eating instincts—sometimes described by his two siblings as those of a starved coyote—invited him to chew right through the paper sack and sink his incisors into the hot sandwich. He was eighteen, though. A legal adult. With that he'd nearly learned to delay his gratification. While traffic hauled past and the Don't Walk sign continued its electronic indifference, Johnny B. chose to give himself a tease. Unrolling the top of the bag, he lowered his nose into the cavity and inhaled fully.

His nose curled in autonomic disgust.

Cheese!

"Korean bitch!" he screeched.

Without a thought or intent beyond his momentary expression, Johnny B. balled the sack between his meaty hands and sidearm-chucked his dinner. In that instant, he saw little more than red, yet seemed to feel the million slights he'd suffered since he could first remember. The sandwich was an afterthought. No more. And his mind would have instantly switched to some other flavor of fast-food satisfaction if it hadn't been for the piercing pitch of squealing tires and gnashing metal annoying his hyper-sensitive ears.

The Philly steak sandwich, balled into a projectile, had blindly sailed across three lanes of traffic before exploding in a red meat and mayo smear across the windshield of an eastbound Hyundai Accent. The startled driver, a cosmetician and part-time coed at nearby Pierce Community College, recoiled in shock. When she reflexively stomped on her brakes, her skidding car drifted left and into an oncoming Mercedes S-Class coupe. The heavier German car practically swallowed the Korean compact. Despite the imparting g-forces, the deployed airbags should have saved both drivers. Only the Hyundai's roof sheered and released like a horizontal guillotine. The sheet metal and carbon fiber Frisbee cut through the Mercedes's windshield and neatly decapitated the Malibu Barbie mom behind the wheel in an eyeblink.

Johnny B. had witnessed every slow-motion frame of it. And the shock of sound to his ears was closer to that of a grand piano dropped from ten stories than of two cars colliding in an ugly spray of metal and shattered safety glass. The smell, though—that puke-worthy cheese and meat mélange was replaced by burnt rubber and gasoline. It fouled his senses and nearly blinded the bulky teen.

With traffic stalled and both drivers and passengers in shock or counting their lucky stars or hopping from their cars to rubberneck or call 911, a scared Johnny B. took the opportunity to run across the street. His stride lacked the coordinated grace of most eighteen-year-olds. He edged between stalled cars and past the smoking rear of the wrecked Mercedes until he had a clear path to his hot black Mustang. There, he shut himself inside with a distinctive Detroit *thunk* and waited for the change in air pressure to equalize his nerves. The silence of the interior calmed him. The new car perfume soon replaced the odor of the street horror he would leave behind. Johnny B. push-buttoned the ignition, geared the Ford into drive, and slung the vehicle east and onto Ventura Boulevard. Miles ahead was Glendale and his bedroom in his parents' 1920s Spanish hacienda. The safety of home beckoned along with his PlayStation and turntable. But first, a fast-food drive-thru to temporarily distract his guilt as well as satisfy his gastronomic pangs. Perhaps an In-N-Out burger—double meat, animal style, and please-oh-please, no goddamn cheese.

2

From Lucky Dey's perspective, Los Angeles and thereabouts were suffering from an overpopulation of headshrinkers. He couldn't recall the last time he'd visited any form of an office tower of three stories or higher that didn't sport at least a dozen psychotherapists on the legend. The Los Angeles sheriff's deputy had turned it into a bad habit bordering on superstition or OCD. He'd enter the lobby of a random building and, even if he knew exactly which floor he was visiting, check the resident list and search for initialisms following a name. PhD, LCSW, CCMHC, MEd-LPC-CDVD. Most of the titles left him without a glimmer of whatever psychology degree they represented. A simple detective's deduction might conclude that there were too many post-graduate programs punching out too many degrees for too many couch-friendly analysts.

"You were saying?" cued Dr. Anna Sandalwood from her soft perch.

"Not sure I was saying anything," replied Lucky, wondering if he'd lost his place while staring out the eighth-floor window. The picture-frame pane revealed the final streaks of what had been a bluebird day. The late-October Santa Ana winds had blown hotter than usual—from across the desert—leaving cotton-ball clouds bearing little moisture hanging low, their fading shadows still dotting the San Gabriel Mountains in ever-moving spots.

"Think it was my turn," said Gonzo, sharing the corduroy couch with her live-in lover, common-law husband, and emotional codependent, Lucky Dey. The space between the pair wasn't nearly as wide as the gaping divide in their relationship.

"Okay," shifted Sandalwood, moving one of her leggy limbs underneath herself. It left one of her favorite heels empty on the floor.

The redheaded psychoanalyst, a former volleyball spiker from Cal State Fullerton, was every bit as tall as Gonzo. It made Lucky wonder why women tipping six feet felt the need to add even more stilt to their already towering frames. Had they been so used to intimidating boys that the fashionable four inches added by their designer footwear gave them an exponential advantage?

"I feel like we're static," revealed Gonzo. "Not moving forward or backward."

"Like you're stuck?" asked Sandalwood.

"I like progress," said Gonzo. "Something quantifiable beyond days or months."

"Commitment," clarified the doc.

"Not like he needs to put a ring on it," said Gonzo. "We're supposed to be a family. But it feels like we're all just really good roommates."

Family.

Lucky had a love/hate conflict with the word. He had no trouble using the word as a reference. He shared their Altadena

bungalow—the former rental they'd finally bit the bullet and purchased—with Gonzo, her fifteen-year-old son, Travis, and Lucky's
emancipated charge, seventeen-year-old Karrie Kaarlsen. But in his
stubborn mind, Lucky still saw the family as something ad hoc.
Made up. Did that make the family only something between temporary and for real? Or was it just Lucky holding Lucky back?

Lucky didn't dare offer that terrible tidbit in that, their third
couple's therapy session. He was still sussing out the therapist's
office trappings as if he were investigating something. To Dr. Sandalwood's right was a small built-in desk, on top of which was a
large computer running a screen-saver slideshow of pastoral photographs. To her left was a bookshelf unit stacked with books on
far-ranging subjects—from criminal sociology to climbing Mount
Everest. Haphazardly strung in and around the bookcase was an
electric garland of friendly ghosts and jack-o'-lanterns. It was a
reminder that Halloween was fast approaching, and also that Dr.
Sandalwood's practice wasn't for couples or adults only. Children
had played in that room, on that same couch. Traumatized. Troubled. And, like Lucky, itching to bolt for the door.

"Bought   the   house,"   deadpanned   Lucky.   "That's   a
commitment."

"And it was practically a deal-breaker," shot Gonzo. "Like you
and rehab. You did it only because I threatened to leave."

"Is that true?" asked Dr. Sandalwood.

"Probably," said Lucky.

"Lucky," pressed the therapist. "Do you need to be pushed in
order for you to feel something?"

"Excuse me?"

"Threatened," clarified Sandalwood. "Pressured. Do you require
ultimatums for you to reach down and find your emotional self?"

"I don't really know," said Lucky. "Not on the street or the
job."

"You know," said Sandalwood. "You're not the first police
officer who's been on that couch."

"She's a cop too," deflected Lucky. "We're a cop couple. You've
seen many of those?"

"No," Sandalwood replied. "You're my first. But where I was going had to do with something I've seen in other police officers. They're guarded. What's that stuff you wear to protect you from bullets? Bulletproof Teflon—"

"Kevlar," corrected Lucky.

"Kevlar," she repeated. "That's right. Cops are often covered in Kevlar. Not just on the job, but once they step across the threshold of their homes. Their families find it hard to get through to them."

Lucky gave a half exhale and faced Gonzo.

"Do you have trouble getting through to me?" asked Lucky.

"I want to go on a vacation," said Gonzo. "And two nights in Vegas isn't what I'm talking about."

"You said that was fun," reminded Lucky. "I remember you saying—"

"You. Me. Travis. Karrie," Gonzo counted off on her fingers. "The four of us. Far away. Anyplace we can't drive to in a day. A cabin. Anything. With no TV and cell phones. I want quiet and board games."

"*Bored* games," Lucky joked. "And Travis hates 'em."

"So do you," argued Gonzo. "And don't use Travis as your excuse. That's not cool at all."

"Travis thinks I'm plenty cool," segued Lucky.

Gonzo twisted away, arms crossed and shaking her head as if to punctuate her point.

"I believe what Lydia is saying—"

"She's Gonzo," corrected Lucky. "We all call her Gonzo."

Gonzo agreed with an annoyed nod. Having been called Gonzo by nearly everybody but the Department of Motor Vehicles since grade five, Lydia Maria Gonzalez, her birth name, might as well have been someone else's official moniker.

"What she's saying," continued Dr. Sandalwood, "is that she needs a connection. Your family needs to connect. All of you to each other. Board games. Hikes. Anything analog you all could do together—as family—might lend itself to repairing those bonds."

"And if the bonds are already okay-fine?" asked Lucky.

"They can always be made stronger," suggested the therapist.

"My daughter," Lucky switched before turning to Gonzo as if to prove something. "You see. I said *daughter*. Karrie. She's got a lawyer because she wants to legally take my last name. Does that count as a *bond*?"

If there were answers from the therapist or Gonzo they would have to wait until the following week. The leggy shrink had already slipped back into her empty pump and stood for the session-ending cross to her desk. Though it was only the third appointment, Lucky had already clocked some of the therapist's physical cues, the most obvious being her way of lowering a curtain on the appointment. Instead of the *de rigueur* "That's all the time we have for today" employed by so many psychologists, the ex-volleyballer would simply rise and pivot to her desktop, where she summoned an electronic calendar.

"Next week?" confirmed Sandalwood.

The cop couple walked in silence to the eighth-floor elevators, both with their emotional skin rubbed slightly raw.

"Where we going with this?" ventured Lucky.

"It's not supposed to be easy," shouldered Gonzo. "Just show up, okay? Go with it."

"Go where?"

"Wherever!" annoyed Gonzo. "It's a process."

"Feels more like a train headed over a cliff," deadpanned Lucky. He triple-tapped the down elevator button again.

"You wanna keep this going?" reminded Gonzo. "You and me? This is what it's gonna take."

"Forgive me if I don't get how peeling off each other's skin helps anybody but Dr. Ka-ching back there." The reference was to the shrink's hourly fee.

"Know what?" stalled Gonzo. "I'm not up for this shit. You keep the car. I'm gonna Uber back to the house."

"Suit yourself," shrugged Lucky, both trying and succeeding to appear as if he didn't give a rip—defensively indifferent to a fault.

No sooner had Gonzo turned her back and swerved toward the stairwell than the lift mechanism dinged a familiar signal.

"Elevator's here!" Lucky called out.

Gonzo's response was no more than the sound of the stairwell fire door automatically sealing shut with a secure *kuh-shunk*.

3

Little Armenia. 10:03 p.m.

"Don't trip over the bodies." The voice, coming from just inside the crime scene perimeter, had a penetrating strain. Male—a cop, most likely. Senior in stature. Uniformed and instructing. The de facto on-the-job authority. CSI Amy, as her social media friends called her, had a little chuckle to herself.

No shit, Sherlock.

Hours earlier, the bodies—seven in all—had been living, breathing human beings. Teenagers mostly, they had been attending a house party so large it had spilled out onto the street. The dead were evenly spread across the mostly concrete front yard. The two-story, mid-century stucco, pock-marked with fresh bullet holes, was flanked and spotlighted with gas-operated construction arrays on loan from the Department of Water and Power. The white-hot lights were so blistering that, to the naked eye, the blood appeared like rivers of coagulating crude oil. The slight pitch, designed to drain rainwater into the street, gutters, and storm drains, acted like an autopsy table, funneling fluids away from the corpses. The non-mortally injured, seventeen in total, had long since been ambulanced to three nearby hospitals. The blood they left behind mingled with that of the dead. Sections of the surrounding white-painted wrought iron were flecked pink with arterial spray.

This was East Hollywood. And CSI Amy Cho was an ardent fan of the zip code and its lurid history.

She referred to her interest as *Hollywood Fringe History*. From the wannabe starlets who'd shed their morality for a shot at immortality to the gumshoes who plied their trade for cash, investigating the dirty secrets of the natives who had piled up on every storied street corner. Since age twelve, Amy had read or watched everything about the topic she could glue her eyeballs to, the sleazier the better.

If only these streets could talk to me.

The thirty-year-old LAPD CSI thought of herself as a lucky girl who adored her job. But that love would elevate into pure goosebumps affection whenever an assignment landed her inside a rope of fluttering crime scene tape anywhere near Hollywood. East. West. Koreatown. Thai Town . . .

. . . Little Armenia.

For the Kenmore Avenue crime scene, the entire block had been shut down from Fountain to Lexington. LAPD units had the street corked at both ends. The murder scene's fronting asphalt was littered with brass. Shiny, ejected bullet casings appeared as if spilled by the bag-load. When Amy's criminalist supervisor was doling out the scene assignments, Amy had volunteered for the painstaking job of cataloging the discarded cartridges. This required first recording a digital series of photographs. Then assigning each discarded shell casing a designated number. Each number corresponded to a readable black digit on a five-inch-tall neon green cone. South to north, Amy placed a single cone next to every discharged cartridge, a count of 116 in total.

Arms wide, she stood a few feet back in her hooded white coveralls, rubber gloves, and shoe covers, every inch of it disposable. The paper suit concealed a willowy frame of five and a half feet, her goggles turning her already wide brown eyes into comical orbs. After admiring her work, the geometry of numbered cones appearing like a constellation atop the blacktop, the kid-in-the-candy-store side of her wanted to skip and slalom through the evidence field. Instead, she took a few admiring selfies before recording her work with her camera phone. Next she began the painstaking chore of bagging and cataloging each individual piece of brass. The activity—marking and signing a single evidence bag for every expelled cartridge—might normally have been dull, but protocol was protocol. And ever since the famed O. J. Simpson trial, the LAPD Crime Lab had tried to keep itself institutionally zealous in all its criminalists' record-keeping in the all-important chain of custody.

Amy, though, had a trick to keeping the grunt work interesting. Magic. Sleight of hand. The age-old art of prestidigitation honed from years of practice. While more popular high schoolers had been partying hard or studying for their college boards, once seventeen-year-old Amy was upstairs, above her parents' Koreatown bakery and grocery mart, she was gorging on pulpy Hollywood history and learning how to palm poker-sized playing cards with her impossibly petite hands. Amy had become so skilled with her close-up magic she'd recently auditioned and earned a card-carrying membership to Hollywood's famed private club for magicians, the Magic Castle.

Of the 116 expended cartridges, Amy had counted twenty-three 9mm, forty-seven 5.56 x 45—standard ammunition for an AR-15 semi-automatic rifle—thirty-five .45-caliber ACPs, and eleven .40-caliber. Most likely four weapons, she guessed, operated by four shooters in two passing cars. But that wasn't in Amy's job description. She wasn't a detective. She was a professional technician—a criminalist—and her vocation was to soldier the simple gathering and preservation of evidence.

Then why am I planting evidence?

Amy's heart purred, accelerating to 120 beats per minute. Inside her Microguard coveralls, she was sweating out every concealed pore. Yet on the outside, she was performing her magic act of replacing eight of the ubiquitous 9mm casings with nearly identical brass. It had taken some hardworking off-hours to rehearse and perfect the moves while wearing latex gloves. Baggie. New casing. Palm. Switch. Box. Repeat. So efficient and effortless was Amy that should there have been a video camera capturing her every maneuver, nobody could have caught her. The exchanged brass would be secretly stored while the planted casings remained locked up in the LAPD's evidence hold awaiting ballistics matches and the inevitable pairing to a weapon in the possession of a designated bad guy.

The performance was so flawless Amy felt it deserved a bow. Which was what she did once out of view of the stacked TV cameras, crews, and local news reporters looking to capitalize on the bloody scene for their respective live broadcasts. Once Amy had finished with her private moment of acclamation, she curtain-called herself back onto the crime scene in search of her next CSI chore. All the while, on the inside she was tingly, warm, and wet at the thought of how proud Miles would be. She couldn't wait for Miles to reward her for what a fine magician she was. Once back at her Koreatown apartment, she'd be counting the hours like sheep until he knocked.

The anticipation was palpable.

Friday

4

Downtown Los Angeles.

After the counseling session, Lucky couldn't stomach an immediate return home. Gonzo had been steaming mad when they'd parted. Following her home felt as if he were being lured into a conflict trap.

Though it was a school night, both teenagers were away for the evening due to a recently instituted citywide grading day, ostensibly a workday for teachers without the actual teaching of students. Added to that was Monday and Halloween. The sum of which made for a four-day weekend to be enjoyed by his pair of high schoolers.

Yeah, thought Lucky. *As if cops got a paid day off not to chase criminals.* From Lucky's perspective, teachers clearly belonged to a more influential union than cops. And for his kids, the weekend had started early. Thus, Gonzo's boy Travis was staying over at a friend's on a video-gamers' all-nighter, while Lucky's legally emancipated adoptee, the soon-to-be seventeen-year-old Karrie Dey, was in Lake Arrowhead on an overnight with her church group. Normally, that would have meant some much-needed private time for the common-law couple. Only Lucky feared that any privacy following the contentious conclusion of their therapy session would lead to more fighting. Only louder and for which Lucky had no worthwhile answers to Gonzo's arguments.

So, instead of turning his '99 Crown Vic toward the Altadena bungalow they shared, Lucky pointed the vehicle toward downtown and the Temple Street headquarters of the Los Angeles Sheriff's Department. Waiting for him there was his desk in the Major Crimes Bureau. It was a recent assignment following his tour of duty as a training officer at LASD's Compton Station. When Lucky wasn't digging through a seemingly bottomless pit of current investigations, he was playing catch-up on a pile of unsolved case files that might benefit from a fresh pair of eyeballs.

To save on after-hours electricity, the windowless office space, painted in the desolate shades of civil service and divvied up into cubicle slices, was only half illuminated by overhead fluorescents. Sharing the stale air and lousy light while listening to her own mix of vintage hip-hop was Detective Zadeh Raad. The always ponytailed pixie, imagining she'd have the office to herself, appeared genuinely startled when Lucky walked up from behind and asked her for help deciphering a pair of identical case codes on non-identical crimes.

"Jeezus," she'd exhaled before setting Lucky straight on the unit's constant coding errors—a temporary nexus between the department's switch from paper to digital. Neither deputy inquired as to the other's rationale for the off-the-clock shift work. Nor did Zadeh politely ask if the volume of the music pouring from her computer's external speakers bothered her cohabitant. She rightly reckoned that because she'd had the space to herself, it was her party to rock. Lucky figured the same, half enjoying the old-school tracks of nineties-era Dr. Dre, Wu-Tang Clan, and De La Soul. It sucked him back to high school and his bad boy days as a Santa Monica surf punk. Certain melodies or beats could even trip an olfactory memory to such a degree that he could smell the brine and mildew of his old wetsuit.

Three hours and two Red Bulls into his case file catch-ups, Lucky's phone buzzed with a text from his former sheriff's trainee Shia St. George. After some teasing exchanges, he eventually agreed to meet her for beer and chips at Casa Vega, an old-school Valley haunt that was as famous for its Cadillac margaritas as it was for being a favorite retreat of the late Marlon Brando. Myth held that the Mexican restaurant had contributed mightily to the great one's girth. It was difficult for some to wander into the joint without imagining Brando squeezed into one of the rear dining room booths alone, yet holding court with a lobster quesadilla, a pair of crab and shrimp enchiladas, flanked by plates of hot rice and frijoles.

Lucky discovered Shia at a small corner table in a bar so dark the twenty-six-year-old deputy and her half-consumed bottle of Corona practically blended into the shadows. The tea candle at the bottom of a red triple-shot glass barely lit a face Lucky had from the beginning thought far too arresting for police work. Shia's beauty was flat-out distracting. Flawless blue-black skin. Gleaming teeth and rosy lips spread beneath impossibly high cheekbones. The woman's face and body seemed sculpted for fashion photographers rather than for putting the boot to the neck of guttersnipe bad guys.

"So, this is your new hood, huh?" inquired Lucky in an awkward attempt at small talk. Chitchat was neither his forte nor conversational preference.

"Close to everything," replied Shia. "Especially the job."

"The job," Lucky repeated with a nod. "And how's that new duty treating you?"

"Department J is my bitch," she bragged with a broad smile. "Truth? I really got a sweet assignment. Great judge. She knows I'm interested in the law. She's already writing letters to law schools."

"I'd toast you, but I'm dry so far." Lucky mockingly held up an empty hand.

Shia waved toward the bar, then pushed her bottle across to Lucky.

"Share mine until you get yours?" she suggested.

When Lucky sipped on the beer he could both taste her lipstick and smell the soap she'd washed with. In the seven-plus months he'd been her training officer—five in the patrol car plus the nine weeks of paid vacation they'd both received pending a shoot investigation—he could count on one hand how many times he'd seen her out of uniform. Without the baggy green slacks and her ballistic vest, she appeared twenty pounds lighter, lithe and poured into black jeans and a T-shirt. And the hair she normally kept in tight cornrows was a gentle spray of soft kink.

"Working the court looks good on you," said Lucky.

"Like this is what I wear on the job."

"It's not the street."

"By that you mean Luckyland?"

He chuckled at that. She'd worked with him just long enough to see the street was where he thrived. In the gutter, he'd often said, was where the world made sense. There were no politics there and what was primal was all that mattered. Lucky had deemed it *Luckyland*, but gave credit to his deceased little brother.

"So, Major Crimes," she segued. "How you likin' that? Or, more importantly, is it likin' *you*?"

Lucky shrugged, explaining how the downtown position was taking some getting used to. As usual, his reputation as a Lennox Reaper had preceded him: the rumor and innuendo of the rule-bending, civil-rights-shaving, and effective but dubious street policing that forever followed deputies inked with a Reaper tattoo. But for one other Major Crimes detective who had spent time on patrol out of the Lynwood station, none of the unit had worked patrol anywhere in the bang-bang neighborhoods of hardcore South Los Angeles.

Two beers in, with the restaurant staff putting up chairs atop the dining room tables, Lucky kept steering the conversation back to Shia.

"Okay," she finally relented. "You really wanna talk about me?"

"That a problem?" he teased.

"Here's my problem," she leaned in, her lips inches from Lucky's crooked nose, eyes locked on his as if trying to read his pupillary response. "When I was your trainee, why'd you never try to get in my pants?"

The come-on line landed with unexpected force. Lucky's resting heart rate, something Gonzo had once remarked resembled something close to a medical flatline, accidentally skipped.

"Let me clarify," she almost embarrassedly grinned. "My less than clinical research has led me to pretty much know that practically every male training officer eventually gets down with his female trainee. Or at least gives it the ol' college try."

"And then there's me?" quizzed Lucky.

"You. Yeah."

"Had somethin' at home," Lucky explained. "You know that. Was tryin' to make it work . . . Still tryin'."

"Hard times on the home front?"

"Any other kind?"

"So, that's your answer? Home-lovin' Lucky was trying to stay the course?"

"Awful personal we're getting at something after what? Shit. One in the morning."

"And you're not home," Shia clarified. "You're here. With me."

"I'm not your training officer any more."

"That change things?" she half smiled.

"What about your roommate?" asked Lucky, referring to Shia's half-blind, disabled father.

"Gone boat fishin'. Alaska. Back tomorrow."

"Right. Okay. So . . ." he segued. "Who told you about this mythical training officer rite?"

"Asked around. My own private investigating."

"I think, though, the way it's supposed to work involves the

TO propositioning the trainee and the trainee wondering if what he's askin' is part of the training. Or is that just a man thing?"

"Like you said. You're not my TO no more. And maybe I got tired of waiting to be asked."

Lucky unconsciously rotated his beer bottle on the cocktail napkin coaster. Counterclockwise. As for Shia, she had a hard time reading if he was pondering her proposition. Or just pondering the way Lucky pondered. Lucky was hard that way. He didn't give much away. Ever.

"Guess I'm still tryin' to make the family thing work," suggested Lucky, not entirely convincing Shia, let alone himself.

"Family is one thing. Not like you're married."

"You know what I'm sayin'. And I may as well be."

"Like you're ever gonna put a ring on it," she said. Then her face slackened with sudden purpose. "Is it because I'm black?"

"Wow. You really just go there?"

"Ha. Shoulda seen your face," she grinned before abruptly changing the subject. "Hey. How's America's most kick-ass teenage girl?"

"Karrie? She's had, like, this late growth spurt. Tall as you now."

"Sixteen?"

"Seventeen in a coupla weeks."

"Ever figure out what she was gonna do with all that money?"

After seven months of the Sheriff's Department's tethering, there was little training officer or trainee didn't know or hadn't figured out about the other. Hard as Lucky was to read, when he did converse or offer up personal information, Shia could bank on it being the God's honest truth. Thusly she'd heard all about Karrie's tale as a runaway, losing both parents, and the millions of dollars left to her in a trust managed by Lucky's billionaire *consigliere*, Conrad Ellis.

"She doesn't wanna touch it," answered Lucky. "Like it's kryptonite. Don't blame her, really. Considering . . . After buying the car and the lifetime Muay Thai classes, she doesn't even wanna think about it."

"Wow," was all Shia could think to say. "Taking after you."

"She wants to legally change her last name."

"To yours? No shit. Gotta make you proud."

The sheepish smile was a new look on him. The warmth from Lucky's face was contagious. Shia's eyes lit up. And in that brief moment, instead of wanting Lucky in her bed, she realized she wanted *him*. Period. End of subject.

Damn, girl.

Shia had to catch herself. Her breath. Lucky was spoken for. And he wasn't biting on her blunt invitation. The conversation devolved into something akin to superficial recitations. Rehearsed answers. Informational trades. When the bartender announced last call, the former training officer and trainee instinctively decided to call it a night.

In Casa Vega's valet parking lot there remained only two vehicles. Lucky's '99 Crown Vic and Shia's pearl white Kia Optima.

"Oh, if your little Korean car could talk," joked Lucky, knowing that if evidence could somehow be culled from the compact sedan, neither he nor Shia would still have their badges.

"Still finding dog hair," she admitted. "And that's not just 'cause I took Mr. Hank off you."

A year earlier, Lucky had come into the possession of four big street mutts, each having been named by their previous master after famous African Americans. Lucky had adopted one, convinced Shia to adopt another, while the remaining two were still serving as Compton Station guard dogs.

"Speaking of that shit, how's that working out with your allergies?"

"It's a whole thing. Take meds every morning and thirty minutes before I walk through the door. Gonzo *Furminates* her every week and the house is still one big Oprah hairball. Ten'll getcha twenty she's in bed with her right now."

"Brings new meaning to the word 'rescue.'"

"Hey. About that," shifted Lucky. "I know you pulled some downtown chain to get me on Major Crimes. Suppose I owe you something more than thanks."

As if cued, Shia stepped up to him, cupped his stubble in her hands, and kissed him fully on the lips. Lucky neither resisted nor acted on the electric charge he felt to his bones. His arms wanted to wrap her up, carry her to his back seat, and finish things off like a hungry adolescent.

"That'll have to be thanks enough," completed Shia, before retreating toward her car with a last-word tease. "At least for now."

Hands in pockets, Lucky remained and watched until Shia was safely locked in her Optima. Her taillights disappeared down a section of Ventura Boulevard that appeared striped in traffic lights all switched to green. Gone until next time.

If there'd ever be a next time.

A sinking feeling came over him—a pulling suction not unlike an ocean undertow. The first time he'd felt it he'd passed it off as grief for his departed younger brother. How long had it been? Three years? More? Despite the passage of time, the undertow had remained. Just beneath. Ready to drag him down. A battle that had begun with his slide back into Los Angeles when he'd chased killer Greg Beem all the way from his cushy Kern County detective's gig back into the heart of darkness. Ever since, Lucky felt as if he'd been a loose pinball pinging in a washing machine. Sure, along the way he'd done some decent deeds. And good things had come to him. Gonzo. Travis. Karrie. Yet there'd also been too much action and too many dead bodies—both in *and* out of Los Angeles Sheriff's policy. The gunfights alone, righteous or otherwise, should have been enough to flag his file and assign him to ride a desk until retirement beckoned. Were it not for Shia and that backdoor leg up into Major Crimes, odds were Lucky would've already been out the door, sheriff's career in his rearview mirror.

Was he good at his job? Sure. Valued? Perhaps. But in a world of body cameras and cell phone video feeding a twenty-four-hour news cycle, cops like Lucky Dey, who had a knack for the darker shades of police work, were fast becoming too great a liability to carry.

Conclusion? Change, quit, or die.

Exhausted, but without muster enough to drive home to Altadena and risk Gonzo smelling another woman on him, Lucky sought a quiet spot to park and sleep with little risk of disturbance. He climbed into his '99, recently upgraded from primer gray to a low-budget black paint job, and pointed it up Coldwater Canyon. Two and a half miles up the hill, he pulled into the entrance to Coldwater Canyon's TreePeople Park. The forty-five-acre hilltop expanse of mostly parking lot and hiking trails was a favorite place for Valley urbanites to catch some outdoor exercise and for paparazzi hoping to photograph makeup-free celebrities walking their dogs or being exercised themselves by personal trainers.

The park's yellow swing gate, open only during daylight hours, utilized a heavy chain and a padlock easily beat with paper clips and a multi-tool. Lucky made sure to re-secure the gate behind him before settling into a space with his headlights aimed north. Below, the entire San Fernando Valley twinkled like a carpet of wall-to-wall Christmas lights. He rummaged through his glove box and found a sheet of paper with a wrinkled, pre-scrawled note. He spit-glued it to a window:

DO NOT DISTURB
POLICE OFFICER ON THE JOB
VIOLATORS MAY BE SHOT

From the back seat, Lucky grabbed a pair of folding screens meant to cool and protect the car's interior, fixed them to cover both the front windshield and driver's and front passenger's windows, and stretched what he could of himself across the bench seat, bunching up a musty sweatshirt for a pillow. The position practically guaranteed future spasms from his surgically repaired back. The best he could hope for was that the beers he'd consumed would turn to ethanol in his bloodstream and offer some natural muscle relaxant. He craved a pain pill, then bit on his tongue for slipping on his fifteen months of twelve-step work with those two cold *cervezas*. Lucky could only hope when he closed his eyes that sleep would overcome his conflict between lust for Shia and guilt for considering cheating on Gonzo, who, for all her conflict and complaints about Lucky, was lovely and loyal to a fault.

You're such an asshole, Lucky.

Despite the mental self-flogging, sleep overtook Lucky in seconds. He was unconscious and bothering nobody whatsoever with
his ground-shaking snores, blissfully unaware that from downtown
to Casa Vega to where he'd parked for slumber, he'd been carefully
followed.

From a distance of two hundred yards, Lucky's parked '99 was
quietly stalked through a pair of Armasight binoculars. The night
vision lenses gathered the faintest ambient light and magnified
the live picture into a green, high-definition image wherever the
wearer pointed them. The zoom function allowed the observer a
chance to watch Lucky lock his car doors and block out his windows in preparation for his short night's sleep. Each action and
the time it occurred was recorded in a voice-to-text memo on a
smartphone. The stalk was so acute and detailed that a recording had been made of the precise moment Lucky and Gonzo had
left their Altadena house to the very last entry marking the early
a.m. hour and minute the windows of the parked Crown Vic had
begun to fog from Lucky's snores. Once encrypted and transcribed
into a digital file, it was safely emailed via a local cellular network
with a trademarked *whoosh*. With that, the shadow-job had
concluded for the night. The assigned stalker returned to the nondescript rental vehicle left at the park's gate, turned over the electric
engine, and silently disappeared into the night.

5

Studio City.

Lucky woke to the annoyance of his phone vibrating. First thinking it had slipped under his ribcage, he reached to find the grip of his .45 before rolling left and discovering the rapid pulsations were coming from his left breast shirt pocket. With his eyesight still somewhat blurred, he ignored the name on the screen and answered.

"Yeah," answered the sheriff's detective.

"Lucky," said Gonzo over the phone, flat and clean. "I need you to very calmly wake up."

"Gonz?"

"Open your eyes," said Gonzo. "It's after eight a.m. already."

"I'm okay," he reflexively replied. As consciousness returned, he was remembering the night before in all its guilty color. He squinted at what pieces of day streaked past the over-sized sunshade.

"Listen to me, Luck," pressed Gonzo. "I need you to put your gun on the deck."

"What about my gun?"

"I need you to be calm right now," she practically pleaded. "Cool and cogent and doing everything I say."

"Jesus, Gonzo," annoyed Lucky. "So what if I didn't come home last night? You don't gotta be so spooked."

"I'm perfectly calm. Are you calm?"

"I'm barely awake," he said. "How much calmer can I be than that?"

"Do you know where you are?"

"Same place I was when I turned off the lights."

"You're at TreePeople," said Gonzo. "Top of Coldwater. You put up that big sunscreen Karrie and Trav bought you with a note that said—"

"Says 'Violators will be shot.' Yeah, I know. I wrote it. Did you follow me?"

"I'm at five hundred feet and circling," said Gonzo.

It was as if his ear canals had only just drained. He heard the staccato thumping of helicopter rotors outside. His common-law wife slash LAPD chopper pilot was above and churning in tight circles. Lucky pried back the shade. The morning light scorched his pupils. In the five seconds it took for them to adjust he was able to catch the tail numbers of Gonzo's whirlybird arcing clockwise against a baby blue sky.

"Jesus," pissed Lucky. "Why the fuck are you stalking me?"

"Stalking you?" angered Gonzo. "I'm trying to keep your ass from getting killed right now. Please tell me your weapon is on the deck!"

The unconscious calculations, momentarily backed up like a sewer line, suddenly came unglued. The helicopter. The location where he'd parked. The blacked-out windows . . .

"LAPD?" he asked.

"Some early morning hikers saw your car and your stupid-ass note, got spooked, and called nine-one-one."

Peeling away two inches of the screen on the driver's side window, Lucky was able to glimpse only the edge of a brigade of LAPD black-and-whites that—once he peeked in the rearview mirror—were parked bumpers to grilles in a cordoned semicircle. Patrol officers in their blue-black uniforms were cocked and locked with pistols and shotguns trained at his '99 Crown Vic.

"You'd think somebody coulda knocked," griped Lucky into his phone.

"With a warning like that on your windshield?" Gonzo was no longer calm. "Lucky. I've talked to you about that!"

"I'm obviously a lousy listener," he deadpanned.

"Are you listening now?"

"Tell me how to play and I will."

"PD knows I'm on the phone with you. So, just pull down the screen, slowly crack the driver's door, and show your hands."

"How about you tell 'em all that you know me and I live with you and to just fuck off and go?"

"Didn't you just tell me you'd play it my way?"

"Yes, dear," Lucky sarcastically droned. "Hanging up now. And popping my door."

As advised, Lucky pushed a shoulder into his driver's door just enough to crack it six inches. He showed one empty hand and, in the other, his six-point Los Angeles Sheriff's badge.

"Hands in place," sounded a voice over a loudspeaker. "Slowly step from the vehicle."

Lucky counted eight radio cars and eleven LAPD uniforms. After carefully exhuming himself from the newly painted car, he kept his hands and arms wide while facing the sky, just in case Gonzo could read the smirk on his face. With only one more half arc to fly, the chopper swiveled south and vanished over the ridgeline.

"Trespassing. Loitering," spoke the approaching sergeant, re-holstering his pistol. The bulky cop sported a full head of salt-and-pepper hair sculpted into a throwback flattop.

"Gate was open when I parked," fibbed Lucky. "We know each other?"

"I think maybe," answered the sergeant with a cryptic drip. "You Lennox boys mighta dropped a carload of Nutty Bloc Crips in Grammercy Park. Blood hood."

"Seventy-Seventh Street Division? That was you guys?" grinned Lucky.

"Wasn't so funny back then," the sergeant said coldly. "But some of us ol' hands mighta had a few laughs 'bout it since."

"Need me to apologize for causing this ruckus here?"

"Shit, you kiddin' me?" guffawed the sergeant. "Prolly made their day drawing bead on a sheriff's."

Lucky's phone buzzed in his pocket.

"I'll leave you to get that," said the sergeant. "Maybe it's your sky wife makin' sure you're not shot fulla holes."

"Thanks," said Lucky without a lot of verve.

"And no more trespassing in my park!" called back the sergeant. "Bust in here again, you might not like what you get."

As the LAPD throng retreated, Lucky answered his phone.

"This is Lucky," he stated, his eyes turning back to the view of the Valley.

"Please hold for Assistant Sheriff Paul McGill," said the secretary.

The feeling of heat prickled the back of Lucky's neck. Calls from the top floor were never good.

Ever.

6

Glendale. 8:31 a.m.

Johnny Boy had seen neither his bedroom nor an ounce of sleep in nearly two days. After his beach visit followed by the tragic Philly steak sandwich fail at the Woodland Hills sub shop, Johnny B. had slipped eastbound onto the Ventura Freeway and patiently put up with the bumper-to-bumper traffic until he had safely pulled off in the City of Glendale. He parked in his usual spot in the side motor court of his parents' salmon-pink stucco turn-of-the-century Spanish manor. Only instead of checking in through the front or kitchen doors, Johnny B. detoured around the side of the house along the gated gravel path usually reserved for the pool man and gardeners. He followed the steps down to one of the old changing rooms he'd converted into his private discotheque. There was no dance floor or even enough space should anybody ever want to cut loose. He'd superglued acoustic ceiling tiles over the tiled walls to dampen the reverb. Inside the shower stall he'd erected an all-in-one DJ setup replete with dual turntables and a computerized lighting array. There were two padded stools, a computer screen for online game play, and a compact refrigerator stocked with Dad's Root Beer, Mountain Dew, and packaged hard-boiled eggs.

Despite Johnny B.'s feeling that the world in general was far too loud, bright, busy, and chaotic for him, when he could control his environs with ear-busting beats and tune the lights to fit the flashing in his brain, a strange calm would ensue. It wasn't merely a form of molecular relaxation that developed within his overactive amygdala. The bass-heavy music was also guaranteed to numb his many fractured emotions.

All that night and into the dawn, Johnny B. had rocked his underground house. When at last his ears began to ache, he shut off the noise and lights and lay down on the cooling tile holding cold cans of soda against the sides of his head. There, in the nearly pitch black, he closed his eyes, hoping the images of those crashing cars had been erased.

Shit, shit, shit!

The moving pictures remained—the swerving Hyundai impacting with the Mercedes coupe—the blast of metal, plastic, and shards of safety glass. Only the sounds weren't there. It was as if Johnny B. had succeeded in only erasing the audio track of his bad sandwich-induced pileup.

He heard voices outside. Familiar. Arguing. His mother, Tabitha, and his father, Vartan. The duo sounded roughly halfway between the sliding French doors of the family room and the eleven curving steps down to his rave cave. He pictured them standing only feet from the pool's edge and wondered if one of them would get heated enough to shove the other into the salt-treated water. His mother, bleached-blonde, sturdy, and Armenian tanned, would have her hands on her hips, elbows bent, defiant in jeans and a silver spangled T-shirt. Johnny B.'s balding dad, affectionately called Vaz by nearly everybody but his three children, would tower nearly a foot above her, his dress shirt unbuttoned down to a proud sprout of ethnic chest hair decorated with a one-inch jewel-encrusted gold cross pendant.

And the argument seemed always the same.

Johnny B. needs to grow up, learn to be a man.

He isn't like normal boys. He needs our help.

How much more help can we possibly give him? More therapy? More meds? More residential treatment? He costs more money than twenty young men his age.

Johnny B. is our son. He has a mental illness.

As the closet DJ focused his ears onto what seemed like the gazillionth marital clash about him, he was hard-pressed to disagree with any of it. After years of eavesdropping, he'd come to understand both sides of the parental pingpong match. Johnny B. saw himself as the net stretched across the table, with a perfect view and recognition of both opponents. All the same, as hard as his mom and dad tried to wrap their heads around the Johnny B. problem, they never quite grasped what was at the center of the teen's being.

Hopelessness.

The self-loathing Johnny B. felt was marrow deep and malignant. Through his lens he would never be normal nor a real man in the truly cultural sense—at least not in his father's Armenian eyes. Johnny B. wasn't smart enough. He wasn't athletic enough. He wasn't tough enough. He would never be accepted into the family's *real* business.

In an atmospheric rush, the changing room door swung open. The white light of day flooded over Johnny B., still flat on his back on the tile floor, staring straight upward, his ears flanked by that pair of aluminum soda cans.

"Get up," demanded Vaz, sounding remarkably gentle despite the force of his words.

"I'm too tired," replied Johnny B. in a flat monotone.

"We work today," insisted Vaz. "And the sweat will help you sleep."

"But I'm not a good worker," continued Johnny B. "You already said that."

"That wasn't a good day for either of us. Let's try again. New day. New job."

"What kind of job?" The teen knew himself well enough to know he'd almost always rise to an interesting carrot dangling from a stick.

"We'll figure it out when we get there."

"I don't like the smell of hot asphalt," Johnny B. argued, with good reason. He was especially sensitive to certain odors. They could trigger him with excitement—or repel—not unlike the melted cheddar that forced his better self into chucking his uneaten cheesesteak into surging traffic.

"We'll figure it out when we get there," repeated Vaz. "C'mon. Breakfast first. Your mother made *choreg* and *bishi*."

"I need coffee."

"Sure about that?" asked the father. "How does the caffeine interact with your meds?"

"I drink Coke. Mountain Dew. They got caffeine."

"Right, right."

The father offered a hand to the son. Which Johnny B. accepted, rising to his feet. Vaz wrapped both arms around his son, more bearish than warm. Yet it was a hug all the same. And despite his father not having a glimmer about the anger-induced car accident, in that morning moment Johnny B. felt nearly forgiven. Loved. A comfortable and worry-free interlude bracketed by a life filled mostly with fear and anxiety.

7

Woodland Hills. 10:01 a.m.

Lucky sat on the bus bench. Alone. His eyes were level and scanning left and right and back again along the parallel striations of Ventura Boulevard. He read the traffic, calculating the average speed of east- and west-moving cars depending on whether the Topanga Canyon Boulevard stoplight was signaling red or green. Scattered across the asphalt before him were the remnants of the deadly accident the day before. Small half-dollar to nickel-sized bits of safety glass, plastic, and some sheet metal shards littered the scene while the nonstop parade of vehicles rolled past, indifferent to the destruction and death that had occurred less than twenty hours before.

According to the photocopies of the accident reports from LAPD and LAFD that Major Crimes had forwarded to his smartphone, the Barbie doll–looking driver of the Mercedes had been decapitated when the Hyundai's roof came loose and axed through her car's windshield. Within hours, the bereaved husband and habitual political donor had reached out to his Saturday golfing buddy, LASD Assistant Sheriff Paul McGill.

"I know it's LAPD jurisdiction," Paul McGill had said in his phone call to Lucky, "but I'd look upon it as a personal favor if you worked a parallel track on this. Did your own detective work. Even maybe get a bit out ahead of the official investigation. Just to make sure of the due diligence."

Strangely, Lucky and McGill had never met in person. Their paths had crossed via internal investigations. It was well known to McGill that Lucky was a former Lennox Reaper. And Lucky had suspected that his move out of Compton to Major Crimes was most likely due to the unlikely and tragic nexus of the Assistant Sheriff's friendship with movie director Atom Blum and Lucky's former trainee, Shia St. George. A few curious questions on Lucky's part might have easily clarified the suspected connections. But that was politics. And in Luckyland, politics was for those who wanted to play.

And Lucky didn't play politics.

The reports stated that an accident had occurred on Ventura Boulevard, two blocks east of Topanga, on Thursday at approximately 6:43 p.m. After the fire department had cut her out of her crumpled compact, the surviving driver of the Hyundai had given her statement at 9:13 p.m. from an emergency room bed at the Kaiser Permanente Medical Center. The Pierce College student claimed that while driving eastbound at roughly forty miles per hour, a large bird had fallen out of the sky and splattered across her windshield. The impact had startled her. She had braked hard and lost control of her vehicle, skidding left into oncoming traffic and striking the westbound Mercedes S-Class.

Witnesses willing to wait around to give their own accounts added little to the student's statement. Because a death was involved, LAPD was required to perform a follow-up investigation. Due to the lack of priority, it could take a week or more before a detective was assigned to research, assess, and write the final report. And whoever the unlucky cuss was to receive that prime assignment would probably crib half or more of his or her notes from the dueling insurance narratives.

With no such assistance, Lucky was expected to deliver his assessment of cause and a conclusion in a matter of a day or so.

A bird, huh?

Lucky spun the odds. A shocking bird strike against a front windshield? Or perhaps the college student behind the wheel was texting while driving and didn't want to eat the blame? Lucky lived in a house with two teenagers. Their cell phones were like limbs with digital nerve endings. Severing teens from their phones and the social connection that came with the devices could be harder than threading a needle would be for a Parkinson's sufferer.

Or find the bird, asshole, and you're done.

A carcass would have made things easy, only most dead animals that weren't disposed of by first responders were usually snatched up by scavengers. In the span between midnight and dawn, coyotes would emerge from the nearby hills in search of house cats, small dogs, and the previous day's roadkill.

Feathers, thought Lucky. If it indeed was a bird strike that had caused the Hyundai driver to swerve, there'd be evidence in the gutters. Lucky walked both sides of the street, a full two hundred yards east and west of the accident scene, and discovered no quill or downy speck of bird fuzz. To totally discount the theory, he'd next need to visit the impound yard and examine the wrecked Hyundai's windshield for bird blood and maybe pieces of trapped feathers. But first, he'd need to visit every nearby establishment with a security camera. He'd already clocked them all. So, beginning with a frozen yogurt shop and finishing with the corner Jiffy Lube, Lucky flashed his sheriff's badge to seventeen different retailers and sidewalk establishments. Eleven businesses had operational security systems versus those using dummy cameras as deterrents. Eight had salvageable recordings while only five had lenses that captured all or part of the actual accident.

It was the recently updated security system at Livingston

Liquors that provided Lucky recorded proof of exactly what had triggered the wreck. The wide-angle digital camera, positioned on the roof to record any robbery suspect's escape onto Ventura Boulevard, revealed what appeared to be a male figure exiting the sandwich shop across the street. While the figure waited for the Walk/Don't Walk sign to give him the go, he inexplicably hurled an object into the passing traffic. The Hyundai could be seen braking, swerving left, and smashing headlong into the black Mercedes S. By Lucky's simple calculations, the combined g-forces of both cars were equal to a car striking a concrete wall at roughly ninety miles per hour.

Lucky boomeranged back to the corner Jiffy Lube to review the security images from its east-facing camera. Rewinding to the minute following the traffic accident, he was able to find digital captures of the suspect hurrying into a black Shelby Mustang. The car bore no visible tags. Instead, there was the dealer's promotional placard—a rolling advertisement stuck to the car until the owner received a permanent license plate. Though somewhat blurry, Lucky had little problem identifying the seller: Star Ford and Lincoln in Glendale.

Without a warrant or jurisdiction Lucky was unable to physically secure the hard drives with the security footage. But with permission, he was able to record it on his smartphone. Screen to screen. Irrefutable visual evidence. All Lucky required to complete his errand was to call the dealer to identify the suspect, hand off his findings to the LAPD and, more importantly, Assistant Sheriff Paul McGill, then return to his overstuffed desk in the Major Crimes Bureau.

Easy, peasy, lemon squeezy, Lucky singsonged. If only keeping Gonzo happy were as easy to accomplish.

8

Van Nuys Superior Court. East Building. 1:49 p.m.

Lee Chapman loathed metal detectors. The onetime TSA Cargo Specialist thought the technology was outdated and cumbersome as hell to manage. More importantly, the devices created long queues wherever employed. And damned if Lee didn't hate standing in line even more than operating the machinery. That, and as archaic as metal detectors were as a security precaution, the instruments prohibited the fifty-nine-year-old from concealing his comfort items: one five-inch KA-BAR spring-operated folding knife, a Smith and Wesson tactical pen, and a black chrome retractable baton. He'd come to love the latter piece during his short tenure toiling as a security guard for nearby Lockheed Martin.

If only the Superior Court hadn't become his daily habit, he wouldn't have had to leave his comfort items in the trunk of his silver and sun-damaged Honda Accord—a.k.a. *the shitmobile*—otherwise known to Lee as the last remnant of his no-good, horrible, awful, goddamned, motherfucking marriage. While sweating in the line with thirty-odd others waiting to enter the eleven-story monolith, Lee's mind rewound through nearly four months of memory tapes, back to the first day of his latest bright idea: to write a courtroom thriller about a custody case gone horribly wrong. Using his tragic life experience, his screenplay would reek of authenticity. He would research his story by attending open court sessions. Learn the legal lingo. Base his characters on real-life lawyers and judges and plaintiffs and defendants. He'd research during the day. Sling words all night. Catch a few winks and be back again.

But in those sixteen weeks, Lee had yet to scribble a single word beyond the chicken scratches in the red-spiral notebook that accompanied him on his daily sojourn into the justice system.

"Mr. Red Book," grinned Delano Flores, one of the five regular security deputies operating the upright metal detector, paddle wand, and X-ray machine. "How goes the movie script? You gonna make me a star in it?"

"It goes," was all Lee could usually muster as he deposited his car keys, loose change, money clip, spiral notebook, and mechanical pencil in a plastic tray. Though he didn't care to be called Mr. Red Book by the all-deputy security crew, it was sure as hell better than Parrot or Parrot Face, the name he'd suffered through much of primary and secondary school. It was also not as dismissive as Mr. Tweedy, the moniker ascribed to him by a certain judge because of Lee's near daily uniform of a brown tweed jacket and porkpie hat. He knew the outfit screamed *old wannabe hipster* more than *I'm a screenwriter*. Yet clothes had always made Lee feel more official. Not unlike the togs he'd been required to adorn himself in for the TSA, or as a security guard, or the short but unhappy stint he'd worked in the electronics department at Target—all of them a far cry from his early years as an electrical engineering recruit at Pasadena's Jet Propulsion Laboratory, a.k.a. NASA/JPL.

Oh, how far the once mighty have fallen.

Instead of lamenting over his almost thirty-year plummet into the sewer, Lee worked at relishing his slippery descent as a life adventure. *And why the hell not?* People living on the down-low were a damned sight more compelling. If he'd remained married with his feet glued in the world of rocket science, he might never have met the likes of Lucinda or Adelina or Gennifer, his three favorite sirens of Sepulveda Boulevard, the prime prostitution corridor of the Valley. They may not have been actual muses, but they were damned good company at the discounted price they offered regulars. One hundred and fifty bucks for an hour of carnal exercise.

Having passed through the Superior Court building's security gauntlet for the umpteenth time, it was a short ride to the seventh floor and Department J, Lee's most desired courtroom. When he'd begun his daily visits, he'd hopped from department to department—both east and west towers—thirty-six courtrooms in all. Though his scheme to script some thrilling *roman à clef* would have best lent itself to observing the process of civil cases, Lee found himself more intrigued by the criminal trials and narrowed his courtroom hopping to the East Tower. Then one August day, he landed in the back row of Department J. Lording over what appeared like a societal assembly line of innocent-until-proven-guilty gangbangers—brown, black, and Armenian-white—Judge Serena Sollocito would serve up her unique style of justice from behind a rosewood bench underneath a wood-carved seal of the great State of California. Short and mousy with a crop of unrestrained black curls, Judge Sollo, as she was called by her staff and the other courthouse regulars, was rarely without a smile for anybody and all, despite the discomfort of their circumstances. She expressed a little extra adoration for the courtroom observer she'd come to think of as her biggest fan.

Lee Alexander Chapman.

"Good morning, Mr. Chapman," Judge Sollo began from the bench before addressing the assemblage of attorneys prepared for a half hour of afternoon motions she'd usually set aside before carrying on with whatever trial was before her. "How we doing so far today?"

"So far so good," smiled Lee from his usual seat, on the right and to the rear.

"And your movie screenplay?" A self-styled cinephile, there was hardly a day the judge didn't ask about, make mention of, or use some motion picture as an example. Judge Sollo loved the movies, especially those of the wildly entertaining popcorn variety.

"Comin' along," Lee lied every day.

"Good to hear," said the judge before motioning to both her clerk and the court reporter. "We are back on the record. Who has the first motion?"

Lee let his eyes drift left to the slender deputy partially perched on a stool, set against the wall only feet from the jury box. While Judge Sollo imagined the wannabe screenwriter was a constant attendee because of her, Lee knew to his loins that Deputy Shia St. George was the true lure of Department J. From the moment he'd first noticed her crossing from the sally port—the courtroom side door leading to the holding cells—to the clerk's desk, Lee was transfixed. In his eyes, Deputy St. George seemed to float, striding with such feminine grace it defied her desexualized sheriff's uniform of forest green slacks and starched khaki shirt.

It's in your face, Lee would say to himself as if telepathically whispering to the deputy.

Attention-wise, the deputy appeared to pay little mind to Lee. Rarely catching him abjectly staring, she mostly regarded his perceived level of threat to the proceedings. Because he relegated himself to that one back row, right corner seat, Lee had practically turned himself into little more than furniture in the eyes of the bailiff. This was preferable to Lee. The last thing he wanted was to be perceived as a stalker. Therefore he confined his obsession with the beautiful sheriff's deputy—dubbed only as his Obsidian Goddess in the pages of his spiral notebook—to Room 703 and Department J.

To this end, my secret affection remains safe, secure, and all mine.
Never mind the Google searches or the online private eye he'd

dropped 295 PayPal dollars on in exchange for all the information that could be gathered on Shia. Lee had learned Shia's former home address, Shia's significant education history, Shia's near-death experience on her first night of Compton patrol, as well as some of the details of the lives she had taken in self-defense on just her third night with a training officer named Lucas Dey.

Perhaps my movie will be about her life instead of my continually failing years.

Lee flipped open his notebook and scribbled the thought. He determined to spend the rest of his day pondering the notion. Hours well spent. Worth even feeling naked and defenseless until court was adjourned and he could return to the parking structure and his shitmobile and rearm himself with his three comfort objects—his spring-action knife, retractable baton, and highly concealable tactical pen.

9

"Stop the game!" shouted an angry voice. "I'm serious. Stop it the hell right now!"

Lucky, standing between home plate and second base, quickly paired the voice with the reddened mug of an angry father, traversing from behind the cyclone fence separating the twenty or so parents from the field of play. As volunteer umpire for the Mid-Valley Fall Ball League, Lucky was beginning to believe in the fence. Ostensibly there to protect the bystanders from foul baseballs, the eight-foot pane of galvanized steel posts and chain-link also defended the seven-year-old players from all the interfering moms and dads.

A quick step between the pitcher and batter and Lucky held up both hands in the universal signature of an umpire calling time-out. The eleven children on the field, their miniature bodies instinctively shrinking further in their oversized uniforms, obediently froze in place. Meanwhile, the undersized father of the equally small little girl positioned as catcher entered the ball field and hooked himself in the direction of his daughter.

"Let's go," he demanded. "Time for Abigail to play another position."

As Lucky approached the father, he motioned to the team benches for calm.

"Sir," cooled Lucky. "Parents are not allowed on the field—"

"She's my child and I'm her goddamn parent," interrupted the father, thin, soft-faced in green corduroy pants and a Sy Devore cardigan.

"Hang on, now," appeared Abigail's coach, bolting from the dugout, a double-sized dog run of a cage for players currently waiting their turns at bat. "Abby *requested* to play catcher for just one inning."

"Inning's over," demanded the father. "Too dangerous for her. She either plays outfield, where she can't get hurt, or I'm taking her home right now."

"Sir, get off the damn field," urged Lucky.

"Forgive me if I don't take advice from some ten-bucks-an-hour loser in a blue shirt," spat the dad. "C'mon, Abigail."

"She's safe in her position," argued Lucky, underselling the fact. The girl, hung with oversized protective gear that included shin guards, a padded vest, and a catcher's mask, had been cautiously fielding pitches a good fifteen feet behind the batter at the rear of the backstop. Out of concern for even greater safety, play was halted after every pitch so the catcher could remove her mask, retrieve the squishy softie ball, and attempt the toss back to the pitcher.

"Hey, shit stain," the angered father pissed at Lucky. "Didn't ask your opinion, did I? I want her out of the game or in right field."

"But, Daddy . . ." cried Abigail.

"Mr. Greenwald," salved the coach. "There's just one more out in the inning—"

"It gets done the way I say or I'm suing you, this league, and shit stain the umpire here and his retard son," said the father, voice elevating beyond the backstop and into the outfield.

In that brief moment, Lucky pictured one of his hands jutting forth and squeezing the man's neck until the bigmouth's head separated from his shoulders and *lollipopped* into the air. Instead, Lucky spun a brief ninety degrees left to ease his nerves. He saw fifteen-year-old Travis, Gonzo's son, trotting in from the outfield. The pimply teen, Lucky's co-umpire, wore a matching blue athletic shirt. Lucky stuck out a palm and shook his head. Travis instantly stalled and held in place halfway between second base and the pitcher's rubber.

No good deed goes unpunished, eh?

The umpiring gig was a volunteer job, loosely organized by a mix of LAPD and county sheriffs. Gonzo got wind of the opportunity and suggested it might be something for Lucky and Travis to share. Though Travis had never played baseball at any level, the fifteen-year-old had become a nut for the sport, its storied history, rules, and the constant panoply of statistics the professional play offered to number-obsessed brainiacs. Gonzo's instincts had proved to be on target for both Lucky and her son. Through the spring leagues, summer, and now the eight-week season of fall ball, the ad hoc father and son team had formed a mutually enjoyable partnership calling balls, strikes, and outs for Mid-Valley.

"Mister," chilled Lucky. He placed a strong hand on the father's shoulder and eased the angry man a few steps back. "You are interfering with the game. The conduct rules—which you signed—state that you are risking you *and* your little girl getting booted from the league. Doubt you want that."

"What's your name?" replied the father. "And you sure as shit better have your homeowners insurance paid up—assuming you're solvent enough to own a fucking home—because you are not gonna like the shit I'll do to you in court."

Lucky's fingers had already begun to clamp a pit-bull grasp into the prick's weak trapezius when a familiar voice carried through the cyclone fence.

"Everybody take a time-out," sounded the tall baritone. Circling around from behind the backstop walked a man in his mid-sixties, balding, pear-shaped, soft in the middle, with a jowly smirk. "Deep breaths, everybody. Remember, we do this all *for the kids*."

Jaime Peralta—Judge Jim or Judge Jimmy, as almost everybody called him—entered the baseball diamond sporting the league's blue umpire shirt identical to what Lucky and Travis wore. His was clingy, though, a size too small and hugging every unflattering curve. The casual Friday outfit was finished off with cargo shorts and flip-flops. The judge was vice president of the local Pony League Chapter and manager of all the volunteer umpires.

"Your Honor," bitched Abigail's father as if by rote, yet without a lick of back-down in his throat.

"Mr. Greenwald? Coach?" asked Judge Jim. "Gimme a sidebar with my umpire and we'll sort this out posthaste."

In a hushed side-by-side stroll to the mound, Lucky recounted the circumstances leading to the conflict. Judge Jim was all nods and understanding.

"Gotcha. Now the dipshit daddio behind us is a litigator," whispered Judge Jim. "Ass-clown of the highest order. But he's a brilliant goddamn lawyer, litigious as fuck, and could shit-stink this league into a legal quagmire if he put his mind to it."

"So?" shrugged Lucky, as if to say, *So why shouldn't I rip out dipshit's tongue and feed it to his own asshole?*

"Let's move his precious little snowflake to right field and get on with the game," suggested Judge Jim. "You talk to the coaches. I'll talk to the lawyer. He'll get a warning letter from the league office and that'll be that . . . Unless, of course, there's more."

There was a small bite more. Lucky had purposely left out the dialogue where the alpha daddy had loudly called him a shit stain and Travis a retard. From Lucky's gutter-high view, name-calling among adolescents was little more than sticks and stones in that ongoing social experiment known as the schoolyard. But if the ass-clown's insult had made its way to Travis's ears, Lucky would have had no problem whatsoever following the attorney into an empty men's room to serve up some attitude adjustments as a public service.

"You with me?" asked Judge Jim. "You're gonna smooth it out with the coaches, yeah?"

Lucky registered the question. He'd even queued up his answer. Only something had caught his eye—a face on the other side of the chain-link, first base side, top row of the aluminum bleachers. Hispanic male. Early thirties. Stout. Neck tattoos and a blue-inked double teardrop at the corner of his left eye. The sudden stare-down wasn't completely abnormal. Cops of all stripes from every conceivable jurisdiction lived with the probability that on any given day they could bump up against someone they'd arrested, testified against, shot, or tangled with. Mr. Teardrops, as Lucky mentally cataloged him, rang no immediate bells. Nor did the face play back anything familiar. Only the man's unwavering glare at Lucky could be measured.

"I hear ya," Lucky finally replied to the judge before peeling himself from the staring contest with Mr. Teardrops and replacing his Wayfarers on his face. If there was beef with Teardrops Dad, it would have to wait until the game was over.

10

"He wouldn't even get out of the goddamn car." Vaz's words sounded more like a recitation than an actual recrimination. He reached and softly snapped his fingers, beckoning someone to pass him another flour tortilla. "He just sat there. Four hours."

"You talk like I'm not sitting here," complained Johnny B.

"I was only answering your mother's question," explained Vaz. "'What'd you two do?' The answer is I worked. He—meaning you—did absolutely nothing."

"He sat in the car without complaining," said Chris, Vaz's eldest son and Johnny B.'s twenty-four-year-old brother. "And that's not nothin' for J. B."

"Has a point," chimed Lizzy, Johnny B.'s bleached-blonde sister. She was twenty-one and thin enough to be an opioid addict without ever ingesting more than the occasional Jack and Coke or party drug. The nose piercing added character to skin so fair that she often joked—but never quite wished—she must have been adopted.

"No ganging up on your father," ordered Tabitha, softly but with the emphasis of a demand. Their stout little mother, slipping back into the dining room with a second plate of hot-off-the-stove *carne asada* and a serving bowl of grilled onions, seated herself opposite Vaz. "All the same, I did ask."

"And I answered," finished Vaz.

Dinner nights at the Kasabians were something never to be missed. Family meals, which became harder as their children grew older and carried on busy social lives of their own, were non-negotiable. The older pair of Chris and Lizzy never so much as bemoaned it. Both Johnny B.'s older brother and sister had full-time jobs, but in the Armenian tradition, still lived under their parents' roof. Meals were rarely shared on nights other than the scheduled Thursday and Sunday when Tabitha would serve more traditional Armenian cuisine. It was on those unscheduled evenings that she would plan something casual like that Mexican-inspired meal. Tacos were one of Tabitha's new favorites. And the constant passing around of sour cream, guacamole, *queso fresco*, and lime wedges felt as shared and exciting to their mother as a trip abroad.

"J. B. said he couldn't handle the smell of asphalt," continued Vaz, attempting to sound agreeable. "So, I showed him what the advance teams did. The engineers. Inspecting and preparing the roadbeds. No dirt. No stink. No hot asphalt."

"Why didn't you get out of the car?" asked Lizzy, hoping to tee up her little brother to voice a valid complaint.

"I dunno," said Johnny B.

"He doesn't ever know," gestured Vaz, not meaning to mock, yet succeeding nonetheless. In response, Johnny B.'s eyes dropped to his lap in shame.

"See there, Papa?" annoyed Lizzy.

"He was laying on the floor of his 'disco room' and I wanted to get him out and into something productive," defended Vaz. "You said you wanted to. Right, Johnny?"

"I don't remember," replied Johnny B., shaking his head.

"Could we stop with the arguing and get on with the eating?" impressed Tabitha. In one hand she held out the plate of tortillas, the other a bowl of chopped Roma tomatoes. "Johnny? C'mon. Grab a tortilla."

"Not hungry," said Johnny B., pushing himself away from the table.

"Stay, buddy," encouraged Chris. "Mom cooked for all of us."

"But I'm not hungry anymore."

Vaz threw up his hands.

"How could you stop being hungry when you haven't eaten—"

"Stop bullying him!" flared Lizzy, leaning forward, eyes peeled at her father.

"Family. Dinner." Tabitha clapped her hands, and that was all she needed to say to stuff a plug in their argument.

Those four succinct syllables stalled Johnny B. before he could make the first landing turn of the stairs. The eighteen-year-old stood stock-still, oddly relishing the brief moment when he was above them. Elevated. The youngest and least of them was almost hovering over the nuclear family amidst all their comfortable opulence. The dark wood veneers. Antique tapestries. The hundred-year-old Spanish oak table had enough leaves to seat sixteen. For family meals, though, it was kept to a cozy circle set under a wrought-iron chandelier. The table was in front of a spectacular multi-paned window that faced southeast and overlooked the sloping hills that stretched all the way down to the few high-rises of Glendale's city center.

"What you lookin' at, Johnny?" asked Chris, hoping to break his brother out of what appeared to be a vacant stare.

"Nothin', really," said Johnny, remote and disconnected. "For a second I was kinda imagining that all of you were midgets."

Lizzy laughed. Gamely.

"Can't say 'midget' anymore," smiled Tabitha, sensing her

youngest was easing back to the family. "Think the correct label is 'little people.'"

"Not PC to label nobody no more," corrected Lizzy. "We accept them as small of stature."

"I hate all this PC bullshit," groused Vaz.

"Johnny needs something to do?" suggested Chris. "Come have him work with me."

"Not *the business*," pointed Vaz.

"Why not *the business?*" argued Chris. "He's eighteen."

"Learns to work first."

"I can work," pleaded Johnny B., his feet still stuck on the landing.

"You had your chance today," snapped Vaz. "Show me you can work the legit side and we can talk about *other* work."

"What if *other* work is all I want to do?" asked Johnny.

"We don't talk family business at dinner," reminded Tabitha. "My table. My rules."

"I'm not hungry," repeated Johnny B. before spinning an about-face and thumping angrily up the stairs.

"Look what you did!" annoyed Chris.

"Look what I did?" Vaz dropped his taco and pointed at his eldest. "You know the rules. Daughters don't work in our business and—"

"Here comes the bullshit again." Lizzy dropped back in her chair. She folded her arms and rolled her significant brown eyes to the hand-carved ceiling.

"No women," continued Vaz before automatically lowering his voice. "And no boys with Johnny Boy's condition."

"What condition?" zeroed Chris. "ASD hardly makes him a cripple. Shit. Steve Jobs had Asperger's, Dad. And you know who Steve Jobs is?"

"Steve Jobs *was*. He's dead," offered Tabitha.

"Steve Jobs was a genius," continued Chris. "For all you know, Johnny B. is just as much of—"

"Of a genius?" sighed Vaz. "Wouldn't that make things easier?"

Easier, indeed. The entire clan was more than aware of all

the help they'd sought and paid for in trying to learn what ailed Johnny B. Misdiagnoses, a half dozen psychologists, and a failed stint at a therapeutic boarding school had left Vartan Kasabian bereft of ideas beyond some old-fashioned tough love.

"C'mon, Pop," suggested Chris. "Let him tag along with me. Maybe it's a repeat of today and he just sits in the car and plays on his phone."

"Or I can offer him something at one of the salons," joked Lizzy. "See which he chooses."

"Not funny," pointed her mother. "I know half those customers."

"You embarrassed by him?" whispered Lizzy across the table. "Shame on you, then."

"I'm his mother," narrowed Tabitha. "And I will always protect him. Even if it's from himself."

"You both are so fucking pathetic." Lizzy stood, dropping her dinner napkin onto her plate of uneaten meat.

"Language, Lizzy," was all her mother could think to say in the moment.

"Sit," demanded Vaz.

"Go. Fuck. Yourselves." Lizzy was so quick and light, her footsteps were like feather drops as she chased up the stairs after her brother.

"Family dinner," moaned Tabitha, disappointed.

"He's with me tomorrow," finished Chris while loading up a tortilla. "I'll get him moving. Leave Johnny to me."

11

Lucky had met with some recent history at Beeps Diner. In those between days after he'd resigned from Kern County Sheriff's Department, awaiting reinstatement with LASD, he'd picked up some private work to keep himself busy and paid. Ever since he'd staked out the unusual fifties-themed turquoise and hot pink diner in hopes of catching up with a slippery subject on whom he'd been hired to drop a subpoena, he kept returning to Beeps for its all-day breakfasts. Then came fall and after months of volunteering for Judge Jim's Pony League, a select few of the blue officiating crew had come to gather at the tacky joint for after-game French fries, onion rings, and old-fashioned milkshakes.

Teenaged Travis enjoyed the testosterone-fueled camaraderie. And but for Judge Jim, the umpiring crew was a top-drawer mix of cops and firefighters who spared the teen little in the way men needle each other. But after Travis's video game all-nighter, Gonzo dropped the hammer. A book report was due the next Tuesday—the day following Halloween—on an assigned tome Travis had yet to even crack. So, when her helo shift ended, Gonzo swung by Beeps, politely interrupted the after-party, and hustled the boy to her car.

There were no telltale kisses or so much as a flick of eye contact for her live-in, Lucky. Despite that, Lucky casually called after her, promising to be home soon after.

"Sheezus," moaned Miles, faking a shiver. "Somebody turn up the thermostat."

The quartet of umpires was seated in the corner of a patio covered in weather-stained corrugated plastic. The overhead space heater *tick-tick-ticked* as if it had overheard forty-four-year-old Miles Czajkowski's request. The classic, head-shaved LAPD homicide lieutenant chuckled and high-five gestured to his beefy pal and fellow Van Nuys Division detective, Charlie "Sugar" Freeman.

"Little cold that was," remarked Judge Jim, more than a little pointed at Lucky.

"Is what it is," said Lucky.

"Seriously, coz," added Sugar. "Put a ring on that shit or get the fuck out."

"Unsolicited advice received," finished Lucky as a way of putting a stopper on the subject. He doubled up an onion ring, swirled it in a serving cup of ranch dressing, and devoured it.

"Okay," shifted Judge Jim, eyeballing Miles and Sugar before leaning in. "Change of subject. You put any thought to our thing?"

"Been a little preoccupied," said Lucky after swallowing and washing the oversized bite back with a Diet Coke.

"Kinda coy, dontcha think?" suggested Miles. "I'd say our *thing* is pretty damn preoccupation resistant."

"Your *thing*," Lucky answered collectedly, "demands some heavy thinking."

"Exactly what it is," agreed Judge Jim. "Wouldn't want you to proceed any other way."

Besides the switch to Major Crimes, Lucky had spent part of the past six months getting to know his fellow diners. From the near-freezing early spring nights calling strikes and outs at the Burbank Catholic league to the summer travel tourneys to fall ball at Mid-Valley, the time span had provided a backdrop for Judge Jim's coppers to get to know one another. They'd shared meals, motel rooms, frothy pitchers of beer, and as police officers were wont to do, endless on-the-job stories—all the dark moments and impossible laughs that only fellow cop brethren could fully comprehend.

Lucky was by far the least talkative of the group. He might have shared some tales, but his actions and reputation were well known to both Judge Jim and Miles long before *the cryptic ask* had landed Lucky in the same restaurant at the same table only one short week before.

"Will you join us?"

The *us* in question was Judge Jim's quiet cabal of police officers and technicians. Exactly who and how many there were, Lucky didn't know.

"We know all about you, Lucky. Where you've been. What you've done. And we like what we see."

The pitch, unwrapped by the judge himself in a calm but calculated conundrum, contained a litany of societal truths, most of which were felt deeply by every self-respecting big city badge.

"We're outmanned. Outgunned. Out-financed. And never before in the history of law enforcement have cops been under such impossible scrutiny. Social media. Smartphones. Body cams. It's a wonder anybody beyond the run-of-the-mill street thug gets incarcerated."

Lucky had listened to it all, baseball hat pulled low, nearly motionless but for the occasional nod of understanding in either empathy or a simple sign of reception. Chilled as his exterior appeared, his brain was a synaptic fireworks show—as if, all at once, replaying his every on- and off-the-job indiscretion to his impossible-to-live-by policeman's oath—all in order to serve and protect those under the security blanket of the almighty US Constitution.

"You might not be one of us. At least, not yet. But we know you are one of us in spirit. In your actions. Your choices. You, like us, are not someone who chooses to suffer—or have others suffer—the injustices dealt at the hands of a badly broken system."

It was likely they knew Lucky too well and had looked him over from inside and out via official channels and those less reputable. They'd run down the fact sheets and the rumors. They'd peeked so deep into his history they could practically feel his rage or imagine having witnessed moments when he'd crossed that thin blue line to right an actual wrong. Lucky had never assumed he was alone in his plight. He never, though, imagined that he'd be invited to join a club of cops with a similar disposition. The difference? To them it was a mission. To Lucky it was a cross to bear.

"We're making cases, Lucky. Irrefutable cases. Against the capos of the regimes. The generals. No more prison and jails filled with nothing but addicts and street soldiers. It's as old as the Greeks. Crime is killed when you cut off the heads of the snakes. That's what we do. Make cases that stick. Make cases that juries and judges like me can't help but drop the hammer down with guilty verdicts and life without parole sentences. And believe you me. We are making a difference."

The inner architecture of Judge Jim's cabal was never precisely revealed to Lucky, nor the measures utilized to "make" cases. Nor would they be unless Lucky came aboard. So Lucky could only assume. DNA. Witness tampering. Crime scene manipulations. The distinct opportunity to put away the *real* villains in the game—the connected and protected desperados who operated beyond Lucky's gutter-high comfort zone—had been served up to him on a white porcelain platter.

"We know you, Lucky. Where you've been. What you've done. As a Reaper or otherwise. And you know what can be done when a brotherhood of the righteous comes together in defense of the defenseless."

Lucky recalled Judge Jim having drawn the fingers of both hands into fight-ready fists—his eyes unblinking and serious while Miles and Sugar added affirmative nods. They were brethren, ready to take on the city. And Lucky was receiving an invitation to join their call to arms.

"We don't need an answer today. You need to think on it. Hard. But know this. What we're doing is real. You heard about Teddy Ryder? That shitbag child pornographer funneling all the guns into South L.A.? Nailed to the cross on a rape charge? That was us. Those MS13 honchos tied into the city council bribes? Went down on decade-old murder beefs. See where I'm going? Where we're all going? Name the bad guy and we have the power and means to put him away."

A full week had come and gone. Time enough for Lucky to mull over the offer, sleep on it, marinate in all its possibilities. Nobody was taking money or getting rich off the scheme. Arguably, Judge Jim's secret posse of case-closers had all the makings of a justice juggernaut. And didn't that fit with Lucky's base talent for separating the good guys from the bad? Wouldn't all that difference-making ease the ills of the collective innocent? Or even at its most simple, relieve the pressure in Lucky's brain that made it impossible to summon sleep on many nights because of what he'd done . . . or what he was willing to do?

The answer was still a resounding no.

For Lucky, it came down to the weight a man could carry. Actions. Consequences. It was, as God might have designed, enough only for one human being to bear—or not. In Lucky's view, when conspiracies formed between men it made souls ripe for a particular flavor of cancer. It was a malignant, contagious rot that could turn a good idea into a negative force—where collusion was guaranteed to turn into corruption. In the end, even a conspiracy for good was doomed to end up as nothing more than an excuse serving only the conspirators themselves.

"I've thought about it," answered Lucky in a spate of feigned over-intellectualizing. "And I keep coming back to the same question. If, for thousands of years, people like yourselves—or ourselves—have been cutting off the heads of snakes, why are there still so many snakes?"

"Why does the sun rise and set?" countered Judge Jim. "Or the tide rise and fall? That doesn't mean that men with a conscience shouldn't stand as bulwarks against evil. Sure, there's a cycle. And like it or not, we are all part of it."

"I getcha," said Lucky. "And I respect it. Maybe it's because the shit I've done—or might do in the future—is mine and mine alone. My yoke, you know?"

"One man against the world," surmised Sugar, unable to hide his disappointment. "Sounds pretty damn lonely."

"Hey. Lucky is who he is," defended Judge Jim. "We're not here to judge."

"Say da judge?" chuckled Miles before putting a comrade's hand on Lucky's rock of a shoulder. "I got five kids and not one is on their own yet. Sugar's got three. Judge here, his kids are all grown and out of the house, so the best he can hope for is saving the world for his grandbabies."

"Is there a point?" prompted Judge Jim.

"You got two, right?" continued Miles. "That Travis boy is a great kid. Little weird, but who wasn't at some time? Point is that we—all of us here—are the stewards of the world they're gonna inherit. S'up to us to make it as safe and sane as we can."

"All for ya," Lucky feigned. "Seriously. We're on the same side. Maybe I'm just the asshole who can't put the *me* in *team*."

"Makin' a mistake." Sugar was leaning back, stretching his meaty arms, shaking his head.

"Enough," interrupted Judge Jim. "Lucky's on our page. Same team. Different methods. And don't think we've misjudged you. Invitation comes with no expiration date. Our door is always open. As we trust our secret is safe with you. And who knows? We may grind on you again next week."

"You bastards should come with a warning," joked Lucky.

"Caution," jibed Miles, dropping into his street rap. "Judge Jimmy don't take no thank you for no answers. No ways. No hows."

"Fine," said Lucky. "Keep comin' at me. Long as you're buyin' the milkshakes."

"We love ya, Lucky," laughed Judge Jim, eyes pretending to be earnest. "Especially 'cause you come so cheap."

The four-man blue crew broke in the reverse order of how they'd arrived, with a quick stop by the hatchback of Judge Jim's black Cadillac Escalade. The gull-wing lid lifted with hydraulic elegance and, one by one, each man reached into a plastic file carrier to retrieve his cell phone, watch, wireless earphones, or anything digital that could be loaded with surreptitious eavesdropping tech. None could be too careful in that department, including Lucky, who, after depositing his electronics into the bin before the meet, had even allowed Miles to pat him down in search of an old-fashioned body wire.

Each man departed in what appeared to be a different direction. As Lucky trekked the half block to where he'd parked, the cast of Beeps's iconic neon fell quickly away into side-street darkness. With every step, he carefully replayed their meet-up. The repeated offer. His polite pass on their solicitation to join their "righteous" conspiracy. Their body language when his rejection landed. Eyes don't lie. The involuntary tics of the human body revealed when contrary news traveled down the ear canal into the human brain's neuro centers was nothing if not informative. He'd read only a few—mostly insignificant tells. Uncomfortable lower body shifts from Judge Jim. As for the LAPD duo—Sugar had popped a pair of orbital pupil shifts in the direction of his partner, Miles, who, in Lucky's practiced estimation, gave away absolutely zero but for a winning grin and the yellowed teeth of a former chain-smoker.

There was a decided itch of danger in the aftermath. They'd showed their colors. Shared their dirty secret. In Lucky, they'd either trusted him to join or keep their game under wraps. It was a big ask—maybe too big in the final estimation. And with Lucky answering in the negative, there might come countermeasures against him. During the week that Lucky had "mulled over" the offer, he'd been both calculating his moves while quietly hoping his initial reticent reply had been enough to put a chill on his recruitment. If Judge Jim concluded that Lucky's refusal to join in the cabal was a threat to his vigilante conspiracy, Lucky would need to be quick with his offensive. He'd already recorded and transcribed his detailed notes from the first meeting to a cloud file. The moment he hit the freeway he planned to dictate part two into his phone. Copies would be emailed to Gonzo, Shia, and Conrad Ellis for safekeeping.

Lucky prayed it wouldn't turn into a shit storm.

He arrived at his parked '99 Crown Vic. He was reaching in his pocket for his keys when he clocked the movement. Top right periphery, a shape behind the wheel of a parked paint-ravaged Dodge Neon. It was the distinct action of a shoulder shove that began a thrust to open the car door. Next came the *flick* of a latch pull and the dull *thunk* of a lock release.

Lucky's play was to cover the twenty feet between his car door and the Neon's before the suspicious male could clear his body from his vehicle. A streetlamp backlit the figure, one boot on the curb and a thick head springing up from behind the window frame. Lucky closed the gap, using the blunt inertia of his body to reverse the swing of the Neon's door. The resulting effect was a vise. The would-be assailant released a wheezing sound as he found himself pinned between his door and the car frame.

The small car rocked from the opposite side. Lucky glanced and saw a passenger throwing off his seat belt. With his left hand, Lucky reached back and unsnapped his concealed SIG and directed the .45-caliber bore at the windshield.

"Tell your friend to buckle the fuck up or I will punch holes in him!" hissed Lucky.

The words reached the passenger, who was already relenting, sinking deep back into the bucket seat. Then—and only then—did Lucky return his face to the unknown male suffering the painful squeeze from the off-duty detective's weight against the driver's door. Six inches from Lucky's twisted nose was the ink of the tattooed double teardrop he'd noted on the baseball dad during the afternoon stare-down.

"Listen and listen good," began Lucky in their face-to-face. "I know you got some beef with me. I knew it from the jump. Right? Either I locked you up or cracked on you or put a bullet in your cousin. But I seriously don't have a fuckin' clue. Whatever it is, I strongly suggest you and your knucklehead buddy have a good

long think before you come at me again. Nod, fart, anything. Jus'
tell me you're up to speed on this shit so far."

"Think my arm is broke," said Mr. Teardrops.

"Not so bad that you haven't let go of what you got."

Not a second later Lucky heard a weapon clatter into the
gutter at his feet. Nothing louder than a .380 pistol, he guessed, by
the sound of the mass striking the asphalt.

"Here comes part two," continued Lucky. "The beef. Maybe
it's justified. Maybe I deserve whatever you got comin' for me. But
not here, not now. So, this is what I'm gonna do. I'm gonna give
you my card. It's got my cell number printed on it in black and
white. If, after you had yourself that serious think, you still wanna
dance? Call me. I know this quiet piece of real estate in the upper
desert. Between Hinkley and Copper City. Just you 'n' me. Guns,
knives, fists. I'll even bring the shovel so whichever of us is left
standing can finish shit right. Fair 'nough?"

". . . Yeah," grunted Mr. Teardrops.

"Say 'fair 'nough,'" repeated Lucky. "Wanna hear it."

". . . Fair 'nough."

"Back in the car, door shut, drive the fuck away."

"My piece . . ."

"Enterprising tough guy like yourself?" smirked Lucky. "Bet
you got more where that came from."

Lucky released the door without ever once shifting his pistol
from the target. As Mr. Teardrops slipped back into his car, pulling the door shut with his opposite hand, Lucky flicked a Los
Angeles Sheriff's Department business card and tucked it underneath the Neon's wiper blade. He waited for Mr. Teardrops to
steer the Neon out of the curbside spot before re-holstering his
gun and retrieving the dropped pistol. Confirmation. The piece
was a bargain-basement Cobra .380 with a ghetto-preferred white
grip and red-metallic slide. Cheaper than cheap, but equally
deadly as any top-shelf model.

He slipped the weapon into his back pocket before returning
to the '99. As he keyed the door, he noticed a small duffel bag in
the passenger seat. At first, Lucky thought it was an item Travis

had left behind from his sleepover. The bag was a slick convention giveaway piece embroidered with a yellow logo for the *Whirly-Girls Association*—a national society of women helicopter aviators. Attached to the handle was a sticky note with Gonzo's handwriting:

Having serious second thoughts about our living arrangement. Do us both a favor and stay somewhere else for the next couple of nights.

Missing were both the addressee and addressor, as well as the usual Xs and Os with which Gonzo usually ended her handwritten communications.

"Shit," sounded Lucky to nobody but the night. He stuffed his wont to phone Gonzo or text her a tell-all *WTF?* Instead, he climbed behind the wheel, shut the door, and tried to wrap his head around just where the hell he might be able to lay his head for the night.

"That's two nights in a row."

"Could say the same for you," replied Lucky, one eye slit open with his stocking feet propped up on his back-against-the-wall cubicle desk.

Ponytailed Zadeh Raad leaned into a partition, feet from Lucky's left, arms crossed, her pixie hard-body oddly balanced by the heavy 9mm she packed on her right hip.

"Tonight makes four for me," corrected Zadeh. "But you weren't here the first two, so I guess that makes you half right."

Lucky didn't think his back could handle another twisted night in his car—nor could he necessarily trust parking it anyplace he wouldn't be rousted. And cheap motel beds were always a risk for bad-back sufferers. Before Lucky arrived at his desk in the Major Crimes Bureau, he'd trolled the Temple Street corridors for an unlocked door and a reclining desk chair he could borrow. Once he'd rolled it to his desk, he adjusted the spring tension. Then he placed a rolled gym towel at the base of his spine for lumbar support. He was moments from succumbing to the sleep gods when the nasal tones of Detective Raad had punctured the air.

"What's your excuse?" she pried.

"Do I need one?" Lucky returned.

"Hey. None of my business is none of my business," teased Zadeh.

"You first, then," said Lucky, once again closing his eyes.

"Simple. I suck at sleep," shrugged Zadeh. "I go through these fits of insomnia just before my period. You?"

Lucky pried one eye open as if to reply, *I'm a dude. I don't get periods.*

"Sleep's usually no problem," finished Lucky.

"So, anywhere you lay your head?"

"Complicated," answered Lucky. "Domestic problems."

"Married?"

"Technically? No."

"None of my business. Sorry."

"Go ahead and play your music," said Lucky.

"Naw, man. You tryin' to sleep."

"I'll put Kleenex in my ears."

Zadeh unconsciously bit her lip, then stepped nearer.

"Hey," said Zadeh. "You really need some shut-eye? I got a place to show ya."

Lucky followed as Zadeh led him across the corridor to an equipment room stuffed with nonlethal tactical supplies such as ballistic vests, chemical masks, and helmets stenciled *LASD* front and back. In the rear was a second door with a passage lock easily beaten with a credit card Zadeh produced from her wallet. With a flick of her tac light, she revealed a closet-sized space that had once housed the floor's electrical panels. On the floor was a foam mattress and a pillow.

"Maintenance guy showed me." Zadeh then admitted, "Time to time I've been known to take a dive here. Or play my music and just zone. Clean enough for a cop flop."

Lucky looked down. In his stocking feet, she was a full foot shorter.

"Cop flop?"

Zadeh lifted her eyes. Instead of a smile she revealed almost a snarl.

"Your wife, your girlfriend, or whatever you got at home . . ." she doe-eyed him. "She like to get fucked hard?"

For a moment, all either could hear of the other was their respective breathing—all nerves and tension and secreting pheromones. Zadeh ran a not-so-soft hand up the inside of Lucky's thigh. And the rest for him was all unthinking and male reflex. He started for her mouth as she pulled him down to the floor. They fumbled at each other's clothes, pushed aside their weapons. He pulled the door shut until it clicked. Somehow, Zadeh produced a condom, ripping it open with her teeth and expertly applying it in the unforgiving darkness. The act itself was as unhinged as it was uninhibited. Wordless. Loveless. And satisfyingly crass.

When it was over, Lucky lay on his back, his mind not yet caught up with his breath while Zadeh found her tac light, squeezed back into her jeans and T-shirt, and re-affixed her gun to her hip. In what little Lucky caught of her, he noted that her ponytail appeared as tight and controlled as when he'd first set eyes on it.

"That was fun, detective," smiled Zadeh before exiting and pushing the door shut. "Now get some sleep."

With the click of the latch, the tiny room snapped back into a perfect blackness. Lucky remained still, eyes wide, waiting for his pupils to adjust. Between his lingering hopes for the most meager of illumination and the onset of guilt for having cheated on Gonzo, sleep crept in and sucked Lucky into a dream-free unconsciousness. It would be some nine hours later until he woke, bleary, disoriented, wondering where he was, what he'd done, and where the hell his pants were.

Saturday

12

Altadena. 7:24 a.m.

Throughout Gonzo's life, sleep had never been as easy as just closing her eyes. Even worse, it seemed the older she got, the busier her mind. Her love of books, both fiction and nonfiction, was her only tonic against her constant substate of worry. She was never more than a light switch away from the last chapter where she'd left her bookmark, a crude handwoven version of the American flag made by Travis for Mother's Day when he was six years old. The colors in the cheap yarn had faded or dirtied into patriotic pink, beige, and baby blue. Yet she was always that much more at home every time she flipped a book open and saw her baby boy's handiwork.

Her current volume, a grind of an old library biography on Irish independence leader and politician Éamon de Valera, had delivered her from three in the morning until five, when she rose, fed a pile of dry kibble to Oprah, their perennially shedding rescue mutt, and tossed in a load of wash before hopping in her Hyundai for the five-minute drive to the gym. An hour later, she returned to the bungalow, sweaty and aching for a shower. As she pulled into the driveway, her phone rang with an amusing custom tone Travis had loaded when she wasn't looking—the theme from the original 1960s cop show *Dragnet*. She considered not answering, but thumb-clicked the button on her steering wheel.

"Morning," answered Gonzo, flat yet still clipped.

"Simple question," asked Lucky. "What the hell did I do? Tell me so I can apologize and we can get back on with things."

"For one," said Gonzo, as if she'd spent her waking hours assembling a list of Lucky's indiscretions, "you stopped going to your meetings. Remember that was the original condition for us moving in together? You think I'd forget?"

"Meetings are for addicts," Lucky replied. "I haven't touched anything more than a beer in almost two years."

"A deal's a deal," dug in Gonzo.

"And this is why you leave a duffel bag in my car? That shit didn't come up in therapy."

"You gotta be committed to therapy for it to work."

"Three sessions. We've only had three goddamn sessions!"

"Who didn't come home Wednesday night?"

"Made it pretty damn clear you didn't want company."

"My fault I needed to clear my head?"

"Yeah? And how's that workin' out?"

"Hanging up," relented Gonzo. "It's too early in the morning for this shit."

"Can I remind you that I'm the one living out of a duffel bag?" forced Lucky. "Can I please get some sort of timeline for when it's okay for me to return to my own house?"

"*Our* house."

"Goes without sayin'," calmed Lucky. "Look. Whatever I did—or didn't do—whatever you think I've done or didn't yet apologize for, I'm sorry. Okay?"

"Excuse me? Blanket apology *not* accepted."

"I'm not a mind reader. Just playing the cards you're dealing me."

"Just worked out. I need to shower and get to it. Let's talk tonight."

"Talk in person? At home? Yeah?"

"I'll call you after work," finished Gonzo. "Now I gotta go."

With the same thumb she had answered with, Gonzo depressed the hang-up button and took a pair of deep breaths with equally long exhales before exhuming her leggy self from the car and up the steps into the side door to the antique bungalow's updated kitchen.

"So, what happened?" burrowed Karrie. The strawberry-blonde seventeen-year-old wore baggy sweats and a coarse Mexican poncho while peeling an apple over the sink.

"Hey," said Gonzo, surprised. "When did you get home?"

"'Round midnight or something."

"How was it?" asked Gonzo, overselling a completely false and upbeat tone.

"The trip? Fine," said Karrie before refocusing her lens. "Talked to Trav. Said Lucky hasn't been home for two nights."

"Yeah, so?"

"So, what up?"

When the teen's green eyes flared over the top of her freckles, Gonzo dropped the happy act and tried to disappear around the corner into the laundry room.

"Not about you, Kar," Gonzo called back. "It's between me and Luck."

"Not about me?"

"What I said, didn't I?"

"What the fuck?!"

"Really?" warned Gonzo.

"We all live here, right?" pressed Karrie, crossing the short distance to the laundry room's threshold. "Like a family? One of us not being welcome home affects all of us."

"Didn't say anything about Lucky not being welcome."

"Then why's he not home?"

"Want me to spell it out?" angered Gonzo. "We're having a fight. Half past seven in the morning, I just got off the phone with him yelling at me. I don't need to be interrogated by you—"

"Breaking news. You can be a real bitch," interrupted Karrie.

Gonzo felt like slapping the teen. Four fingers, hard, and across the face. She even pictured the mark she would leave on the girl's right cheek before her cognitive brain kicked in. Instead of striking, Gonzo wrapped both hands around the handles of the laundry tub, lifted from the knees, and stood as if waiting for Karrie to give way.

"Sorry," said Gonzo, her voice lowered to just above a whisper. "Bet this is how it sounded with your mom and dad."

"Not about my dead effing parents!" barked Karrie. "Jeezus. You both need to get your shit together. Either that or we're just a pretend family!"

Gonzo watched the teen stomp off. Inside her gut, a rage boiled. But was it about Lucky, her damn impatience, or realizing she might have just flushed months of time and the trust she'd earned trying to parent the former runaway? Though seventeen, Karrie was still a child—or at least as much in Gonzo's compassionate view. The girl was barely mended and held together by little more than faith, willpower, and an unyielding affection for her surrogate father, Lucky *goddamned* Dey. The couple had rescued her, protected her, and loved her up with the unwritten promise that while under their roof she'd find something stable and comforting. In essence, the polar opposite of the discordant life she'd bolted from just two short years before.

And that deadly dynamic parenting duo was deceased. Instead of rebuilding her life with some distant Midwestern relative, Karrie had sought legal emancipation and a home with her favorite cop couple—Lucky and Gonzo.

For a moment, Gonzo contemplated crying liters into that basket of unfolded laundry. She regretted every angry word and action she'd taken against Lucky.

"She's right," whispered Gonzo to nobody but herself. "You *are* a bitch."

13

Glendale. 7:55 a.m.

Lucky couldn't precisely calendar the last time he'd suffered a hangover. Yet the way he felt that morning was practically equal to his bone-aching recall of what alcohol poisoning felt like. He'd slept. He'd already pounded back two large cups of coffee. Despite that, the only three explanations he could muster were: A. dehydration; B. the onset of flu; or C. the toxic guilt of sexual indiscretion. The latter fit as the most obvious reason while at the same time was utterly intangible. As in how the hell would an angry romp outside the fidelity loop manifest in such clearly visible symptoms?

On his trek up the sloping walk to 208 Valencia Court, Lucky briefly imagined himself visiting his physician.

How've I been feeling? Some pissed-off dirty sport sex last night. But aside from that, Doc, things have been pretty normal.

Lucky rang the doorbell, retreated the standard three steps backward, and angled his body forty-five degrees from the hinges. He called it a cop knock. And statistically speaking, it was one of the most dangerous and exposed actions a police officer could make, second only to a traffic stop. So, by keeping to the dead-bolt side, if Lucky were to be surprise attacked, the doorjamb would provide perhaps an extra second to a second and a half for a defense—ergo time for an aware deputy to juke, skin his weapon, and survive.

The front door of the turn-of-the-century Spanish manor was aptly arched and neatly painted in a black semi-gloss. Overnight, his email to the fleet manager at Star Ford and Lincoln had returned the name of the Shelby Mustang's registered owner: John Bartholomew Kasabian of Glendale. The address the eighteen-year-old had given the DMV was precisely where Lucky stood waiting for someone to answer the doorbell.

He was inches from completing his assignment—the favor for the Assistant Sheriff. All he had left to accomplish was to meet the Mustang owner, size him up to see if he fit the character in the security videos, and inform the suspect that he was investigating a car accident and the possible felonious violation of Section 23110 of the California Vehicle Code. Lucky would follow up with a few questions about what he'd already coined as a "chuck and run," then include the suspect's answers in his informal report.

And the rest would be up to the almighty LAPD.

At the sound of a thrown deadbolt, Lucky instinctively brushed the butt of the weapon holstered behind his right hip. Bracing herself against the cracked-open door was a short woman in a bathrobe, forties, hardly five feet tall, with a well-tended pair of dark brown eyebrows beneath a volume of bleached-blonde tresses.

"Yes?" asked Tabitha Kasabian.

"Morning," said Lucky. "My name is Detective Dey. I'm with the Los Angeles Sheriff's Department."

"Yes?" she repeated. "Do you know it's not even eight yet?"

"Mrs. Kasabian?" Lucky guessed.

"Yes?" she said for the third time.

"I'm looking for John Kasabian. Is he your son?"

"Yes."

"Does he drive a black Shelby Mustang?"

"Yes."

"Is he home?"

"Left for work with his brother."

"And when was that?"

"What is this about, officer?"

"Detective," corrected Lucky. "Nobody is under arrest. I have no warrant. Just would like to speak to your son. If you could have him call me?"

Lucky offered Tabitha his business card. She reluctantly pinched it between her fingers before giving it a cursory read.

"Our attorney will contact you," said Tabitha before pushing the door shut and re-throwing the bolt. From the other side she finished, "And don't come back here again."

Yet another career door-slammer, joked Lucky to himself. Given enough years, all detectives lose count of the impossible number of doors that have been shut in their faces. Some civilians, no matter what the flavor, didn't care to cooperate or assist for fear of being a witness, getting involved, or simply being bothered by any such authority. The petite woman at the Valencia Court address possessed, in Lucky's estimation, two aggravating factors. For one, she admitted to being the suspect's mother. Kids often confess to their permissive parents, who follow suit by auto-switching into defense mode and checking to make certain their homeowners insurance is current and paid up.

Aggravating factor number two was more obvious.

Armenian.

As Lucky retraced his steps down the curving path to his '99, he replayed for himself the glaringly obvious. He was in a mon-eyed section of Glendale, visiting the residence of a well-to-do Armenian family. The mother, by Lucky's educated guess, bore an accent that sounded fully assimilated and yet still in touch with the native language of the old country. Armenians had been flooding into the US in a mass migration ever since the Ottoman-led genocide of the early nineteenth century. And as a culture, they had risen to great heights in California society and politics. Clannish to a fault, they populated significant swaths of Glendale and East Hollywood. Lucky recalled a patrol deputy of Armenian descent who, over a midnight lunch of greasy tacos and cinnamon-flavored *horchata*, declared that there wasn't anybody he knew with a last name ending in *-ian* or *-yan* who didn't have a close relative somehow connected with the Armenian mob.

Effectively, though, Lucky had completed his off-book assignment—his personal favor to the department's number-two brass. He'd identified the cause of the accident and a suspect and his home address. The car dealer had even provided a cell number. There was plenty enough for Lucky to sandwich between a pair of file covers—one for the LAPD and the other for Assistant Sheriff McGill. Lucky's guess was that some Valley Assistant District Attorney would plea the felony down to a misdemeanor with little or no jail time, but with culpability enough for the aggrieved Malibu family to mount a slam dunk of a wrongful death suit.

Over and out.

When Lucky's key slid into the ignition of his Crown Vic he should have been thinking of his next official chore. Another cold case from the pile on his desk? Or would the bureau's lieutenant have something fresh with a stink trail for him to run down?

So, then why am I thinkin' on these damned ten digits?

The mobile phone number the Ford dealer's fleet manager had provided kept tripping across Lucky's frontal lobe. Sure, he thought. I could dial it. Chances are, it would come up unrecognized and unanswered by teenaged suspect John B. Kasabian. Or even more likely, in the mere thirty or so seconds since the bleached bantam lady had shut the front door in his face, mommy dearest had phoned up her precious baby boy and relayed the warning.

"Whatever," replied Lucky to himself, reaching for his phone and searching his menu of contacts. He spun through the list until he landed on the one he needed.

"Em," replied Lucky to his former booty-call buddy at the other end. Emery, an MDMA-loving, tattooed, save-the-earth geekette with a telecommuting job and security clearance, was his go-to gal when it came to geo-locating suspects without a warrant. "Wanna find a cell phone for me?"

"I dunno," she moaned, having been rousted from a coma-like slumber. "How's married life?"

"Not a quid pro quo call," said Lucky, still sloughing off the guilt of last night's tryst. "Just a favor."

"You willing to owe me?"

"C'mon, Em. You can or you can't."

"I. Can." The sleepy sound of capitulation in her voice was almost sad. "You at least flattered?"

"Em?"

"C'mon, Lucky. Look at me."

"How can I? You're in Playa. I'm in Glendale."

"You know what I'm sayin'," she explained. "Look like a dyke but I still crave dick. And to make matters even shittier, I work in the land of socially stunted dudes with zero freakin' game."

Lucky found it none too difficult to picture Emery's copious tattoos. She had such affection for vintage comic book characters that Lucky likened sex with her to getting dirty with the Sunday funny papers.

"Awright," she whined, a notch more alert. "Text me the digits and I'll get you close as I can."

"Comin' to you," replied Lucky, clicking off and transferring the ten-number sequence into a text. He pressed send, keyed the car's ignition, spun a wide U-turn, and backtracked to the 7-Eleven he'd mentally marked before winding up that southeastern slope of Glendale. He was itching for a Slim Jim and a Super Big Gulp full of even more caffeine.

* * *

"Don't do it," begged Johnny B.

"Do this every damn day," declared Chris, flicking back the switch that auto-lowered the driver's window of his deep gray Lexus coupe.

"I watched a TV thing about this," warned Johnny B. "It's a scam."

"But for the grace," replied Chris, pinching a folded twenty-dollar bill between his middle and index fingers. He stretched his arm out of the window.

The Burbank Boulevard overpass with two off-ramps, three sets of traffic lights, and six east- and westbound lanes arching over the 405 Freeway was a bumper-to-bumper jam. Posted at each stop were impoverished-looking panhandlers, all holding their own small cardboard signs, their plights usually inked in a black or red Sharpie:

Homeless vet.

Need money for food.

Have children to feed.

Each vagabond varied in age, sex, and dress. While most looked the part, as bedraggled or itinerant as their advertisements, others were kempt, clean-shaven, and appeared interview-ready for a job at the nearby Costco.

"But for the what?" asked Johnny B.

"'There go I but for the grace of God,'" quoted Chris. The designated scrounger at the top of the off-ramp bore wild white hair stuffed under a deformed felt fedora, a scruffy face, and a corduroy jacket. The man pressed his palms together in a prayerful pose and returned a small, grateful bow.

"You don't believe in God," said Johnny B.

"Went to church just last Easter."

"Anyway, that douche was wearing a brand new pair of Skechers."

"So what? I just gave him a twenty."

"Told you I saw this thing on TV," said Johnny B. "These stop-light guys average, like, a dollar for every light change. Twenty-five or thirty light changes an hour? That's, like, thirty dollars cash. Per hour. No taxes."

"Sayin' I just got scammed?"

"Just sayin', that's all."

"My money. My thing," explained Chris, wheeling left at the green arrow. "I do my pickups, what? Every other day? I give a buck back there every time. It's a thing for me. Like, for good luck."

"You got a superstition?"

"You can say that. Yeah. Maybe I do."

"And we're doin' pickups?" grinned Johnny B. He unconsciously rubbed his hands together.

"Don't go tellin' on me," warned Chris. "I know what Poppa said about you and family work. But he and I talked after. Not like he gave permission or nothin', but the way I see it, you're almost twenty."

"A year and four more months."

"Just keep your mouth shut and watch today. All right?"

"Where we goin' first?"

"Just makin' my stops. Checkin' on my boys. Collectin' some envelopes."

"But, like, where first?"

"What I say about keeping your mouth shut?"

The drive west brought them past a pair of municipal golf courses rimmed by a rambling bike and walking path. Johnny B. gazed out the window, joy on his face, marveling at all the weekday morning adults either cycling or jogging.

"Bet none of them have a job as good as mine," remarked Johnny B.

"Most of those assholes probably don't have a job at all," agreed Chris, firing a good-natured poke at his brother's bicep.

"I got this idea on how to become a big earner," shifted Johnny B.

"Hey. You're here to *learn* the biz," said Chris. "Not start any."

"Was thinkin' about all the stealing going 'round," continued Johnny B. "You know. People gettin' their, like, UPS and FedEx boxes stolen off their doorsteps—"

"Porch pirates," corrected Chris. "That's what they're called. And it's the kind of thievin' left for addicts and such."

"I know, I know. Saw all about it on YouTube. But what's stoppin' someone who sees the bigger picture?"

"Bigger?"

"Why not *follow* the delivery trucks? If the box they drop is little or light, you forget about it. It's probably, like, socks or stuffed animals or plastic flowers. But if the box is bigger? Something obvious like computer components and TV screens. You know. Electronics and stuff. Write down the address, come back later with a crew and a truck, and hit the place. Brand new merchandise. Maybe even still in the box."

"You think of that yourself or you just see that on TV?" Chris looked across at his brother, half serious, not yet fully impressed.

"It was *my* idea!" said Johnny B., almost insulted. "I figured I thought of it because I was Armenian Power now. And that's how we think."

Chris gave Johnny B.'s curly scalp a happy rub.

"You my lil' brother," said Chris proudly. "But you still gotta keep your mouth shut today. Watch and learn. If you feel like talkin', zip it anyway. Feel me?"

"I'm your brother," grinned Johnny B., thumping a fist to his flaccid chest. "And I feel you in my heart."

Technology. Damn.

To Lucky, the leaps in tracking humans were awe-inspiring—and terrifying as well. He'd performed only a single phone call and a text to gal pal Emery and in a matter of minutes she was able to geo-locate the suspect's mobile phone. And just like that, Lucky was receiving real-time updates on John Kasabian's movements throughout the central San Fernando Valley, courtesy of the private government contactor who employed Emery.

Lucky imagined what the feds could do—or already did—legally or otherwise. With mobile phones alone, they could monitor the movements and real-time audio of any city, county, or state police officer. Screw the body cameras, Lucky thought. The technology was there to identify any cop and spy into his or her most private conversations. What tales his phone could tell if targeted by Internal Affairs, a US Attorney, or even Gonzo, for that matter.

In little more than the sweep of the hour, Lucky had caught up with his subject, getting eyeballs on John Kasabian visiting a Panorama City tire shop. The eighteen-year-old, easily spotted in the same black T-shirt and jeans from the security videos, appeared to be hip-tied to his peacock-like older brother, a lissome young gangster with a buzzed head wearing a tailored paisley dress shirt. The teen appeared to be awkwardly hanging back a few feet while trying like hell to listen in on a hushed conversation between the young gangster and three taller rubber-jockeys in dirty coveralls.

From the tire joint, Lucky trailed the suspect riding shotgun in the Lexus coupe to a consistent queue of auto supply and repair shops. The scenes were repeated, with the brotherly peacock in the paisley shirt accepting the occasional envelope, beginning and ending every encounter with a mix of Eastern European men with handshakes and American-style bro hugs.

Armenian or Russian mob, Lucky confirmed his suspicion. Adding up all the stops, the running theme was clearly blue-collar and mostly automotive. Fronts, probably. Semi-cash businesses—all legitimate—but most likely masks for criminality. Lucky knew auto theft rings often centered on the car repair business of some form or another. And the Eastern European style of organized crime syndicates required their soldiers of all stripes to work bona fide aboveboard day jobs as covers. Through Lucky's prism, every face and posture fit the underworld profile.

Except for the young turd in the punchbowl.

John Kasabian. Lucky's accident suspect. He didn't fit, never looked the least bit comfortable in the various situations, not to mention his own skin, and with every consecutive stop, took on the growing affect of a bored puppy dog.

On the split second each meeting broke, the hulking teen who presented as nearly twice the bulk of his older brother, couldn't wait to return to his oversized smartphone to—in Lucky's non-clinical guestimate—continue playing some genus of online game.

The collections tour paused near one p.m. After the central Valley circuit of meet-ups and envelope pickups, the Kasabian brothers shifted into lunch mode at a North Hills liquor mart. The former fruit-packing space, retrofitted to accommodate an ethnic mix of grocery store, butcher shop, and every imaginable brand of imported vodka, featured a small corner deli decorated with Armenian soccer posters and looping strings of Slavic flags hanging from the high ceiling. Upon Lucky's entrance, he spotted a gathering of small tables pulled together, accommodating what appeared to be yet another meet-up. The paisley-shirted gangster sat back, relaxed and sharing jokes and hits on an electronic cigarette with four muscled men of equal age and casual dress. Peers, it seemed. Like fellow mob lieutenants.

Lucky's ears culled a name. Mikayel. He'd clocked the lieutenant as the tallest of the crew. Maybe six-five or six-six. Athletic. Winning grin. After the peacock, Mikayel was the second alpha.

At the deli counter, Lucky perused the chalkboard menu, ordered a lentil soup and coffee, added the morning issue of the *Daily News* to his tab, and settled into a corner table set up near a display of herbal teas for sale. Hard as he tried to clue his ears into the conversation across the space from him, he picked up only the occasional string of English. The rest, he concluded, was Armenian. Entirely left out of the jokes and obvious camaraderie was his suspect, John Kasabian. As platters of food were served, the awkward teen never touched a bite. He jittered his right leg anxiously, kept his nose to the game on his phone, and sucked back can after can of Dr Pepper until he eventually asked his brother if he could be excused to go to the restroom.

Opportunity had just knocked. Lucky counted to thirty in his head, slurped a final spoonful of soup, stood, and left a two-dollar tip under his coffee mug. Behind him, the laughter trailed as he followed the overhead sign leading him between the whisky and tequila aisles to an industrial bathroom marked with the international figure for male. A toilet flushed. Lucky's suspect exited the single stall, glanced left at Lucky, then stopped at the sink to wash his hands.

"You're John Kasabian?" asked Lucky, though it didn't sound at all like question.

Johnny B.'s body stuttered as he jerked around to get a second look at Lucky. The moment their eyes met, the teen slung his view down and away.

"John Kasabian who drives a new black Shelby Super Snake," continued Lucky. "Nice whip."

"Who you?" asked the teen, looking everywhere but at Lucky. His arms defensively wrapped around his body. Not so much closed off, but as if he needed to hold himself in place, otherwise he might just melt. Johnny B. rocked in place.

That's when it clicked for Lucky. He'd been observing Johnny B. for hours already. The odd social cues. The tics. The inability to mix with peers.

Asperger's. Spectrum disorder.

The revelation explained so much. Until that moment, Lucky had been trailing somebody he'd just assumed was some entitled, selfish ass-bucket who'd accidentally caused a fatal car wreck and blithely walked away. Up close, though, young John Kasabian reeked of somebody entirely different. Like a middle schooler trapped in an adult's body.

"Name's Lucky," he softened. "I'm a detective with County Sheriff's."

"'Kay," rocked Johnny B.

"Not here to arrest you," eased Lucky. "Just wanted to put the face to some video I have."

"What video?"

"The accident," said Lucky. "Woodland Hills. You remember? You chucked a sandwich into traffic."

"Philly cheesy," Johnny B. nearly whispered as if to remind himself.

"First off, lemme tell you that I *know* it was only an *accident*,"

Lucky impressed. "I know you didn't mean to get anybody hurt. Maybe I can get you to come out to my car. Just you 'n' me. We can have us a talk about it. Okay? Can we do that?"

"Get in your car?"

"Just wanna hear your side of things."

"I dunno 'bout that."

"Look. I'm not even LAPD. They got jurisdiction on this. You know what that is?"

Johnny B. shook his head.

"Jurisdiction means it's their investigation. LAPD's. I'm Sheriff's. I'm just writing a report. Words on paper. That's all."

"'Kay."

"I have video, though. Of you. The sandwich. What happens after."

"There's video?"

"Come out to my car. We'll talk. I'll show you. And I promise we'll only talk."

The teen's eyes hadn't lifted since first making contact with Lucky's. They'd remained at half mast, waist high, rapidly scanning at nothing in particular until they made a sudden flick up and to Lucky's left. Johnny B.'s mouth appeared to be forming into a word when the first blow landed.

Lucky's lights went out.

The force of the fist—and whatever may have been clenched in it—temporarily cut Lucky's motors when it landed above his left ear. The blackout lasted nary a second, with consciousness resuming as the cracks of the bathroom floor looked to be racing at him. He'd barely folded up onto the tile when the first boot struck him between the shoulder blades.

"Fuckin' perv!" Lucky thought he heard.

The invectives that followed—*Faggot! Cunt! Fucker! Shitknob!*—reverbed off the bathroom surfaces in percussive concert with a flurry of kicks and foot stomps from what he pictured was a trio of assailants. He desperately wanted—and surely would have barked—*I'm a cop!* Only that would've required air from his lungs to force a sound. He'd already lost his breath with a smash to his solar plexus. The wind gushed from him like gas from a popped balloon. All he could muster was a wheeze, his arms involuntarily bracing to save his ribs, unable to reach for his .45.

Lucky's eyes, though, flashed across the men's faces. He'd captured each grimace, smirk, and grin. The most familiar was the big, athletic gangster they'd called Mikayel. Yet even more arresting than the flashed visages of his attackers was poor Johnny Boy. The teen had recoiled up against the urinals, his face contorted in a mash-up of excitement and fear.

"Pervert's got a piece!" shouted a voice.

There came a pause in the attack. Before Lucky could make a grab for his pistol, he felt it tugged clear of his holster.

"Badass faggot with a SIG .45?"

"Thinks he's a fuckin' Omar."

"Johnny!" shouted a voice from the open door. "Let's go! Now!"

Despite the hard echo, Lucky clearly remembered the voice as belonging to the older brother—a memory that would end up as bruised as his body.

The assault ended after Lucky saw Johnny B.'s Converse All-Stars beating a straight path for the exit. He heard his .45 splash into the toilet bowl, followed by an automated, industrial-sounding *whooosh* of the toilet's flush.

14

Lee Chapman's midday habit was to be the very last spectator to exit Department J. When Judge Sollocito adjourned her court for lunch, the wannabe screenwriter would purposefully remain rooted in his rear corner seat, pretending to be making notations in his trademark red spiral notebook, his head tilted and his eyes guarded under the felt brim of his hat. He listened for the snaps of lawyers' briefcases, scraping dress shoes, clicking high heels, and the rustle of defendant denim as the courtroom slowly emptied. The act usually left a breathless thirty seconds when it was only himself and the bailiff, Deputy Shia St. George, in the baffled chamber.

"Hey, you," she'd usually sound out from some thirty-five feet, never venturing beyond the rail. "Gotta lock it up for lunch."

She knows my name, Lee would remind himself, instantly forgiving the deputy because he guessed she was required to behave within the strictest measures of professionalism. A less familiar Shia St. George would've called him "sir." Referring to Lee as "you" was friendly-like. Pally. Affectionate, even. And almost . . .

. . . *Intimate.*

In order to avoid the annoying reentry through the first-floor security gauntlet, Lee packed a light lunch—usually a lean *cotija* chicken salad packed in a disposable plastic container. He set down his backpack underneath one of the polished concrete benches that stood against the courthouse building's floor-to-ceiling windows. He ignored the central Valley view that he'd come to know by rote—the hardpan semi-urban sprawl beneath a cloudless blue-sky banner. From inside the air-conditioned high-rise, the outside conditions could be anywhere between sixty degrees and a hundred and ten and Lee wouldn't have felt a degree of difference.

"Kiddin' me?" Lee said aloud, picking through his Vallarta Market lunch sack. The plastic utensil he'd expected to be included was nowhere to be found, an obvious oversight on the part of the lazy-ass *ese* working behind the deli counter.

Fer fuck's sake!

Without an instrument to neatly eat his lunch, Lee pondered for a silent few seconds before choosing to toss his salad and head downstairs for a two-dollar hot dog from one of the sidewalk vendors who worked the midday courthouse exodus. With his backpack awkwardly slung over his shoulder like some kind of deformity, Lee hiked to the elevator bank, pressed a down button, and was instantly favored with an empty car. No sooner had he stepped aboard than he heard a familiar voice.

"Hold that, will ya?"

Lee stuck out his arm, reversing the direction on the automated door, and watched her slide past him—the closest he'd ever been.

"Thanks," Shia smiled, stepping aboard.

Her fragrance—hardly more than the remnant of herbal soap—tickled his nostrils. The door finally closed and once again they were alone. Lee was a breath away from mentioning the obvious—if even as a lighthearted parry in hopes of instigating banter—then *ding!*—the car slowed to open on the sixth floor. Two uniformed cops slipped in along with a taller, elder gent speaking with friendly surprise.

"Well, if it isn't Mr. Tweedy," acknowledged Judge Jaime Peralta with a dismissive nod before turning his body to include only Shia with his attention. "*Aaaand* lest I forget, Deputy Shia St. George. How is everything in Department J for Justice?"

"We're holdin' up our end," Shia replied.

"Hey," said Judge Jim. "Have you met my friends Miles and Charlie? They work across the plaza."

"LAPD?" nodded Shia, offering a hand. "I mighta seen you around."

"Lieutenant Czajkowski. Sergeant Charlie Freeman," introduced Miles. "And believe it or not, think we might be acquainted with your former training officer."

"Small universe, your cop world," remarked Judge Jim.

"Maybe," said Shia. "Or Lucky Dey gets himself around. That man's got himself some serious rep."

"You don't say?" feigned Judge Jim.

"Don't let the old guy fool ya," teased Miles. "We know Lucky from doin' the blue man crew thing with the Mid-Valley Ponies."

"Ponies?" quizzed Shia.

"Little League," said Sugar. "All of us. We volunteer umpire together."

"Oh," blushed Shia. "Was thinking you were talking about some kind of strip joint."

The quartet laughed as if Lee wasn't even there. Invisible. His tweedy self squished into a corner. Once again resigned to nothing more than observer status.

But that smile of hers.

She was so close to Lee. Closer than ever. And so damned radiant. As if her playful demeanor with the two suited men stripped her of that awful defeminizing uniform. She reeked of estrogen. Her posture softened, curves accentuated. She was all woman and . . .

. . . flirting?

Lee felt blood rush into his face. Embarrassment. Anger. It surged upward and presented with prickly sweat underneath his felt hat. He feared she would look at him and see him for all his flaws and ugly failures. He imagined himself a chalkboard covered in his ex-wife's scrawl detailing his every guilty fault. He lowered his hat brim, sunk deeper into the corner, and waited for the ghastly ride to end.

With a jolting stop, the door opened and Judge Jim and his two cop pals stepped aside to let Shia clear out. If the foursome had spoken anymore or uttered polite goodbyes, Lee never heard, his ears having shut in a sphincter-like squeeze. His stomach churned and demanded release. Head down, he rushed into the lobby and swerved toward the bathrooms. All thoughts of lunch, his tossed salad, or the promise of a two-dollar hot dog vanquished from the onslaught of shameful feelings.

Shia missed so very little, especially when it came to small details. In her months of tutelage under Lucky Dey, her sense of the unusual—the off-kilter and out-of-the-ordinary—had gone from keen to highly focused. The tweedy little man who'd sat daily in Judge Sollocito's court had become a curiosity to her, maybe even a slight concern. At her mention of the man with the red spiral notebook, Judge Sollo had merely shrugged it off.

"Mr. Chapman?" she'd replied. "Not close to a threat. Just another man with a screenplay. And in L.A.? That's, like, half the damn city."

Indeed, Shia knew the man's name. But when it came time to hustle him out of the courtroom—at either lunchtime or day's end—she'd made a choice not to let on or appear that, at least from her perspective, he was welcome beyond his legally protected status as John Q. Citizen and his right to sit in and observe American due process in all its transparent glory. Initially, she'd politely called him "sir." After a week, she'd chosen a more dismissive tone, saying only "hey, you" to get his attention—not at all unlike when she rolled the streets of Compton in a sheriff's black-and-white, windows down, to interface with the community.

Her plan was to meet up with a group of deputies at the nearby Sam Woo's BBQ for lunch. Only before the short bus ride, she changed her heading for a quick pit stop in the ladies' room. When she pivoted left toward the back of the downstairs lobby, she saw Lee Chapman trotting a beeline for the men's bathroom. Poor little parrot man. He was clearly on a mission to expel something rotten. Perhaps it was a viral thing. Shia thought twice as to whether or not she'd touched anything in the elevator other than Judge Jim's or the LAPD lieutenant's hand. Miles, she remembered, not missing the man's white gold wedding ring. There'd been a lingering squeeze on the handshake as well as some impressive eye contact. Nothing Shia wasn't used to. Especially with male cops, most of whom she rightly knew were dogs—nearly to a man.

But not Lucky.

Never once had he tried to bed her, despite their obvious chemistry and shared sexual tension during all the tedious wee hours they'd spent together in the front seat of a radio unit.

Not once. Until we kissed.

It was then that she knew for sure there was indeed *something* there. Palpable. It lay barely beneath the surface, a connection beyond that of just training officer and trainee. Yet a kiss was all it might ever be. It was a bitter pill that Shia found impossible to swallow.

A love thing?

No, she insisted to herself. It was a sex thing—that never-allowed-to-digest notion of *what if?* Her time with Lucky was stuck to her. And the further and longer they worked apart, the harder it seemed for Shia to shake her need to reach out even if only to discover the attraction was mutual.

Sucks for you, girl. But prolly not so much for him.

After all, Shia kept excusing, Lucky had Gonzo. Gonzo had Lucky. And the two of them had built a provisional family out of both necessity and affection. So, why compete? The last thing

Shia wanted on her personal résumé was the title of Miss Deputy Homewrecker.

Shia reversed her thoughts back to her grumbling stomach, the finite time allotted by Judge Sollo for her lunch break, and to sinking her incisors into a phallic-looking beef rib at Sam Woo's BBQ.

Damn it, bitch, Shia complained to herself. *You need to get yourself laid.*

Lucky lay on the bathroom floor of the liquor mart, cold from the tile and sticky wet from blood dripping out of his nose and split lower lip, waiting for the vision in his left eye to realign with his right, which remained crisp and in focus. The view from his left was shadowed and snapping back and forth. Concussion, he reckoned. *Shit.* He found himself employing unusual patience to collect his brain, his agenda, and more acutely, his errors. His reflexive self would have had him dialing 911 on his mobile phone, identifying himself as an assaulted sheriff's deputy, and setting off a domino effect of cops flooding into the zone. The assailants would be hard to ID, let alone snare, but for that peacock young gangster in the Lexus. He and teenaged John Kasabian were sure to get scooped, cuffed, and deposited into some form of police custody within the hour.

Johnny B.

That's what the peacock had called him. Lucky had been struck by the young man's awkwardness, his socially inept condition. And when Lucky replayed the conversation, most likely overheard by one of Johnny's tablemates, he could comprehend—even appreciate—the depth of the misunderstanding. The goons had rushed in to protect their weaker charge from what appeared to be a pervert suggesting a sex tryst in his nearby parked car. Hell, thought Lucky. It was the kind of righteous ass-whooping he might've dealt—and probably had—back in his Lennox days.

"Ow, fuck!" he cried at the pain.

With barely a chuckle, Lucky sent himself into spasms of

stabbing pain. Busted ribs, he worried. Maybe worse. Flogging himself with third-person curses, he crawled to his feet and shouldered himself into the toilet stall to retrieve his soaked pistol. Temporarily useless, Lucky popped the magazine, cleared the chamber, and used paper towels and a heated hand-dryer to retard any immediate rusting. As soon as he could return to Temple Street, he'd strip it and drop the pieces into the dehumidifier for an overnight bake. Then he'd glue himself to his desk, tap out the unofficial accident report, forward it to both McGill and the LAPD's CID, and be done with the stupid-assed assignment.

But first, a doctor.

Hitching his aching body across the gravel parking lot, Lucky tried to mentally assemble a list of urgent care facilities where he might be able to hop the line. Then he remembered his location. North Hills. The deep Valley. His orthopedist was only a quick jog south to Tarzana. With luck and a willingness to talk a little cop shop, Lucky bet his true-crime-loving spine doctor would return some VIP attention.

"Nothing broken," the aloha-shirted doc announced after a review of Lucky's X-rays. "Obvious bruising to your right intercostals—that's the muscle meat between the ribs. It can hurt worse than a broken rib, so go easy and up the anti-inflammatories. What kinda post-surgery painkiller I used to have you on? Percocet?"

In a finger snap Lucky realized he hadn't been treated by the good doc since his days of abusing opioids. Arguments with Gonzo about whether or not he was truly addicted aside, Lucky didn't care to tempt his system and imbibe. He informed the doctor and settled for some sample packs of prednisone. He purposefully failed to mention the head trauma. Lucky's vision had returned to something passing for normal and, he rationalized, if he could survive a .25-caliber bullet in the head, he sure as hell could handle the idiot headache and faint but lingering dental drill-like whine lodged in his ear canals.

By four o'clock Lucky had returned to his Major Crimes Bureau desk, having crept in via the freight elevator and through the rear door of the windowless unit. With his skull feeling twice its usual size, he wasn't keen on the customary cop banter. Considering his demeanor and physical affect, someone regarding Lucky from a distance might've assumed he was hungover, a slightly better excuse than the embarrassing truth.

Oh, yeah. I got rolled by four Armo gangbangers who mistook me for a toilet hawk.

Flashes of the beatdown returned in living color. Lucky recalled clocking two forearms bearing identifying ink. Cyrillic crosses. The *de rigueur* mark of one of the two Armenian gangs: Armenian Power and Armenian Pride. As much co-conspirators in crime than rival sets, Lucky knew enough to remember there were training academies for the larger and more insidious Armenian mob, a Los Angeles subsect of the internationally powerful Bratva Brothers—a.k.a. the Russian Mafia.

But only the identity and Glendale address of Johnny B. was pertinent to his report. It was, after all, only the accident that Lucky had been tasked with. Johnny B., who based on his condition would probably be diagnosed with a low frustration threshold, had only hurled his sandwich in some kind of fit. Had he meant to disrupt rush-hour traffic? Or set off the chain reaction of braking, skidding, and converging g-forces leading to the tragic death of a Malibu Barbie mom? Doubtful. Or as the lawyers liked to identify an innocent act resulting in human injury, it was *absence of malice*. After Lucky washed his hands of the quick investigation, it would be up to the blue-black-clad men and women of the LAPD and, more than likely, some high-test personal injury attorneys looking to line their pinstriped pockets with insurance money.

Because the report was unofficial, he wasn't required to upload it into the L.A. Sheriff's system. A detailed email from his lasd.org address would suffice. Lucky tapped out his notes, hours, and investigative chronology up to Glendale, where Johnny B.'s mother shut the door on him. The rest of his two-day adventure was nobody else's business. With the document complete, all Lucky had to do was press send, feign a stomach virus as an excuse for his early exit, then return his rattled brain and body to just how the hell he was going to extricate himself from Judge Jim's invite to join the illegal case-making cabal.

Press. Send.

The chair creaked loudly as he sat back and waited for a confirmation receipt for the sent email. Instead, his electronic out-box revealed the message hadn't left. After three more failed attempts to send the email, Lucky slapped the top of his desk with a louder than expected *thwap!*

"Oh, c'mon, you b—" he griped, swallowing the last word of his outburst. The last thing he needed to ice his cake was to be written up for sexually offending his computer—or others within earshot.

"You too?" replied a voice. It was a detective called Carmac, Lucky's immediate neighbor on the other side of the cubicle.

"Email won't go," complained Lucky.

"Half the building's off the grid," stood Carmac, eyeing Lucky over the partition top. "Shit, dude. Didn't even know you were in today."

"Anybody say when shit's gonna be working?" Though he was speaking to Carmac, Lucky kept the bill of his baseball hat angled downward.

"Nope. I'm just loading my out-box and hoping it goes when we're back up again."

Lucky finally glanced upward. Carmac, the career detective with the prematurely gray hair and a gin-blossomed nose, was like a whack-a-mole character, popping out of his chair to speak then dropping back down before Lucky could lift his chin. And thanks to Lucky's audible outburst, any chance of him ghosting back out of the office was in doubt, later to be confirmed when the unit commander pulled in every available detective for an unscheduled case conference. During the team meet-up, a roughly twice-monthly surprise event, chairs were pulled into the center of the room and all active folders were talked through, cover to cover, with each non-participating detective invited to weigh in with an investigative opinion. During Lucky's short tenure, he'd found it equal parts elucidating, butt-numbing, and exposing as to which investigators were the ass-kissing busy-makers versus the detectives who could grind out a quality arrest.

Making matters gleefully uncomfortable was Zadeh. She was forty minutes late to the meeting and, upon arrival, spun up a chair behind and slightly to the left of Lucky. Every so often she'd tilt forward and, in a breathy hush that smelled of a garlic hummus snack, lend a personal opinion for seemingly no other reason than for him to hear her whisper. Lucky wondered if she could count the standing hairs on the back of his neck or make out the bruise forming in the shape of a boot print.

Then came the texts. All from Gonzo who had a bad habit of using her send button as a thought-ending period. They were make-up sentences without apologies. She'd found an online recipe under "best meatballs ever" and was planning a family meal. Of course, she claimed to understand if he was busy, angry, or indifferent. He acknowledged with a shorthand *okay*, informed her of his current meeting-without-an-end-in-sight and promised to let her know the moment he'd cleared Temple Street's underground parking and was pointed home.

"Got Advil?" Lucky semi-twisted around to Zadeh.

"Why? I leave you sore and wantin'?" she leered.

"You got 'em or you don't."

Zadeh pushed off and over to her desk without leaving her chair. She returned with a double shake of a pill bottle.

"How many?" she asked.

Lucky held up four fingers, returned his eyes to the puffy detective reciting his case in a dusty manner resembling testimony in front of a jury, and flattened his palm until he felt the capsules land. He fisted them and, in an addict's move, popped them to the back of his throat and dry-swallowed a pair at a time.

"Sheezus," said Zadeh, catching an angle on Lucky's split and swollen lower lip. "Who'd you throw down with?"

"Caught one sparring with my daughter," lied Lucky. "Muay Thai. Last time I go without headgear."

"And to think I was so proud of my own moves," she quietly giggled.

"Thanks for the meds," replied Lucky without even the slightest eye contact. He wasn't outright rejecting her. After all, as much as she was a reminder of his moral weakness, she was a colleague with whom he'd require a working relationship. He'd rather keep his faithless indiscretion in his rearview mirror. Only five minutes shy of a break point in the individual presentations, Zadeh quietly excused herself to use the women's restroom and never returned. Lucky paid little attention to her convenient exit beyond justifying that she was a Major Crimes veteran with a personal relationship to the captain.

And *why* was none of his damned business.

As promised, the moment the grille of Lucky's '99 cleared the threshold of Temple Street's underground garage, he released a pre-composed text to Gonzo and swerved north toward the nearest entrance to the Pasadena Freeway. The city was slipping into twilight and the downtown skyscrapers, a polarizing contrast to the topography's seemingly endless horizontal sprawl, were a geometric collage of sky-reflecting windows and gold-lit rectangles.

Lucky stuffed his trepidation. After two nights of banishment, he'd been invited home. If there was subtext to Gonzo's texts, it was a plea for normalcy. For her and the kids. It wasn't for Lucky to ask. Only to deliver. He knew there'd come a quiet moment between them. Chock-full of tension, which he'd have to break with gentle hands and a heartfelt apology. Something authentic. He could only hope the guilt of his tumble from the fidelity wagon didn't arouse Gonzo's bullshit detector.

Before it was the Pasadena Freeway—the world's oldest expressway of its kind—the four-lane ribbon was called the Arroyo Parkway. Its snaking route was designed as much for its scenic path as for delivering passengers to the mounds and hollows of neighborhoods called Montecito Heights, Highland Park, and historic Garvanza. Lucky kept his eyes on the darkened spans, only guessing he was traveling at just shy of seventy miles per hour—this on a blacktop better suited for speeds around fifty-five with on- and off-ramps shorter than four car-lengths. The antique overpasses, decorated with concrete arches and chest-high rails, were infamous for shielding vandals as they made targets out of passing cars, hurling everything from overripe persimmons to bricks to bags of wet mortar.

Nice damn neighborhood.

The rest of Lucky's route home was a zigzag cut up through Pasadena's lower residential blocks until he struck Lake Street. From there, home in Altadena was less than a ten-minute roll up a slow-moving slope. The red, yellow, and green traffic lights mixed with the uniform streams of taillights and headlights were so straight up the hill they could've been drawn with a ruler. A chirp came from his mobile phone. A glance told Lucky it was from Gonzo. He waited for the next stoplight before giving it a read, only able to lodge the first six words of her request before the accident happened.

plz cld u pick up 4 . . .

It started with the tires. Locked wheels followed by the familiar squeal of rubber sliding across asphalt. Before Lucky could flick his eyes up to his rearview mirror, he felt it. The *slam!*—a sudden shock from behind—the plastic crunch of distorting car bumpers. The '99 was shoved nearly a foot before it rocked back to stillness.

"Shhhit," pissed Lucky. "Really?"

The offending car filling Lucky's rearview mirror was too close to fix a make or model. The driver's silhouette was clearly that of a male with two arms lifted in ugly frustration, hands pathetically atop his head as if to say, *What did I just do?*

"Let's get this over with." Lucky shouldered his car door, intending to step out only momentarily to direct the other driver over to the curb. Southbound cars whizzed to Lucky's right and horns from cars stuck behind the fender bender were already sounding. The driver responsible for the rear-end collision was behind the wheel of a green Volvo wagon, 2002 model year. Two passengers. With the firmness of his authority, Lucky pointed to the driver, then swung his finger to the curb.

The driver gestured back a shrug and open palms. Lucky twirled a finger and took two steps forward.

"Roll down your window!" instructed Lucky.

"S'cuse, what?" sounded the driver, his window only lowered a third.

"We're blocking traffic," pressed Lucky. "Meet me over at the curb."

"Sorry," said the driver, his bald dome and squeezed pair of eyes barely clearing the window. "Can't hear you. Horns and all. What again?"

Enough, thought Lucky. He was automatically reaching into his belt for his sheriff's shield. A simple authority play was generally sufficient to cut through the crap.

"Step to the car, get in the back," said the voice, hushed and to his near right.

Before Lucky could even glance, he felt an arm on his back and a firm gun muzzle in his ribs.

"Volvo. Back seat," repeated the voice. "Don't worry. We got your car."

The moment slowed into micro-beats as Lucky quickly thought. If it was to be an assassination, he'd have been dead already. He could fight back, sweep the gun muzzle with a twist and an elbow, and probably survive the first shot. But then again, he'd never know who wanted his attention so badly to hijack him in the middle of mid-evening traffic. As Lucky stepped to the Volvo he heard his car's door slam followed by the Crown Vic's familiar eight-cylinder rumble. As a kidnapping, it was slick, utilizing no fewer than six men by Lucky's estimate—three in the Volvo, one in his '99 Crown Vic, another in an unknown assist vehicle, and the deadly sixth with the gun in his side.

Inside the Volvo's rear seat, a man reached across to push open the door. As the face neared the window, Lucky flushed with recognition. It was that little peacock. The paisley-shirted gangster with the buzz cut shoved the door open, then slid over to make room for Lucky. Once both Lucky's feet were inside, the atmosphere turned into a vacuum as the car door *thunked* shut behind him. The car lurched ahead. Through the windshield, Lucky could see his '99 leading the route, signaling and executing a safe turn at the first available right.

"You're not in danger," began Chris Kasabian, his own palm-sized Beretta pistol pressed gently against Lucky's temple, "but I'm gonna need your metal."

As Chris worked a free hand behind Lucky's shirttail for his .45, the sheriff's deputy was examining the burly features of the fortyish man in the front passenger seat. The mustache was a tell. Old country. Armenia. But would his English come with an inflection of home?

The .45 was dropped in the well at Lucky's feet. A pat-down of his pant legs revealed the same caliber backup pistol he strapped above his right boot.

"Wow. You carry two," said Chris. "Certified badass."

"Apologize," grumbled Vaz from the passenger seat.

"Right," said Chris. "Sorry, man. This afternoon. The bathroom thing. Thought you were—"

"A toilet hawk?"

"What?" asked Chris.

"Pervert," clarified Lucky.

"Yeah. Oh, yeah," chuckled Chris. "Looked really wrong. My guys got out of hand."

"Just protecting your brother," Lucky guessed.

"You can understand," chimed Vaz. "He was only looking out for his own."

"Figured as much," said Lucky. "But it's not like I wound shit up. Put the dogs on you."

"Yeah. But you seriously had me going," admitted Chris. "Spent the rest of the day checking my rearview mirror."

"That's what this is?" asked Lucky. "You hijack me to say I'm sorry? That's a new one."

"I begin with apology," said Vaz, revealing a slight accent as he pushed the short O sound into a longer, guttural *ooohhh*. "We come as friends."

"Since we're practically giving each other bro hugs and shit," asked Lucky. "You got names?"

"That is Christopher," said Vaz. "Johnny's older brother. And I'm Vartan Kasabian. But everybody calls me Vaz."

The father twisted in his seat and offered an open hand. Lucky slowed things down before he accepted. Both grips revealed to the other an understandable male resolve.

"Now, my youngest son," continued Vaz. "He's in some trouble?"

"Concerned dad," acknowledged Lucky. "Okay. I get it. How about I make it easy for you and just forward you the unofficial report?"

"Unofficial?"

"The accident. In Woodland Hills? It's LAPD jurisdiction."

"That's right," Chris remembered. "You're Sheriff's."

"Let him talk," admonished Vaz.

"Victim's from Malibu. That's Sheriff's country," Lucky said. "I was instructed to investigate and write. An assist to the PD. That's all it was. All it still is."

"You deliver this report?"

"Stop dancing and tell me what you want," pressed Lucky.

"My son . . ." began Vaz, his voice dropping so deep it sounded as if he might choke. "Johnny B. He's different. Not so normal, if you know what I'm saying. He's weak. Fragile boy. With his own very personal problems. You hear of something called Asperger's Syndrome?"

"Not Asperger's anymore," corrected Chris. "They changed it to Autism Spectrum Disorder."

"My normal son," an annoyed Vaz gestured. "Not weak. Not fragile. Who thinks he knows more than his father. Is that right?"

"Just sayin', Poppa."

"This car accident," continued Vaz. "My Johnny is the responsible party?"

"Appears that way," said Lucky. "Emphasis on accident. And that's it. An accident."

"So, there's no crime?"

"Vehicle Code is 23110. And depending on the DA's office? It can go low as a misdemeanor. Or because he fled the scene with knowledge, he can be charged with felony manslaughter. Not my call, though. Like I said. Not even my jurisdiction."

"But you were the police who knocked on my door," implied Vaz. "Followed both my sons."

"You're gonna wanna talk to the DA," repeated Lucky. "Or the LAPD."

"But they aren't in my car," said Vaz coolly, his agenda revealed with every careful word. "They are not you. You are a father?"

"Yeah," said Lucky, though weirdly feeling that it was a lie. Even under pressure, the family thing felt fake.

Or maybe you're the fake, you asshole.

"My son," continued Vaz. "Believe me when I say to you he is not strong enough for prosecution, let alone incarceration."

"It's out of my hands—"

"It's not anybody's fault!" burst Vaz. His voice cracked, betraying all the pain he kept at bay. "Nobody's fault. Not yours, mine, his. Johnny was born with it. Since he was five—his mother and I—we have done *everything* we could. Therapies. Treatment. Hospitals. The group home . . . He is who he is and I love him no less than Chris here. So, you see, whatever happened, it wasn't his fault."

"Listen," calmed Lucky. "I've met your boy and I'm on your side with this—"

"But it is not under your control?"

"LAPD will investigate. They will meet your son. There is a record of his condition and treatment so they will most likely—"

"No, no, no, no," corrected Vaz. "There is no 'most likely' for Johnny Boy. A family cannot risk 'most likely.' You too are a family man. I can't believe you would allow 'most likely' to define their future."

"Life is a risk," hard-lined Lucky. "As a parent or father I do only what *I* can do."

"Then we have an understanding," Vaz grinned, so pleased he slapped the top of the console.

Lucky's eyes squeezed shut, if only briefly, in a gesture of frustration. The Armenian gangster had clearly misunderstood him. Lucky was preparing his rephrase when he noticed the Volvo had come to a complete stop in the middle of a residential street.

At a glance, in the darkness, it could have been anywhere. Yet the configuration of porch lamps, driveway lights, and lit windows made Lucky reflexively snap his head a hundred degrees to his left. Their little convoy was stalled outside his renovated Craftsman bungalow. Through the living room shades he could see shadows in the dining room—Karrie and Travis setting the table for dinner.

"We *don't* understand each other," Lucky corrected emphatically.

"No?" asked Vaz. "You know where my family lives. Now *we* know where your family lives. Nice bungalow, by the way. I'm a fan of Arts and Crafts. You a collector?"

"Just the mortgage," replied Lucky, the gist of Vaz's shift in attitude sinking in with the man's every pleased-with-himself syllable.

"Question," restarted Lucky. "Is there something about me that suggests I can be bent?"

"We're fathers," quipped Vaz. "And when it comes to our children, we are all bent. Yes?"

In what ways am I not *bent?*

With the thought stuck in his head, Lucky paused at the threshold of the bungalow's kitchen door and collected his jangled nerves. This before delivering himself to those close to him whose lives had just been threatened—albeit indirectly—by a supposedly equally concerned father.

An Armenian mob father.

Though Lucky had questioned his authentic connection to his concocted family, his current desire to protect them seared at every sinew. The second he'd stepped from the kidnappers' Volvo, he'd busted out in a sweat. It soaked through the front of his Tommy Bahama shirt. Silk. An unworn gift from Gonzo that she'd packed in that overnight bag. If he wasn't the center of calm walking into his home, each and every member would be throwing queries about his health, his demeanor, or his commitment to hearth and home.

He painted on a smile, tried not to wince when his lip

stung, and pushed the door inward. Instantly, he was accosted by the smell of slow-cooked meatballs and sweet basil.

"Daddy's home," quipped Travis loudly, as if trying on the sound of the word tripping over his tongue.

"Lucky Dey to save the day," added Gonzo, tossing a salad. Only she looked up and saw he'd walked through the door empty-handed. "Did you forget something?"

"Could be . . ." said Lucky, not at all certain what she was saying. He was busy giving some quick attention to Oprah, who'd come barreling at him, all fur and wagging tail.

"Pasta?" she reminded. "Spaghetti noodles? I sent you a text."

"Sorry," pleaded Lucky, dipping for his phone. "Didn't see it."

"All the extra time you took gettin' home," she continued. "Thought where could you have been other than the market?"

"Fender bender," shrugged Lucky, starting with the truth before fiction. "Got me from behind."

"The Vic?"

"*No hablo.* No insurance. No registration," lied Lucky.

"God bless America," jested Travis before shaking more Parmesan cheese onto his palm and licking it.

"That's so disgusting," careened Karrie into the kitchen. She threw her arms over Lucky's shoulders from behind, pulled herself up, and kissed his cheek. "Welcome home."

"Owwww?" Lucky tried to joke, only the pain was terribly real.

"You got whiplash?" asked Travis.

"I'm old," Lucky replied. "Everything hurts."

"Not even forty, you big pussy," grinned Gonzo, well aware of Lucky's injury-prone career, as well as all the permanent steel screws in his back. She pecked him on the lips softly, then flicked a look across his pupils as if to say, *I see your split lip and I know that shit didn't happen in a fender bender.* Then in an eyeblink, she was whisking past with a finished salad. "So, it's meatballs with no spaghetti."

"Hold off twenty minutes. I'll go get it," apologized Lucky.

"And risk you not coming home?" Gonzo jibed to the amusement of Karrie and Travis.

"Owned," laughed Travis. "That makes you her *bitch*."

"Trav," warned Gonzo. "And bring the cheese, please?"

Lucky washed his hands in the sink, toweled off, and joined his crew around the circular antique dining room table Gonzo had purchased because she said it "matched the house." As his elbows touched the tabletop, he thought of Vartan Kasabian and his question: Was Lucky a collector of the Arts and Crafts era?

I collect bad guys' scalps, asshole. And yours could be next.

Then came the inner conflict. He glanced at each of their faces—from Karrie to Travis to Gonzo—and was flushed with both affection and a soul-busting care for the trio. None were his blood. Yet they were his just the same. What must Vartan Kasabian have felt for his troubled son? A boiling DNA-need to protect his last-born and most innocent?

"What?" asked Gonzo.

"Dunno," quizzed Lucky, confused. All three were staring back at him as if he had been caught at something.

"What happened to your lip?" asked Travis, only now noticing.

"Totally fake," winked Lucky, putting more spin in his reply than the actual truth. "Halloween party at the office. Didn't have a costume, so I smacked myself into a door."

"I call bullshit!" said Travis.

"Trav." Gonzo looked down her nose at her son.

"Are you crying?" asked Karrie, invested in Lucky's odd demeanor.

"Lucky doesn't cry," insisted Travis.

"Only when Lucky loses," Gonzo teased.

"Just a little whiplash." Lucky forced a smile. "Why aren't we eating?"

"Grace first." Karrie held out her hands, taking Lucky's and Gonzo's. The rest of the foursome uncomfortably followed suit. Praying before meals was new, speared on by Karrie's infectious zeal. Nobody was up for denying her. "Dear Lord. We thank you for this food, this family, this warm and comfortable home . . ."

Family, thought Lucky. Was it so? Was it true? Did he really belong to a clan that didn't come with a Reaper tattoo? While Karrie prayed, Lucky found himself making a personal appeal to God.

If you're there, Mr. Jesus, Lucky silently asked. *How about some goddamn personal clarity?*

15

Koreatown. 10:57 p.m.

The condominium units were Amy Cho's father's investment—a four-unit 1930s apartment building with high ceilings and hand-carved antique moulding. After an efficient renovation, he'd sold off three and held back the upstairs fourth as a lure to bring his only child closer to home. It was another success for the neighborhood baker.

Growing up in Koreatown, Amy had spent many nights imagining her life once she turned eighteen and was free to escape her ethnic boundaries. During much of her junior year in high school, Amy obsessed over East Coast colleges. She openly joked that it was because she pictured three thousand miles as a sufficient distance to put between herself and her well-meaning but soul-suffocating traditional father and mother. But after Cal State Long Beach offered up a nearly full four-year scholarship, Amy's sensible side chose to stay local and study for a forensics degree at the school's Department of Criminology. Graduation led to her LAPD job and a roomie situation with a pair of wannabe actresses in a two-bedroom apartment up in Beachwood Canyon below the famed Hollywood sign. Considering her burgeoning affection for learning sleight of hand in classes at the Magic Castle and collecting Hollywood fringe stories, the location was more than a good fit. The annoying roommates weren't.

Thus Amy couldn't resist her father's offer to move back to Koreatown, less than two city blocks from the above-the-bakery apartment where she'd spent her initial eighteen years. Her rent was free, and the digs were nothing less than a spectacular 1,700 square feet of prewar plaster, arched doorways, and original hardwood floors. The young CSI had decorated with swap-meet finds and retro movie posters and turned the second bedroom into a cluttered shrine to her passions.

The joint gave her fleshy goose bumps nearly every night when, after work, she climbed the ivory-painted steps to her front stoop. It was her home. And she prided herself that she belonged there. Exhausted from a slow afternoon and evening of re-cataloging old evidence into the department's new database, she keyed the lock on the condo's heavy door and, with an easy push, let it swing inward. The instant she crossed the threshold, the follicles on her forearms went taut, as if magnetized.

Hungry and craving a bath, Amy squelched the feeling and swerved around the Chesterfield sofa she'd rescued and restored before crossing into the kitchen at a dead-reckoning for her refrigerator. She knew exactly what she'd find: the second half of the barbecue chicken pizza she'd brought home from CPK the night before. She was already reaching before she realized the container wasn't there. The top shelf, where the white, yellow, and black box should have been, was empty but for three cold cans of coconut water and a jar of Best Foods mayonnaise.

Amy screamed when a hand grabbed at her hair.

"Ssshhh," calmed the voice at her ear—the speaker's other hand already caressing the flesh of her belly.

"Your breath smells like my dinner!" pissed Amy.

"And your vodka."

Without thinking, Amy yanked open the freezer door. Along with the rush of cold came an obvious reveal. Her fifth of Tito's Handmade Vodka wasn't where she'd left it.

"Didn't believe me?" quizzed Miles.

Amy twisted ninety degrees clockwise and shoved the cop, touching nothing but bare skin. Wearing only a semi-drunk grin, Miles stood naked in the refrigerator light, his Polish skin hairy and pale.

"With a boner, no less," regarded Amy, hands on her hips.

"What all that waiting for Amy does to me."

"I'm hungry."

"I'm not."

"So?"

"So, after."

"After I eat."

"No. After," reminded Miles. "You know I can't stay."

"I smell like a crime lab. I need a bath."

"You smell immensely fuckable," argued Miles on his approach. He began by unbuttoning the top two buttons of her blouse. "Wash and I won't be able to lick you clean."

Amy gathered up her arms in an unexpected defense, only to have Miles wrap her in a bear hug, lift her clean off the floor, and kick the refrigerator door shut.

"Miles!" she squeaked.

"Me first, eat later."

Amy loathed surprises. Once at fourteen, she was so easily startled that her older cousin convinced her to spend a day letting him hide and jump out at her, guaranteeing her that in the end it would cure her. It didn't. Instead, Amy had learned to live with her fear of being crept up on, developing a girlish giggle that only encouraged more of the same scary attention. Her boyfriends had become merciless.

Married Miles was no different. Only he wasn't at all like the boys she was accustomed to dating. He was, in her eyes, both dangerous and a superhero in dark blue LAPD togs. That and he'd made her his sidekick of sorts. Their own private Super Team. Though she hadn't yet met any of the others in their justice league, her world with Miles had turned into something between the comics she grew up on and the fringe Hollywood history that kept her company.

That, and Miles had made her the banker—the keeper of all evidence, which she stowed away in a secret temperature-controlled vault.

With Miles on the prowl, those frightened giggles had graduated into an entirely new degree of thrill. So, squeak as she would every time he crept up on her, she gladly relented to it as sordid foreplay. As per the usual script, he hauled her to a bedroom adorned in Spiderman, Hulk, and Avengers posters, stripped her naked, licked her as promised until she was wheezing from tickles, then maneuvered her until she was astride him. Only he refused to enter her.

"Stop teasing me," she pleaded.

"But you like it," he kissed her. "And I like it."

"Want me to get you a condom?"

"Not at all what I want." Miles grinned, still underneath her, his eyes fixed on her face—her deep brown, wanting eyes. He didn't want to miss her reaction because it would only happen once.

"You don't want me tonight?"

Then Amy felt it. First the hand on the back of her neck, squeezing. This quickly followed by a calloused palm sealed against her petite, sex-expectant mouth.

Amy screamed. The fear sounded in muffled yet resonant cries from the walls of her chest. Her eyes were blown in wide horror, searching Miles's face for answers.

"Ssshhh," Miles calmed her, index finger to his lips as if slowly blowing out a candle. "It's only my man, Sugar."

The hand on the back of Amy's neck moved around her torso, lifting her away to allow Miles to ease from underneath her. He slid to the edge of the bed and swiveled back to her. Meanwhile, Sugar Freeman pushed Amy to her stomach, his weight at least double hers.

"Let it happen, sweets. This is all part of being in our little justice league," said Miles, stroking her hair. Then his voice dropped an octave, playing off the moment with some ghetto street talk. "We a team. And we all shares alike. Feel me?"

Choked with fear, Amy watched Miles retreat into her Fantastic Four folding camp chair. Her cousin had given it to her after he'd used it to wait in line at San Diego's Comic-Con. He'd even succeeded in getting the back strap signed in gold Sharpie by the legendary Stan Lee. Huge, Hulk-like forearms flanked both Amy's shoulders. Only this beast of a superhero was black-skinned instead of CGI green.

"Go with it," whispered Miles, relaxed and ready for a show.

She wanted to speak, demanding Sugar wear some kind of protection. Anything to mitigate the . . . the . . .

Violation of trust.

Was it rape? she asked herself as she somehow disconnected from most of her physical feelings. When her lover was watching? Pleasuring himself while his police partner plowed her from behind. One thing for sure, she was hell-bent on staring down her lover with the stranger's every thrust. She wanted him to wallow in her discomfort, remember it for a lifetime. At least, that was until Miles produced his smartphone, horizontally aiming the tiny, high-definition lens to capture the ingloriousness of the moment. Amy's only defense was to twist her view in the opposite direction, giving the camera the satisfaction of only seeing the back of her head.

"Ahhh," sounded Miles, disappointed. "Since when is my slanty-eyed sidekick camera shy?"

Instead of staring back at Miles, Amy chose to level her gaze on Spiderman and his comic-book, silver-blue eyes. The superhero was depicted hanging in the air from one silky strong strand while releasing more of the same from his free palm. Amy refused the sexual connotations of the image, instead imagining that if she chose, she could just reach out and grab the sticky strand and pull herself out from underneath the sweaty brute before he could finish.

Only she wasn't in a comic book or a magician's act. Her life, though, was fast becoming a Hollywood fringe tale. She was, at last, part of the story.

16

Glendale. 11:58 p.m.

The Newport burned. With every prolonged draw, the hot ember glowed and ate away at both tobacco and paper while briefly igniting the paleness of her face. Elizabeth. Or Lizzy. The sister of the family. The middle child, a.k.a. the cool girl in an extended clan of Armenian men and their old-school rules designating women as second-class citizens. The cigarette, effortlessly pinched between her filigree-tattooed fingers, was calming, the nicotine a welcome inhibitor to her anger. Her stare was fixed on the knobby topography of Glendale's south slope. The nonstop headlights and taillights of the cars and trucks speeding along the Ventura Freeway appeared like a pulsating vein breathing life into the nightscape.

"It so seriously sucks," she said with a slight shake of her head. "And I'm so tired of things sucking for *him*."

"I'm trying," replied Chris.

The brother-sister pair sat in a couple of Adirondack chairs painted pink on the balcony outside her bedroom. Chris's thin legs were stretched to their utmost tensile, bare heels hooking the wrought-iron rail, while Lizzy appeared cold, her knees pulled up under her crocheted cardigan. Below was the family swimming pool, and underneath that, those former changing rooms turned into Johnny B.'s personal discotheque. The beat worked as an underscore, not loud, but present, always rumbling through the mansion's turn-of-the-century beams.

"Pop can't see past none of it," excused Chris. "John's the way he is, and that's it."

"It's fucking cruel," she said. "That's what it is. J. B. can't help how he is. But that doesn't mean he's gotta live like he's less than what the BHA considers a man."

The BHA. The nickname was a long-held private joke between the two eldest siblings and was based on Lizzy's favorite children's book by Roald Dahl, *The BFG*, or Big Friendly Giant. For years the young pair had kept their giggle-worthy secret from the rest of the family.

Translation: *Big Hairy Asshole.*

"I know. But this accident thing ain't helpin' things," excused Chris.

"Pop's got him lower on the food chain than me," she continued.

"Yeah," agreed Chris. "But you found a work-around. And I'm still workin' on John's."

The two had long agreed that the dictated tradition forbidding Armenian women from participating in "family" business was arcane, unfair, and antithetical to profit-making. By day, Lizzy managed a chain of hair and nail salons, all owned by various family members under a great number of Armenian names. Though each acted as a convenient front for laundering cash, Lizzy's feminine hands were never allowed to touch the accounting books.

Her job was the legit side—hiring, firing, and keeping the regular customers satisfied with coifs and lacquer.

But satisfied lady customers weren't satisfying enough for Lizzy. With assistance from her elder brother she'd set up a clever extortion scheme where she'd handpick attractive Eastern European women to date equally unappealing single men with bank accounts spilling with disposable cash. Once the marks fell in love—which was usually at a significant velocity, considering Lizzy's acumen at targeting the men via their social media profiles—a scripted tragedy would befall the girl's family. The love-blind men were usually quick to assist in fixing whatever ailed their lady love. Cash would be wired to an offshore Armenian collection depot and once the target was sufficiently sucked dry, the high-cheek-boned trophy chick would disappear into the Southern California ether. Lizzy paid her girls twenty percent of the take. And any one of her well-paid honeypots was known to work up to five lonely men at a time.

The scam grossed upwards of a million dollars a year. Every dime, as well as the tribute, passed along to the Russian mob's moneymen was credited to Chris and not Lizzy, who quietly simmered in the shadows waiting for the old-world organized crime biz to catch up with her twenty-first-century game.

"Swear to Christ," claimed Lizzy. "J. B.'s gonna self-immolate if we don't get him moving with the family current."

"You're not officially 'in the current' and look at you," argued Chris. "You're okay with it."

"I have the capacity to handle my shit," she angered. "Johnny doesn't. If he doesn't find a place to fit in . . ."

Lizzy's brown eyes were lit by the pool lights below. A pair of uniform tears trickled over the top of her pale white concealer.

"You know Pop means well."

"Yeah. Means so well, he's gonna suffocate his own son to death. You know, J. B. tells me shit he won't tell you. Scary shit. Doesn't want you or anybody else to know he's afraid of himself. What he might do."

"And what if he already did it?" Chris asked.

"The car accident? He told me. It was an *accident*. I'm talkin' much worse. Like pour a can of gas over his head and light a fucking match just so Pop'll take notice."

"You're making Pop's argument for him."

"Whose side are you on?" It wasn't so much a question as an accusation or demand that Chris choose a team and fight for it.

"I'm on everyone's side," played Chris. "That's my job. Make everything right for everybody."

"Well, things are gonna be made right for Johnny or I'm gonna show my claws," warned Lizzy. "I'll cut out the old man's spleen if it's between him and *our* lil' brother."

For punctuation, Lizzy flicked the nearly finished cigarette. It spun and sparked, arcing until it landed in the swimming pool.

"Sweet," said Chris. "Now Mom's gonna be on your ass if she finds that shit in the filter."

Lizzy was already relighting another smoke.

"Might as well finish the pack," she smirked. "Give her something to be *really* pissed about."

"Johnny-wise, she's on *your* side."

"She'll never—*ever*—cross the BHA."

"FYI. Tomorrow I'm gonna pick up where we left off today. Bring J. B. around the other guys. He'll find something that makes him comfortable or he'll change his mind about wanting to be with Power."

"What do you wanna bet Pop asks me to put him to work in the salons?" Lizzy laughed before Chris joined in. "Can you picture that?"

"Might get him laid," joked Chris.

"Something else he needs," said Lizzy, pointing with her cigarette. "Girlfriend. Hooker. Right hand's probably sore from all that pud he pulls."

"Right hand strong!" ripped Chris with a purposefully bad accent. "Like all Armenian men."

"And hairy as shit," she giggled. "Except you. Anybody know?"

"What? That I wax? Hell effin' no. And don't let me find out you're spreadin' rumors."

"You're sooooo pretty. And your secret's safe enough. For now . . ."

Lizzy laughed some more, open and unfettered. The tension in her belly was momentarily relieved. But not resolved. With every day as a successful—if not lauded—member of the crime family, her confidence grew. Johnny B. had become a priority. If it meant leveraging her father into the most uncomfortable of positions, so be it, decided Lizzy.

So fucking be it.

Vaz could have easily muted the swells of sibling laughter that mashed with the waves of sonic thumps resounding from Johnny B.'s subterranean rave cave. The French doors to Vaz's first-floor study were glassed with sound-insulating panes, mostly to keep the neighborhood from hearing the pre-dawn racket when he watched his beloved soccer. *Futbol,* as the rest of the world called it. He'd stay up until all hours enjoying the matches on his big screen with Dolby amplified audio, sometimes barking as loudly as the massive crowds attending the live events.

On that night, Vaz kept the TV muted to the Fox News Channel and chain-smoked Sancho Panza cigars while tripping through Internet searches for treatment options for his youngest son. Though he'd applied pressure to that overreaching sheriff's deputy, he couldn't trust a cop to deliver. His most back-pocket defense was the oldest of devices: an extended overseas vacation to Armenia or Russia. Long enough for the statute of limitations to run out on whatever crime the authorities might charge—assuming the negotiated charge was less than involuntary manslaughter, as the family attorney had already advised. The thought of sending Johnny B. away for an extended period scraped at Vaz's stomach lining, sending his gut into such a riot that he'd been popping acid reducers like they were Tic Tacs. Vaz's other option included committing Johnny B. to an inpatient treatment in an out-of-state home. The obvious mental health optics might be defense enough for Johnny B. to escape with survivable probation.

Vaz put a pause on his Google searches, momentarily breathing in the moment. The sweet Cuban smoke combined with the sounds of all three of his children—from above and below. His affection for them felt blinding. In that moment he realized there was nothing he wouldn't do for them, including, perhaps, betraying his allegiance to the Eastern European power structure that had fed him, his father, and his grandfather before that. The roots were generations deep, all the way back to the Armenian genocide when the Ottoman Empire—or as Vaz called them, *those fucking Turks*—had laid to waste a million or more of his blood before twelve-year-old Vartan Kasabian had ever set foot on US soil.

There came a brief flash. No more than a second or two in length. It was a subconscious wish in which Vaz imagined the victim of the car accident. Could Mrs. Malibu or her husband be of Turkish descent? If they had even the faintest remnant of that black-hearted Anatolian DNA, maybe young Johnny B. had done a service for the cause. Perhaps that would even satisfy his boy's dumb-lust for joining the family business. But the odds were remote. Impossible. It sucked Vaz back into the reality of the moment.

And what the hell to do about Johnny Boy.

Sunday

17

Altadena.

"Well, that explains things."
Explains what?

"The bruises," continued Gonzo, as if reading Lucky's thoughts. "I thought maybe last night we'd end up having, like, this epic make-up sex."

She'd caught Lucky in the shower. In lieu of a hot, scraping steam, he'd opted for an extended blast of cold water in hopes that it might reduce the inflammation. His body had screamed in pain most of the night. Sleep was, at best, intermittent. If he'd had a half hour more forethought, he would have hit up the nearest corner market for bags of ice and filled the bathtub before reclining in it. The frigid shower and a quadruple dose of Advil would have

to suffice before he and Travis hustled off to another half day of
volunteer umpiring.

"Bar fight?" Gonzo was only half joking.

"Assumes I was in a bar," groaned Lucky.

"Wanna keep secrets? Be my guest," said Gonzo, although there
was little forgiveness in her posture or tone. She turned and stood
at the sink, applying whitening paste to her electric toothbrush.

"Made a dumb move," admitted Lucky. "Followed a suspect
into a bathroom. Got jumped by his crew."

"Any arrests?"

"It's complicated."

"When isn't it?"

The buzz of Gonzo's toothbrush trailed off as she wandered
from the bathroom, engaged in her usual multitasking. And
by the time Lucky had toweled off and dressed, she'd vanished
into the morning, no doubt on her way to a pocket-list of errands
before a split day-into-night shift piloting her helicopter for LAPD
air support.

With Travis riding shotgun, Lucky hit a McDonald's drive-
thru for a morning dose of coffee and carbohydrates. The pair
arrived at the Mid-Valley ballparks six minutes before their first
game, a coach-pitch barnburner where a seemingly equivalent
number of parents openly complained that keeping score was
either self-esteem killing or paramount in building character in
their eight- and nine-year-old spawn. So sore from the beatdown
the day before, Lucky could barely lift his arms, so he left the calling of balls and strikes to Travis while he signaled outs from a
grassy patch behind second base.

The headache was merciless.

Behind the league's snack shack, the blue crew of umpires
gathered for the between-games break under a shady trio of large
big-leafed maples. The leaves had half turned to gold in the cold
snap preceding the four days of hot Santa Anas. Judge Jim sat atop
his orange and white Igloo cooler, occasionally standing to dole
out an ice-cold bottle of his beer of the week. On that Saturday

morning it was a craft ale with a bright red label that read *Blind Pig*.

"Russian River Valley Brew," bragged Judge Jim.

"Can I try?" braved Travis.

"Now, there's some breaking news," popped Sugar. "Superior Court Judge busted for issuing liquor to a minor."

"Not liquor," corrected Travis. "It's just beer."

"Just as illegal," smiled Judge Jim.

"Get yourself somethin' and me a Gatorade, will ya?" suggested Lucky, peeling off a five-dollar bill and stuffing it in Travis's fist. As the teenager shuffled away, Lucky waved off Judge Jim's offer of a cooling Blind Pig. Miles stepped in, snatched the beer from Judge Jim's grip, and applied his key-chain bottle opener.

"Heard you got your ass kicked," grinned Miles, an index finger to his mouth, indicating Lucky's painful split lip.

"Word travels," said Lucky, none too pleased to share. His hackles were already up. Suspect. Who exactly would know of his run-in with Johnny B.'s peacock of a brother and his gang of Armenian leg-breakers?

"Wanna talk about it?" asked Judge Jim.

"*It*?" asked Lucky, preferring Judge Jim, or even Miles or Sugar, to first show a few more cards.

"Your AP thing," cued Miles.

The answer got Miles a swerving glance from Lucky. Harsh. Unwelcome.

"You having me followed?" asked Lucky, his glare back on Judge Jim.

"I'm on the bench for over a decade," reminded Judge Jim with a not-so-innocent shrug. "Before that I was a prosecutor. Before that, a cop. Lotta friends in a lotta places. I can't help it if they whisper things in my direction."

"Shit," added Sugar. "Judge won't even tell me 'n' Miles all the eyes 'n' ears he got."

"Girl's gotta have her secrets," winked the judge.

"Weekend drag queen?" ribbed Sugar. "Ugly-assed one too."

"You wish," said Judge Jim. "But if I was, I'd be the belle of the tranny ball."

"Seriously," segued Miles back to Lucky. "The AP thing."

"Vartan Kasabian," said Judge Jim. "What's your relationship to him? And more importantly, what do you think you know about him?"

On the spot, Lucky recognized he needed to choose his words with extreme care. What and where and how much Judge Jim knew about Lucky's off-the-book errand was a categorical unknown. And like a good trial lawyer, the judge rarely asked questions to which he didn't already know the answers. In the time it took to tilt a beer, the game had changed. There would be no room for Lucky to delay Judge Jim's solicitation to join all the vigilante fun. No time to plan his extrication. So far, the most he'd contemplated was to turn over what he knew about the cabal to some discreet FBI agent. The problem was, the *Feebs* and US attorneys Lucky had encountered in his recent career were as trustworthy as a roomful of bankers.

No, decided Lucky to himself. He'd have to play.

At least for now.

In short order, Lucky detailed his past two days working the Woodland Hills accident. From the phone call from Assistant Sheriff Paul McGill to the Armenian market men's room assault to his brief hijacking the night before. None of it was a secret. McGill had never suggested Lucky work under a shroud. *The truth*, Lucky thought, *is way easier to remember.* The poker-faced judge gave away little if nothing during Lucky's sparse yet accurate summation.

"So, the report you wrote up," Judge Jim asked, prying the cap off another bottle of Blind Pig. "You deliver yet?"

"No," answered Lucky. "Still in my out-box."

"Walk with me for a minute," requested the judge. He stood and shook out the aggravating popping sounds in his aging knees. "Miles? Phones."

With a nod, Miles collected both Lucky and Judge Jim's mobile phones.

"Promise not to do a device search for dirty pictures," Miles joked to laughter only from his pal, Sugar.

A picket line of eighty-year-old eucalyptus trees was the northernmost demarcation between the baseball complex and one of the Los Angeles River's many concrete tributaries. The trees formed a man-made windbreak, dating back to the time when the San Fernando Valley was nothing but farms and citrus groves. The two men strolled a sandy jogging path between the trees and a rusted chain-link fence.

"I'm sharing this because of a certain history particular to you and yours," qualified Judge Jim. "Vartan Kasabian, besides his laundry list of criminal accomplishments, likes his playthings young and blonde, if you follow. Wherever the working girls are shipped in from—and I'm talking Ukraine or Slovakia or back-assed Bumfuckistan—he and his Armo cronies get first taste of the *baby dolls*. Yeah. Those kind of babies. As tribute? As a personal fetish? Who knows? But I know me a federal judge in San Diego who sat on a case that had this Wall Street *pedo* dead to rights. I'm talkin' in the bay, on a yacht, covered in Crisco and a pair of fourteen-year-old sex kittens. Kasabian's fingerprints were all over the party, the manifest, the cargo ship they floated in on. And the slippery prick walks after a car with the two key witnesses and their FBI wrangler gets bumpered to death off a cliff on Route 18."

"That the Big Bear thing?" asked Lucky, remembering both the dangerous winding road and the news story that had accompanied the murder back when he was a Kern County sheriff.

"Is there a direct connection between whatever happened to your nearly adopted daughter and the Kasabians? I don't have proof. No smoking gun. But math is math and some shit just adds up."

If the judge was hoping to tweak Lucky's nerves, Karrie was ground zero. The father-daughter relationship had begun with Lucky as detective and the fifteen-year-old runaway as no more than a photograph. The duo had survived fire and worse. Their mutual affection made it evident they would kill for each other.

"Don't need to remind you that, on our best day, what we do

on our side of the law is opportunity," explained Judge Jim. "You turned down my offer. I respect that. But now there's this—this gift to the both of us. Kasabian's asked you to fix this thing for him. With his boy?"

"*Asked?*"

"In the Armo way, yeah," clarified the judge. "Does it matter? He's twisted your arm and will twist it again. But. If you come through for him? You get to twist back. And when you do, we'll have him."

"And you got a plan for that too?" Lucky cued.

"I can fix the accident thing. With the eighteen-year-old kid, at least on the criminal side. No charges. You have a sit-down with Kasabian over something as simple as a beer. Bring him the good news. Bend him back the other way with something he can do for you—otherwise he won't trust a second of it. After he departs, you bag the evidence."

The judge held up his half-drunk bottle of Blind Pig.

"DNA," said Lucky.

"Not just DNA," added the judge. "The Almighty DNA. Right crime, right body, right place? We prepare, we watch. And when Vartan Kasabian has no worthwhile alibi, we plant a swab of irrefutable, billion-to-one, silver bullet of DNA somewhere in a murder scene. The kind of DNA evidence that makes modern juries cum with judicial ecstasy."

Judicial ecstasy? Jesus, thought Lucky. *Only a lawyer could come up with that kind of fetishistic phraseology.*

But Lucky wondered what the judge's play was. To further coerce him to join the secret charter? Or set him off on some kind of revenge bender? The mere whiff of finding the stink of human traffickers who'd tried to steal Karrie's future was a killer carrot Lucky might not be able to turn down.

Then came the squeeze—a pressure that started from the top of Lucky's skull and worked downward to his core. But it wasn't the inflammation from the beatdown or something he could ease with a double dose of Advil. The feeling was neurological and cold, as if he were being screwed into the barrel of a syringe and forced through a hypodermic needle. Through the discomfort, Lucky could see Judge Jim's perspective. Yet there was something about *the ask*. Without the context of Karrie, the query would have come off as a request—one requiring little more than a yes or no. Instead, Lucky felt whip-herded into a singular direction. As a man and a cop, he wasn't beyond portioning out the occasional judgment and sentence. He could live with that. And if mistakes were made, they were his to pay for in the present and the happy hereafter.

If there even is a happy hereafter for dirty ball sacks like me.

But never in his thirty-eight years had Lucky meted out a lick of street punishment due to another man or woman at chain-of-command's suggestion or instruction—let alone because of blackmail. There was a piece of Lucky he had never fully jettisoned—his angry anti-authority side—that reflexively wanted to grab that sweaty bottle of designer ale, wrench it from the judge's grip, and shove it up Jaime Peralta's fleshy crack.

18

Sherman Oaks.

Hav u ever felt invisable B4?

So read the sign, the words thickly crayoned on a worn square of cardboard. The woman holding the placard was so tan and weathered, her skin appeared to be melting from her face. Where her hair wasn't a premature gray mess, it was sun-bleached to a fine frizz. Yet her teeth told most of her story, the enamel demolished from years of smoked methamphetamine. For Chris Kasabian, his usual donation seemed somehow insignificant. And his money clip held only a wad of singles. He snapped his fingers in hopes his brother, Johnny B., could supply him with an extra twenty or two.

"Hit me with some Jacksons."

"Ohmygod!" gasped Johnny Boy.

"Dope fiends call that 'meth mouth,'" replied Chris. "C'mon man. Before the light changes."

"But I killed her!" wrenched Johnny B., who had been paying zero attention to the needy woman outside his brother's lowered window.

Just like the day before, the duo was near the top of the Burbank Boulevard freeway off-ramp. It amazed Chris that no matter the day or time, he never seemed to discover the same panhandler at the same stop—as if the homeless and street hustlers were on some kind of organized rotation to guarantee that a driver would never be able to say, "Hey, I already gave you a buck two days ago."

Yet when he heard his brother cry out, he snapped his attention away from the homeless woman. Johnny B. was already cramping into a fetal ball, his feet on the seat, knees pulled up. In front of Johnny B.'s face was his ever-present smartphone with the oversized display. His face contorted in fear. Chris was so concerned for his little brother that he impulsively withdrew his left arm back in the car before the beggar could pinch the bill from his fingers.

"Green light," barked Johnny B.

"What's wrong?" asked Chris.

"Green light!"

Chris gassed the Lexus into a hard left turn and, in practically the same move, snatched the mobile device from his brother's grip. A quick glance to the horizontal screen revealed a clickable headline and a candid headshot of a thirty-five-year-old blonde.

LAPD SEEKS ANSWERS IN VENTURA BLVD ACCIDENT KILLING OF MALIBU WIFE AND MOTHER

The publisher was one of the local online *Patch* feeds and linked to a blurb in the online edition of the Valley-centric *L.A. Daily News*. After cutting across three lanes of traffic and cursing at every driver with the nerve to sound his car horn, Chris parked the Lexus on a sandy shoulder. Johnny B. was folded up in full body tremors.

"It's okay," calmed Chris. "Wasn't your fault!"

"WAS MY FAULT!!!" screamed Johnny.

Chris tried a hand on his little brother's shoulder in an effort to soothe. As he'd done so often, Johnny B. jerked away, only this time he'd unhooked his seat belt and was throwing his considerable weight into opening his car door. The distraught teen stumbled to his knees, righted himself, and spun a three-sixty as if seeking a way out of an imaginary corner. Chris popped his own door, scrambled around the front end, and caught up with Johnny B., who was almost blindly preparing to rabbit into the busy boulevard. Instinctively, Chris lowered a shoulder and butted into his out-of-control sibling, bouncing Johnny B. a half step backward.

"STOP IT!" barked Johnny B. "LEMME GO!"

Despite being outweighed by no less than seventy-five pounds, the years and familiarity with dangerously dissociative episodes gave the older brother two distinct advantages: preparation and practice. Chris had been forced to grapple his troubled brother protectively so many times that he'd transferred from the privileged acres of Studio City's Campbell Hall School to Burbank's rough and tumble Birmingham High just for its wrestling team. Competing at 140 pounds, Chris had made the All-City team twice before hanging up his singlet, an outfit Johnny B. couldn't help but snigger at.

Chris shot for Johnny's legs, wrapping the big teen up in a practiced move that was nearly indefensible. Gravity provided the rest of the equation. Johnny B.'s body slapped the road's shoulder with a decided *thud!* Dust billowed. When Johnny B. twisted and tried to crawl away, Chris gained the advantage. He damned his street shoes and designer black denims to mount his younger brother's back. From there, Chris hooked his legs and arms in a hold guaranteed to subdue.

"LEMME GO, LEMME GO!" pleaded Johnny B.

"I will when you're calm," Chris whispered into his sibling's ear.

"I'm calm!"

"No, you're not," chilled Chris. "Just breathe, okay? In. Out. Nose. Mouth."

"Can't breathe when you're on my back!"

"You can breathe. Just relax and promise me you'll get back in the car."

"Phone's in the car," cried Johnny. "Phone's got the truth. They're going to arrest me for what I did."

"You didn't do nothin'."

"I chucked my cheesesteak."

"And that's all you did. What, bud? They gonna arrest you for littering? Sheeeiiit."

"Killed the lady."

"Accidents happen. All it was. Even the cop said that, right?"

"Cop in the bathroom." Johnny B. eased, allowing Chris to submit him.

"And he and Poppa made friends," fudged Chris. "Nobody's gonna take you to jail."

"But what about the lady?"

"We don't know her. And she's not family."

"She's got a family. That's what it said on my phone."

"And she's her family's problem."

"Yeah," wheezed Johnny B. "Like I'm *our* family's problem."

"You're my brother," reasoned Chris. "Like you're Lizzy's brother. And we won't ever let anything bad happen to you."

"Ever?"

"C'mon, bud. Let's get up." Chris let go and gently slapped his brother's back.

"Ever?" repeated Johnny B., needing one last ounce of assurance.

There came a loud electronic *whoop!* Amplified. It so jolted Johnny B.'s nerves, he nearly tossed Chris off his back. Both young men had missed the sound of crunching gravel and the shadow that had come across them. It was an LAPD black-and-white—one of the new Ford Explorer radio units designed to both intimidate and offer more room for the ever-expanding variety of crime-fighting and crowd-control equipment. Two uniformed officers stood ten feet apart, white ballistic vests poking out above the top buttons of their dark short-sleeve shirts.

"Everything okay here?" asked the nearest uniform. "If not, suggest you take it to the nearest octagon or a motel room."

"You promised nobody was gonna arrest me!" squeaked Johnny B.

"We're fine," cautioned Chris. "Just helping my brother out."

"Somethin' wrong with him?" asked the uniform.

"He's fine," said Chris.

"I got the Asperger's," Johnny volunteered.

"Got the what?" asked the other uniform.

"Asperger's Syndrome," explained Chris, rising and dusting his jeans.

"You're brothers?" asked the first uniform, pointing to Johnny B. for an answer.

"Brothers. Yeah," he answered. "Are you gonna arrest me?"

"For what?" replied the first uniform.

For killing the woman in Woodland Hills, thought Chris, hoping to hell his little brother wouldn't spill anything that might require further explanation.

"Is your brother under medical care?" directed the second uniform to Chris.

"Yes," nodded Chris. "His episode is over. I'm taking him home now."

"Road shoulder is not the safest place for freak-outs," reminded the second uniform.

"We're good to go," nodded Chris. "That right, J. B.?"

"Good to go," saluted J. B., appearing weirdly sunny and ebullient, the anxiety episode clearly in the past.

By their expressions, both LAPD uniforms looked somewhat mystified as well as relieved the stop hadn't ended in some kind of altercation. While the officers retired to their air-conditioned SUV, Chris and Johnny B. returned to the driver and passenger seats of the Lexus. The dust and sand smudged what had been a pristine black leather interior.

"We dirtied your ride," said Johnny B., flat and affect-free. As if no wrestling match had ever occurred.

"Why they made car washes, buddy," assured Chris. "How about we go do that?"

"We got time? Isn't there business to do?"

"Hey. We're the Sabs," reminded Chris. "And everybody waits on us. Don't ever forget that."

19

North Hollywood. 12:11 p.m.

It never failed to fascinate Shia. Travel a mile and a half north of NoHo—a.k.a. the hipster section of North Hollywood—and be it native or tourist, one might wonder if he'd somehow gotten turned around and crossed the southern border into Mexico. The street signs remained in English, as did the ever-present franchise names: Burger King, FedEx, 99 Cents Store. But from the bill-boards to the bus benches, non-locals might find it confusing that nearly every ad space was occupied by Spanish-language advertisements. An obvious appeal to the zip code's dominant population, be it legal citizens, green card holders, and the ever-present undocumented hordes.

Though not a native speaker, Shia spoke and read Spanish fluently as well as five other foreign languages. She adored

L.A.'s poly-ethnic landscape. *Her* Los Angeles was a true melting pot—only too much of the damned multicultural stew had yet to emulsify and conjoin with the rest of the meal.

"My decree?" she'd sometimes volunteer at social events. "If I were Queen of Los Angeles, of course . . . I'd allow only breeding between opposing ethnicities. The race lines would blur and disappear within two generations. And everyone in Shia Land would live happily ever after."

Generally speaking, her assertion would be greeted with guffaws or agreement or, better yet, open deep-rooted discussions from friends of already mixed blood. It had been months since she'd dropped the favored party line. The thought had only returned when she was steering her Kia Optima into the Sherman Way entrance to Home Depot. Crowding the concrete corner was a sight ubiquitous to most of the So Cal do-it-yourself stores with lax loitering enforcement. Dozens of Hispanic men ranging from eighteen to sixty years old—each wearing manual labor duds— and nearly none a legal resident—stood around hoping to catch some cash for a day's construction work. Shia hated the sight of it. There were days she wished she was a general contractor with a job for every available man. She pictured herself pulling up in an extended-bed pickup truck, waving all of them into the rear, and driving off into a sunrise of full-time employment.

A girl can dream.

It was already past noon. Shia was painfully aware the men's hopes of finding even a half-day gig was dwindling with every sweep of the minute hand. The sun acted like bleach against the surrounding stucco, cement, and asphalt surfaces, but seemed to darken the day laborers' hopes, their eyes unreadable below their painters and baseball caps. She wondered what they'd think of her cocktail party conversation starter or, more importantly, how often they'd regretted their journey north of the border to the land of milk and social welfare.

Perhaps it was this momentary distraction that prevented Shia from checking her rearview mirror. Her years as a head-turner, as well as under Lucky's hard tutelage, had taught her to be aware of her personal geography. Had she not been daydreaming about the lingering day laborers she might have marked the driver practically tailgating her into the parking lot. Once out of her vehicle, Shia's awareness returned with a chilly vengeance. Only her three-hundred-and-sixty-degree sweep of the lot showed little, if anything at all, out of order. She recorded mostly men, either headed into the store in a hurry or loading their vehicles with the likes of cut lumber or lengths of PVC pipe.

Her Sunday mission was all about rosebushes, which was why she bypassed the main entrance and carved a path directly to the outdoor garden section. She quickly oriented herself toward the larger stands of plants, aiming for the pricier five-gallon offerings. Robust as the selection was, each bush was marked at just south of fifty dollars.

"Jesus," she said, disappointed.

"You want my employee discount? Try addin' some tears first."

The voice was dangerously close. Shia swung to her left and popped with surprise.

"Frosty!" she giggled. "The hell?"

Despite what Shia called him, the man's employee name tag plainly read "Lamar," the letters officiously carved into a plastic badge clipped onto the familiar orange bib.

"Workin' dog," smirked Frosty. "Gettin' my nursery shit on for fifteen an hour."

"All the way up here?"

"No more Compton," said Frosty. "Me and my moms got out and all the way here. Set up by some church folks we know."

"Out of the hood? Outta the game?"

"Tryin's all this nigga can do. Hey. You talkin' to Lucky?"

"Every so often."

"He good?"

"He's Lucky," said Shia, eyebrows arched in a facial shrug. "Hey. He know you moved to the Valley?"

"Didn't wanna bug him no more than I already done. Figured in time, you know?"

"He'd wanna hear. He'd be really proud."

The subtext of Shia's words had a resonance with Frosty. Though Lucky hadn't introduced her to the young man until after what could only have been described as a come-to-Jesus moment during the remaining months of her South L.A. training, the trainer-trainee duo would break for a late-night "lunch" every so often and meet Frosty at either a taco stand or for iced tea and sandwiches at the community's Greater Zion Baptist Church. The specifics of Frosty's conversion were never discussed, nor was his confidence betrayed by Lucky. But something earth-shaking had occurred for the youth. And it was clear that Frosty looked upon Lucky as some kind of human touchstone.

"Checkin' out my roses?" asked Frosty.

"Yours?"

"Ain't trees, but until I get my own farm, this is Frosty's kingdom."

"You set the price?"

"Wish I did," said Frosty, "but you wanna buy rosebushes anywhere else, them five-gallons gonna cost you sixty, seventy. And mine are healthy and ready to rock your garden."

"Kinda stuck, then."

"One-gallons go a lot cheaper."

"I moved too," explained Shia. "Ever tell you I lived with my dad?"

"I remember. He in a wheelchair, right?"

"Exactly. He wants to garden. So, I thought I'd get the bigger plants to make it easier for him to do from his chair." Shia regarded the one-gallon plants and their barely eighteen inches of height. "Still, these we'd have to grow for a year or so before he could comfortably get at them."

"Wheelchair-access rose garden?" pondered Frosty. "Like that. Did I tell you the Frost-man moonlights as a custom landscaper? What if I said I can build your ol' man some elevated planter boxes? That way he can start his roses young—and on the cheap side."

The look on Shia's face—it was the picture of elation. *Brighter*, thought Lee Chapman, *than all the flowers in the Home Depot garden section*. She beamed, excitedly cupped the black man's face,

and kissed his cheek. She followed with a girlish bounce from the
balls of her feet. In all his hours and days and weeks watching her
every tick from his perch in the back right corner of Department J,
he had never once seen anything he could remotely call *giddy* from
the deputy. Seeing her smile with such unhitched abandon sent a
rush of red to his already ruddy face. Though it landed with a stab
of jealousy. Who was the man in the orange bib? He was nearly
as ebony as her, with yellowed wide-set eyes. Alien-like. Did they
know each other well? Was she attracted? And if so, why? Because
he too was black-skinned? Lee couldn't imagine how. He'd seen
her interact with other African American men—from convicts to
attorneys. None made her smile like the skinny gardener in the
orange bib.

Should've known better, thought Lee.

He hadn't meant to follow her in the first place. It had started
late on Friday afternoon. The front wheels of his aging Accord
had just touched the pavement of Sylmar, the street fronting the
four-floor parking garage serving the Van Nuys Superior Court.
That's when Lee saw her motoring past in her white Optima. *Of
course it's white,* he first thought. What would look better on Miss
Shia St. George than white? Lee imagined her house, her carpet,
her wardrobe. White was all he could picture. Perfect, blank, clean
white. Before he could put the brakes on his subconscious, Lee
noted he'd already shifted his course from west to east and was
into the follow. It felt like his shitmobile was being pulled by her
Optima. Magnetically. Like it was meant to be.

I'm just curious, he'd excused. No harm in that. What's a
screenwriter if not inquisitive to a fault? It was all the rationale Lee
required. Then, just as he realized how close he'd ridden up on her
rear bumper, he panicked, backed off, dropping a car behind as a
way of keeping his actions stealthy.

In what had felt to Lee like only a few city blocks, Shia had
pulled into a driveway. Lee was struck at how close to the job she
lived. The nondescript home was small and badly stuccoed in a
stained battleship gray, landmarked as straddling the boundary
between Sherman Oaks and Van Nuys. Lee had pressed himself so

hard in order to avert his obvious stare, worried that her neighbors might be keeping a lookout for prowlers and stalkers, he'd missed both the house number and street name. At the first intersection, he made a squeaky U-turn, the belt of his power steering slipping into a hard-to-miss whine. So panicked and distracted by his easily identifiable car, he again missed the street sign he'd meant to mentally record. The domicile, though, it was sixty yards ahead and on the right, hardware-store house numbers screwed vertically onto the wooden mailbox post.

14005.

One last glimpse at her house and Lee thought he'd seen a curtain move. His eyes might well have been attached to his right foot. He put gas to the engine and Shia in his rearview mirror, surging west until he could clearly capture the street name.

Califa Street.

A reminder on his smartphone sounded.

"Shitballs!" shouted Lee. He was worse than late. He'd been so in his hypnotic moment that it had slipped his mind. The job.

My new goddamned job.

In late August, Lee had answered a Craigslist ad for a roaming souvenir vendor at the Los Angeles Coliseum. The gig was parttime and paid minimum wage. Demeaning for a former JPL rocket scientist? Sure, figured Lee. But such was his adventure, his decline into life's underbelly. That, and he had fond memories of attending NFL games as a boy in San Diego. But those hellish stairs of the Coliseum? Miles and miles of them divided the twentyeight sections, each with a vertical ascent of twelve floors from field level. His aging quadriceps still ached from last week's game when the University of Southern California Trojans had hosted the Oregon Ducks. Despite the week-old residual pain, the rest of Lee felt downright jubilant, buoyed by thoughts of Shia. So, when he donned his souvenir basket that Friday night, it felt light, and no longer was he obsessed with calculating the average number of steps climbed per foam finger sold. Lee had a different immovable number in mind.

14005.

"Souvenirs here! Who wants a souvenir?"

All the while, between his ears, Lee was repeating: *Fourteen double-oh five Califa. Fourteen double-oh five Califa.*

After the game clock counted down to zero and he'd turned in his receipts, reality had returned to Lee. Perhaps it was because during his shift he'd passed so many coeds. Young. Beautiful. His twin daughters, whom he hadn't seen since age ten, should have been graduated from college. They'd be peers of Shia's. Similar in age. When the Southern Cal coeds barely met his eyes unless they were seeking a souvenir, he imagined how old he must look to them. Pathetic. A middle-aged loser predisposed to a life of scratching depravity. Lee drove himself back to his dirty rent-by-the-week motel room, tuned the TV to a *Law and Order: SVU* marathon, and slowly drank himself into a coma on a mixture of Popov vodka and Sunny Delight. He didn't wake until nearly dark the next day. Once the fuzziness of the hangover dissolved into lucidity, he'd found the same mantra tripping from his mental tongue.

Fourteen double-oh five Califa. Fourteen double-oh five Califa.

Unable to shake the obsessive loop, Lee dared himself to once again drive past Shia's house. One last time.

Just a little sniff of a look-see, he excused.

It had been just shy of midnight on Saturday when he'd parked across the street, two driveways to the west of Shia's stucco rental. He'd killed the shitmobile's engine and lowered himself and the bill of his USC cap and watched for shadows to pass in front of the curtains. The anticipation. The excitement of his proximity to her had sent his heart into an uncontrollable flutter. To calm his guilty jitters he had swallowed some Xanax, twice his usual dose. Only the drugs had served up another deep sleep, fast and hard, and when he finally woke, it was in Sunday morning daylight and Shia was climbing into her car. That impossible magnetism had pulled. And for the rest of that morning, Lee allowed himself to be dragged along on Shia's errands. Starbucks. Hot yoga. A respite at the Sherman Oaks Jamba Juice. And lastly . . .

Home-depressing-Depot.

On Shia's first three stops, Lee remained inside his car. He smelled of body funk and was concerned that with a peek into any enclosed building his reek would warrant him unwanted attention. Yet when Shia beelined from the Home Deport parking lot to the open-air garden section, Lee absolved himself and his private stink and thought perhaps he might get a better angle on her than through the dirty windshields of his shitmobile—and perhaps even a keeper of a snapshot through some plants: Shia in just a sports bra and yoga pants. He was breathless as he walked. His heart throbbed bass notes all the way to his ears.

Like a horny damned teenager.

Shia had been browsing the potted rosebushes for less than a minute when she'd been approached by that black man in the orange bib. To get the picture he'd hoped for—mental and otherwise—Lee maneuvered himself counterclockwise, ending up in a wide aisle reserved for fifty-pound bags of tree bark and mulch. The stench of peat and processed manure overwhelmed the space, doubly masking his worrisome odor. And through a triangular window of stacked lattice and rolls of three-foot steel garden fence, Lee watched. Frozen. Mesmerized. Never once acting on the impulse to record or snap a phone pic of her. After all, he'd watched her for weeks—learning most of her tics and expressions. He'd memorized them all. Or so he figured until he experienced her beaming at the yellow-eyed young man. Her expression was full of grace and the wonder of surprise. Unforgettable.

Shia's nine-minute encounter with the Home Depot man concluded with an extended hug before she trotted for the parking lot as if late for yet another appointment. Lee snapped his eyes away and instinctively about-faced his direction in an effort to exit the DIY store.

"You lookin' for a piece of that?" Frosty stood, legs shoulder-width apart and braced, blocking Lee's path.

". . . Sorry," replied Lee in a feeble attempt to appear surprised. "I'm not looking for anything."

As Lee tried to sidestep the awkward situation, Frosty slid with him, arms thrust out, and popped Lee backwards with a not-so-gentle shove.

"Asked you somethin'," demanded Frosty.

"Minding my own business," said Lee, eyes unwilling to meet the young man's.

"The shorty," pressed Frosty. "You wantin' to follow that shit? What's with you? You follow her here? You some stalker or somethin'?"

"Asshole, you work here!" switched Lee, eyes finally forward. "You can't touch a customer like that. I can get you fired—"

"If it's about protectin' my people?" shot Frosty. "They can fire my nigga ass ten times over. But you still be maimed for fuckin' life."

Frosty bent at the knee and hooked his finger in a decorative pink cinderblock. When he picked up the brick, the vein striating his bicep pulsed, practically blinking a warning in Lee's face. In what was supposed to look like an insecure posture, Lee's hands found the deep pockets of his cargo shorts. He'd practiced the move so many times in his bathroom mirror. In his left, his fingers found the steel of his tactical pen. Lee's right dipped and grasped the handle of his retractable baton. His brain repeated the instructions. He'd rehearsed for such an event, more expecting to defend himself against an angry pimp or mugger rather than an overprotective garden associate at Home Depot.

Right foot back.

Snap baton.

Swing at knees.

Left hand attacks neck with the tac pen.

The online videos had been very educational. Empowering. The little man in Lee felt safe when armed with his one-two punch. Protected. Brave, even. Yet there he was, under mortal threat, face-to-face with a potential assailant. And Lee was stuck. Not just for action, but for words. His heart, which had earlier fluttered from excitement, rattled like a freight train inside his chest. Sweat surfaced. Fear had overtaken him, turned him into marble.

"Hey, Fros?" sounded the managing cashier, an Amazonian-sized woman with huge, veiny hands. On his entry to the garden section, Lee had registered her as a tranny caught between sex-reassignment surgeries. She was five yards behind Frosty and half concealed by a stack of fence posts. "When you're finished with your customer, could you please help the lady with the toddler load her five bags of soil prep?"

"That's . . . uh . . . er . . . oh—" Lee faked a throat-clearing cough to cover his word stumble. Next he wisely pointed at the cinderblock in Frosty's grip. "Not the, you know, kinda brick thingy I was a looking for. You know, my garden. But, hey, thanks for the help anyway."

Lee retreated two steps, turned a one-eighty, and nearly performed a face-plant as his toe caught the edge of a wood pallet. Chagrined, he caught his balance without looking back. He tried not to hurry to his car as a matter of escaping further notice. Once inside the shitmobile, he auto-locked the doors, having difficulty inserting the car key due to the residual tremors. Once the engine turned over, he took a breath and scanned the parking lot to see if anybody was approaching or staring back in suspicion.

Nobody but nobody. Thank God.

He dropped the Honda into gear and searched for an exit. He'd nearly cleared the parking lot when he had to quickly brake, coming to a full stop to allow an over-thinned, middle-aged woman dressed in teal from head to toe lead her toddler—and Frosty—to a waiting SUV. The garden associate dutifully pushed a platform cart piled high with bags of compost and appeared to pay no mind to Lee. Frosty's lack of notice—or indifference—didn't quell the chill tracing Lee's spinal cord. He was reminded of his failed defense. The tactical pen and retractable baton—neither had cleared his pockets. The weapons may well have been an unnecessary pair of flaccid phalli. No, decided Lee. They wouldn't suffice at all in a fight. He was going to require an equalizer. Something equally as compact and concealable.

A gun.

20

Pasadena.

"I'm assuming Lydia knows you're here."

"She doesn't. No," replied Lucky. Though he'd only visited Dr. Sandalwood's office three times, the room seemed larger without Gonzo seated next to him. That single north-facing window from which he'd watched the sun setting over the San Gabriels was practically opaque from some unseen reflection, the shimmering heat coming off like a flaw in the glass.

The Sunday appointment was unplanned by both patient and analyst. Lucky had dialed her without much thought as to the day or time. Dr. Sandalwood, as it worked out, was spending her Sunday afternoon catching up on annoying office chores when her office line buzzed. When she heard Lucky's voice on the answering machine she instinctively grabbed for the handset and agreed to meet him within the hour. That was before she remembered that she was unprofessionally garbed in a Hüsker Dü T-shirt, college sweats, and flip-flops. Whoops. She briefly considered calling Lucky back to alter the last-minute appointment, but instead chose to simply explain her attire with the truth.

"I expect there's a reason she doesn't know?" asked the therapist, one of her flip-flops dangling from her toes.

"Didn't want her to think I was going behind her back."

"And that's not what you're doing by seeing me without her?"

"My call was not about her," said Lucky. "Or us. As in Gonzo and me."

"Don't usually see clients on short notice. Sundays especially. If I'd have known it was going to be just you—"

"Want me to go?"

"Not at all. You're here. I've staked out the hour. What's on your mind?"

Lucky turned his gaze toward that sun-struck window, feeling the heat tickling the tips of his unshaved hairs.

"Think I asked you before if you knew cops." Lucky intoned the question with a dulled tongue.

"Think you asked if I'd treated cops," answered Dr. Sandalwood. "And yes. But I don't necessarily *know* them."

"Or me, for that matter."

"We only just started a few weeks ago." Dr. Sandalwood waited for his response. Lucky's gaze remained fixed out the window. "Something you want me to know? About you, perhaps?"

"Sure."

"'Kay."

"Guys who become cops are wired for it in three general flavors," began Lucky. "Adrenaline junkies lookin' for on-the-job thrills. Control freaks who can't handle their own real-world shit. And bad guys who don't see themselves as bad guys. You know? If it weren't for their shield, they'd be in the gutter, doin' what they do."

"Okay, I'll bite." Her reply earned a sideways glance from Lucky. She shifted uncomfortably. "Which of those three are you?"

"Good question," answered Lucky, clearly not entirely certain. "One of the above. All of the above. You pick."

"But it's *your* session. It is about you. Why you're here without Lydia."

"Gonzo," corrected Lucky. "Nobody calls her Lydia."

"Okay. Gonzo it is. What kind of cop is she?"

"A woman. Guy rules don't apply."

"Is that what this is about? The differences between you?"

"Not about her in the least. It's about a decision I need to make."

"Regarding?"

"Dilemma. Choosing."

"Between?"

"Bad guys."

"What have they done?"

"Everything," shrugged Lucky. "In the name of justice. In the name of family. Usually, that's not a problem for me. I'd just pick sides and make a move."

"What kind of move?"

"The kind that solves the problem."

"These solves . . . legal? Moral? Neither?"

Lucky met her eyes, not so much looking for trust, but for a semi-objective arbiter. Dr. Sandalwood shifted again, depositing the dangling flip-flop on the floor and tucking her bare foot underneath her other leg.

"What about making no move at all?" she suggested. "You have your family to consider."

"Believe me," grumbled Lucky. "They're my primary concern."

"Okay, then. Why must it be you who makes the choice?"

"I'm the one getting squeezed."

"By whom, if I may?"

"By those who apply the pressure." Lucky's body language added an "obviously." All the while his eye contact remained steady, confident in his own skin. Not so in his indecision.

"You say this is about your family?" she segued. "Gonzo and . . ."

"Karrie and Trav. Yes."

"May I ask about your own family? We haven't talked at all about that." Dr. Sandalwood positioned the stylus against her electronic tablet. "Just for my own reference."

"Sure," clipped Lucky. "Father's a no-show. Mom's passed away. Little brother's dead."

Dr. Sandalwood added a pause, letting the brevity of Lucky's family lay there, the door open for him to elaborate. He didn't.

"Okay," she finally said. "They're all gone. Is there a particular family member that comes most to mind?"

"What does that have to do with anything?"

"We don't know yet," she softened. "What strands existed from the loss of your nuclear family and how they may affect the family you've made with Gonzo? Perhaps the answers lie there."

"Or maybe they don't," said Lucky. "Why do therapists always have to go there first?"

"Where?"

"Childhood shit."

"Good place to start. It's where we all started, yeah? Childhood?"

Lucky's gaze leveled on the freestanding shelves of books to the right of her chair, happily lit up with those smiley ghost and pumpkin faces. The books were stacked both vertically and horizontally, a potpourri of titles, only a few of which touched directly on the subject of psychotherapy. Lucky wondered how many she'd actually read or if their true purpose was to stir thoughts in her patients.

"You're not my first therapist," remarked Lucky.

"No?" she asked, though nothing about her appeared at all surprised.

"Policy," continued Lucky. "After even a good shoot, a deputy's gotta do so many hours with a department-approved shrink."

"Shoot?" she asked. "You mean, like, with a gun?"

"Like with a gun."

"And this happened to you?"

"If a cop's lucky or doing his shit right, most of what really happens is to the other guy."

"As in the other guy gets shot?"

"Or dead."

"And you've done this," forged Dr. Sandalwood. "Been in a good shoot?"

"I killed a man, yeah," said Lucky, bluntly. "Rookie season. All in the green."

"Green as in go?"

"Green as in everything was within policy." Lucky shifted, shrugged. "Traffic stop on a suspected stolen vehicle. Passenger went rabbit on us. I put down the foot chase. He showed his piece and popped off at me. Three shots. I drew down on him and put two in his chest."

"Musta been scary. How'd that make you feel?"

"Ya see?" pointed Lucky. "That's exactly what the department shrink asked. Now, even though I was still a trainee, I knew that if I ever wanted to work a black-and-white again, I'd need to dig up some bullshit about feeling bad, wrestling with my guilt, the pain my defending myself musta caused this asshole's family. So, I blah blah blah'd my way through five sessions and that was that."

"That was that," she repeated.

"Yeah. But truth is that I haven't lost a second's sleep over it. Scumbag was already suspect on two murders the PD detectives at Southeast Division couldn't make stick and he still spun three bullets at my head hoping I'd be his next vic. Think he'd have cried over my dead body?"

"Guess we'll never know," she said, masking her discomfort.

"How about I simplify my earlier question?" offered Lucky. "You have a family?"

"Yes. I do."

"'Kay. If your family was threatened. And the only true solve was outside procedure, morality, PD policy. How would you handle that?"

"That might take a lot of thought," admitted Dr. Sandalwood. "I might even need to make an appointment with my therapist."

"You're no help."

"Truthfully, I'm not entirely certain I feel comfortable with where this conversation is going."

"So?"

"Unpacking your personal history, your circumstances, your feelings—as they may or may not apply to your present circumstance—is one thing. You seeking advice on whether you should or shouldn't do something illegal or immoral?"

"We're just talking. Just talk."

"Here's my advice," she cautioned. "Don't do it. Whatever you're considering—whoever you're imagining doing it to? Don't. Make the right decision."

"Right," said Lucky, dismissively. As if to say, "Swell advice from eight floors above Planet Reality."

"Just an observation?" she offered. "You don't strike me as a man who vacillates over much. My take is that in your career . . . life . . . whatever . . . you've made hard decisions. You know? Something that would require you to 'make a move.'"

"Yeah. So?"

Dr. Sandalwood unhooked that foot from underneath and reinserted it into her flip-flop. Knees together and fingers splayed, she bent slightly at the waist for emphasis.

"What makes this one different?" she pressed. "Why this dilemma? This day? With these particular parties? What in this whole emotional stew led you to me? Here? Right now?"

Lucky had no immediate answer. Nor did he attempt to fill the rest of the hour. He simply excused himself, eased out the door without making a follow-up appointment, and rode the elevator down. He'd hoped that by the time he arrived in the basement garage he would have reached a moment of decision. Only there was no blinding flash. Nor was there some magical fog-clearing clarity. As much as Lucky loathed self-vacillation, he remained impaled on the horns of his dilemma.

Do for Judge Jim? Or do Judge Jim by ratting him out to the Feds?

The underground garage was mostly vacant, the gate arms that barred entry and exit without a paid ticket or validation were raised and vertical. There was no attendant on duty. Instead of taking the short stairwell that cut from the elevators, Lucky followed the concrete downslope, his sneakers spanking the tire-slicked surface with distinct footfalls. Some six paces before the hairpin right turn that led back to his restored Crown Vic, he heard another set of feet. Two pairs. Running. The trailing steps were followed by the slam of a heavy steel fire door and, beyond that, the fading pounding of shoes climbing a metal staircase.

And the hits just keep comin'.

Lucky fully expected to find his car had been broken into. Busted window. Marbled shards of safety glass littered inside and out. Because there was little to steal in the main compartment, Lucky wasn't that worried, thus his unhurried pace. The only true valuables were in his tactical kit in the trunk, including a fully loaded Benelli combat shotgun and a Heckler & Koch 5.56x6mm assault rifle with four spare magazines. Though both weapons were well within the law for Lucky to possess, an argument could be made that the trunk latch booby-trapped with two exploding tear gas canisters crossed some statutory lines. But better to break the law than have his weapons on the street in the mitts of some gangbanger.

Lucky's rules.

Despite the stenciled warnings on the walls, Lucky had left the '99 parked tail to the wall, as was his habit. The flickering fluorescent above revealed no shattered glass nor any other telltale marks of an attempted break-in. The only evidence of something amiss—besides the retreating footsteps Lucky had heard—were the fresh footprints surrounding the vehicle. A nearby puddle of condensation from an air-conditioner had been splashed by the comings and goings of the would-be thieves, leaving fresh impressions in a horseshoe-like trail around the Crown Vic.

He wondered if he'd arrived just in time to thwart a basic smash and grab—or if the unseen duo had an altogether different purpose in mind.

Lucky weighed both arguments and stuck with the former. It was, after all, greater Los Angeles, where auto burglary was a felony that nearly always pled down to misdemeanor theft due to the non-violence of the act. It was practically a non-crime for meth heads seeking to snatch anything that might be turned into cash for crank. His cutting short the session with Dr. Sandalwood might have earned its only benefit. His car hadn't been breeched. There would be no phoning and waiting for an auto glass repair truck to service his aging Crown Vic, let alone having to explain the lingering stench and eye irritation from the expended gas grenades he'd rigged to protect his trunk's stash.

Bonus.

The brief relief was replaced by a creeping notion that he was being followed.

The actual prickly feel of paranoia didn't click for two full blocks after Lucky had exhumed his '99 from the office tower's basement. After a half-mile stretch of checking both his rear- and side-view mirrors, he'd picked up nothing obvious. No vehicles shifting lanes two to three cars back. No tires riding the lane dividers as a way to keep eyes on him. One by one, he utilized all his tricks to discern if he'd picked up a tail. He slowed, sped up, made four right turns in a row followed by four left turns. To check if he was being tag-teamed, he memorized cars, drivers, distinguishable dents or scrapes, license plate tags, bumper and window stickers, looking for anything that repeated. When that failed, instead of merely shrugging off the annoying sensation, Lucky wheeled into the nearest Starbucks, set the parking brake and entered, casually ordering a small black coffee and standing sentry behind the smoked glass between the café and the street. He stared outward for five full minutes, examining the patterns of traffic, keying on all passersby, trusting his instinct to spot any confederate with an interest—police officer, Armenian, or as yet to be determined.

Nothing sparked.

Before abandoning his concern and climbing back into his Crown Vic, Lucky stood five paces from the car, then rotated counterclockwise, examining the new paint for defects, recent palm prints, or a disturbance of road dust. He got down to his hands, knees, and back. With a tactical light he checked the under-sides of his bumpers, inside the wheel wells, even fitting his fingers into fender crevasses for anything resembling a magnetic GPS device. He did the same to his engine, quitting only when his arms and umpire's blue shirt were black and smeared from grease. He wanted that GPS device.

Nothing was discovered, though, leaving him to second-guess himself and those senses he so thoroughly trusted. He wiped his hands on his formerly clean jeans, then fired an angry foot into the rear door panel, leaving a dent, evident and clean. A scarlet mark of his failure.

Lucky sighed, squatted to his haunches, and traced his fingers along the new defect. The scalloped shape wasn't unlike the remnant bullet wound at the base of his skull.

"That's right, ol' girl," said Lucky. "Now we both got one."

Despite the clouds of indecision continuing to hover over him, his patience—or lack thereof—pushed him towards less of a choice and more of a pathway. It wasn't quite a plan, but it was a route—a direction.

A possible way out.

21

Glendale. 5:01 p.m.

God bless those crazy Kardashians.

Aside from giving the occasional heavenly thanks, Lizzy generally regarded the Calabasas clan with animosity. In her mind the Kardashians had made themselves famous by suborning viewers into hundreds of hours of mindless and grotesquely shallow reality TV. Though Lizzy would admit that in doing so, America's favorite Armenian family had shown some serious media and business acumen. But they weren't anything close to real Armo. Not in her hard-to-satisfy opinion. Beyond some annual social media post regarding the Armenian Genocide, the ridiculously rich West Valley fame whores shared nothing ethnic or culturally relevant with Lizzy Kasabian beyond the nearly all-encompassing affection for making bank.

Thus it was *God bless the Kardashians* for bringing attention to the Armenian beauty biz.

Besides the purple awning and pink neon script, there was little remarkable about Glendale's Lazy Suzy's Salon. It was one of the eleven businesses she "managed" from La Cañada to East Hollywood. Each always had a few native-speaking hairdressers on hand, promising the very best in 'dos for ethnic sweet-sixteen parties. Generations moved through the front doors—grandmothers to mothers to daughters. And out the back doors? Wheelbarrows of laundered cash.

"Asshole," complained Lizzy, dropping all one hundred pounds of herself into the bucket seat of her Jaguar. She dragged her cobalt blue Givenchy purse towards her, pained by the weight of it no thanks to a Glock 26 pistol and perhaps thirty dollars of loose quarters to feed the parking meters that fronted most of her salons. Out her side window was a car equally as low to the road as hers: a vintage Ferrari convertible. Red. The 1973 model Dino 246 was parallel to her and halfway forward. Behind the wheel was a well-heeled-looking man of sixty-five or so years, his untrimmed white hair creating a Caesar-like crown around his tanned dome. The man absolutely knew Lizzy was there. She'd caught him checking her out in his rear- and side-view mirrors. He hadn't missed a lick of her short walk from the salon to her car. Despite that, he didn't deign to move his precious Ferrari enough so Lizzy could safely extricate her Jaguar from the curb.

She did some quick math.

It was Sunday. *Babka Sunday.* For the past month, the Jewish bakery next-door to the salon had started selling its chocolate and cinnamon sweet cakes for half-price on Sundays. The simple reduction from $13.99 to $6.49 for day-old Babka had created a stampede of sorts. Business was so brisk, the salon manager had complained to Lizzy that customers were having difficulty finding street parking.

Luxe prick! You're too cheap to buy your sweet cake at full price?

The thought of it! A man driving that kind of ride, double-parked and waiting for wife number two or three to return with a half-price Babka? Lizzy wanted to retch right there. She gave a sharp but still friendly chirp from her car horn, eliciting little more than a backhanded wave. He inched forward no more than twelve measly inches. Once again, the classic Ferrari thrummed in idle.

"Really?" pissed Lizzy. She rolled down her window and forced enough air over her tongue to believe he could hear her voice over the whine of his Italian-tuned engine. "Hey!"

That's when her eyes dipped down to the Ferrari's vanity license plate.

JUSTS3

"Hey," shouted Lizzy again. "Mr. JUST-S-3!"

The man in the Ferrari neither heard nor moved a muscle.

"'Kay, JUST S," she pissed.

With fewer than six inches of room to her rear, Lizzy dropped her Jag into drive, cranked the wheel to turn her tires, and gave the gas pedal a poke. The Jag leapt and struck the sports car's right rear taillight like a snapping alligator. There was an unmistakable crunch. The Ferrari driver, both rocked and shocked, twisted angrily in his seat.

"Sorry, sorry, sorry!!!" pleaded Lizzy, shrinking in her seat, feigning the part of a bleached-blonde mess. She held up her hands, shaking them in pretend fright, her heavily inked mascara drawing circles around her white-eyed orbits. "I just got my license, so . . ."

"Jesus fucking Christ!" bitched Judge Jaime Peralta. He set the parking brake and climbed out, buzzing around the rear to check the damage.

"I have insurance!" cried Lizzy, having incorrectly pegged the man to be as equally short as he was vain. But the man who approached was rather tall, albeit frumpy, wearing a dark blue T-shirt with *Mid-Valley Pony League* embroidered on the pocket. "Please don't be mad! It's my daddy's car and he's gonna be so pissed at me!"

"Can't goddamn believe this shit!" griped Judge Jim, before throwing his arms up in the air.

"We need to exchange information, right?" played Lizzy.

"Stupid bitch."

Judge Jim's words might have been mouthed under his breath and swallowed by the Ferrari motor's constant lament. But Lizzy had been able to read lips since she was six years old. Despite the slight, she waited for him to climb back into his seat to pop the glove box in search of his registration and state-mandated insurance card.

Then Lizzy slapped it again.

Foot to the gas. Lurch. Crunch. In a repeat maneuver, the Jag bucked and smacked into the Ferrari. This time, a direct hit below the sports car's famed chrome horse insignia.

"Oh, Jesus! Sorry, sorry, sorry!" she bellowed.

"WHAT THE FUCK ARE YOU?!!"

"I forgot to put it in park! Please don't yell at me."

With that, Lizzy shrunk even smaller, willing herself to appear even more helpless and pathetic than seconds before. She summoned her entire body to shake with mock fright.

"Please don't hurt me!" Lizzy pleaded.

"Just calm down!" yelled Judge Jim. "I WON'T hurt you!"

"Hate me," corrected Lizzy. "I mean PLEASE DON'T HATE ME."

"PUT YOUR GODDAMN CAR IN PARK!" the judge pointed. "AND GET OUT YOUR INSURANCE SHIT 'CAUSE DADDY IS GONNA PAY!"

Again, the man she called JUST-S—as in *Just Shit*—dug back into his glove box for his registration. And again, Lizzy dropped her act long enough to slip the Jag into drive and nudge the accelerator. This time, her tires squeaked, if only slightly, before the Jaguar's grille jumped and took a final bite out of the Ferrari's rear end.

"YOU INSANE LITTLE CUNT!" shouted Judge Jim, launching back out of his car with a fistful of papers.

"I'm having a really bad car day!" faked Lizzy, her face practically buried in the Givenchy purse.

"Do you have a clue what it costs to fix a vintage Ferrari?" he gesticulated between the Dino Sport's damaged tail and Lizzy.

As Judge Jim swung closer to her, Lizzy lowered the purse and revealed the muzzle of her baby Glock. The barrel rested on the window frame, oriented directly at the crotch of the man's khakis.

"Not close to what it's gonna cost to build JUST-S a new package," she smirked, all pretense erased. "Like there's anything down there that works without a little blue pill."

At a loss for both words and the muscle to move, Judge Jim sucked in a lungful of air and held it.

"I hate Turks, hipsters, and double-parked assholes like you— in that order," continued Lizzy. "Now get back in your little dick-mobile and fuck off."

"Miss," lowered Judge Jim. "You have no clue who I am."

"Know who I am?" spat Lizzy. "I'm the cunt with a nine who doesn't give a shit. Now do as I say and FUCK. OFF."

"Jimmy? What's going on?" Standing at the passenger door of the Ferrari was a forty-year-old brunette in a glittered tank top. Attractive—extremely well-tended with a surgeon's nose job. In her hands was a baker's box with her half-off babka.

Perfect, thought Lizzy.

"Just get in the car, Ruth."

"Jimmy?" pressed Ruth, her mandible already set.

"Get in the car, Ruth," chimed Lizzy. "And enjoy the bargain dessert. Really."

Lizzy smiled as JUST-S stumbled back to his driver's seat. How far would he drive before pulling over to dial 911? Would he tell Ruth first? Or explain after? It didn't really matter because the rest was going to be easy for Lizzy. There were any number of secure places she could ditch the gun. And if JUST-S or his wife had description enough of his alleged assailant, the make and model of her damaged Jaguar, or even a partial license plate, the cops dispatched to find her would be from the Glendale Police

Department. And thanks to her father and his extensive tentacles into the local PD, that would be that. A dead end.

22

That crazy little bitch.

She'd left the judge's stomach in spasms. In his forty-plus years in law enforcement—from street cop to prosecutor to justice— Jaime Peralta had prided himself for facing down all matter of bad—from the poor-intentioned misfits to the downright evil. Never once, though, had Judge Jim been point blank with a gun muzzle aimed at any part of him, let alone his crotch. In fact, he'd never been confronted with more than a screwdriver in the hands of a serial wife abuser on PCP. His cop career had consisted of cushy assignments divided by nights in law school. His political trajectory had led straight to the Superior Court bench. And from that high dais he'd dispensed justice to the worst of the worst. Until he'd organized his one-man star chamber of backdoor justice, the courtroom was where and how he faced down the bad men of the world. Between himself and the criminals were that giant raised desk, lawyers, railings, and lest anybody forget, the sheriff's deputies who manned the metal detectors at the courthouse entrance.

The pain in Judge Jim's gut felt as if the mouthy bleached-blonde in the Jaguar had pulled the trigger. The memory of the moment, the image of the gun muzzle pointed at his groin, and the fear that had struck him to his bones, cast a pall on what was, in his opinion, the most incandescent and perfect of moments. He cherished his Sunday evenings. He would sit on the redwood deck just outside his upstairs home office and observe the setting sun on three distinct focal planes.

The furthest plane—the backdrop—was the distant and famed Vasquez Rocks. The sideways jutting formations courtesy of the San Andreas Fault reached hundreds of feet off the high desert floor, slashing into the sky, their colors changing in the slow descent of the sun.

Mid-plane was the back half acre of his Canyon Country home, much of which was occupied by a custom swimming pool faced in hand-cut flagstone. The sounds of children's squeals and splashes as they plunged down the built-in slide completed the picture. His daughter and three grandchildren were there, plus the usual handful of neighborhood friends. His son Jim Jr. worked the outdoor kitchen barbeque like the maestro he had once been.

Occupying Judge Jim's closest plane was a clear tumbler brimming with sweet Kentucky rye on ice. Knob Creek, his preferred Sunday elixir. The nose of the American whiskey blended perfectly with the scent of flank steak on the grill. The ice swirling in the golden liquid was a sensory and visual complement to the distant rock formations.

My life is gooood. Or so he would usually exhale on those heavenly Sundays. But instead of sipping his whiskey, the judge gulped at it and wished for his muscles to settle into his throne, a heavy-beamed Adirondack chair. He wiggled his bare toes to shake off a slight numbness, worrying it was the onset of type 2 diabetes. That would mean some asshole doctor telling him he'd have to curb his evening cocktails. But maybe it was just nerves from facing down that little bitch and her 9mm.

After the uncomfortable encounter outside the bakery, the shaken judge had climbed back into his vintage Ferrari and tried like hell to look calm in front of Ruth while flicking his eyes to the rear mirror to read the Jag's license plate. His vision was shaky and the numbers and letters were a backwards jumble. By the time he'd turned enough street corners and felt safe to pull over and dial 911, he'd already listened to five minutes of his wife all spun up with excitement over the evening's planned festivities. On top of their usual Sunday evening social, it was their youngest grand-child's birthday.

Thus Judge Jim had momentarily swallowed the indignity of his showdown and let the hot wind chap his face all the way to their homey Santa Clarita hacienda inside the gated safety of a private community called Mesa del Sol. Once in his office, he'd dialed the Glendale Police Department, leaving a detailed report with the duty officer and a strongly worded message for the Chief of Police to call him during business hours the following day.

He also took the unusual step of backing his Ferrari into their four-car garage so that his wife wouldn't notice the damage to the right rear of the vintage Dino.

It might have been the only imperfection in his Sunday. Only no day was perfect. Not while society's flotsam was out there. The gutter scum, they lived beyond his property line and the private walls of the gated community, where he planned to reside until his eventual death from natural causes.

"Papa, look!" shouted his daughter Patsy.

Judge Jim leaned forward to peer over the deck rail. His daughter was below, already seven months pregnant with his next grandchild and holding the half-price chocolate babka over her head. There were three unlit birthday candles stuck in the cake.

"Beautiful babka," she voiced with adoring gratitude. "You must give us the name of the bakery."

"My secret," joked the grandfather. "If I told ya . . ."

"You'd have to kill me," she rolled her eyes. "I know, I know."

With the picture of his pregnant daughter in his head, Judge Jim recalled his moment of clarity. Even after all his years serving the city, he'd never felt entirely satisfied. Whether hanging up his gun for the day or his judge's robe, his mind would always spin. He imagined it as an inaccessible hard drive that couldn't rest. Despite trying, he was never able to distract his gray matter into submission. The most he could accomplish was drink the itch away until he—or it—was duly numbed.

Then came a night like this . . .

A nearly perfect evening. Families spread across the lawn. Grandkids barreling down the slide into his freshly re-plastered pool. Midnight blue. The color of tranquility. So the salesman had said. Yet the judge felt nothing close to the peace he'd hoped for. If anything, the world felt as if it were slipping through his fingers into a deeper morass of incivility and suffering. There was no being content to *just do his part.*

So had come Judge Jim's unifying moment of clarity.

I can't make the world perfect. But I can sure as shit leave it cleaner than I found it.

"And I will protect mine," added Judge Jim, offering a solitary and solemn toast to his country, his home, his property, and most importantly, his family.

He hadn't expected anybody to be observing, let alone joining in his liquid tribute. From the corner of his eye, he recognized the cue-ball dome of Miles Czajkowski, the sole invitee to the birthday barbeque who wasn't family or a neighbor. As Miles lifted his Heineken bottle to the sky until he caught his host's attention, his wife hooked his bicep and pulled the arm down. The ever-strident Mrs. Czajkowski, a quasi-masculine figure in an unfortunate bikini, appeared perturbed at her husband's lack of attention. Coupled with the embarrassed look on Miles's face, Judge Jim inferred it as a strike-two tiff—one more foul-up and Miles might be walking home. The pair seemed to always be feuding. Judge Jim rescued Miles with an approach-the-bench wave.

"You're such a control freak," his first wife Angelica used to complain with a wagging finger and a smirk. It had been five years since she'd passed. Ovarian cancer.

Talk about a fucking trial.

Jaime thanked God for Ruthie and the likes of match.com, the dating site where he'd found a dead ringer for his dearly departed wife, only twenty-two years younger.

Judge Jim summoned Miles with a come-upstairs gesture. A small mercy, he reasoned. De-escalate the tension. Miles directed his wife's attention to the judge's deck, shrugged as if he had no choice but to obey, and quickly disappeared around the property's northwest corner to the kitchen door. Miles's wife squared her swimmer's shoulders to the judge, arms akimbo, and forced the thinnest of smiles beneath a volume of Italian black hair.

"And fuck you too," toasted the judge, speaking only beneath his breath, his mouth barely moving to make certain she couldn't read his lips.

"Judge!" sounded Miles, climbing the back stairs. "I owe you big time."

"Only gonna piss her off that much more," answered Judge Jim. "Wanna cigar? Smokes are in the box."

"Cuban cigar stink?" chuckled Miles. "That will sure as shit put a bullet in my marriage."

"Ruthie used to complain. But that's why I began showering at night before bed."

"And gargling with what? Moonshine? My wife can taste that shit for days."

Miles joined the judge in a second Adirondack chair—the queen's chair, as his first wife used to call it. From there they'd watch those magnificent hill country sunsets and plan their next home improvement.

"Peralta Party Palace," said Miles. "That's what you should call this joint."

"Angie woulda liked that," smiled the judge, referring to his deceased wife and toasting with his diminishing tumbler of rye.

"Stacy says we gotta wait for her old man to drop dead before we'd be able to afford anything close to this. Either that, or my consulting biz takes flight."

"And what was that again?"

"Tech adviser for movies 'n' TV," reminded Miles. "And that sometimes leads to all sorts of other income. Small acting parts. On-camera news analyst."

"Your kids are young still," segued Judge Jim. "We built this place for our grandkids."

"I'm not so patient."

The brief conversation was quick to stall, the judge content to let his eyes focus on infinity and the changing colors on Vasquez Rocks. Part of him wanted to confide in Miles. Tell him of the game of bumper to bumper with the Armenian blonde in the Jag. The nine-millimeter aimed a foot from his junk.

Relaxed as the rye was making the judge's muscles, the man's stomach was still a knot.

"Think he's with us?" asked Miles.

"Think *who* is with us?"

"Deputy Dawg. You know. Lucky Dey."

"He is or he isn't," replied the judge, glad to switch his mind from the afternoon encounter to other matters. Then dryly, without a scintilla of recrimination, "No matter which way it goes, Lucky Dey's been circling his own drain for years now. Disposable, I'm afraid. Sad too, 'cause it's all his own doing."

"Yet we asked him to join our club."

"Because we are his only redemption. If he can't see his way to that, then . . ."

"We put him out of his misery," nodded Miles. "Yeah. Guess I'm good with that."

"And we're all set just in case?"

"Just in case."

"So, we wait. See if he comes through for us." Judge Jim raised his whiskey. Not in a toast, but to examine the shade of amber in his glass. "If he doesn't? We put Lucky Dey down."

23

Lucky had learned a trick or two from his year attending Alcoholics Anonymous meetings. Though it wasn't quite with the lasting result he or Gonzo had intended—him coming to grips with his untreated addiction—he had to concede there were some handy tips found in Bill W.'s twelve steps to sobriety. His favorite was Step Four: completing a personal inventory. The set of hard questions asked and answered of oneself had the probing quality of a gifted interrogator. State the problem and answer with unvarnished honesty.

Applying the fourth step to his Major Crimes casework, Lucky would try to take an unflinching inventory of any given problem. Catalog every fact to its flaw, then string it out. Extrapolate.

Conclude. Then beat on the conclusion with a hammer until it broke.

Only there was a problem with the Judge Jim quandary.

Hard as he tried—and as much as he wanted to drop some kind of self-serving indictment against his Honor Jaime Peralta—it was impossible for him to divine all the connective threads the sixty-five-year-old jurist would have sewn throughout his forty-plus-year career. Police brass. Feds. US Attorneys. Everywhere Lucky imagined he might stretch for an assist felt like a potential trap door. Hell, he thought, even going to Assistant Sheriff Paul McGill felt like a reach that might just as likely be met with a meat cleaver than a sympathetic hand.

"Sometimes the only way out is through." Lucky recalled the sage advice from his training officer and fellow Reaper, Flip Bledsoe. "Only problem with that plan is sometimes you end up shot and bleeding out."

So be it, decided Lucky.

The neighborhood of Atwater Village was defined as much by its east and west boundaries—Interstate 5 and State Route 2—as by being a partial bridge between Little Armenia and the more affluent Glendale. The former fertile flatland along the eastern tributary of the concrete Los Angeles River had long ago evolved into a polyethnic suburb, equally close to downtown, Hollywood, and Pasadena.

That, and the Atwater Village Denny's had sustained its liquor license.

The diner was attached to a Best Western motel. A recent facelift had hoped to give it a Santa Fe flare. Instead, it merely made the two-story roadhouse appear as sandy and ubiquitous as every other strip mall found at most of the busier intersections.

Lucky's instructions were to find a seat in the bar and wait for Vartan Kasabian to arrive. The restaurant hostess, a motherly beauty with sky-high cheekbones and an Eastern Euro tune to her voice, implored Lucky to order whatever he liked and it would be on the house. The prospect of ordering a double vodka martini to wash down a Grand Slam breakfast amused Lucky. In how many Denny's, from sea to shining sea, was that even an option? Lucky picked a corner bar table underneath a faux stained-glass window and ordered a Diet Coke and a side order of bacon cheddar tots.

There he waited, certain he was being observed through one of the two security cameras he'd spotted flanking the bar. No doubt Vaz and his Armenian crew were casing him. Careful. If he were Vaz, he would have had teams of gangsters circling the block in search of backup deputies or FBI or any clue whatsoever that might lend to the notion that Lucky was wired or setting up the Kasabian chieftain for some kind of surprise arrest. Whatever Vaz's reason, Lucky sat alone, polishing off Diet Cokes for nearly an hour before Chris Kasabian waltzed in from the restaurant, broad smile, an unrepentant falseness to his exuberance. The only thing shinier than Chris's teeth was the ivory silk of his shirt.

"Deputy," said Chris, offering a hand. "You mind? I gotta check you."

Lucky stood, striking out his arms like a crucifix. The pat-down was perfunctory, as much looking for a wire as weapons.

"My ol' man is old-school," said Chris. "I tell him listening devices are way more advanced today. Aim a laser at that window there and you can listen to anything in the room."

"Important safety tip," replied Lucky, offering up his cell phone. "Thanks."

"Speaking of that, Pop's comin' in with muscle," warned Chris. "Just keep your hands in view and nobody gets their shit all ruffled."

The young gangster retreated to a stool at the empty bar. A mounted television tuned to a replay of a Premier League soccer match was overhead. Tottenham versus Arsenal. With a remote control, Chris turned up the volume until the sound of the raucous crowd bounced off the imitation hardwood paneling.

As if cued, Vaz swept into the bar, trailed by three obvious bodyguards, though none were clichéd suited thugs. These were Armenian Power—jeans, Timberlands, tattoos, and size-too-small polo shirts that better revealed their muscled necks. Vaz had attired himself in tennis whites, partially sweat through from a recent workout.

"Did you eat?" asked Vaz. "I left instructions."

"Floating in soda," remarked Lucky.

"And your Sunday?" asked Vaz. "Was it good for you?"

"Denny's with a full bar. Thought I knew L.A."

"Glendale. We're a small town in the big town."

"Sound like you're the mayor."

"That was my father's fantasy." Vaz snapped his fingers then twirled his index. "More Coke?"

"Diet. But I'm good."

"Bring me a Stella," said Vaz to Chris, who instantly slid off his stool and stepped behind the bar. "My poppa had this thing he'd say all the time. 'If I was mayor I'd fix the sidewalks.' Or 'Tell the Koreans to speak English.' Not that his own English was so good."

"Mayor? Glendale?" probed Lucky.

"East Hollywood. Little Armenia. Where they have no official mayor, of course. It's L.A. proper. Which is why he wanted to fill the void. My poppa was good at that. Filling voids."

Chris served a pint glass of draught beer, the foam spilling over, leaving a wet ring on the small table.

"You're from here?" Lucky confirmed.

"Armenia." Then Vaz corrected, "Technically Azerbaijan. Across the border there was a Russian hospital my mother preferred. So, I was born there. Lived in Armenia 'til I was thirteen before my parents emigrated."

"Parents still alive?"

"My poppa is. He moved back."

"America didn't take?"

"Oh no, no, no. He loved America. Everything about it." Vaz leaned in as if imparting a secret. "Used to compare the United States to the ultimate orgasm. Yeah. Like that. I shit you not."

The statement required no retort from Lucky, who only cocked his head as if to say, "Aaannnd?"

"American Bang, he used to call it," carried on Vaz. "Like this country was a big wet pussy. The weather. Lifestyle. Hell, the supermarkets—the fucking abundance of everything. Kinda stuff you and me take for granted."

With no reply from Lucky, Vaz carried on.

"'A-*More*-ica,' he would also say," continued Vaz. "My poppa, you understand, grew up on the Soviet side of the Iron Curtain. And as Armenians go, we lived well. But the wealthiest of Armos were like the ghetto poor we have here. In Los Angeles."

"Lemme guess," segued Lucky. "He eventually retired and left the business to you."

"No, no." Vaz wagged an index finger. "He still runs it. From Armenia. Me? I'm just management." Vaz allowed his chest to swell with pride. "This diner? The hotel? This was his. Where he started. He bought this place back in the seventies. Ran girls in and out of here. Perfect location. Halfway between Pasadena and downtown. Freeway-close. If a businessman or politician wanted a little somethin', he could dip his willy and be back at the office in an hour."

"Girls," repeated Lucky. "Young ones?"

"Young ones, old ones, black ones, brown ones, yellow, green, blue. Fuck it. You wanted it. My poppa would get it for you." Vaz leaned it yet again. "Hey. We're married. Family men. But we're men all the same and we like what we like, yeah? So? What does Lucky like?"

"Yeah . . ." Lucky took a generous pause, pretending to be thinking about his reply. "You wouldn't trust me to come back to you with a positive outcome on your son's issue if I didn't ask for more. Girls. Money. Favors."

"Would you trust me if all I came at you with was threats?"

"Against my family," Lucky reminded.

"Like I just said. We're about our families. We both know each other's soft spots."

Lucky applied his lips together. His jawbone added an extra cut to his visage.

"I could be less delicate," shrugged Vaz. "My poppa used to refer to a moment like this here as two men with hands around the other's testicles. It was all about who could squeeze the hardest."

With a nod, Lucky finally sat back. Left both his hands on the table. Flat.

"I like young girls," lied Lucky, acting like it was an admission of preference rather than guilt. "Blonde. Freckles. Fifteen."

"We can do that," agreed Vaz. "We could do younger if you want. Right here. At my old man's hotel. You stay for a few drinks and Chris'll bring you a selection."

Though he felt as if infected microbes were crawling under his skin, the trick for Lucky was not to scratch. Not even feign an itch. Lucky felt he had warrant enough to shove the barrel of his .45 in Vaz's mouth and force-feed the bastard a single serving of lead. Though the aftereffects would more than likely be fatal, in the grand scheme of mankind, the load might be that much lighter.

Sometimes the only way out is through.

"Another night," Lucky deadpanned, then shrugged. "Bad timing. Family shit. You understand."

"But we *have* an understanding, yes? And that's an excellent start. Better than a surprise meeting in a car." Vaz gave a wink and a nod. "Now do you have something for me? Or is it too soon to ask?"

"Nope," said Lucky. "My report's still parked. And I have a certain somebody with the juice to make your son's accident go away. Permanent."

"But this certain somebody wants something for themselves," suspected Vaz. "From me, I expect."

"You know the game."

"So?" Vaz gave a two-fingered beckoning gesture, revealing his impatience.

"What they want?" Lucky teased.

"Let's get it done." Vaz slapped his hands on the table with an optimist's glee.

Lucky's plan wasn't fully formed. It couldn't be, because when attempting to get *out by going through*, there were always unseen obstacles, dangers, setbacks, even collateral damage. If he'd had more time to think, an entirely different solution might have presented itself.

No, thought Lucky. *It's time to give everybody precisely what they want.*

"Kitchen got some plastic wrap?" asked Lucky. He looked past Vaz to Chris and the three muscle-heads. "The stretchy stuff. Saran Wrap. Cling-something?"

"You serious?" asked Vaz.

"As hot lead," finished Lucky.

Before Vaz could ask, Chris reached over the bar and retrieved an industrial-sized box of Stretch-Tite.

"This work?" asked Chris. With a permissive chin tilt from his father, Chris crossed the floor and handed the thirteen-inch box to Lucky.

He accepted the box with one hand, then with the other took hold of Vaz's half-supped pint of beer, turned the tumbler over, and dumped the rest of the brew onto the floor before returning the glass upright in front of the gangster.

"Now work up some saliva and spit in it," ordered Lucky. "Three times."

"Is this a joke?" asked Vaz after a few staggered breaths.

"That's what they want." Lucky pointed at the bagged pint glass.

"My beer glass with my fingerprints?"

"Your DNA. See? You squeezed me in hopes to get the crosshairs off your Johnny Boy. Meanwhile, these other assholes are squeezing me to get your Armenian DNA. You know. To seal the deal on some future crime you did or didn't commit."

"Wait, wait, wait," said Vaz, not at all liking being off balance. "The certain somebody who can take care of my Johnny wants my DNA?"

"They told me to tell you Johnny would be taken care of. Get close to you. Pretend we're pals 'n' shit. Then when you weren't looking, walk away with a sample."

"Like my beer glass."

"Exactly like your beer glass. The extra spit is for good measure. Just to make sure."

"So, why tell me?" wondered Vaz. He leaned back as if to try to take in a bigger picture of Lucky, the man across from him who was making very little sense. "This is bullshit. You're not stupid enough to fuck up your own deal."

"What my certain somebody don't know is what he don't know," pushed Lucky. "But that same certain somebody is the real deal. I give him the glass, your spit in it, he makes Johnny Boy's problem disappear. Poof. Gone. My guy's a real live magic man."

"But . . ."

"But what? Thought you said that as parents we would do anything for family. That *we* shit. I figured that you meant you *and* me." Lucky put his thumb to his sternum. "I know what I'd do to protect what's mine. And this is it right here. Betraying my brothers in blue for my family."

Vaz had his hands up in the air as if under arrest. Only his gesture was the halting kind, signaling for the world to slow its roll.

"Okay . . . Right . . . So, let's pretend you're not bullshit," reasoned Vaz. "Why tell me? Why not just wait for this sit-down to finish? Bag my beer glass after I leave. I'm none the goddamn wiser."

"Nope," firmed Lucky. "You don't need to know anything more than this. I do for my family the way I do. You do for yours the way you do."

The air was so still, Lucky could smell the hours-old sweat on the mob boss. As well as a brand-new profusion of perspiration that had appeared on Vaz's matted hairline. He was a man accustomed to being in control. Lucky knew that. In his experience, most captains of industry, criminal or otherwise, were pretty much hooked up with the same kind of wiring. Lucky was banking on as much by pushing Vaz off-kilter. It was only a matter of how or what the gangster would reach for as he attempted to regain a sense of mental equilibrium.

I know what I'd do.

Vaz stood, rising quickly, his chair sliding away. He gazed down at his empty pint glass, the inside walls of the tumbler coated in foam. For a moment, Lucky was almost certain that Vaz would snatch it up, toss it to Chris, turn, and exit. It would be up to the three muscled goons to finish with Lucky.

"My son Johnny," stated Vaz. "His problem disappears?"

"Yes," replied Lucky.

A single nod, then, with the glass in hand, Vaz swished up some saliva between his cheeks and spat into it.

"Twice more," requested Lucky.

After hocking up as much saliva as he could spare, Vaz added a gob of snot to the beer glass, then slapped the cocktail onto the table with an emphatic *clunk!*

"All you get," finished Vaz.

Lucky unfurled a sheet of Stretch-Tite. He first sealed the top of the beer glass, sufficiently securing the evidence. Then in a bit of overkill, Lucky laid the beer glass on its side and wound enough plastic around it until it resembled a plastic cylinder capped at both ends.

"This certain someone . . . this magic man," sneered Vaz. "You make sure he delivers on his promise. Or I will find out who he or she is, gut them, and hang them from the Hollywood Sign."

Vaz's hastened exit from the bar created a vacuum of sorts, sucking along Chris Kasabian and the three musclemen. Lucky was left alone with the wrapped glass and the crowd from the soccer game on the TV.

He made sure to leave a tip.

24

Sunland-Tujunga. 7:00 p.m.

The lot for the Mexican restaurant was roomy by Los Angeles standards. In the land of ten million cars, parking was always at a premium. Most popular restaurants, even in the outlying suburbs, required valets to keep the vehicles in order. Not so at the Mucho Max Cantina on Foothill.

Per their instructions, the Armenian duo of Eriq and Tavet had spent the day stalking the strawberry-blonde teen in her lime green Prius. They were to watch and wait. If and when the order came, they were to move from stalk to snatch. After observing her from a distance, pummeling her way through a three-hour Muay Thai workout, they realized the task was easier ordered than accomplished. A short pit stop later and both thugs were armed with stun guns powered with six million disabling volts.

"Overkill," Chris Kasabian had laughed upon hearing the request. "She's what? A hundred ten pounds?"

Better overkill than bruised faces and egos, reasoned the kidnappers. It was equally easy to imagine the shit they'd get from their Armo comrades if the freckled teen left a single visible welt.

The furthermost reach of the parking lot was rimmed in eight-foot-high cinderblock, against which were the employees' cars. Four hours earlier, Eriq and Tavet had observed Karrie back her Toyota into a corner space, headlights pointed out, another clue to her hyperawareness. The teen partially undressed before pulling a frilly white frock over her head, emerging from the Prius only moments later in a traditional Mexican dress trimmed in red and gold embroidery.

"Day-um," said Tavet, miserably failing to sound ghetto. "Shorty's got more moves."

"Hey, man," added Eriq. "She ain' no Mexican. So, wha' da fuck she doin' dressin' like?"

"Workin', maybe," decided Tavet. "Like you and me."

Eriq chuckled, then counted to thirty once Karrie had disappeared through the rear door of the restaurant. The rented panel van fit snugly into the open space next to Karrie's car. In case the snatch order came, the sliding door was poised opposite the Toyota's driver's side. The distance from the girl's car into the van was a matter of only a few feet.

"What if the order comes while she doin' whatever she do in there?" asked Tavet.

"We make something up. Give her a reason to stop what she doin'," reasoned Eriq.

The sun finished the last of its daily arc, sinking behind the scrubby walls of Big Tujunga Canyon and leaving the twilight sky in changing hues of vanilla, peach, and azure. The twinkly white Christmas lights affixed to the low arches of the Mexican cantina clicked on at exactly 7:15 p.m. Behind the property, the parking lot slowly filled in a testament to the restaurant's popularity. The sound of recorded mariachis played to the parked cars through tinny patio speakers mounted under the restaurant's eaves.

Seventeen-year-old Karrie had desperately wanted a job. A *real* job, she had explained to her friends and family. Part-time. A place where she would clock in and out in the manner of a normal worker bee and earn a paycheck with her new name on it.

Karrie Anne Dey.

This despite the multimillion-dollar trust the emancipated teen had partial access to. But for her Toyota Prius and shelling out a two-year advance for a five-day-a-week habit of Muay Thai training, Karrie had touched nary a dollar of her inheritance. Nor had she any plans to.

I soooo crave the normal.

In her young life, she could recollect very little that she could categorize as normal. Was she adventurous? Yes. Reckless and stupid? *A double yes.* While she struggled to accept God's forgiveness for her responsibility regarding her former life, she kept her eyes forward to the traditional landmarks ahead—high school homecoming, prom, graduation, college.

"So, how many are there in your party?" asked Karrie, the newest Mucho Max hostess.

The middle-aged Hispanic man, teacup small, with a respectively tiny wife and two middle-school kids, held up for four polite fingers. Karrie gathered an equal number of menus and delivered the quartet into the dimly lit dining room with heavy wood furniture and faux Spanish frescos painted on the plaster walls. Karrie guessed the family spoke little to no English. Dining out on a cash budget. The father probably made a similar assumption. That the strawberry-blonde hostess probably knew little, if any, Spanish.

Karrie seated the family at a booth under a hanging piñata of a red pig.

"*Ocasión especial?*" asked Karrie to the family's surprise.

"*No, gracias,*" replied the father, the wide grin on his face revealing chewing-tobacco–stained teeth.

"*Disfrute de la comida,*" Karrie replied, so pleased with herself she practically squeaked her words.

She recalled little Spanish from her early years in private school.

But with Travis at her side, she'd successfully shamed Gonzo into rediscovering some of their language heritage as a family activity. Working at the restaurant provided even more topspin to her burgeoning skills—this despite the cantina manager's suggestion that she stick to English. After all, he'd hired her for her apple-pie looks as much as her personality. No sense in confusing the mostly Anglo customers.

The worst part of the job was the requirement that she deposit her cell phone in the hostess locker before clocking in. Good for a teen's self-discipline, she excused. Both Gonzo and Lucky had echoed the sentiment. To Karrie's bewilderment, upon her return to the hostess stand she discovered the assistant manager, a bosomy Latina whom the entire staff called Mama, thrusting the restaurant's wireless phone handset in her direction.

"What's the rule 'bout getting calls at work?" Mama accused.

Karrie could only shrug and shake her head in return.

"Man says it's urgent." Mama gave Karrie a knowing wink. "Exactly the kinda shit my daughter's boyfriend would say."

A quizzical look remained stuck to Karrie's face as she accepted the phone and placed it to her ear.

"This is Karrie," she said, utterly indifferent.

Mama drew a close eye, reading Karrie for telltale giveaways that she was somehow flouting workplace rules. Though Mama could hear nothing of the voice on the other end, she recorded a wince on Karrie's face, the muscles on the teen's forehead tightening with concern, eyebrows squeezing at the top of her upturned nose.

"'Kay," said Karrie into the phone, her face slackening further with every understanding nod. "'Kay. All right. I get it."

Karrie returned the telephone to its base.

"Everything okay, *mija*?" asked Mama, shifting from suspicion to genuine concern.

"Sorry," said Karrie. "I . . . I gotta go."

"Go where?"

The teen gave neither answer nor apology. She struck out, vanishing through a pair of swinging kitchen doors. She juked past the kitchen staff without regard for the slinging of hot fajita skillets, barely whispering *disculpe por favor—excuse me*. In a single maneuver she tugged her bag from the locker and reversed her way into the panic bar release on the rear exit. The latch popped and the door swung free and into the back parking lot. Karrie slowed ever so slightly as her eyes adjusted to the amber dim cast across the rows of parked cars. The lime green shell of her Prius stood out like a distant Easter egg. Instinct led her eyes to shift a few degrees to the right to the white panel van with "RENT ME" and a local telephone number emblazoned across the double rear doors. A slicing cold cut through Karrie. Goose bumps formed. Then headlights flared from her left. A black GMC Yukon surged at her. A cautious step backward and she flattened against the cantina until the big SUV slid to a stop. She knew to question nothing and do only as instructed. The rear passenger door popped and swung out under Karrie's power. She practically dove inside, pulling the heavy door shut behind her.

"Seat belt, miss," requested the driver.

"Okay," answered Karrie, clicking in, then digging into her backpack for her phone. She speed-dialed a number before reading a single notification. "I'm in the car. Where'm I going?"

"No questions," replied Lucky at the other end of the call. "Just stay put until you reach your destination."

"I will, but what's going on?" begged Karrie. "Where's Gonzo and my brother?"

"Explain later," cut Lucky.

"Are you safe?"

"Love you," said Lucky before clicking off.

The Yukon whipped a wide counterclockwise loop around the parking lot. Karrie, meanwhile, kept her head on a swivel. Through the tinted windows her eyes instinctively remained glued to the rented panel van. And through one of the van's large sideview mirrors she could've sworn she caught eyeballs tracking her. As she twisted to look out the rear window, she saw a figure skate out along the wall as if to get a better look at the retreating SUV.

"I think we might be followed," feared Karrie.

"Not a problem," promised the driver. "I've been instructed to get you home without incident."

"My home?"

"Bel-Air," said the driver.

That was all the information Karrie needed to hear. The luxe enclave of Bel-Air was home to but one person in Karrie's life. Conrad Ellis. The eccentric billionaire and acquaintance of her dead father and mother had proved himself as a strange nexus in the former runaway's life. Aside from being the executor of her trust, Conrad Ellis was the man who had introduced Lucky Dey into her mix.

"Gawd," she accidentally said aloud, as only a teenager could. "And I'm gonna be so fired from my job."

25

South Los Angeles. 9:12 p.m.

The air was crystalline, nary a wisp of smog or mist. Gonzo loved flying nights, weekend nights especially. Action was guaranteed. But when visibility was so stark and crisp, it was like watching TV in high definition after a lifetime of viewing in the old standard resolution. At a cruising altitude of five thousand feet, the entire city was in readable relief. Even from as far south as Watts, she could see from the Port of Long Beach all the way past the Hollywood Hills and into the San Fernando Valley. The summer-into-fall marine layer remained offshore, hovering beyond the island of Catalina, held at bay by the Santa Ana winds.

"Still on 'em?" asked Gonzo, her voice playing back inside her headphones.

"Five o'clock, turning south on Wilmington," replied Bobby,

her wet-behind-the-ears observer, whose job was to eyeball and operate the variety of high-tech lenses the helicopter was equipped with.

Gonzo tipped the stick of the Bell JetRanger, gently feathering the rear stabilizer with her feet. The chopper dipped slightly into a bank steep enough for Gonzo to glimpse her prey. Far below, traveling like a trifecta of ants chasing each other were three cars of identical persuasion, grille to tail to grille, all nineties-era Honda Accords.

"That's so not sexy," remarked Bobby. "If I'm gonna triple-jack cars, it's gonna be something in the Corvette genus of rides."

"Knock yourself out," grinned Gonzo. "Make you some kinda high-wire criminal."

"I like to make me a strong impression."

The game unfolding on the blacktop below was well-known to LAPD's air support division. The Southland's most popular stolen vehicle was a nineties model Honda Accord because of both its ease of theft and street ubiquity. Gangbangers looking to pull a crime or a drive-by shooting would most often express their act in a stolen car that could never be traced to the offender. For street cops or helo-units, seeing a pair of Honda Accords driving in tandem was a suspicious tell. Encountering three Accords moving across the city asphalt in a uniformed roll was a veritable jackpot. A delivery to someone who wholesaled in ripped cars was obviously taking place.

"Me likee this job," nodded Bobby.

Gonzo glanced at him sideways. Smirked. Someone at Parker Center had a sense of humor, pairing Lydia Gonzalez with Roberto Gonzales.

Me of the Z and he of the S.

Both cops had spent their lives nicknamed Gonzo. Lydia had put any competition over the moniker to rest the moment they'd been introduced at LAPD's Hooper Heliport. Thirty-year-old Bobby had just moved over from Traffic Division and was bent on getting his pilot wings one day.

"I'm Gonzo," she'd introduced herself with a cool air of seniority. "And from now on, you're not."

And that had been that.

The night had been relatively quiet. But it was a Sunday, the last night of a warm weekend. Criminal activity and the subsequent 911 calls were sure to pick up the pace. Until then, Gonzo and Bobby had fish nipping at the line.

"Time to drop the net," advised Gonzo, so Bobby would radio call in nearby ground units to gather and corral the three suspicious Accords.

"Air six, this is base," crackled the radio.

"Air six," replied Gonzo.

"Return to Hooper."

"Fully operational," returned Gonzo, doing an unconscious visual sweep of her instruments. "We're three hours from fuel."

"Air eleven will cover. Return to Hooper. Repeat. Return to Hooper."

"Affirmative," answered Gonzo, temporarily lost. "Do we get a reason why? Or do we wait 'til we're outta the air?"

Five seconds of static passed, followed by suppressed dead air.

"Base—" keyed Gonzo.

"Something urgent to do with your son," said the dispatcher. "Sorry Gonzo. All I know."

That was all Gonzo required. She throttled the helicopter while arcing a hard banking turn one-hundred-and-seventy degrees to the north. To increase her speed, she nosed the aircraft on a downward slant until she was at an elevation of one thousand feet and aimed directly at the downtown skyline. Bobby, who'd earlier felt that he'd mastered the touch of flight after only ten hours behind the yoke of a single-engine Cessna trainer, had to put a clamp on his esophagus or else he might have tossed up his Whopper and French fries lunch.

The Bell JetRanger covered the 7.8 miles to the LAPD's Hooper Heliport in under three minutes. What appeared like barely seconds to Bobby felt like an eternity to Gonzo. Her stomach was a growing knot, her musculature at a near cramping tensile.

Fucking fear!

Gonzo hated fear, despite living with it on a daily basis. Every time Lucky left their bed for work, she'd whisper a rote-like Hail Mary.

Hail Mary, full of grace. The Lord is with thee . . .

Then there was parenthood. Someone had once described mothering teens as standing at the edge of a mile-wide abyss, arms outstretched, trying like hell to keep the babies from throwing themselves into the void. So, she distracted herself—with her work—with books—with gym workouts to loud, pounding punk rock blowing through her ear buds. Anything to keep *the afraids* at bay.

The afraids. Jesus.

That's what four-year-old Travis had coined his bedtime worries. She could count the minutes until he'd creep into her bed with a case of *the afraids*.

Gonzo ignored half of the safety protocols for her approach on the heliport, a three-story structure just north of where the 101 Freeway cut across the top end of downtown. She'd checked the sky for bogie aircraft, swung the bird wide over the edge of Chinatown, and delivered her skids to the concrete X corresponding with her helicopter's number. She powered down the engine and climbed out while the rotors were still spinning.

"Get a pad crew to lock us down," the pilot ordered before her helmet hit the seat and her boots the tarmac.

Bobby saw little more than her jumpsuited silhouette rushing for the door to the pilot shed.

"Downstairs," waved the air unit's watch commander the moment she caught wind of Gonzo. "There's a car."

"Do you know?" she asked, not missing a step.

"All I know, G. You got all our prayers."

Three flights of stairs and Gonzo emerged into the tiny lobby, white with fluorescents, the walls colored only with enlarged photos of LAPD air units in flight. The posted sentry barely glanced up from behind the sign-in desk as the languid helo pilot charged past, arms forward and elbows locked, pushing out the exit door with an atmosphere-sucking force.

Before Gonzo, a black Mercedes stretch limousine gleamed, rear door already swung wide open. She froze, trying to shake off what she thought must be a temporary illusion . . . or a mistake . . . or—

"Get in, Mom!"

A head popped into the frame of the limousine's open door. It was Travis, still wearing his blue umpire shirt, a crazy wide grin exploding across his face.

"What the hell, Trav?" asked Gonzo.

"It's Lucky," Travis defended. "He told us we had to."

Gonzo's abject fear morphed into heartburn in a matter of seconds. After a long exhale, she dipped her head and slid into the limousine alongside Travis. Expecting to find Karrie inside, Gonzo registered surprise when she encountered Conrad Ellis seated on the leather-upholstered side bench, designer-suited as was his habit, a tumbler of scotch on ice cradled in both hands. The billionaire returned a warming smile.

"Ms. Gonzalez," acknowledged Conrad.

"Connie," nodded Gonzo with another disappointed exhale. "This your idea? Or Lucky's?"

"Don't try 'n' touch Mr. Ellis," reminded Travis in a not-so-quiet whisper.

Conrad chuckled at the boy and his self-acknowledged germophobia. Gonzo suspected nobody touched the businessman unless he had personally washed and disinfected them. The man's Italian suits appeared like armor. Crisp, tailored, no doubt threaded with anti-bacterial fabric, if there was such a thing.

"Where's Lucky?" asked Gonzo.

"He asked me if I would please look after you," explained Conrad.

"That doesn't answer my question," pressed Gonzo.

"Then I don't know," shrugged the billionaire. "He asked. I said I would. All I know."

"Dontcha think he should have explained it to me?"

"I'm certain he will."

"Damn right, he will." Gonzo unzipped the breast pocket of her jumpsuit, removed her mobile phone, and speed-dialed Lucky.

The Altadena bungalow was dark when Lucky crept his car into the rather slim driveway. Even the front porch light was extinguished, leaving the antique house looking as lifeless as a discarded cardboard box under the faint streetlamps. He wheeled into the driveway, crossing from his driver's door to the side kitchen door in a matter of three seconds. Once inside, Lucky never touched a light switch. Before parking, he'd already surveyed his street twice, marking two cars as suspicious and belonging to either the Armenians or associates of Judge Jim and his cabal of vigilante cops.

Or both . . .

He maneuvered by memory in the dimness. When that failed, he availed himself of the low light cast from his cell phone's screen. Thirsty, he reached behind the refrigerator and unplugged the appliance before searching inside for something resembling a beer bottle. He flicked the twist-off cap toward the sink. It rattled and sounded as if it had settled in the garbage disposal.

"Of course," muttered Lucky. His hands were too large to reach directly into the disposal to rescue the cap. After calculating the cost of installing a new unit, but still not keen on playing plumber and disassembling the guts to save it from chewing on the metal bottle cap, Lucky reached around beneath the sink until he found a grip on the power cord. His bruised ribs screamed at him as if to say, *You deserve the pain, asshole.* He ripped the cable free of the power outlet, then bent back the tongs of the plug until they snapped free. *There*, he thought. Nobody would be using the disposal until the offending bottle cap had been removed.

Lucky heard scratches at the back door followed by a familiar canine whimper. The big mutt Oprah wanted in. Sweet as she was, and probably hungry as hell, Lucky had forgotten to pre-medicate. So, he put some kibble in her bowl and slipped it out the back door without much more than a *good girl* before returning to the kitchen table, where he guzzled half the beer, hoping the ethanol would find his bloodstream and relax the muscle spasms forming at the base of his spine. A freakin' Bud Light Lime, guessed Lucky from the citrus aftertaste. Unlike those snooty craft beers preferred by Judge Jim, the ale quenched. He pictured the beer in his hand, bottled by machine only miles to the west at the behemoth of a Budweiser brewery smack in the center of the San Fernando Valley. Lucky wondered if he'd even sniffed the actual ingredients used to make the very beer he was imbibing. The odds were remote. But why not? It was Los Angeles. And despite the vast horizontal expanse, millions of people seemed to find strange and disparate ways to cross paths, encounter each other, cross-pollinate. Blacks and whites. Christians and Muslims. Armo and the Five-Oh.

From his jacket pocket Lucky removed the pint glass cloaked in layers of plastic wrap. He set it on the table next to his beer bottle, followed by his .45 pistol, laying it with the butt facing him for a quick grip and shoot. Beside it he placed three spare magazines, each stacked with fifteen body-dropping rounds. Including the cartridge in the Sig's chamber, Lucky was armed with forty-six squeezes of the trigger. And that's just what he carried on his day off.

Upon his reinstatement as an L.A. Sheriff's training officer—in a Compton black-and-white, no less—he'd forgone his classic, M1911 pistol for the larger capacity SIG Sauer. Lucky's rationale had been that he was not only defending himself, but also his trainee Shia St. George. When he ditched the uniform for plainclothes duty, he never returned to his old standby. The 1911 was slimmer, concealed snugly inside his beltline at the small of his back, and its heavier barrel leveled easily on a target.

But then came the New Wilmington Gardens.

After the epic meltdown in the Compton housing project, something had shifted in Lucky. The younger version of Lucky had thought a cool head, a Kevlar vest, and accuracy was all a cop required in a gunfight. But since the New Wilmington Gardens,

Lucky had begun to believe as much in the volume of lead he could put in the air as in punching holes in his target.

From his kitchen perch, he was two steps away from the pantry, where a twelve-gauge shotgun piped full of double-ought buckshot was propped behind the door. Any retreat to the rear of the bungalow would allow him to rearm with a further variety of stashed weapons.

Body armor, Luck. You forgot that.

Lucky went outside and grabbed his ballistic vest from the back seat of his Crown Vic, pulling it over his head and noisily fixing the Velcro straps. The meat between his ribs throbbed as he cinched the vest tighter.

Back in the kitchen, Lucky regarded the pint glass.

Veiled in so much plastic wrap, it looked mummified, an antiquity unearthed. The eight-inch sarcophagus contained maybe a tablespoon's worth of a bad man's spit. A father. Vartan Kasabian, in that game-of-chicken moment, had proved his affection for his son, Johnny B. Yet despite the macho display, Lucky fully expected Vaz wouldn't leave it there. A worthy gangster would choose to leverage his bet with the fulcrum being family. Lucky's family. Thus Lucky's call to Conrad Ellis. The billionaire, whom Lucky owed so much to already, promised to send cars to hastily gobble up Gonzo, Travis, and Karrie. It was agreed that Conrad would care for Lucky's trio at his Bel-Air estate and employ an extra blanket of private security. Only as a precaution, Lucky had insisted. Just in case Vaz made a move to double down.

Lucky turned to his phone and opened an encrypted text app Miles had provided him. He tapped out an instant missive to Judge Jim:

> got what u asked for. where do i deliver?

In practically no time at all, Judge Jim replied:

> **You're kidding me. That was fast. How?**

dont ask how. just tell me where.

Reaching out to Miles. He will handle.

sorry. my agreement is with u. i will deliver
DNA evidence to u. only.

There was a pause in the judge's communication. Lucky settled back in the chair, continuing to nurse the sweaty beer bottle closer to empty until his smartphone jiggled on the tabletop.

Tomorrow AM. Bring package to the courthouse.

tonight better for me.

Out of pocket until late. Monday 845 AM. Private security entrance on Delano St. See you then.

The judge had spoken. As was his habit, he grabbed the last word and delivered it as if from his elevated bench. Lucky looked at the digital clock on the oven. It was 9:45 p.m. Lucky quickly calculated he had roughly ten hours to kill before he delivered the DNA. His plan was to shake Judge Jim's hand and look him eyeball to eyeball to see if the man's words matched his promise to bury any criminal liability on Johnny Kasabian's behalf in regard to the car accident in Woodland Hills.

Emphasis on accident.

Christ, thought Lucky. How the ramifications of such a tragic but unremarkable event could turn so dire, swallowing up entire families in a potentially mortal conspiracy.

Lucky's phone danced, the screen igniting with a warm snapshot of Gonzo's smirking face, a result of Travis constantly stealing Lucky's device and assigning images to his immediate contacts. He reached over and answered.

"Hey there," said Lucky.

"What the fuck!" ripped Gonzo.

"Back it up," he defended, flat and with minimal affect, something he instantly regretted, knowing how she hated that even-to-a-fault tone he could take. "Sorry. It's for your protection."

"Think you coulda run it by me first?" she complained. "I was in the air. They called my bird back saying something about a family emergency. I nearly had a heart attack!"

"You safe?"

"I don't know. Am I? Are we?"

"Simple question. You at Connie's yet?"

"I'm in his limo with Travis and, you know, him."

"You should be impressed. Connie doesn't leave the bubble for just anybody."

"Right now I'm not impressed with shit. What's going on?"

"Short version? I'm being squeezed. Someone's using you and the kids as leverage. So, I'm taking you out of play."

"Forgive me if I never knew we were ever *in play*."

"We all are," topped Lucky. "Bad guys like to hit us where we're soft."

Lucky could hear Gonzo huffing at the other end of the call. She knew he'd spoken the truth, and that was the closest he'd ever come to saying he loved anyone or anything without condition. Still, he could feel the strings that held them together fray that much more.

"So . . . this a Major Crimes Unit thing?" she shifted.

"It's a favor thing," Lucky replied. "And it's already way too sideways."

"Ya think?" Her sarcasm was thick. "A personal favor or an on-the-job favor?"

"Undersheriff asked me to investigate a car accident. Turned out to be a bucket of scorpions."

"Sorry, but I gotta ask. Why aren't we in Sheriff's protection? Or LAPD?"

He slowed himself before answering. He worried about sharing too much. That, and who knew if anybody else was listening in electronically.

"Like I said. It's a squeeze play. Until I clear it up I can't trust anybody on the inside."

"Yeah. Guess that includes me too."

Lucky heard her click off the call. Her voice was never raised, though the flat-out hang-up punctuated with a clear finality, as if to say the argument was over and whoever delivered the last word scored the winning point.

Goddamnit, Gonzo.

He spun the phone back to the tabletop, then glared at it, half thinking she'd call him back to apologize for finishing their conversation with such immature flair. The other half of him was pondering if he should perhaps snatch up the phone, dial her back, and mea culpa until she begged him to shut up and get on with cleaning up another one of his messes.

Neither action transpired. Lucky chose instead to relax his aching body and put his feet up on the table. He regarded the mummified pint glass as he began his long wait until dawn.

Boom, boom, boom, boom.

Though music played over the top of the beat, it was the throbbing bass thumping in incessant four-four time that gave Johnny B. his sonic thrills. It also acted as a mask. He could either turn all of himself over to the sound cranked inside his tiled audio mausoleum and allow himself and all his worries to be sucked in by the swirling electronica—or he could set the volume to some earthshaking crunch in a bit of magical misdirection. While the EDM tunes were cranked, the rest of the Kasabian clan were relatively certain young Johnny B. was occupied and out of trouble. Out of sight, out of mind.

Because I have me a big secret.

Nobody in Johnny B.'s family knew that sometimes, while the bass beats jumped off the walls of his cave, instead of vanishing inside his little DJ fantasy world, Johnny B. would sometimes creep out of his hole to spy on his family. It was, in his opinion, both his birthright and his continued education.

During his undercover sorties Johnny B. learned that he wasn't the only Kasabian with secrets. He discovered his sister, Lizzy, had an affection for the party drug MDMA and also her preference for trading tongues with some of the women she employed in her lovelorn extortion scheme. Johnny B. also learned of his mother's private sex toy collection and how his brother, Chris, instead of club-hopping and chasing tail like most young gangsters, would often while away his stress by spending late-night hours alone, blowing smoke signals of medical-grade marijuana, swilling can after aluminum can of Bud Light, all while losing himself in socially connected video games like *Gears of War*.

But it was Johnny B.'s success at espionage against his Pops that satisfied him the most. He figured it this way: the more he could learn, store away, and digest through his unique prism, the greater the chance he'd be able to impress his father one day with his acumen for the family business.

Directly above the changing-room-turned-private-discotheque was an eighteen-inch elevated deck built from pressure-treated cedar. Atop the deck was a pair of patio tables under matching burnt orange umbrellas overlooking a canyon of Glendale homes. Soon after Johnny B. assembled his underground sound system and began spinning his collection of vintage EDM music, he discovered the pool deck was his father's favored spot for discussing family business. As it worked out for Vaz, Johnny B.'s pounding music served as a convenient veil against electronic surveillance by the likes of the FBI, local authorities, or even a distrustful Russian mob.

"Your brother is the problem right now," muffled the voice, a timbre Johnny B. recognized as his father's.

The conversation snippet was easily overheard as Johnny B. had purposefully chosen not to cross-fade between tracks by Basement Jack and Skrillex. In those three seconds, the amateur DJ could hear that the above deck was occupied. Anybody who visited the mob boss knew in advance to clip their talking when the music stalled and continue only when the beats returned. Once a spying opportunity availed itself, Johnny B.'s method of listening in was ingeniously analog.

He would cue up a playlist guaranteed to run in an infinite, pulse-churning loop. Next he would shut the door to the bathroom, stand atop the toilet, plug his ears into a doctor's stethoscope he'd purchased on Amazon, and place the device's diaphragm through a fist-sized hole he'd poked through the ceiling tiles. By pressing the bell of the stethoscope against the deck's support timbers, Johnny B. discovered he could follow the conversations with relative ease. The aluminum alloy patio tables acted as additional microphones, conducting the vocal vibrations, and transferring the sound waves into the wood and eventually through the sensitive stethoscope's tube.

". . . none of this is his fault," defended Chris.

"If you don't count the mess he made in the West Valley, then no. Nothing's his fault," agreed Vaz. "Still. What I tried to do with that cop to keep him safe was a mistake. Can't imagine it working out."

"We tried, Pop. You're not alone in this."

"I'm Johnny's father. My job is to keep him safe from himself and the rest of the world. So, it's decided."

"I say we wait to see if the cop comes through."

"And I say you do as you're told!"

"Armenia? I haven't even been. Lizzy neither. Can't imagine how J. B.'s gonna handle it."

"He's going to have his sister to watch over him."

"Lizzy? Fuckin' kiddin' me. She know this?"

"She doesn't have a choice. I need you here. And Johnny's her biggest goddamn cause. Won't be a hard sell."

"Wanna bet? She's gonna be all claws."

"Why don't you try helping me on this?" angered Vaz, his voice elevated.

"I just don't think we've exhausted all our options yet."

"Do we have that cop asshole's family as leverage? No. Zero leverage. He's got my spit in a glass and all I got is his promise—"

"And sending J. B. to Armenia is kinda nuclear, dontcha think? First of all, we don't even know how bad the Woodland Hills thing is. First offense for him. Ever. J. B.'s got his doctors to say he's got—"

"No. What J. B. has is for our family to know about and there it ends. No talk of mental illness outside these walls."

"Birth condition, Pops. Stop with the mental illness bullshit—"

"Thought I couldn't say 'retarded.' Now mental illness isn't PC enough for you?"

"Trying to be fair, Pop."

"Armenia. He's going tomorrow morning. End of argument. Now, where are we with the cop? We got eyes yet?"

"Sitting on him," answered Chris. "Waiting for the green light. Which I strongly suggest we wait on. He may come through."

"Willing to bet your family on it?"

As much as Lizzy Kasabian didn't care for her younger brother's taste in music, there was a strange comfort in it. To a person, including the house staff, when the floorboards rumbled they knew one thing for sure: Johnny Boy was safe and sound in his underground bunker.

She twisted the hot water knob to the off position, allow-ing the shower's icy spray to raise gooseflesh on her skin. She needed the tingle to further wake her after an afternoon nap that had left her practically comatose through the dinner hour. She'd woken up to the dark and Johnny B. spinning Skrillex. From there she'd wandered into her bathroom, reconnected with the con-scious world, recalled her evening plans with a particularly yummy tattoo girl, stripped off her clothes, and showered. By the time she was toweling off, she'd noted an incongruous bit of stereo. While the dance music permeated through the timbers of her upstairs bedroom, she caught the newly familiar roar of Johnny B.'s Shelby Mustang.

Lizzy wiped the steam from her bathroom window, creating a slash of visibility to see her younger brother backing his car out through the electronic gate.

So weird, she thought.

It was very unlike her little brother to leave his music playing. He was fastidious that way—completely OCD about binary things like hot or cold, on or off. When he left a room, Johnny B. never left a bulb burning.

Wrapped in a pastel blue robe, Lizzy padded down the stairs and out the French sliders to the pool area. The pool and spa lights were snuffed. Through the shadows she was able to spot her father and Chris in close conversation at one of the umbrella-topped tables.

"Hey!" she called out while navigating the outline of the pool. "Where'd J. B. go?"

Chris merely shrugged, gesturing to the edge of the deck and the stairs that angled down to the changing rooms.

"Nuh uh," she shook her head. "He's not down there."

"Hello?" answered Chris. "Or can't you hear the thump, thump, thump?"

"Just saw him drive off in the Mustang," she pointed. "Seriously. He's not down there."

"We're talking business," barked Vaz. "Wanna know where your brother went? Ask your mother!"

"Wait, wait, wait," said Chris, alerting to his sister's tack. "J. B. *never* leaves his music on."

"Exactly!" reasoned Lizzy, palms in the air.

In an instant Chris was up and descending those back steps two at a time. Meanwhile, Lizzy had closed the gap between herself and her father. She stalled once she read the worry on Vaz's face.

"What'd I miss?" asked Lizzy.

"Just a little family business—" Vaz stopped himself when the music waves ceased.

"She's right!" called Chris as he ascended from below. "J. B.'s not here."

"Okay," relented Vaz with a hard exhale. "Probably just went to the 7-Eleven. But get someone to find him. I'll talk to your sister."

"Right," said Chris.

"Talk to me about what?" Though Lizzy was asking her father, her neck swiveled with Chris as he hurried back to the house.

"A decision's been made," began Vaz. "Unavoidable. But it's the right thing to do. For your younger brother—and you, I suppose."

"And me what?"

"You love your brother?"

"Please stop with the stupid questions."

"Perhaps. Anyhow . . ." There it was again. Strains of fatherly worry striating his round face. "No easy way to say this, Lizzy. You're going on a trip."

26

Altadena.

The dashboard clock in the stolen Corolla was nearly as archaic as the car. Complete with a creeping second hand, the electric-powered motor swept the needle back to the top position and, with it, the device clicked into 11:00 p.m. As he entered the last hour of that Sunday, Mikayel began thinking about overtime pay. He would never ask. That wasn't Armo. But he still couldn't help but believe that after adding up all his hours for the week he'd be earning less than minimum wage.

"Gonna need better perks," he croaked to nobody but himself before shifting in the seat. His six-and-a-half-foot body didn't fold well into the '89 rendition of the vehicle. That, and the velour seats were ripped and smelled of cat pee.

Mikayel's eyes flicked ahead, picking up the headlights of an oncoming panel van. As it slid past a streetlamp, he picked up the black-on-yellow *Rent Me* decal on the side, instantly recognizing it belonged to Tavet and Eriq. Mikayel grumbled to himself, barely acknowledging the slight two-finger wave from Eriq as the van rolled past. This wasn't the replacement crew. They were the rest of his assassination team—should the order come at all. Mikayel considered the pair barely capable of shaking down gamblers who owed money. In his view, Tavet and Eriq were at best subpar kneecap breakers. Not hit men. That's when Mikayel began to hope that his disposable cell phone remained silent and that no kill order ever came.

With a glance in his rearview mirror, Mikayel watched the panel van make a U-turn at the intersection, flip off its lights, and park behind him. The analog dash clock read 11:04.

At 11:12 the disposable flip phone buzzed.

"Yeah. He's still inside," Mikayel answered, before acknowledging with a nod. "Yes. They just arrived in a panel van. And I'll just say, I don't care if it's stolen, I don't like the way it stands out with 'Rent Me.' Really, Chris?"

Despite Mikayel's concerns, the order came. He acknowledged, flipped the phone shut, then reached into his peacoat's pocket for a stocking mask. He pulled it over his head and stepped from the vehicle as a signal to arm up and move briskly. Before he popped the trunk lid he heard the squeaky doors of the rental van.

"*Kak*," muttered Mikayel through the wool mask. An error already. Odd sounds drew unconscious attention. He was already worried about eyeballs or security cameras on him. He withdrew a SPAS-12 shotgun with a sling from a black canvas bag. His second gun was another Israeli weapon, an X95 sub-machine pistol, equally compact with a thirty-round clip. Though not a fan of the Jews as a religion or race, he admired their products, especially their weaponry. Elegant *and* efficient.

Geghets. Beautiful.

Tavet and Eriq stepped towards Mikayel.

"Three doors into the house. And a dog," informed Mikayel. "I'll take front, you two split the side and back. Lights are out, so he's either sleeping or watching. Try not to shoot each other. Most of all, don't shoot me."

In the earlier twilight hours, as Lucky had walked out of the Denny's in Atwater Village, Deputy Zadeh Raad was ready and in place to pick up the tail. With Oakley wraparound sunglasses pinned to the temples of a San Francisco Giants baseball cap pulled low, Zadeh considered herself unrecognizable enough. If Lucky began any obvious maneuvers that revealed any suspicion that he was being followed, she'd break it off, dial up Sugar Freeman, and he'd put her back on a looser track based on GPS coordinates pinging from an electronic locator carefully sewn into the rear seat upholstery of Lucky's '99 Crown Victoria. While parked between cars in the Taco Bell lot across the busy boulevard, Zadeh had carefully observed Mikayel, the tall, sandy-haired goon hanging at the southwest corner of the Denny's, smokestacking on imported cigarettes. Zadeh had a certain fancy for long-legged men, especially Euro-white volleyball players. If the goon had ever been a spiker, Zadeh figured his cigarette-smoking habit would've killed his lung capacity to keep up with her some time ago.

Then Lucky had eased from the Denny's onto the sidewalk.

Zadeh was ready to roll the tires of her new Chevy Cruze when she noted Mikayel crushing his cigarette and quick-stepping to a beater of a Toyota Corolla with the driver's seat cranked so far back his face nearly disappeared behind the door pillar. Zadeh kept her cool as Lucky pulled out of the Denny's lot, the smokestack goon in the Corolla sliding in not far behind him.

"He picked up a tail," said Zadeh into a portable radio.

"Yeah, you," crackled Sugar over the speaker.

"Not just me no more," keyed Zadeh. "Armos are on him as well."

"Popular dude," replied Sugar. "Be careful. Don't get swept up into any AP shit, know what I'm sayin'?"

That was earlier in the evening.

At nearly 10:45 p.m., Sugar arrived to relieve Zadeh from

her post. The tires of her Chevy Cruze were tightly tucked up against the curb approximately 280 feet west of Lucky's Altadena bungalow. Sugar eased into her passenger seat, quietly pulled the car door shut behind him, then passed off his car keys to Zadeh.

"It's the gold Hummer," he said. "End of the block and make a left."

"You're shittin' me," laughed the deputy. "You drive a gold Hummer?"

"Wouldn't think it so funny if you knew what I paid for it," grumbled the detective.

"Bet you made up for that in what it sucks back in gas. What's it get? Eight miles per gallon?"

"Ten. Twelve if I'm lucky."

"Hummer. Shit."

"So, the Armos still on him?" switched up Sugar.

"Corolla," pointed Zadeh. "House and a half past the address. Guy's a fucking smoke machine. Just wait for the glow and you can almost see him."

Sure enough. Practically the second Zadeh identified the car, Sugar saw the cherry red ember of the cigarette peak and fade low behind the windshield of the distant Corolla.

"All night long," she added. "Has to be a pack and a half in since I got here. Least he's not littering. Haven't seen him toss a butt yet."

Though she had his keys, Zadeh was aching for company. Once she hiked her way to Sugar's gold-pimp Hummer, her plans for the rest of the evening were to settle into the long drive out to Simi Valley, where she shared a house with her two brothers, both firemen in the LAFD and currently on call at their respective and faraway stations. So she carried the friendly cop banter past the top of the hour until the arrival of that low-budget, *Rent Me* panel van.

Both Zadeh and Sugar froze in instinctive unison, their eyes fixed on the slow-rolling mystery van making an end-of-the-block U-turn before pulling up behind the lanky goon in the Corolla.

Zadeh's heart began to pound. It pushed up against the top of her ribcage.

Uh oh.

"Could be a big nothin'," cautioned Sugar, putting a calming palm on her forearm. "Change of the guard. Like how we just do."

"Like 'how we just do'?"

"With a big goddamn difference," joked Sugar. "We the good guys."

As if cued, the doors to both the Corolla and the panel van swung wide. Three men were on their feet assembling at the trunk of the Toyota.

"Jesus, fuck!" barked Sugar, one hand grabbing for his pistol as quickly as the other touched the passenger door lever.

"Radioing for backup." Zadeh was switching channels on the walkie-talkie when Sugar stalled her.

"Backup, shit. We ain't supposed to be here."

"Then what—"

"Shut up and lemme think!"

Zadeh fumbled and found her Bushnell night specs. The scene at the Toyota's trunk came into green and black relief. All three men were armed with at least one assault weapon each, masks pulled down to the chins.

"It's a fucking kill squad!" she charged. "Three men. Masks."

With that Zadeh threw her shoulder hard into her door. The dome light flicked on. She had one foot on the pavement when Sugar hooked her with an overhand right, his big grip pinching her at the triceps. He was pulling her back in when headlights blasted from behind, followed by the eight-cylinder thrum of a black Shelby Mustang. The car accelerated past them and braked hard. Its taillights flared panic red. Then quick as it appeared, the muscle car swung into the driveway of Lucky's bungalow.

"*Dadar!*" *Stop!* spat Mikayel, thrusting both arms wide. "*Babar gleer!*" *That empty dickhead!*

The Mustang shut down, turning as black and pitch as the unlit bungalow. In the shock of spotting Johnny B.'s familiar car, Mikayel missed the sudden movement further down the street. In a Chevy Cruze, a dome light had flicked on, revealing a pair of unseen confederates in the midst. Had the big goon spotted them, he would've surely pegged them as police, aborted the kill decision, and ordered Eriq and Tavet to return to their van. Get lost and don't forget to dump the guns. Instead, through the eyeholes in his mask, Mikayel kept his gaze on Johnny B. as he hoofed from the Mustang.

"*Kak!*" pissed Mikayel. "Fucking retard!"

Sometimes the only way out is through.

Lucky had begun to wonder if that phrase he'd oft repeated to himself was an actual truism or just another self-justification for hurtling himself headlong into trouble instead of seeking a less aggressive resolution. Over his career he'd been reprimanded for headstrong behavior. Privately, he'd been assigned harsher words like "reckless." "Suicidal," even. Much of it was excused as a byproduct from working some of L.A.'s toughest real estate. But Lucky knew to his soul that the how and why of who he was had formed long before he'd buttoned his first uniform.

If only I'd give Dr. Sandalwood a peek.

Lucky remained at the kitchen table, marinating in his thoughts, expectant, prepared for a crash of glass, the jamb-busting crunch of a door being kicked in, or the sound one could never prepare for—bullets penetrating glass, Sheetrock, and wood. He'd survived a cornucopia of close scrapes, some of which he'd written reports on. But when he had to describe the shock and awe of being the target of gunfire into words it proved impossible. The high-pitched whistles, the snapping sounds, like yellow number two pencils breaking next to a receptive ear. Nearly everything a bullet touched either cracked or slapped—all but flesh. Skin and muscle absorbed the acoustics, practically welcoming the projectile with a silent whisper.

Oprah, her canine instincts fully in play, began barking loudly. Incessantly. The dog's noisemaking was followed by a heavy fist pounding on the front door, interspersed with a staccato of doorbell rings.

Lucky's right hand had already found the grip of his .45. He heard the *click* as his thumb pulled back the hammer into a light firing position while he put his feet underneath him. He slid right into the side corridor, checking the passage back to the rear bedrooms before easing into the living room and toward the front door. The curtains were drawn, revealing nothing in the way of human shadows laying in wait, ready to release a hail of gunfire into the house.

The pounding carried on, followed by a muffled, yet plaintive, "C'mon, c'mon!"

The front entry, though solid oak, wasn't dense enough to stop a heavy-caliber bullet. So, Lucky approached from the left, semi-crouched, using the gun muzzle to ever so slightly push away the sheer drape covering one of the twin, six-inch sidelights framing the door.

"Pleeease!" cried the voice. The doorbell continued to play in a panic of rings.

Then Lucky recognized the caller on the top step.

You're kidding me.

With the bolt thrown, Lucky cracked the door and withdrew into a dark corner, on his haunches, sighting down the top rail of his pistol.

"Hello?" asked Johnny B.

"Shut the door behind you," replied Lucky. "Throw the deadbolt."

Hanging at the threshold, Johnny B.'s silhouette was all nerves. Vibrating. All the while Lucky scoured his gun sight, searching beyond the hulking figure for secondary targets.

"You said you'd help me," pleaded Johnny B.

"Three seconds to shut the fuckin' door," said Lucky. "Three, two, one . . ."

"'Kay, okay!"

If three quick steps could have been described as unathletic, such was Johnny's shuffling move through the front door, followed by a pivot and a fluster of hands as he slammed the door shut and felt for the deadbolt.

Click-clack! Lucky's arm shot past Johnny B.'s and twisted the deadbolt's knob. He hooked the teen's shoulder and swung him wide and into the dark of the corridor. Johnny B. thumped hard against the paneling, slumping halfway to the floor.

"'Kay, please!" squealed Johnny B. "You said you'd help, you said you'd help, you said you'd help!"

"That why you're here?" pressed Lucky.

"Said you'd help!"

"My house!" hissed Lucky. "How'd you find my house?"

"'Cause I know things, okay?"

"This address? You know this address?"

"My dad knows. So, I know, okay? I know things. Nobody thinks I know much, but I know a lot more than anybody thinks—"

"Your father sent you?"

"Fuck my dad!" angered Johnny B. "He's sending me away. You gotta help me make all this stop."

"Where's your father? Your brother?"

"Where I left 'em. Don't tell 'em I'm here. Please—"

"Left them where?"

"Home . . ."

"Who sent you, then?"

"Nobody, but nobody, but nobody," cried Johnny B., breathless. "I sent me—I mean, I know where you are. So, I came 'cause you said you can help me!"

"I can help you only if you help me first," calmed Lucky. "Now. How did you find my house?"

"My dad. He wrote it down. I read stuff on his desk when he's not home. Please don't tell him I'm here! He's gonna send me away."

"To where?"

"Armenia. I don't wanna go to Armenia."

"Why is he sending you away?"

"Cuzza the thing I did. You know? The thing. Why you said you'd help me."

"The car accident?"

"I'm bad, 'kay? I did a bad thing. But I don't wanna go to

Armenia. I don't know Armenia. Nobody Armo knows it but the old men—"

"I hear you. Just gotta know. Did anybody come with you?"

"Here? No! Please don't tell anybody I'm here. Please, please—"

Johnny B. began a descent into tremors. Uncontrollably so. He swerved left then right in the corridor, bumping into walls, seeking escape as if drowning and requiring air to breathe.

"It's okay. Calm down," tried Lucky.

"Gotta go, I gotta go!"

As Johnny B. began his steps toward the back bedroom, Lucky snagged him by his waistband and swept his foot, knocking the big boy to the floor.

"Don't hurt me, don't hurt me, don't hurt me!" squealed Johnny B.

"Ssshhh!" Lucky pinned Johnny B. with a knee across his shoulder blades. "I'm gonna help you, but I need you to be calm, okay? Can you be calm? Breathe in and out."

"Can't breathe—"

"Yes, you can. In 'n' out. In through your nose. Out through your mouth."

"'Kay . . . 'Kay. In 'n' out. Nose. Mouth." Johnny B. sucked in half a lungful of air and wheezed it out. In the meantime, Lucky twisted, checked all angles, dropped the hammer block on the SIG, then secured the weapon into his waistband.

"You calm yet?" asked Lucky.

"I'm calm," huffed Johnny B., appearing anything but.

"You gonna let me help you?"

"I don't wanna go to jail . . . I don't wanna go to Armenia neither."

"Long as you're with me, it's neither, okay?" soothed Lucky.

"Promise?" Johnny B.'s face was turned sideways against the floor, eyes squeezing out tears, his doleful mouth more in tune to that of a ten-year-old than a 240-pound man of eighteen years.

"Promise," relented Lucky. Yet in the moment he might have said anything to gain a better grip on the situation. Johnny B.'s landing on his doorstep was an unexpected obstacle to Lucky's plan to get out of his circumstance by going through. Somehow it felt like Lucky had just added a ball and chain to his already heavy load.

"Mnal, vortegh yek' duk'!" Stay where you are! blasted Vaz into his mobile phone. The kitchen chair spun as he snatched his jacket from the back. *"Kak!"*

Lizzy chased her father down the stone steps to the canopy-covered motor court, where the remaining stock of Kasabian family cars was parked and kept to a waxy shine by the day staff. Vaz chose the nearest vehicle, a gray Bentley GT, pulling the door open.

"He ran off cuzza you!" screeched Lizzy.

"I take care of my family," Vaz defended. "You get your things together and be ready."

"I'm not going to Armenia to fix *your* problem!"

"You will take care of your brother!"

"Why? Because you never could?"

"You don't know what you're talking about," he said, pointed at Lizzy, then waved her off dismissively.

"You're making deals with cops for him!"

"Shut up. I'm saving him from what shit he can't handle!"

"That's just it! You don't know what he can handle! You don't know anything about your family!"

"You're taking your brother to Armenia. That's enough of you!"

"I'd rather fucking die!" spat Lizzy. "And so would Johnny!"

"Whatever." Vaz waved her off again, dropped into the bucket seat, and pulled the door shut.

Lizzy, in denial and already dressed for her night out, pulled off one of her brand-new pumps—studded in black with silver and jeweled skulls—and from the bottom step, hurled it at the Bentley. The spiked heel ricocheted off the windshield and disappeared over a six-foot hedge.

"*Fuuuccckkk. Shiiiitttt,*" howled Lizzy, watching her father back through the automatic gate before she spun a U-turn and raced back toward the house.

Standing at the top of the steps was her brick of a mother, arms crossed, scowling face raining disappointment.

"He's an asshole, Mom," complained Lizzy.

"He does his best," urged Tabitha. "And so should you."

"And what's that supposed to mean?"

"For you to decide." Tabitha turned and vanished back inside the house.

For the duration of his call to Vaz, Mikayel had hung on the line, overhearing the entirety of the private family squabble.

"*Boosh lesbiner.*" *Stupid lesbian,* muttered Mikayel, before double-checking to make certain the mute function was still engaged on his device.

"Are you there?" asked Vaz, accelerating the Bentley into the downhill turns of Glendale.

"*Ayo,*" replied Mikayel, remembering to unmute his phone before repeating the affirmation.

"Anything?"

"Still here," said the big goon. After dismissing Eriq and Tavet, Mikayel had withdrawn back to the cramped Toyota, waited about a minute before he cranked up the engine, backed into the nearest driveway, and slowly accelerated away from the bungalow. It was only a minor ruse as Mikayel simply circled the block before returning to rest the Corolla behind a newish Chevy Cruze parked two homes to the west of the residence.

"Nobody goes in or out before I get there," ordered Vaz. "I'm clear on this, *ya?*"

"And if Johnny tries to leave?"

"Just make sure he doesn't!"

"How far are you?"

"Five minutes."

If birds were to fly the route, the trip from Vaz's Glendale home to Altadena was barely three miles. Only between the point of departure and the destination were foothills, canyons, and a scenic expanse called the Arroyo Seco, a mostly dry watershed that served as home to parks, two golf courses, the historic Rose Bowl Stadium, and residential streets fronted with multimillion-dollar homes. If he'd owned a helicopter, Vaz would have flown it, dropped the skids into the middle of that *Lucky goddamn cop's* suburban street, and reclaimed his troubled son with a flourish nobody would soon forget. Instead, Vaz suffered what felt like an interminable drive east by freeway and then north by boulevard. His speeds topped eighty-seven miles per hour and, but for heeding red lights, he disobeyed a laundry list of traffic rules. *Damn the police*, he repeated, fully aware. He was armed, breaking traffic laws, yet damning all consequence.

Damn the police and damn my fucking spit!

Vaz had gone from fence-sitting to fully regretting that he'd allowed Lucky to bully him into giving up his precious saliva. He had hoped it was a cheap trade in exchange for his youngest boy's safety. After all, he would have even more leverage with Lucky's goddamn family. Only while Vaz was hocking up two gobs of DNA-infused saliva he'd been outmaneuvered. Now Lucky had *his* son.

"I'm here!" Vaz announced once he whipped the Bentley onto Lucky's street. He streaked past Mikayel's Corolla without notice and stopped, blocking the driveway where Johnny B.'s Mustang was still parked.

Mikayel needn't have heard the order. He sprung from the cramped compact, quick-scanned the landscape, then began what should have been a fifty-yard jog. The towering goon didn't consider the Chevy Cruze behind which he'd set up his second position, let alone perceive it as a glimmer of a threat. The two cops concealed inside the new-model Chevrolet were unseen and unaccounted for and would surely like to have kept it that way.

27

Sugar Freeman had begun to cramp. He blamed it on the tension. At first there had been the moment Zadeh had spotted the Armenian kill crew through her night specs. Her instinct had been to emerge from the vehicle and reveal herself as a sworn LASD deputy. Sugar read her body language, fully understanding her motive. She was reflexively going to place herself and her body between her fellow sheriff's officer and the trio of assassins. And why not? That's how cops rolled their rock.

Only Sugar had reached out and snagged Zadeh, wrenched her back inside, pushed her head down to the center console, and pulled the door back shut in the frantic hopes of dousing the dome light.

"We ain't supposed to be here!!!" he'd repeated.

Zadeh's first instinct was to argue for Lucky's safety. She wanted to say, "Christ's sake! I had sex with that motherfucker! Not gonna watch him get dropped!"

Whatever result might have come from their quarrel turned irrelevant once the Shelby Mustang had roared into their midst. The un-sub—a.k.a. the unknown subject—had acted as an instant repellent—like a skunk that sends prey into flight. The kill team had pulled an about-face and fled back to their vehicles—while Sugar and Zadeh peered between the dashboard and the lids of their baseball caps.

"Swear to God, I almost just shit myself," admitted Zadeh with a nervous giggle.

The pair chattered, mostly in play-by-play mode, with Zadeh calling out the movements of the two would-be assassins in the panel van as they extricated themselves from the neighborhood. Sugar ciphered her accounts via encrypted texts to both Miles and Judge Jim. More relief came when the man she'd coined as Mr. Volleyball fired up his compact Toyota and, with headlights dimmed, backed into the nearest driveway and slipped away into the night. Neither Zadeh nor Sugar imagined Mr. Volleyball was only shifting his position with an around-the-block rotation to a secondary spot. He'd returned with his headlights on full beam, easing his 1980s import so close he kissed Zadeh's Chevy Cruze's rear bumper.

"That asshole!" she hissed, slumped impossibly low in her seat. "Only bought this car two weeks ago!"

Sugar twisted around, sinking his knees into the footwell and facing the seatback. His Glock rested on the center console, prepped and ready to spray the rear windows with a magazine-load of 9mm lead should Mr. Volleyball reveal himself to be a threat.

"This is just the tits," complained Zadeh.

"Anyone ever say you talk way too much like a dude?" added Sugar.

"Never in complaint," she sighed.

"Call into the Altadena sheriff's station," suggested Sugar. "Get a black-and-white to swing by, roust Mr. Volleyball as a suspicious character."

Zadeh agreed, produced her phone, and began dialing 911.

"My fucking back—" bitched Sugar, biting his tongue when, once again, the car cabin was awash in a second pair of headlights. And mere seconds after the pass, the clunky sound of the Toyota's door popping open was clear to each cop.

"911 operator."

"Hello," whispered Zadeh. "I'm calling to report a strange man in a Toyota Corolla parked on my street—"

"He's out of the car," interrupted Sugar, his body tensed, the push of adrenaline putting a temporary chill on his back cramps.

Zadeh stopped her jaw from moving. Her breathing ceased. The only sign of life she revealed was in her eyes as they tracked the muzzle of Sugar's 9mm following the target outside the window. Any question as to whether Mr. Volleyball would continue his walk—or stop dead if, and when, he made the pair of contorted cops concealed in the compact car in front of his—was answered when Sugar's pistol rose from its left-to-right arc. Zadeh's instinct to slam her eyes shut in full expectation of a muzzle flash, discharge, and downpour of safety glass was interrupted by the shadow outside the window. Mr. Volleyball had stopped dead in his tracks. When the shadow loomed closer, she could see the stoop of the tall goon straining to see what might be inside.

The window tint! she realized.

Zadeh had paid a pretty penny extra for it and ever since had felt skinned by the dealer for the up-sell on the option. Clearly, Mr. Volleyball was fighting the dim light outside the car as well as the factory-installed charcoal-gray privacy glass. She watched the big man tilt adventurously closer to the pane. In equal measure, Sugar defensively pushed his Glock's blockish muzzle ahead until it nearly touched the glass.

What Zadeh recalled after was practically in still images—like a slideshow with bright flashes of projector light between staggered film frames.

Mr. Volleyball partially straightened, threw his left hand defensively forward, fingers splayed like jazz hands. His right mitt, though, slipped toward his waistband. Zadeh never saw his fingers touch a gun. Nor did Sugar. But as cops were oft to remind naysayers, *the dumbass wasn't reaching for his dick.*

Pop! Pop!

Zadeh couldn't recall if she so much as blinked. She must have, though. Otherwise how could she explain the lack of injury to either of her corneas? There was a yellow-hot burn of powder in her nostrils. Before the second bullet left the barrel, the safety glass released in a jigsaw of puzzle shards. Worried she had swallowed glass, Zadeh bucked and spat, and followed with a preventative cough.

"He's down, he's down!" cried Sugar. "Fucking drive!"

"What?"

"Go! Now! Drive!"

She punched the ignition button. The engine turned with a hum. Zadeh straightened and made a curb-to-curb U-turn, the tight wheelbase making a clean arc to the left. Through her empty window cavity, the shaken deputy caught a quick but close enough view of Mr. Volleyball, flattened on the asphalt, his six-and-a-half-foot frame splayed, eyes to the sky, right arm crooked to his waist, his left above his head as if caught waving hello.

Or goodbye.

Vaz thought Mikayel had stumbled and tripped backward over his humongous feet. Though the big man appeared athletic, Chris often retold the story of Mikayel's "wipeout" after slipping in blood he'd personally spilled from a loudmouth Turk. It had all been over a drunken jibe regarding whether or not the Armenian Genocide of 1915 was truth or some made-up myth. The scene had taken place in a downtown Russian nightclub named Krov. Mikayel had followed his victim into the men's room and, while the Turk was relieving himself at the urinal, drawn a razor across the unsuspecting man's throat. Though he had successfully avoided the geyser of blood, Mikayel had lost his footing in the slickening gore when rotating for the exit. He had fallen hard, fouling his black pants in his victim's blood. Despite the murderous detour, the crew had moved on to another bar, Mikayel wearing his stained trousers with Armo pride, even excusing his accident by insisting the blood of Turks was extra slippery—that every evil descendent of Osman the First had olive oil mixed with the sweat of fetal pigs pumping through their veins.

But when Vaz saw Mikayel's body strike the asphalt, he witnessed no attempt by the servile goon to break his fall. The languid man slapped the pavement, his head snapping backward and striking with a resonant, melon-like *thud*. Somehow, Vaz's ears hadn't registered the sound of gunshots. His eyes, though, froze in the sudden sweep of headlights as the Chevy Cruze whipped an efficient one-eighty and sped from the neighborhood.

Shot dead, worried Vaz. One of his loyal soldiers was down, felled by who knows what or why. Instead of rushing to the street—or dialing 911—Vaz stood frozen in the middle of the bungalow's lawn, dew oozing over the tops of his Gucci loafers.

I have maybe one minute to save Johnny.

Vaz's legs acted like they were trapped between the instinct to take flight and the fight to protect his family. Altadena was L.A. Sheriff's territory. They *would* be coming.

Save who? asked his conflicted psyche. *Mikayel, Johnny, or myself?*

Then the answer came.

Johnny. My son.

Vaz's plan was to knock first. Just walk up from the street, bang a couple of fists against the bungalow's door, and call out for his son. His voice, let alone his proximity, should be violence enough to snap the hardheaded teen back onto the right track. But that was before the gunshots—before Mikayel had been mysteriously felled and was probably bleeding to death in the street.

The father's mind accelerated. It wouldn't just be Johnny on his way to Armenia. After the violence he was about to cause, Vaz would have to disappear with him. As the mob boss charged toward the bungalow's antique front door, he was prioritizing his subsequent moves.

Grab my son.

Call the pilot. Secure private jet.

Bypass home for Van Nuys Airport.

Fly to secure airfield in Mexico.

Wait for passports to arrive via second aircraft.

Once in the air again, refuel in Greenland or Iceland.

Final destination, airstrip at Jermuk. Cousin Gor greets them with changes of clothes and a bottle of mulberry vodka.

As if the final entry had been checked off his list, the bear of a father charged the bungalow's front door, lowered his shoulder, and felt the lock give way in a spray of splinters. A call for his Johnny B. was rising from his chest when his head jerked toward the snarl of an equally angry beast. Vaz heard the scraping of large paws and nails seeking immediate traction. From the black of the entryway he saw only eyes and bared canine teeth.

Is he dead?

When she'd peeked out her shattered window, Zadeh couldn't exactly see. The compact Chevy's U-turn was too crisp and quick to check for the rise and fall of Mr. Volleyball's chest cavity. *Probably not yet*, she answered herself. Gunshot victims, even those with holes blown in the ten-ring—center-cut shot in the chest—could breathe and blink through blank stares for up to a minute or two before fully expiring.

And Jesus Christ. We're in my car!

"But we're in my car!" announced Zadeh, somehow repeating her thought aloud.

"And whose fault is that?" fired back Sugar.

"Fuck me!"

The wind whistled through the shattered window. Zadeh was unconsciously leaning heavily on the accelerator, braking hard into a pair of intuitive right turns, then back on the gas.

"Slow your sweet ass down!" bit Sugar.

"Right . . ." she heaved. "Speed limit."

"Shit was dark. Bad guy down. Ain't nobody but nobody gonna bring it back to us if you keep your shit."

"My car. But *your* gun!"

"Nobody's gun!" corrected Sugar, already wiping down the weapon with his undershirt. "Pulled it offa some jammed-up knucklehead in Pacoima."

"Miles . . ." Zadeh found herself saying.

"What about 'im?"

"He's gonna crap a gasket." Zadeh was making an effort to obey every traffic rule. After working her way two miles east, she engaged her right-turn signal. "Shit. Your Hummer."

"Miles ain't gonna cry nothin' over no dead Armo." Sugar snapped his fingers across her nose. "Pay attention. Not goin' back to my ride. Pick it up tomorrow after the crime scene's scooped."

She switched off her turn signal and continued on her original trajectory, cautious, but with a survivalist's purpose of putting distance between herself and the crime—even if it felt like she was crawling by the linear inch. The passing of each streetlamp streaked across the new paint of her Chevy's hood.

"And my stupid window," she remarked.

"Shit happens," answered Sugar. "Your new whip got broke into, that's all. Come up with somethin' stole. Make a proper police report. Claim the insurance."

"Got, like, a five hundred dollar deductible."

"Claim it no matter. Catalog phone calls. Emails. Believe me when I say nothin' beats a good paper trail."

Sugar directed Zadeh to merge onto the nearest freeway pointed west, fully expectant she'd taxi him all the way west to the Ventura County burg of Camarillo. He'd bought a mini-mansion out of foreclosure during the great recession of 2009. The house was seven thousand square feet, had its own guest suite for visiting relatives and, in Sugar's opinion, was worth the sometimes ninety-minute drive to the LAPD Van Nuys Division. Zadeh replied neither yay nor nay to his invite. She didn't even attempt to calculate whether there was the prospect of sex in his suggestion. Her head was swimming, her breathing shallow. Zadeh had to settle her heart rate with the view ahead.

Freeways. God love 'em.

Zadeh had great affection for the ubiquitous L.A. auto arteries. At least when they weren't choked with stop-and-go traffic. Nights were best. Gazing forward, Zadeh lifted her view a few degrees above the jockeying taillights to a horizon in gradation—city lights to the ambient gray dissolving into a deep blue-black. The section of freeway, which banked ever so slightly right then left, appeared as alive as any organism, its cellular body made of banded streaks of light. Red. White. Forward. Reverse. Like blood pumping to and from the animal's heart.

Entering Pasadena's city center, the freeway appeared to sink into the earth, decorated concrete walls flanking either side. Completing the picture was the electrified Metrorail commuter system that ran on two tracks down the median. The trains, generally only four cars in length, were lit up from the inside like glowing metal caterpillars with sleek gray skins and repeating rows of emerald eyes. Though the cars were tied end-to-nose on steel rails, they appeared to float on a cushion of air as they approached the Lake Street station. Zadeh backed off the gas to keep the moment alive and fluid as the train slowed. It was calming, almost transcendent. Like being inside a momentary bubble of urban beauty.

It couldn't last, though. As the commuter train automatically eased to its next stop, Zadeh, with the wind from her open window rattling her eardrum, settled in for the long drive with a focus toward her next nocturnal object of fancy. Had she not been temporarily traumatized—or transfixed—she might have taken a last look to her left. It was, after all, her cop habit. Checking faces. Reading the lies they tried to tell.

But not that one moment on that one night.

If Zadeh had looked—or even if Sugar had turned his chin to address her—perhaps to attempt to sell her again on the Camarillo sleepover—either of the dirty duo might have performed an involuntary double-take and, for a second or so, laid eyes on Lucky

Dey and that un-sub who'd burned up the Altadena neighborhood before inserting the black Mustang into the bungalow's driveway. Man and teen were seated facing forward—both Metrorail passengers nearly caught in the midst of their great escape.

"I used to like trains."

Johnny B.'s murmur of an admission was something closer to a whispered lament than an effort to restart the conversation. He tilted his mop of hair against the Metrorail car's window. It felt cool against his scalp. With one eye open, he could scarcely see beyond the reflection of the train car's interior. He would occasionally glimpse the forward coaches when the rails swerved. Then with a heavy exhalation, his breath fogged the view.

The grossly out of shape teen was exhausted. The proof was in the short but speedy trek Lucky had led him on like a sloth on a leash. From the moment Lucky had unpinned Johnny B. from the bungalow's hardwood floor, he had practically been dragging the reluctant young man by his shirt collar. Johnny B. made a mental catalog around the house as Lucky collected items into a ballistic black backpack. Handguns, ammunition, toothbrush, underwear, T-shirt, and what looked like a small vase wrapped in plastic wrap. All the while, Lucky was peppering him with questions:

Were you followed?

Did you recognize any of the cars out front?

How soon before your old man comes for you?

Lucky shoved the back door open to let the big mutt he'd called Oprah into the house. The animal was all slobber and tongue at the sight of Lucky and the new guest. Before Johnny B. could utter a simple "Nice doggy," Lucky had maneuvered the dog inside and himself and Johnny B. into the backyard. In the limited light, they had climbed over a rickety rear fence and under a blitz from a neighbor's barking animal, and rushed along a gravel path leading to a street that looked nearly identical to the bungalow's. As they fast-walked block after block of sidewalks, Lucky's hand never seemed to let go of Johnny B.'s shirt, always hustling the teen ahead. When Johnny B. repeated his overall plea for help, he was simply hushed.

By the time the pair boarded a southbound city bus, Johnny B. was sucking for breath and relieved to finally find a seat. The short ride had led them to a Metrorail stop and a commuter train destined for downtown's Union Station.

"'Fore I got into deejaying, I had this really radical train set. Best around. Lionels 'n' Bachmanns. Wanted to sell it on eBay but my dad just put it in boxes in the garage. Said if we hung onto 'em for twenty years they'd be way more valuable."

"How many years ago was that?" asked Lucky.

"Christmas," answered Johnny B., flat as a pancake. Then his tone shifted. "Think she likes trains? Or she just homeless?"

Lucky's eyes followed Johnny B.'s. Across the aisle and two seats up was a woman in veritable rags. Heroin-thin. The seat next to her was stacked with plastic grocery bags chock-full of dirty garments.

"Couldn't say for sure," answered Lucky.

"My brother, Chris, loves the homeless people," continued Johnny B. "Or he's just superstitious. Can you be both superstitious and full of charity?"

"I dunno. What do you think?"

"Think Chris is both," droned Johnny B. "Every time he does his pickups, he stops at the same off-ramp. Burbank 'n' the 405. No matter who's begging for a handout—man, lady, young, old fart, good shoes, bad shoes—he gives 'em money. Good money. Usually a whole twenty bucks. I tell him he's getting hustled but that's where he says he's superstitious. Calls it paying his toll."

Lucky couldn't help but swing a second look at his seatmate. In physique, Johnny B. was every bit a man down to the back hair creeping over the tag inside his shirt collar. The roundness of the big teen's shoulders revealed muscles as pronounced as a rugby player's. Yet everything else, from posture to tone, was all boy. Soft. In demeanor and posture, Johnny B. seemed no more mature than an outcast fourteen or fifteen years old.

"Where we goin'?"

"A friend's," said Lucky.

"I be safe there?"

"You will."

"Promise?"

"How old are you?"

"Eighteen," replied Johnny B.

"Legal grown-up. Nobody can make you go to Armenia."

"My dad can."

"See your dad anywhere around here?"

"We're on a train. He doesn't like trains."

Lucky let it hang. He knew that in a matter of minutes, Johnny B. would ask the question again. *Am I safe?* It was as if there was a loop running in the kid's brain. When the fear element circled back to the frontal cortex, the mouth was re-engaged and the words were sure to be repeated. How long until the worried cycle was derailed was a guess better asked of a mental health professional.

Shit changes, Lucky. And you just go with it.

Lucky recalled another over-abused adage oft uttered by Flip Bledsoe—the very same son of a bitch who'd eventually nominated and inducted Lucky into the Lennox Reapers. The thought was on the heels of Lucky's realization that barely an hour earlier he had been seated at his kitchen table, armed for Armageddon and prepared to stay locked and loaded until Monday morning, when he'd deliver the pint glass full of saliva to Judge Jim. He had no more of a plan than that. Nor had he summoned any countermoves beyond the delivery and *now what?* His plan to exchange some prized Armenian DNA for Judge Jim's transactional assurance that young John Bartholomew Kasabian receive a prosecutor's pass on a manslaughter beef was not the precise endpoint. It was merely the next entry point to his direction *through*. There would certainly be some kind of negative reverb. Either another squeeze from Judge Jim and his vigilante cabal or an attempt from the Armenians to suck a little more quid pro quo out of the deputy. Lucky's answer would be a firm "No thanks." Neither party was likely to be pleased with his answer. And they could choke on it, for all Lucky cared. In the time between his rebuff and their retaliation Lucky hoped to solve the rest of the puzzle and, in doing so, extricate himself and his family from the danger zone.

In the meantime, I'm on a fucking train.

If Gonzo could have seen Lucky she would've quit on him right then and there. Instead of leaving Johnny B. to huff and puff at his front door, he'd opened the door to their home and let the proverbial fly in the ointment inside, tossing his initial plan and who knows what else into the grinder. Lucky both loved and loathed the tingle at his hairline from not knowing a lick just how the hell the game would conclude. And that was explicitly what Gonzo feared most about him—his unfailing knack for upsetting the status quo.

Damn you, Lucky. Goddamn you.

Monday

28

Sherman Oaks. 1:03 a.m.

It was like a radio jingle playing in Lee Chapman's head. Over and over again, the words fit to some unknown melody he'd picked up sometime during his lifelong descent.

He didn't wanna do it. He didn't wanna do it.

The singsong of his made-up self-mocking lyric had been on permanent replay ever since that menacing garden associate had chased him from Home Depot. It had begun as a whistling falsetto as Lee had scampered back to his shitmobile and had played on repeat all the way back to his Sepulveda Boulevard rent-by-the-week motel room. Once there, he'd tried to steal a nap, hoping the sounds over the radio of the Los Angeles Clippers away game against Oklahoma would push him over the edge into restorative slumber.

Lee woke up to a dark room and a digital clock blinking 9:11 p.m. *Shit*, he rubbed his face and smiled, *I ought to get my ass scared more often.* That's when the singsong jingle returned, only revised from third person to first.

I didn't wanna do it. I didn't want to do it.

The pull remained strong. His thoughts of Shia, so feminized out of uniform, had clearly infected him. Imbued him, even. With action? If so, what? Hell no, he eventually clarified to himself. Interest in her? Yes. Affection? Certainly. Obsession? Leading to sexual congress? Impossible. Dangerous.

Danger, Will Robinson. Danger!!!

Jesus Christ, he complained. Now he had the robot voice from television's *Lost in Space*, a show he'd adored as a kid, jabbering inside his skull. It was no real surprise, though. He'd more than once credited the sixties' black-and-white TV series as his first insight into a future in robotics, his consequent engineering degree, and then a soaring career at NASA's Jet Propulsion Lab in Pasadena.

That was then.

Lee needed to exorcise his uncontrollable thoughts. He began by speed-dialing his favorite prostitutes, Lucinda, Adelina, and Gennifer. He didn't need to leave voicemails. The trio knew his digits. The first lady to call back would win the hundred-dollar prize of riding him into exhaustion. He might add a few bucks to pay for party favors. Ecstasy, molly, meth—the latter a last resort to purge the enslaving thoughts of Shia from his system.

He didn't wanna do it. He didn't wanna do it.

Fucking third person again, bitched Lee at himself. Sated from chemically charged sex and still semi-afloat in the euphoric effects of the methylenedioxymethamphetamine—or MDMA— the singsong in his head had returned to the third person, like some shadow self outside of him was lobbing grenades.

Or you can just go with it, dipshit.

As if permission had been granted—and feeling rested from his epic nap—Lee found himself easily transported back to Shia's quiet street, the follow route and address still etched on the insides of his eyelids. *Fourteen double-oh five Califa.* He extinguished his headlights and parked at the curb under a massive, spreading live oak that blanketed him under a near-black shadow only a few strides east of her driveway. The remnant of the drug had left him feeling fearless and unconcerned that she or anybody else might make him out as a threat, let alone the stalker he'd clearly become. If anything, Lee felt more like a fatherly protector. A guardian angel. Yes. That was it. Maybe the excitable urge inside him wasn't so much sexual—though he wouldn't entirely lock the door on the fantasy of the dark deputy in shiny handcuffs—but perhaps an instinct that Shia needed protection. From what? Surely not Lee Chapman. No. Something else. Somebody else. His spidey senses told him so. Therefore, he was right to be rested and armed . . .

Oh, shit. Was gonna look into getting that gun.

Gennifer had been the first of his ladies to return his call. The moment she'd landed at his threshold, she'd been so quick to take control that Lee had forgotten to make the ask. *I need a gun. Can you get me one?* Surely, Gennifer would've known a hookup. Lee filled with regret for having missed a step. There Shia was, a shadow moving inside the curtains of her house, and the man who'd sworn himself as her protector was technically impotent as her bodyguard. He'd need the gun. And soon. Tomorrow, he promised both himself and Shia. Tomorrow he'd get himself "strapped," as the street gangsters in recent movies would say. Until then, he'd have to defend her with what he had on hand. Ballistic pen. Spring-action knife. Collapsible baton. And his newly discovered will.

Then, *slam!*

Lee snapped his head up. He'd been staring down at the baton in his hands. He hadn't heard the hybrid-powered yellow cab swerve to the curb only yards in front of him. Had he fallen asleep again? Fallen into a foggy comedown from the drug?

"Shit," he spat aloud. His shoulder blades reacted, pinching hard at the peak of his spine, his fingers tensing around the hardened steel rod in his grasp.

A man climbed from the rear of the cab. Six feet, fit, every movement appearing as if it was business. Police, Lee quickly guessed. All those hours as a courthouse observer had taught him how to spot an out-of-uniform cop. They walked with a crankshaft for an axis, like they were on twenty-four-seven alert. Stepping out behind the cop was a big fellow, much younger, equally tall but soft and awkward. As the younger man trudged the short walk toward the front door, the cop fella stalled atop the curb and quickly swept the landscape, his eyes absorbing the scene with practiced efficiency. As Lee found himself trying to blink away the grogginess, he caught himself frozen in a dead-on stare down with the cop. It was as if Lee's nervous system released an electric jolt. Could the cop really see him under the cloak of darkness provided by the ancient oak? Lee remained locked in, terrified to breathe. The cop's eyes were black holes in a hard-to-read face—impossible to decipher from Lee's perch. Yet after what felt like an eternity, the cop broke off and sauntered toward the front door, already opened by precious Shia. She was in a ribbed muscle shirt and sweatpants, her un-relaxed hair a kinky spray falling on her shoulders. In the porch light, she'd never looked more beautiful.

Or fuckable.

Lee corrected the libido side of his addled brain. Again, he blamed the drugs, then held on tight as his emotional pendulum swung deep into an unsettling jealousy. After cordially greeting the awkward young man, Shia stood on her tiptoes and wrapped her arms around the cop in a lingering embrace. This wasn't the friendly familiar hug she'd afforded the Home Depot prick-with-a-brick. This was a clinch. Lover-like. Reserved for . . . *him.*

The son of a bitch!

His face flushed in a prickly heat. His teeth grit while tears trickled from his eyes. The hurt of it was a surprise. Informing. All his mental gymnastics and self-rationalization were stripped away by Shia's single act of affection toward the cop. Even at a distance, he could read her adoration. In Lee's existential *now* he'd pictured something unexpected. Love. It appeared pure, without condition, complete with a tippy-toed girlishness that betrayed the de facto indifference Shia revealed in her daily chores working as Judge Sollo's bailiff.

Anger swelled within Lee. It was a fuel unlike any he'd felt before. Destructive. Without an ounce of care, even. Lee imagined himself in public, gripping the collapsible baton with both hands, and peeling back the skull of that asshole cop with one thrashing blow after another.

Wow, thought the wannabe writer in Lee. The rush of feelings spoke to one of the primal motives of why a man kills.

For love.

"When was your last tetanus shot?"

"I don't remember," groused Vaz, low and throaty in his reply. He'd asked the nursing staff and the attending doctor for privacy, showing concern that the emergency room stall's plastic curtain be kept closed at all times.

"Nasty coupla bites," noted the doc, a gaunt man around thirty years old with a long face and tired eyes.

"You should see the fucking dog," deadpanned Vaz. He was seated at the edge of a hospital bed, his right pant leg cut open to the knee, the puncture wounds on his calf slowly oozing blood. His salmon pink shirt had been snipped to the shoulder, his left forearm bearing similar punctures, only with more stitch-worthy skin and muscle torn away as if it had been worked over by a hungry animal.

"Your dog?"

"Neighbor's," lied Vaz. "Please. Just fix me up and let me get home to my bed."

The emergency room visit had been just shy of midnight. It was well after one in the morning when Vaz had finally limped out of Glendale Adventist Medical Center. He'd paid the bill in full with an American Express card, at that point unconcerned about the trail he'd left in his wake. In nearby Altadena he'd left a broken front door and a trail of his blood and DNA back to his Bentley, along with the dead body of one of his best soldiers in the middle of the suburban street. No doubt there'd been witnesses. Lookie-loo residents peering out their windows. Perhaps some home security camera footage of his arrival and escape. Hell. His son's impossible-to-miss Shelby Mustang was still parked in the bungalow's driveway. Any numb-nuts detective would be able to pull the strings together in a matter of hours. In no time at all, Vaz fully expected the Sheriff's or LAPD to make a show of force at his home for questioning, custody, or some manner of arrest. Any pull he had through the Glendale chief of police would be utterly moot.

And I was worried about my DNA in a fucking beer glass? Vaz berated himself. He phoned Chris and made a demand that his immediate family meet him in an upstairs room at the Atwater Village motel fronted by that Denny's. The location was poetic, considering it was there he'd made his first mistake in an afternoon and subsequent evening of colossal errors. To slow down any immediate police chase, Vaz met another soldier on a quiet residential street in Highland Park, switched his high-profile Bentley for a less identifiable Ford Explorer, and drove the last ten minutes to the motel. Tabitha, Chris, and Lizzy were already waiting in what was advertised as a smoke-free mini business suite. Despite that, cigarettes burned in each of their hands.

"Jesus. The family that smokes together . . ." began Vaz before a nod to his wife. "And I thought you quit."

Tabitha was seated, back straight, in a cutout nook with a desk and office chair, the lone reason the otherwise nondescript motel room could be advertised as some kind of suite. Chris was leaning in the bathroom doorframe, occasionally reaching back to utilize the sink as an ashtray. Lizzy was cross-legged on one of the two queen-sized beds.

"Just 'cause I'm smoking this once doesn't mean I'm a smoker again," excused Tabitha.

"Yeah. Go, Mom," added Lizzy, her sarcasm as droll as a cup of decaf.

"Switch cars okay?" asked Chris.

Vaz nodded, shut and latched the door behind him, then hobbled his way to the corner of the second bed.

"I've made some significant mistakes," began Vaz, unwilling to retell the night's events. "I admit them and instead of cataloging them all right now, I'd rather just begin with the fresh plan of action."

"New plan?" wondered Tabitha, her suspicion failing to conceal her long-simmering anger.

"It's good news for you," explained Vaz, directing the remark at Lizzy, who despite her casual posture looked ready to pop up and return to the party from which she'd been plucked. "You won't be going to Armenia."

Lizzy merely harrumphed. "I was *never* going to Armenia," she scorned.

"Be. That. As. It. May." With his painfully slow delivery, Vaz wanted to remind all that he was still the headmaster of the clan. "I've already ordered up the jet. I'll be the one going to Armenia. Soon as we're done here, Chris will drive me to the airport."

"Whoa, whoa, whoa," straightened Chris, more the son than obedient lieutenant. "What about J. B.?"

"It'll be up to you to make sure he follows me as soon as physically possible," explained Vaz. "But the situation will need to get unraveled without me."

"You're an asshole," accused Lizzy without even knowing what Vaz had done.

"What I did was for Johnny!" pointed Vaz. "And the family. You? Who's ungrateful? All I do is for this family!"

In the silence, eyes either dropped, averted, or focused on the inanimate. For decoration, the artless space relied exclusively on the pair of chianti red bedspreads, a forest green carpet with patterned gold filigree, and a table vase with a bouquet of plastic wheat.

"So . . ." began Lizzy, emphasizing her syllables by drawing in the air with her cigarette. "You fucked J. B. every which way when you were around. Now you fuck him up by quitting on him."

"Listen to me, you little bitch!" snapped Vaz, gesturing wildly with his uninjured arm. "I can't help him from jail. I can't help Johnny if *he's* in jail. We both gotta get to Armenia. I will be there to meet him at the airport once your brother gets him on a plane."

"Fuck you," spat Lizzy, flicking the remainder of her cigarette at her father while springing from the bed. "You're just a self-serving prick."

"Do *not* talk to your father that way!" barked Tabitha.

There was no beeline for the motel room door. Lizzy had to serpentine around the corner of the queen bed where her father sat. With his good arm he snagged her around the bicep.

"I know you think you love him more than the rest of us combined." Her father's grip was tight, but his voice softened. "But I've done everything for your brother."

"Keep lyin' to yourself. You're good at it." Lizzy wrenched away from her father, gripped the doorknob, and flung the door wide and charged out.

"You're not going to Armenia," grunted Chris to his father, flat as if giving an order while chasing after his sister. "Not without J. B."

Vaz looked as if he was going to offer a sharp reply, only his eyes caught Tabitha with one finger pointed at him like a gun, the other to her lips.

"What?" shrugged Vaz once Chris had left the room.

"If you're gone, Chris is in charge," reasoned Tabitha. "So, let him be in charge."

"But I'm still here!"

"You wanna abdicate?" she pushed. "Then abdicate and let *Chris* fix this!"

If Chris had heard any of the terse exchange between his mother and father, he didn't let it shift his tack to catch up with his sister. Lizzy was halfway across the asphalt surface of the parking lot when she allowed her brother's calling to slow her escape. She swiveled a one-eighty and held out her arms in a resignation only reserved for her brother.

"He's an asshole, okay?" pleaded Chris. "We both know that."

"So?"

"So, right now you might not know everything."

"Like I need to know more!" Full of sarcasm, Lizzy spun a slow three-sixty. Her gesture appeared to encompass the entire horseshoe of the two-story motel, including the liquor-licensed Denny's, as if she knew all the lurid stories they could tell.

"Hear me out," pleaded Chris, closing their gap so tightly that, to any of the low-rent onlookers choosing to ogle, the pair looked like a squabbling couple. "This one isn't all on Pop. There's this sick cop who's messing up everything. Playing games. Using J. B. as leverage. It's seriously sick. Really."

"Cop?"

"Sheriff. It's Pop he's after. J. B. just got caught up." Chris paused. His eyes swerved as if accessing a thought. "Or maybe it was cuzza . . ."

"Because what?"

"Few days ago. Same cop approached J. B. in a bathroom. Me 'n' the boys thought he was some kinda toilet fag, you know? So, we gave him some what for."

"You beat the crap outta him?"

"Not so bad he couldn't walk away," shrugged Chris. "Meantime, once Pop found out the dude was lookin' into that accident shit J. B. got in, Pop tried to turn it around. Get the cop to bury it."

"You're saying the BHA fucked with the wrong cop?"

"It gets even weirder. I saw it, don't get it, and I don't like it," Chris said, referring to the DNA spit in the pint glass. "And now this shit with Mikayel getting dropped and then Pop wanting to up and run to Armenia?"

"And Johnny's with the cop now?" queried Lizzy. "We at least know that much?"

"Last eyes," replied Chris through a tightened jaw, his thoughts momentarily stuck on Mikayel. "Mike saw it. Called us. Pop went running to grab Johnny like his pants were on fire."

"Yeah . . ." recalled Lizzy, as if remembering hurling a shoe at her old man's departing Bentley in the dark of night. She hadn't yet retrieved the other half of her favorite pair of shoes from the hedge.

"You got a way you want to handle it?" she asked.

"Working on it," assured Chris. "It's all about getting Johnny back home and safe."

No shit, Lizzy thought. *Get Johnny back home and safe. Then retrieve my lost kick.*

In that order.

29

Inside the gates of Conrad Ellis's estate, nobody slept. The four-and-a-half-acre property was lit up like the real estate surrounding a prison, only the lights and cameras were there as a defense against intruders instead of to deter an escape. Modest by billionaire standards, the residence and variety of outbuildings—pool house, gymnasium, guest cottage—were multi-leveled to fit the gentle slope on which it was built, the grounds meticulously landscaped by a small troop of Japanese-born gardeners in full-time employ. Conrad, the notorious germophobe and night owl, was known to cruise about his private domain in a suit and tie, that tumbler of single-malt scotch on ice as a constant accessory.

"You too?" remarked Conrad, standing on the gravel path in a pair of polished power wingtips.

"Can't," replied Karrie, referring to her inability to sleep. She was seated on the guest cottage's balcony, bare feet up, iPad on her lap, smoking a joint.

"Lucky know you smoke that stuff?"

"Legal now, you know. I mean, I'm not eighteen yet, but . . ."

Conrad dipped his eyes, smiled, and gently shook his head as he remembered the daughter he once had and the many secrets she'd kept from him.

"Science on that stuff isn't so good," offered Conrad.

"Not so good for liquor, either." She forced a smile. "Yet here we are."

"Worried about him?"

"I'm on the Altadena *Patch*," she said, elevating the tablet and dropping some sarcasm. "Dead body on my street. White. Unidentified. But why should I worry as long as I'm the one that gets to break the neck of whoever hurt Lucky?"

The cynicism, thought Conrad. Then again, who was he to define how a teenager processed danger, even death? Especially her.

"Your mom?" asked Conrad before he caught himself. Karrie was emancipated, her real mother and father a lousy memory. "Gonzo. Sorry."

"You can call her mom," she said. "She may as well be."

"Saw her walking around. Phone up here." Conrad gestured to his ear.

"She's trying to find out if Lucky's dead."

"And if he's not?"

"Yeah. She'll probably murder him."

"My guess is he's okay," offered Conrad. "He's kinda got a knack."

"For making big fat messes?"

"Staying alive."

Karrie took a drag, pulled the smoke back into her lungs, held it, then exhaled.

"I wanna be there with him," she admitted. "Wherever he is."

"Lost my little girl when she was about your age. So I get why

Lucky would want to bubble-wrap you, your mom. Travis, who is where . . . ?"

"Think he found your pool table. Promise you when he's done with it, it'll never be the same. He's not good with analog."

"Wood can be refinished. Felt replaced," said Conrad. "Your brother can't. I'm glad you're all here. Safe. You. Travis. Gonzo. And soon, Lucky. I'm sure of it."

Gonzo had second thoughts. Moments after hanging up the telephone she'd decided Lucky's plan had some seriously stinking thinking on it.

Stinkin' thinkin'.

It was another clever term Lucky had gleaned from Alcoholics Anonymous. He'd used it to describe not only his errors and bad brainwork but also that of others. Gonzo was now applying it to Lucky. If the family was unsafe at their Altadena bungalow, she could've easily used her cop connections to temporarily park a black-and-white at the front curb. After getting off the call from Lucky, she'd sunk into the Italian leather seating in the back of Conrad's limousine. As luxurious as it was, Gonzo felt as if it didn't fit her, let alone her blue-collar values of living life on a canned beer budget. It was Travis's thrill at the idea of getting a plush ride and spending the night in a billionaire's house that had convinced her to put a check on her better judgment.

More than seven hours had passed and a hard-to-count number of times that she had swung between anger and abject worry. It was, in her words, *a goddamn emotional rollercoaster.* And the revelation of a dead body dropped on her street had sent her into overdrive—dialing everyone from the Altadena sheriff's station to nearby hospitals and the county coroner. She even convinced a neighbor to risk crossing the crime scene tape to inquire as to the identity of the victim. Nobody but nobody had an adequate answer to salve her fears. She cursed Lucky up and down for causing such heartache and was then on her knees again praying for his deliverance.

Gonzo ignored the low battery warning on her phone. She'd found temporary solace under a small grove of decorative citrus trees planted on a gravel patch graded perfectly level. Her footsteps performed a satisfying crunch as she carved figure eight slaloms around a pair of grapefruit tree trunks. Phone at her ear. Waiting for a human being to answer after what seemed an endless line of automated transfers.

"Hi. My name is Lydia Gonzalez with the LAPD. I'm looking for information on a murder that took place in the last few hours in Altadena."

Not a person she'd contacted mentioned any visitors to the Altadena bungalow. No lanky Armenian in a compact Toyota, masked predators in a rental panel van, anxious teen in a Shelby Mustang, unknown subjects escaping in a Chevy Cruze, or a barking dog—let alone a stranger who'd left a trail of blood from the bungalow's front door to his smoke-silver Bentley.

All that and friggin' Lucky wasn't answering his friggin' phone!

In the fevered dash to vacate himself and Johnny B. from the bungalow, Lucky had misplaced his mobile phone. It wasn't until Shia bolted shut her front door and Lucky had dumped the backpack into a front room easy chair that he reached into his pocket for his device. Instinct told him it would need a charge and that he should touch base with Gonzo to make certain she and the kids were safe and settled in Conrad Ellis's care.

Shit.

Both front pockets were empty and his back pockets only contained his wallet and shield. About the time he decided to search the backpack, Shia was apologizing for the clear vinyl slipcovers on the living room furniture.

"I know. It's ugly as hell," Shia admitted. "But it's how my mom always had her living room."

"My phone," pissed Lucky. "Musta left it behind."

Shia introduced herself to Johnny B., noting his frail condition. The teen was averse to all eye contact. His shoulders were hunched and his arms wrapped about himself like he was holding in his guts. She patiently waited for him to notice her welcoming smile before leading them both into a tiny kitchen that hadn't been upgraded since the early 1970s.

"Your father?" asked Lucky.

"Bourbon coma," she replied. "No worries. He'll ping me at five a.m. to help him get his day on."

Johnny B. was stalled in the middle of the kitchen, staring at the wheelchair perched under a small, card-sized dining table awkwardly pushed up against a knotty pine cabinet shaped to conceal an ironing board.

"Spare set of wheels for my father," explained Shia. "For when the batteries on his hot rod get low."

"He's a cripple?" asked Johnny B.

"Paraplegic, you mean?" she kindly corrected. "You hungry? Thirsty?"

"Mountain Dew?"

"Night owl, huh?" smiled Shia. "Got Pepsi. Diet and sugared. Either of those work?"

"No Diet Coke?"

"Pepsi girl. Sorry."

"You got lemon to go with it?"

"Got a tree full of 'em in the backyard if you wanna go pick one."

"I don't know Gonzo's number," Lucky realized aloud. "It's been loaded in my phone for forever but . . ."

"Sure she's fine," calmed Shia. "Not her first rodeo. And she's plugged in where? Bel-Air?"

"She's workin' on a plan to cut me a new asshole." Lucky sat. The friction of the steel-legged chair against the aged linoleum made a tone resembling a duck passing wind.

Johnny B. released an uncontrolled giggle.

"Sure he's not half deputy?" Shia laughed.

"Me? No," Johnny defended.

"Fart jokes," she smirked. "Important to laugh when you're sharing a black-and-white for months on end."

"That's what you did?" asked Johnny B. "With her? Fart jokes?"

"I survived," Lucky smirked. "So did she."

"He was my training officer," added Shia with a chuckle. "He made me the badass cop I am today."

"So, you're one of the good guys too?" asked Johnny B., more suspect than innocent.

"Like to think so." Shia took it on herself to brave a touch. Just a gentle hand to Johnny B.'s forearm still defensively pressed to his wide frame. He half stepped back.

"We're enemies, you know," he said, flat but emphatic. As if his assertion were a science factoid.

"We are?" asked Shia.

"Sure we are," said Johnny B., showing his new tattoo. "I'm Armo. AP for life."

"Family business," eased Lucky.

"Know what?" Shia shifted gently. "I'm all about family first. Live with my daddy. Lucky's got family. You got family. Me 'n' Lucky? We're like family too. And what we do best? We take care of family."

"So, that means . . ." Johnny B. hesitated, choosing the words in his head before they crossed his tongue. ". . . that means I'm safe with you? Here? 'Cause I don't wanna go to jail 'n' I can't go to Armenia."

Jail? Armenia? Shia regarded Lucky without obvious alarm. His returned gaze said there was no easy explanation.

"Nope," assured Lucky with an uncharacteristic vocal up-lilt. "No jail. No Armenia. Not as long as you stick with the plan."

With a two-liter bottle of Diet Pepsi and two red Solo cups—one to drink from, the other brimmed with fresh lemon wedges—Johnny B. settled into the lean-to of a den, an obvious and inelegant add-on to the rental property. He amused himself in Shia's father's spare wheelchair, learning to do wheelies while remote-controlling the big-screen TV.

Outside, Lucky and Shia sat in collapsible camp chairs in front of a wrought-iron firepit centered on an almost useless twelve-by-fifteen-foot slab of cracked concrete, ostensibly the decking for a small swimming pool long since filled in with earth. The only remnant of its former glory was the red-bricked coping that formed a small, kidney-shaped ring.

"Stick with the plan?" repeated Shia, a direct reference to an earlier conversation.

"Yeah," nodded Lucky. "As if it's a real plan at all."

Shia sent sparks into the sky with a fresh log, a lightweight piece of sappy pine. Under flame it snapped like distant, small-caliber gunfire.

"Too warm for a fire," played Lucky.

"My dad likes it no matter what the temperature. Smokes his cigar. Listens to sports on the radio. Routine." Shia shifted forward in her seat, bent at the waist, and repeated the word again. "*Plan?*"

Lucky hadn't bargained on confessing much. He wasn't entirely sure that once he'd recited the domino-like events leading up to his phoning her with his request for temporary sanctuary, it would make any kind of sense to anybody other than himself. Yet recite he did. From the phone call from Assistant Sheriff McGill and the favor he'd been asked to Johnny B.'s knock on the door of his bungalow.

"Judge Peralta?" Shia mouthed the man's name for the umpteenth time, interchanging it with either Judge Jim or Judge Jimmy, as he was known to nearly everybody around the courthouse. "Jesus."

"And his private league of justice."

"Fuck me."

"You're not in this," reminded Lucky. "Safe harbor. Tonight. That's it. Tomorrow it's done."

"Today it's done. Gotta be three in the morning already."

"You should sleep."

"Like I could if I tried."

"Rest, at least."

"What if Judge Jim doesn't come through for the kid?"

"He made a bargain. If I don't press him hard to live by it, then I'll have even less room to maneuver."

"Maneuver where? How? They got you in a vise."

"Beats me. At least for now."

"And Johnny in there?"

"I'll run it by Conrad. Got my family looked after. What's one more?"

"Lucky and his strays," she smiled.

"Not a dog," reminded Lucky.

"And technically you're not allergic to people." She amusingly recoiled off his sideways look. "Well, most people."

"Boy's a legal adult. But he deserves some protection for now. At least until this shit gets sorted."

"Judge Sollo," announced Shia.

"Who?"

"My judge. Maybe she can weigh in?" Shia paused, looking across the fire and through the sliding glass door separating the patio from the den addition. Johnny B. was getting better at balancing wheelies in the wheelchair. "I mean, not to fix the potential charge against him. But she knows the system. Gives really good advice. Might make him feel safer."

"Safer from the system? Or his old man?"

"Either . . . Both."

Lucky didn't follow up with anything, preferring the sound of the pine log burning over his sour voice. He felt Shia's hand touch his. Assuring and full of care. He allowed his fingers to interlace with hers. Their mutual affection was real. Connected. It wasn't without guilt on either's part. In the moment, though, it felt right and protected.

But the feeling wouldn't last.

30

The Santa Anas had finally abated. It was as if the entire city had fallen asleep on a warm summer night and awakened to a moist and dewy fall dawn, just in time for Halloween. The morning had offered the first sweater and jacket weather in months. From city, county, and state employees who were bustling to their appointed jobs, to the prospective jurors arriving for duty, to the vendors who serviced the Monday-through-Friday business of meting out criminal and civil justice, all were picture proof of the ethnic melting pot that was the San Fernando Valley.

For Miles Czajkowski it was an easy morning errand. The mostly horizontal, four-story concrete monolith that capped the east end of the courts plaza was home to the Van Nuys division of the LAPD. So, the walk from his desk to his appointed rendezvous with Judge Jim was little more than a quick stroll and a chance to suck back another Red Bull chased by a filtered Marlboro. It had been an all-nighter for the PD lieutenant. Sugar and Zadeh's Altadena adventure had turned from a fever of texts to an all-out fire drill. By midnight he'd ordered the duo to his Chatsworth home. The trio gathered in Miles's converted garage, a multi-purpose gymnasium and man cave replete with a ping-pong table and twin BarcaLoungers front and center before a curved television screen. After setting up his shaken compatriots with liquor and video game controllers, he quietly sat at his desk and worked the phone for information regarding the dead body on Altadena's Atchison Street. The most important intel remained static: deceased male in the middle of the street; shot twice; California ID with an Armenian last name; no actual suspects; only one suspicious vehicle recalled by a neighbor walking his dog—a dirty white panel van with *Rent Me* emblazoned on the side.

And all was calm.

With Zadeh curled up and sleeping on a stack of foldable exercise mats, Miles and Sugar set out on a pre-dawn commute to the Van Nuys Division. Once there, while Sugar showered and sought out a comfy chair to nap in, Miles thought he'd revisit his growing email list of Hollywood production companies, producers, and even casting directors, and compose a new reminder of his status, experience, and readiness to avail himself as a movie and television technical adviser. In the missive he directed interested parties to a video link of him in various cop roles: uniformed, plainclothes, and even as a hostage negotiator. To the casual observer, the high-definition clip looked more like an amateur actor's audition reel than that of an expert in all matters of policing. Miles was pleased with the three-minute video, watching it for the umpteenth time before attaching it to the email reminders.

It was a productive few hours.

At 7:30 his phone alarm sounded. Miles searched for and found Sugar and poked the exhausted cop awake. He gave Sugar until he'd returned from the men's room to ready himself for their appointed collision with Judge Jim and Lucky Dey.

"Collision?" mumbled Sugar.

"Gotta better description for somethin' you don't know how it's gonna spin out?"

"Asshole. You just described my last twelve hours."

"Need coffee first."

On the short walk to the east tower court building, Sugar was already lagging a step behind.

"Let's do this hand-off shit first, then we get breakfast at Four 'N 20," offered Miles.

"Yeah, yeah. And I'll even pay," agreed Sugar. "But I gotta get some caffeine in me or my head's gonna melt."

Sugar made a forty-five degree cut to the right, beating a new path toward the center of the plaza, where he knew he'd find a man known as Java Juan, a Guatemalan coffee vendor with a mobile kiosk. Miles knew Sugar well enough not to turn a fellow cop's caffeine dependency into a fight. Depending on the length of the coffee queue, the five- to ten-minute delay was tolerable enough— that, and within the few seconds it took for Miles to switch gears, he'd already begun to taste the special sweet chili and cinnamon bite of Java Juan's special *café leche con fuente*.

"You're buyin' my coffee," announced Miles. "Since you're being all generous 'n' shit."

"Whatever," groused Sugar.

"All aboard the Sugar train," jibed Miles, pretending to pull the chain on a steam whistle. "Whooooo, whooooo!"

"You're worse than a hangover."

"All that plus tax, *pardner*."

After only two hours sleep, Johnny B. came to with a grip on his shoulder. Lucky stood over the couch, shaking the teen until his eyes opened.

"What?" asked Johnny B., momentarily lost as to where he was.

"You can either come with or nap it off here."

"Come with who?"

"Me. We talked about this last night."

"Talked about what?"

"The judge," snipped Lucky. "The one who's gonna take care of your problem."

"But can I stay here?" asked Johnny B., still barely awake. "I'm too tired to move."

"Fine. Stay put. Mr. St. George needs anything, you help out, okay?"

"Mister who?" The muscles in Johnny Boy's eyes squeezed his optical nerves into focus. Past Lucky and parked in the corner of the room was a chunk of a man in a motorized wheelchair. Skin black as night. Manicured beard. Strong eyes behind thick horn-rimmed frames. Seated obediently next to him was a large bushy dog of too many mixed breeds to guess.

"Dog's friendly. Name is Hank," said Lucky. "He's friends with my dog, Oprah."

"Think I wanna come with you," switched Johnny B.

In the kitchen, Shia had finished preparing a pile of scrambled eggs and bacon. The incongruity of the woman cooking, an apron defending her freshly pressed Los Angeles Sheriff's uniform, wasn't lost on the teen. He was stuck and staring. Shia knew as much, yet continued to concentrate on keeping the eggs from burning.

"Hope you're hungry," she said.

"You gotta spare charger?" asked Johnny B., his dead mobile phone held up in his ham hock of a mitt.

"Think we gotcha covered, big man," Shia replied sweetly. "With food and your electronic needs."

Johnny B. wolfed back his breakfast plate, asked politely for seconds, and carried a paper plate full of thirds out to the back seat of Shia's Optima.

"Your dad's a racist," volunteered Johnny B. the second he was buckled.

"Why's that?" smiled Shia.

"'Cause all he did was stare at me 'n' Mr. Lucky."

"That 'cause we're white?" From the front passenger seat, Lucky winked over at Shia.

"I'm not white, exactly," defended Johnny B. "I'm Armenian-American."

"You're a stranger in my daddy's house," explained Shia. "He may be a paraplegic, but he still's protective of his baby girl. And that don't make a man racist. Makes him a good daddy."

"My dad's not a good daddy," replied the teen. "He wants me to move to Armenia."

On Shia's six-minute drive to work, her short but usual routine revolved around picking the perfect pair of tunes to play at volume. It was all about setting the mood for the day. Her tastes were eclectic and could fall anywhere between classic rock and recent hip-hop. But recently she'd discovered K-pop, the hyperactive electronic dance sound imported from South Korea. She decided to spin a song just to see Lucky's reaction. It was a girl group called BlackPink and the song was "Boombayah." To Johnny B.'s delight, she cranked the volume before wheeling a ninety-degree turn onto Kester Street. When Shia swiveled her view to collect Lucky's reaction, she found him hunched and distracted, gathering what he could from her right side-view mirror. Then with a sideways look at her, he gestured—four fingers together, horizontal. The same with the other hand, only behind. It was the hand signal for having picked up a tail.

Shia eyeballed her rearview mirror, instantly picking up the nineties-model Accord keeping pace. Though she didn't recognize Lee Chapman's self-described shitmobile, the parrot-faced man behind the steering wheel struck her as familiar.

"Shit, really?" she found herself saying aloud.

"Shit what?" jumped Johnny B., his anxiety piqued.

"I . . . uh," stammered Shia before saving the moment by switching off the music. "I forgot Lucky hates K-pop."

"I was gettin' into it," shifted Johnny B. "But my likes are usually nineties EDM. That's electronic dance music. You like that too?"

Recognizing Lucky didn't want to alarm Johnny B., Shia finger-gestured to her rearview mirror before pointing her thumb at herself and mouthing, *Mine.*

Yours? mimed Lucky for confirmation.

She rolled her eyes and again aimed her manicured right thumb at her breastbone, nodding in the affirmative. It was the same occupied car Lucky remembered parked under the live oak. Anybody could've been inside. The Armenians. LAPD. Instead, it was tweedy little Lee Chapman.

Shia had long suspected the backroom court-sitter had a crush of some kind. At twenty-six, Shia had amassed a manifest of admirers, distant and otherwise. The curse of being born beautiful, her father had often explained. Learn to live with it or become a hermit. Lee Chapman, she'd reasoned, was just the newest man on the stat sheet. Never had she imagined that he'd up his game from fan to stalker. An annoyed sigh escaped her chest with the overwhelming realization that a new wrinkle had become part of her life.

Lee Chapman was going to be another problem for Shia to manage. Once Judge Sollo heard the sad news, she'd most likely act with swiftness. Lee Chapman, whom the judge imagined was *her* biggest fan, would be forever banned from Department J and the Van Nuys court buildings altogether. The only exception to the new rule would be if Lee Chapman the stalker one day returned as Lee Chapman the defendant.

Lee's Honda appeared to keep a safe, four-car-length buffer as Shia zigzagged her way through a grid of tree-lined surface streets, all residential and formerly middle-class. With each block she traveled closer to her destination, the rent and general upkeep decreased and most of the lawns turned from green to brown. Confirming Shia's suspicions, Lee kept up his stalk, turn for turn, finally peeling off to what she presumed was the Sylmar Street public parking structure, which serviced both east and west court buildings. Relieved at last, Shia guided her Optima into a small slotted parking area for Iceland, the warehouse-like ice-skating and hockey center.

"Nice parking space," muttered Lucky, unbuckling and shouldering his door.

"Owner's a fan," agreed Shia.

"Everywhere she goes." Lucky winked at Johnny Boy, who was unplugging his phone from the car's charger.

"Are we here?" asked Johnny B. "This place is for ice-skating. I really hate ice-skating."

"Important safety tip," nicked Shia, stealing one of Lucky's favorite retorts. "Short walk to the courthouse. Promise."

As was his habit, Lucky quick-scanned the topography for anybody who might be watching. Appearance-wise, it was little more than a cool Monday morning. Fall was finally in the air. The entrance to the ice rink was festooned in cheap Halloween decorations, the faux spiderwebs glistening in overnight dew. If anything, the not-so-scary display added some cheer to the dismal and dingy locale. Lucky one-shouldered his backpack, briefly feeling for the shape of the plastic-wrapped pint glass. Somehow, Lucky felt the glass contained more than just Vartan Kasabian's DNA—perhaps the beginning of a way out?

31

Panorama City. 7:43 a.m.

"Ssshhh. *P'aket's zuygvel minch'yev.*" *Shut the fuck up,* hissed Arkady.

Climbing the last steps to the loft were Tavet and Eriq, tired, hyped on Dexedrine tabs, and blathering in their shock over the hard news about Mikayel. They instantly lifted their glassy gazes to Arkady, his bared, gold-capped teeth appearing ready to take a bite out of them. Arkady pointed across the office toward the boss's desk, where Chris Kasabian was seated and expecting silence.

Off Chris's left shoulder was his open laptop, the cast of the screen competing with the burgeoning dawn. Daybreak filtered in through the 360 degrees of windows of his father's third-floor asphalt company office. Chris had been pondering how much more alike he was to brother Johnny B. than anybody had ever realized. Other than the slightest variation in his personal genome, Vartan's first-born might have also been relegated to a life in the back seat. Driven around. Told where to go, how to think, when to take his meds, resigned to never measuring up. But as fate planned it, Chris was the heir apparent—a heartbeat away from taking over the reins of the family crime business. Or as close as his father's escape on a private plane bound for the old country.

The perch overlooked the four-acre equipment yard and beyond, a dead-center stake in the heart of the San Fernando Valley's flatlands. The neighborhood industrial yards were slowly coming to life, the hum of the nearby cement trucks spinning up their barrels with fresh concrete was all that penetrated the quiet. Tavet and Eriq were making themselves comfortable on the corner unit couch. Joining in the vigil were more of the most trusted musclemen: Vasrik, Sark, and Arkady, a forty-year-old mob veteran. They sipped on coffees or hot tea, slumped or paced, wordless as the boss-in-waiting sat at his laptop's screen, keeping tabs on all his immediate family but for one.

Since the technology had been available, a younger Chris had surreptitiously installed GPS tracking apps on his mother's, father's, sister's, and brother's mobile phones. The self-professed tech wizard of the clan, Chris put himself in charge of all upgrades. Thus any new phone came through his hands. And before he delivered it, he'd made certain the tracking was intact and working. What began as a means to track his siblings' comings and goings had dissolved into a comfort zone feeding his self-diagnosed obsessive-compulsive disorder. There'd even been nights at home, when he couldn't sleep, that Chris would turn to his phone screen and punch up the geo-location app just to be soothed by the visual image of all his immediate family residing inside of the walls of their Glendale fortress. Then he'd pull up a digital record of their individual movements of the day. Times. Addresses. It was like a warm blanket.

The sun pierced a stake of light through the east-facing windows. As Chris raised a hand to cut the glare, his computer pinged. Before that moment, there'd only been four family icons on the screen map of Los Angeles—father, mother, and sister, with Chris at ground zero. Now a fifth icon had popped into play, sprouting from the north side of Sherman Oaks. In the center of the icon, a scruffy pic snapped years before of Johnny B. in full grin on Christmas morning. Most every time Chris saw the photo, he was gladly sucked back to the micro-moment he'd captured his little brother, unaware and without his usual brooding expression.

Chris broke the silence when he speed-dialed his sister.

"Got him," Chris said. "He's in Sherman Oaks. We're getting our move on right now."

"I'm in Hollywood," replied Lizzy, her voice groggy but on point.

I know you're in Hollywood. Chris bit his tongue. Lizzy would've stuck an ice pick in his ear if she knew he was surreptitiously tracking her movements.

"What's the address?" asked Lizzy.

"Already sent it to you," said Chris.

"Wait for me, will ya? Please?"

"Just gonna get us within range," assured Chris. "I need you to be the closer on this."

That much was agreed upon. When it came to talking Johnny B. out of a panic state, Lizzy had a knack. A sister's gift. If their diminished brother was still tied to Lucky Dey, she was going to be the best of all lures.

With a circling wave of his arm, the crew was on their feet and surging down the stairs, Chris at the lead. Along with the footfalls came the familiar strains of weapons being readied—safeties engaged and chambers checked, locked, loaded, and prepared to take back what was theirs.

Johnny B.

Judge Jim was well aware of the lawyer jokes passed around by the county sheriffs who worked the criminal courts building. As a cop, he'd told his share and had continued to collect them as he'd climbed his way to the top of the legal ladder. His favorite had a personal spin. It regarded the secured attorney parking in the Sylvan Street parking structure. The ground floor, easiest to access, was reserved for the lawyers, judges, prosecutors, and criminal defense and civil trial attorneys.

Question: What do you call an earthquake that pancakes the Sylvan Parking structure, killing all the lawyers inside?

Answer: A very good start.

As the gate's mechanical arm lifted, so did the paw of the sheriff's deputy assigned to the guard booth. Judge Jim was easily recognized by most of the sheriffs on security rotation; if not by his face and familiar morning smile coinciding with his hands-on-the-steering-wheel three-fingered wave, then by his vehicles and their quickly identifiable license plates. The vintage Ferrari was the easiest to spot, followed by his Cadillac Escalade—OVRULED. And then there was his second wife's Corvette—MRSHNOR. But Judge Jim had just dropped the damaged Ferrari off at a nearby body shop, so on that Monday morning he was driving a Ford Focus from Enterprise Rent-a-Car. The judge had to wait until his driver's window was alongside the guard booth before he was recognized.

"Sorry, Judge," said the extra-large lady deputy, appearing so comfortable on her padded stool that Judge Jim had no doubt she'd be hard-pressed to do any more than radio in a suspected threat. "Didn't recognize you in that lil' thing."

"You know what they say about men driving small cars?" the judge asked.

"Don't think I wanna know the answer to that one, sir." The lady deputy raised her eyebrows. "Get us both in big trouble."

Judge Jim double-raised his eyebrows in reply and gassed the compact rental into the garage. Because he didn't own the vehicle, he didn't feel the need to seek out a single one of his favorite parking spaces—those with the most swinging door room and least likely of earning a ding in his precious paint. As he climbed out of the car he felt a mix of lightness and trepidation. It was his practice not to bring home his work on weekends, entering each Monday with a clean slate. He carried nothing with him, no briefcase or backpack, and found equal enjoyment in counting off the number of attorneys he encountered in the garage emptying their trunks of legal files and assembling the collapsible hand trucks they utilized to haul their office with them.

Good morning, your Honor, they'd call out, voices echoing off the million pounds of concrete slab just waiting for a seven-point-plus shaker to come along and squish them into a gooey pulp. All court commuters, including Judge Jim, aimed for the northwest corner of structure, where the primary common stairwell fed the jurors, bailiffs, civil servants, and observers like Lee Chapman into a blended judicial river of day laborers streaming toward the plaza.

Lee was hurrying down the steps, not so deftly slipping past some of the slower movers in hopes of catching up to Shia. If he was lucky and made it through the security line in short order, he might even manage a ride up the elevator with her. Despite the odds against such a close encounter, the prospect of it would normally leave him breathless with anticipation. But on Halloween Monday, he found himself breathless with fear. She'd traveled to work with two passengers—the cop and his awkward young friend. Who were they to her and what did they mean? What is it? he kept asking himself. Bring a cop and a retard to work day? Normally, his joke might've made him laugh. Instead it was replaying in another endless loop. Like when he couldn't stop with that third-person singsong, *He didn't wanna do it. He didn't wanna do it.*

At the bottom of the stairwell, Lee didn't see the man entering the flow from the structure's ground floor. Lee's speedy descent didn't mix with the man's longer strides coming in from the left. Off-kilter as he surged onto the walkway, Lee thumped the taller man hard, not unlike a body check in ice hockey.

"What the—" exclaimed Judge Jim.

"Excuse yourself!" spat Lee, his tweedy jacket and porkpie hat distinguishing himself as familiar to the judge. And off Lee ran in a slalom pattern, using the slower court workers as if they were his downhill gates.

"Tweedy little turd," mumbled Judge Jim, unconsciously brushing himself before regaining his step and marking the time with his watch. 8:03 a.m. By his account, the perpetually prompt Lucky Dey should already be waiting for their meet-up at the non-public security entrance at the rear of the criminal courts building. By now, he reasoned, Miles should also have arrived to keep the rogue deputy in check. If there was something of the DNA variety to pass off, the judge hoped Miles would convince Lucky to follow the recommended protocol. The face-off with Lucky handing over whatever the hell he had had the air of something arch. The idea of Lucky joining the ranks of Judge Jim's justice league had begun to smell like ill-conceived rot. The untamed deputy was a liability and needed to be put down. Permanently.

Out of both his and my misery.

"He's moving," relayed Chris over the phone. "Northwest. Heading into Van Nuys."

"You better wait there for me," warned Lizzy, driving in a borrowed Fiat and weaving between cars on the Hollywood Freeway. She held her cell phone to her ear. Her Peet's hot coffee in a large to-go cup was cradled between her legs, a brake stomp away from a painful accident.

"Wait where? I don't have a clue where they're going yet!" argued Chris.

"Well, when you do I'm sayin' wait!" barked Lizzy. "Don't want you to spook him."

"Not gonna spook shit."

"He sees Arkady and the rest of 'em, he's gonna think they're there to pack him up for Armenia!"

"Wait a sec," said Chris. The automatic limiter on his end of the phone amplified the surrounding sounds. Lizzy heard the squeaking brakes and the rumble of a diesel truck outside her brother's car. "Think he stopped someplace."

"Where?"

"Is that Iceland?" he asked a nearby compatriot.

"*Ayo*," replied Arkady. *Yeah.*

"Did you say Iceland?"

"Skating place. Yeah."

"J. B. is going ice-skating?"

"Still moving," said Chris. "Crossing Delano."

"Fuck!" she cried.

"What?" asked Chris.

"Do you know where he is?"

"I just told you. Crossing Delano and—"

"Headed to the courthouse!" busted Lizzy. "That's the fucking court there! LAPD too. Van Nuys division!"

"Aw, fuck."

"I'm there in five minutes! You wait for me, okay?"

"Can only do what I can."

Lizzy hung up and dropped the phone into the passenger seat, only to have it bounce into the channel between the seat and the door.

"Damn it," she heaved, eyes filling with tears. She adjusted her rearview mirror, discovering her mascara had been running. She already *had* been crying. For how long? she wondered. Her normally heavy eyeliner was bleeding black onto her vampire-white cheeks.

At least I look ready for Halloween, she decided. I can go under the guise of "Hell Hath No Fury."

The judges' entrance to the courthouse was at the rear of the building. With its nondescript set of tinted glass doors it looked like an emergency fire exit rather than a private entry. The unmarked doors bore an outdated magnetic-key-card lock. Security was comprised of a single camera with a fish-eye lens that covered the doors as well as the half basketball court–sized patio of pebbled aggregate concrete. Deciduous dogwoods flanked the space, the big leaves of the non-native trees not yet slipped into their fall colors. The patio offered a pair of rusted, round outdoor tables with attached benches, generally occupied later in the day by smokers or lunch-time brown-baggers seeking some midday sun.

On days when the key-card lock was down for repair—a

chronic issue—a sheriff's deputy was pulled from the security gauntlet at the building's public entrance to man the back doors.

Such was the case on that Monday morning.

Deputy Delano Flores, a sturdy, jowly faced local, was named after the notorious Van Nuys street on which he was born and raised. Delano Street was famous for being both rife with drug dealing and gangbanging even though it was just three short blocks from the Valley's seat of justice, not to mention the uniform-heavy Van Nuys Division of the LAPD. And though Flores had eventually chosen to raise his family in the city of Burbank, he thought it poetic that his job had returned him only a stone's throw from home. Flores's wife and mother to their three young children worried that the duty might be more prophetic than poetic, kissing her husband goodbye with a daily reminder: "Please wear your body armor."

But body armor was hot. The extra layer trapped the sweat against the skin and gave Flores an irritating rash. So, by noon on most workdays, he would excuse himself to the men's room to strip and change his T-shirt. On that Monday he'd remembered his Kevlar vest, yet fully forgotten the extra T-shirt, which was why he was first to volunteer for the backdoor post. The duty lacked obvious danger, as the only chore was to interface with sitting judges. Or so he rationalized in his disregard for department protocol.

Through the morning glare filtering through his wraparound sunglasses, Flores spotted a trio peeling off from the morning throng, resetting their course directly toward his post. Cupping his eyes, he was able to single out the lithe strides of Deputy Shia St. George. Amongst the courthouse corps, she was as famous for her stunner looks as for her unavailability. Single cops were known to complain of her constant rebuffs while keeping hope alive that she'd return their attention someday.

Thank Jesus I'm married, thought Flores.

"Morning, Deputy," called out Shia.

"Back atcha," returned Flores, disarmed by her smile. "Who's your friendlies?"

Shia introduced Lucky and Johnny B. Flores shook hands with the pair, noting Johnny's tepid grip and insecure posture.

"What brings you to the back door?" asked Flores.

"Meet-up with Judge Peralta," answered Shia. "X marks the spot."

"On approach," gestured Flores with a nod to the southeast.

Lucky twisted ninety degrees at the waist. There was a pinch in his ribs and he silently cursed himself for forgetting to dose up on anti-inflammatories. Back at the Altadena bungalow, he'd left behind a half bottle of prednisone. *Probably right next to my cell phone*, annoyed Lucky. Whatever happened with the tête-à-tête with the judge, Lucky resolved to make a beeline to Bel-Air for a much-needed family reunification. Gonzo was sure to be apoplectic over his hours of incommunicado.

First reading Judge Jim's sidearm wave, Lucky zeroed in on the man's face, seeking more than just recognition. Lucky had brought a total stranger, the boy in question, as well as Shia. But the quizzical look on the judge pertained more to who wasn't there. The tall jurist, his white crown of hair whipping up in a gust of wind, was searching further left and right of the small gathering at the court building's rear door. It was, in Lucky's view, an indication that the judge was expecting others. *Miles*, thought Lucky. *Or Sugar Freeman. Or both.* It seemed Judge Jim was caught unprepared for what was about to transpire.

Thus they began with small talk.

"You brought Deputy St. George," said the judge. "What a great way to start my Monday."

"How are you, your Honor?" greeted Shia. "You know Deputy Dey, of course."

"Damn right, I know Lucky," said the judge with a slap to Lucky's shoulder.

"This is Johnny Kasabian," introduced Lucky. "Johnny? Meet the Honorable Jaime Peralta."

"Hi," said Johnny B. weakly. "You the judge who's gonna help me?"

"I'm here to help *everybody*," acknowledged Judge Jim before stalling. "Delano. Is the card reader on the fritz again?"

"'Fraid so, sir," replied Flores.

"Wife know you're not wearing Kevlar?" spun the judge.

"Please don't rat me out, your Honor," quipped Flores. "That shit gets ugly underneath. Anyway, who's gonna shoot me today *other* than my wife? And she's not here."

"Least as far as you know," returned the judge.

"That would be a shit show nobody wants to witness," agreed Flores.

The punch line gleaned a polite laugh from all but Johnny B., who had begun to rock from side to side like a little boy holding a full bladder.

Lucky nudged the judge with his backpack and feinted toward the double doors. Once again, Judge Jim swept the visible landscape for more familiar faces and then nodded in agreement. His mouth turned down in visible disappointment.

"You mind?" the judge asked Flores, who instantly took a step forward and unlocked the doors. Judge Jim led the way. Lucky motioned for Shia and Johnny B. to hang back.

They stood in a long, thin corridor that ended with a second glass door that led to the security gauntlet for the public entry. The moment the door swung shut and they were alone, Lucky unslung the backpack and began digging for the pint glass.

"You oughta know this is not how I do—"

Lucky stuffed the cling-wrapped tumbler into Judge Jim's hands.

"You asked for it, I delivered. Vartan Kasabian's DNA in a glass. Outside there? That's his boy. Your turn to hold up your end of the bargain."

"Done," shrugged Judge Jim, acting like all was hunky-dory despite his obvious lack of comfort. "Gotta ask. What's Deputy Hot Stuff have to do with our business?"

"Not a thing."

"Then why is she—" Past Lucky and through the smoked

glass, Judge Jim picked out Miles and Sugar circling onto the patio. "Whadda you know. There's Miles. Told you before, this DNA stuff is his bailiwick."

"I said just you and me."

"And so it was. I hope you're grateful." Judge Jim slipped past Lucky and pushed the door open, fully intending to wave Miles and Sugar inside. But then he froze at what he noticed beyond his blue-uniformed pals. Three more men in black leather jackets were entering the patio from the sidewalk. None appeared the least bit lost.

Instinct followed. Human nature. From Shia to Flores to Miles to Sugar to Johnny B. himself, each spontaneously tracked the path of Judge Jim's eyes. As if choreographed, their heads turned in unison toward the men in leather jackets. Johnny B. discovered the face of his brother.

"Chris?" he whispered.

"What's up, buddy?" called Chris, forcing a smile to cover up the sudden pit in his stomach. Chris's eyes kept swerving from his brother to the two LAPD uniforms just to his left.

"No, no, no!" replied Johnny B., his body catching up to the fear exploding in his brain. He began to backpedal. "I'm not going there!"

"Nobody's going anywhere!" assured Chris, hands up, fingers waving.

"Judge?" called out Miles, fingertips moving to his holstered pistol.

From in the hallway, the unfolding drama revealed itself to Lucky in slow motion. The morning sun blazed through the open door. Through its closed mate everything was dark and harder to make out. Both Miles and Sugar automatically pivoted toward the three Armenians, the pair to the right of Chris with hands pulling at their coats. Johnny B. was already in reverse. After five months' training under Lucky Dey, Shia flipped on like a light switch. She squared herself, putting the arch of her hand to the butt of her service pistol while unhitching the safety lever on her retention holster. Only friendly Flores, feet from the open door, appeared flat-footed and without his synapses fully engaged.

In a single maneuver, Lucky dropped his backpack and unskinned the .45 bootlegged against his right thigh. As he stepped by the judge and out onto the patio, his first instinct was to diffuse the skyrocketing tension. He raised his left arm high, palm open.

"S'all good here!" called out Lucky in an attempt for calm.

"NOT GOING TO ARMENIA!" screamed Johnny B., tripping so hard into Flores that the deputy threw two arms around the big teen in a bear hug. The teen thrashed, requiring Flores to wrestle him up against the building.

"Chris! It's cool, it's cool!" pleaded Lucky, his eyes zeroed in on the hands moving inside those leather jackets.

"You know my brother!" returned Chris. "Tell the cop he's gotta let go!"

Wheeling to address Flores, Lucky thrust a hand forward.

"S'okay, Deputy," cooled Lucky. "Johnny. He's gonna let you go."

Ears plugged and eyes shut from feral fear, Johnny B. squealed and wrenched at his binds, his arms pinned to his sides in the deputy's vise of a hug. The open door and adjacent wall made a convex corner of sorts, accumulating the sounds and bouncing them on top of each other. Flores heard little more than the pitch of Johnny B.'s screams.

"Take your fuckin' hands off my brother!" bit a new voice. It was Lizzy's. The petite bottle-blonde in fresh pigtails and dripping mascara had somehow appeared from nowhere, slipping into the patio from the dogwoods. Her giant purse was slung across her like a bandolier, minus that Glock 26, which was in her hand, cocked to two o'clock.

Johnny B. saw the gun and froze, his eyes as white as marbles. The heavy teen's knees gave way. His body slumped. The dead weight of Johnny B. quickly slithered from Flores's arms, leaving him exposed against the wall, broad at the chest and wearing no Kevlar.

Lizzy didn't know why she squeezed the trigger. Perhaps it was because she still saw the deputy as a threat. Perhaps it was that she was tired of her brother taking the brunt of everything.

Perhaps it was her built-up rage.

Yet pull the trigger she did, aiming for the widest stretch where the deputy's buttoned shirt pulled across his torso. The first bullet was a kill shot, penetrating Flores's unprotected sternum and severing his aorta. The projectile exited his back, painting the concrete wall in bright, aerated blood.

Not waiting for the deputy to fall, Lizzy continued left, pulling the trigger as fast as she could, swinging hot lead in an arc toward the double doors and Judge Jim. Lucky pivoted and hooked the judge behind the one closed door as slugs snapped across the bullet-resistant glass. Into Lizzy's periphery came Shia, who was pulling her weapon and traversing along the same axis as Lizzy's killer swing. Lizzy would've kept firing had a picture not stuck in her brain. It was the man at the door, with the bald crown and wild white hair.

The half-price Babka man?

Why was he there and did she just shoot him? Lizzy's odd pause left her momentarily lost and searching the insides of her eyelids instead of the landscape. She heard her name.

"Goddamnit, Lizzy!!!"

It was Chris yelling—in a berating tone, not unlike her father. She felt a brief impulse to twist and shoot at the voice—a fevered desire to finish off her loudmouth father. Her eyes opened, her gaze lifting further left. She saw Tavet crouched and scurrying away while Arkady was standing his place, turned to the side in silhouette, unleashing his full clip. Fire flared from Arkady's pistol and spent powder filled the air. Lizzy couldn't pick out her older brother. Was he dead? Had he fallen already? To her right, she saw a uniformed body drop. Slapping the sidewalk. Were there one or two LAPD? Lizzy couldn't remember. Her head felt foggy, a permanent whistle stuck in her ears. Then as she forced her eyes to find another target—anything or anyone—on which to draw a bead, she saw the muzzle of a pistol rising, behind it a Los Angeles sheriff's deputy, skin like ebony, a model's cheekbones, eyes zeroed back at her.

Lizzy squeezed the trigger.

32

On that morning, the security line was remarkably short, even though the squad of deputies working the metal detectors and X-ray machine appeared to be shy one man. By Lee's quick count, there were only eleven people in line—the normal everyday civil employees and attorneys—all queued up for their electronic frisking.

"No notebook today?" asked Jerome, a towering deputy who was usually relegated to standing sentry versus working the paddle on the other side of the metal detector. Aside from his height, Jerome stood out for being the only deputy not to call Lee Mr. Red Book to his face.

"Oh, man," realized Lee. "Musta left it . . . in the car . . . whatever. Get it at lunch."

"Keepin' it all up here?" Jerome tapped an index finger to his razor-smooth temple.

"Where's Delano?" asked Lee, using the obviously missing deputy as his excuse to manically scan the lobby in hopes his eyes might land on Shia.

"Workin' the back door—" began Jerome before dropping the wand at the sound of gunshots.

It was the snapping sounds, high-pitched with an echo, that caught all four deputies unaware yet prepared by their training. Their necks instinctively twisted every which way in an immediate and urgent search for a potential mass shooter.

Lee, on the other hand, didn't have to search. At the time the gunfire started, he'd already spotted Shia. She was at end of that long corridor that fed to the rear door where the judges entered. Though two men were partially obstructing his view, Lee found his obsession spotlit in the eight-in-the-morning sunshine. Not quite in focus, but still recognizable. Lee began his run toward the gunfire.

Toward *her*.

As Lee approached that pair of tinted doors, one of them swung shut. A man was crouched behind it, seeking cover. Lee heard shouts from behind. Warnings to take cover. Fast and hard footfalls on his heels. Yet *she* was out there. *In mortal danger*. Who better to save her but him? He arrived at the door, shocked to recognize Judge Peralta, on his knees with an elbow hooked over the release bar, as the man cowering behind the bulletproof glass. The laminated glass was marred with three hockey puck–sized bullet strikes, turning what had been see-through into opaque saucers. Lee wanted to kick at the judge to let go of the door. His eyes screwed past the glass to the picture outside. He saw one body down already while another buckled. Two others scrambled to escape. A third figure wearing a leather jacket had a pistol raised, calmly leveled, squeezing successive muzzle bursts like it was target practice.

And there she was: Shia. Front and center beyond the bullet-proof glass. Lee cried, "No!" It wasn't much more than a helpless

whimper, drowned by nearby shouts from the three deputies rushing up behind him. He was forced to the floor. He felt the rush
of the door opening and the crunch of waffle-iron soles climbing
over him.

Lucky was acting on remote. His plea for calm had lasted no more
than ten or fifteen seconds before the bottle-blonde in the braided
pigtails had appeared from behind the dogwood trees and opened
fire. He hadn't a flicker who she was. For all Lucky knew, she was
Flores's wife, there to prove the sweaty bastard wrong for having
forgone his protective body armor.

After wrangling Judge Jim behind the protective door, Lucky
had glanced right to spot the shooter—just in time to watch a bullet smack the laminated glass as the plastic and silicon compound
deformed around the projectile, stopping it a mere two inches
from the bridge of his oft-broken nose. Once the shooter continued on her arc toward Shia, Lucky reversed direction, exhumed
himself from behind the door, and began to train his weapon. The
pigtailed shooter was to his left at ten o'clock, her swing moving
away from him. Shia had already freed her service pistol in defense.
And on the other side of her, thirty feet and in full flame, was one
of the muscle-heads Lucky remembered from Denny's. The man
had already gunned down Miles and had re-jiggered his aim for
Sugar. The thick black cop had tugged his gun, but his shoulders
were already forward as if he'd been struck dead center.

Him, said the .45 in Lucky's hand, as if the pistol had chosen
the target instead of its owner. Arkady was on the other side of
Shia, so Lucky jerked right and squeezed. The .45 erupted. The
escaping slug spiraled and hissed merely inches by Shia's head and
struck Arkady in the neck. A pink mist issued, followed by an
arterial spray with Arkady pulling his trigger twice more before he
buckled at the knees and surrendered to gravity. Meanwhile, Sugar
stumbled backwards and flopped down on the patio. Through his
gunsight Lucky picked out Chris and the other hood scrambling
away—one to the left, the other to the right.

Last was Shia and the pigtailed shooter. Lucky realized he'd let his weapon's sight choose his first target—Arkady—in lieu of offering Shia a first defense. From the jump it had been a breathtakingly confusing situation. First Johnny B. bolting from his brother only to get wrapped up in Flores's bearish grasp. Then his screaming fit to be let go. Next had come the appearance of the pigtailed shooter. The first burst of gunfire. Saving the judge. Taking out the leather coat with the pistol. Then last had been Shia—his former trainee—his rookie girl.

Why was she last?

And so it was that a single gunshot ended the conflagration. The last strike, a dirty exclamation point in a ten-second battle royale. Geographically speaking, Shia had been dead center in the conflict—an always dangerous hurricane eye of confusion. It was that precise circumstance Lucky had often warned her about. *Don't get your feet stuck in a crossfire. At the sound of the very first shot,* he'd said, *choose a direction. Any direction. Either toward the gunfire or away, just don't get trapped in the fog.* Shia clearly hadn't remembered or been able to access her training. The shooter had released a stream of bullets in an arc moving in her direction. Behind Shia and to her right had been more muzzle pops, splitting the morning air. Her right hand had released her weapon from the holster. She had drawn down on the pigtailed shooter, sighting the target with her eyes and lifting her .40-cal into position when she had seen Pigtail's muzzle freeze in her direction. Fifteen feet was all that lay between the two women.

I'm dead, were the words that had quick-played inside Shia's brain. *So, fuck it, bitch. Die and go down shooting.*

Shia pulled her trigger, releasing successive shots and letting the recoil elevate her aim. Her first bullet spanked the dirt just beyond the pigtailed shooter's hips. The next pierced the girl's yellow varsity-style jacket just below the letter. The third and last creased the part in her bottle-blonde locks before burrowing through the top of her skull. The air behind Shia's target turned pink with mist as her legs gave and she crumpled amongst the few fallen dogwood leaves.

Lucky stared for a minor beat. Shia was alive and untouched, mannequin-like, in a shooting stance. Academy perfect. She moved only when she heard the most bloodcurdling of screams from Johnny B.

Having slid from Flores's grip seconds before his sister shot the deputy, Johnny B. had watched the rest of the ugliness unfold from a sideways perspective, his left cheek pressed to the dusty concrete. What he'd seen was cockeyed and like a bad dream. He released a belly-shouting screech when he saw his sister fall. There was no doubt of her condition. The teen had seen the top of his sister's scalp dislodge when the final bullet struck. Johnny B.'s legs were pulled up to his chest in a fetal ball, his mouth wide and tongue retracted, his body heaving in the most painful wail.

The deputies from the security gauntlet broke past the door, guns thrust, ready to join a fight that had already ended. They spread out across the back patio in a slow-motion deployment, late to the party and calling for cleanup. As Lucky eased up on Shia, who appeared transfixed on Johnny B.'s painful lament, he gently touched her, one hand on her back, the other guiding her pistol back into her holster.

"What just happened?" she uttered.

"Another shit show," answered Lucky. "And we're right in the middle of it."

At first inconsolable, Johnny B. soon shifted into a catatonic lump, refusing to move off the four square feet of concrete where he sat cross-legged, rocking and unwilling to communicate, let alone retreat, fixed on his sister's dead body. Unable to process the crime scene until Johnny B. had been removed, LAPD had summoned a city PMRT—Psychiatric Mobile Response Team—and the teen had been put on a 5150 mental health hold for seventy-two hours at the West Valley Mental Health Center in nearby Canoga Park.

Anti-terrorism protocols demanded the criminal courthouse be shut down for the day. But for necessary personnel, the building was evacuated and swept by the Sheriff's Department Counter

Terrorism Unit. Bomb-sniffing dogs were deployed. All witnesses to the crime were walked over to the LAPD's Van Nuys Bureau. This included Lucky, Shia, Judge Jim, and Sugar, who'd suffered only a pair of bruising gunshots to his body armor. Divided and left to stew in individual interrogation rooms, they were all interviewed and re-interviewed by LAPD detectives with Deputies Dey and St. George asked to make both verbal and written statements to visiting sheriff's investigators. Both their weapons were bagged as evidence for the formal inquest that follows all deputy-involved shootings.

Lucky, his arms crossed and feet up on the gray metal table in a room no bigger than the average jail cell, dutifully recounted the entire tale, excising any and all information regarding Judge Jim Peralta's vigilante squad or his meet-ups with Vaz Kasabian. As Lucky carefully retold it, he'd encountered John Kasabian during the investigation of a deadly Woodland Hills car accident that he'd done as a favor to Undersheriff Paul McGill. The troubled young man, in fear of his parents sending him to Armenia, had sought him out. On their way to plead for advice from his friend, Judge Jim Peralta, Johnny B.'s family intervened, leading to the bloody shootout.

It was all a crock of hooey.

Though Lucky fully expected Judge Jim and Shia and Sugar to confirm his tale—their motives being self-preservation from Judge Jim, and sheer loyalty from Shia—he knew any follow-up investigation would more than likely lead to suspicions of some deeper corrupted nexus. With that depressing conclusion, Lucky sincerely doubted his cop career would survive. *So be it*, he continually repeated to himself. He'd always known the dark day would arrive, either due to his own undoing or untimely death. He'd been on borrowed time since his days at Lennox and surviving that .25-caliber bullet to the back of his impossibly hard head.

Whatever the result, Lucky was still making moves in his mind. Four LAPD detectives took turns with him, followed by two Los Angeles Sheriff's investigators and then fifteen minutes with a rep from ALADS, the union covering all L.A. County deputies. He answered each of their questions in a rote monotone, all while playing out the endless strings of potential outcomes, not a single one in regard to his personal or career safety. Chris had been at the scene, clearly there to corral his little brother. The pigtailed dead girl must've been the middle sister. How and what would Vartan Kasabian's reaction be to the bloody event? To flee? To strike back in revenge? Or to hunker down behind layers of lawyers? The answer could've been a mash-up of all three or none of the above.

Then there was Judge Jim and how he might reply. Though Miles was dead, Sugar Freeman remained in play. That, and how many others were connected to their vigilante cabal? The unknowns were endless and acting without more information might prove more calamitous than the violence he'd just survived.

Survived? Or created?

News vans had already descended onto the courthouse plaza. Cameras were sure to be aimed in every which direction, hoping to catch an exclusive live snippet to feed the crime-loving masses. One glance out a third-floor window of the Van Nuys Division had sent Lucky to the opposite side of the building and down a northeast corner stairwell. He followed the signs to the motor yard and slipped out a gate. All he carried with him was Johnny B.'s cell phone.

While wrestling with Flores, the troubled teen's mobile phone had accidentally fallen onto the pavement. In the confusion following the gun battle, Lucky had scooped the device before the crime scene could be locked down and photographed, coolly pocketing it as if it were his. Nobody and nothing saw him but for the video camera above the rear security door, another problem Lucky couldn't control. He added it to the ever-evolving fractious list.

Lucky kept an even but quick pace as he hurried on foot east from the courts plaza into a grid of fifties-era streets practically indistinguishable from any other lower-middle-class neighborhood in L.A. Watts. Compton. Panorama City. Van Nuys. Those flatland communities were populated by tiny single-family homes faced in stucco or paint-needy clapboard. Interchangeable, thought Lucky. Humble. Homey. Miles and miles of sidewalks, buckled by the roots of old-growth trees seeking shallow water, fronted the residential swaths, a gentrification wave away from pushing the black, Hispanic, and poor white classes further into the county's outer rings. Lucky, who'd always felt more at home where the cars were rusty and the street numbers on the curbs too faded to decipher, worried more about what Gonzo would think of what he had planned than what he had just done.

"I'm looking for Emery," said Lucky to the fifth operator he'd connected with. He'd recalled the name of the telecom firm who employed his former tryst buddy, or at least the letters it was known by. FNW. Utilizing the little battery life left on Johnny B.'s phone, he'd been handed off from one department operator to the next in search of the comic-tattooed girl. "Emery. Sorry. Never got her last name. But promise she knows me. My name's Lucky."

He had hoofed nearly a mile before he finally connected with her. A helpful colleague had pulled her out of a tech meeting. Emery was quick to call him back from her mobile, keenly avoiding any corporate ears.

"You want me to run down *another* number?" she asked. "Twice in a week, Luck. If this doesn't earn me a visit from you, I don't know what does."

"That supposes I survive the week," he deadpanned. The first number she'd run had been Johnny B.'s. Now Lucky wanted to crack brother Chris Kasabian's phone. At least, Lucky suspected it was Chris's. On the device it was listed as "CK" and appeared to have been dialed copious times. "Seriously. What can you do for me?"

"What do you need?"

"Track it for me like last time?"

"If it's not encrypted, I can get you practically anything off the phone."

"Without risking jail?"

"Sounds like you're risking way worse," she jibed. "Gimme the digits."

Within a minute, the voice on the other end of the phone had geo-located the cell number.

"Currently in Glendale," said Emery. "On the move, so the user is in a car."

"Which direction?"

"I don't have time to turn-by-turn you like I did last time. But looks like the user's gobbling data. If it's a GPS program like Google or Waze, maybe I can see where they're going."

"You can do that?"

"You have no idea what we can do. Just say there's no such thing anymore as privacy. Least digitally speaking."

Lucky heard Emery firing off expert strokes on her keyboard. It sounded like rat feet running across a cardboard bridge. In a matter of seconds she'd accessed the phone's mapping program and was sending screenshots to Johnny B.'s device. Lucky stopped walking and stepped under the nearest tree to cut the glare on the screen. He wanted to be certain of what he was reading in the turn-by-turn instructions.

"This is in real time?" he asked Emery.

"By the second," she said. "Wherever they're headed, by the app's estimation, you got forty-two minutes to get there."

33

Altadena. 3:11 p.m.

Gonzo had insisted. This in spite of Conrad's polite protestations that she, along with Karrie and Travis, remain safe inside the walls of his Bel-Air compound. But too much had happened since the night before. Though Gonzo had finally received confirmation that the dead body dropped on their street was a departed soul other than Lucky, the morning's multiple shootings at the Van Nuys courthouse had taken over so much of the local media bandwidth that names had begun to leak, Lucky's included. Without even a phone call from him to assuage her worries, Gonzo had turned full commando, demanding Conrad ferry them back to Altadena or else they'd order up a taxicab.

The Mercedes stretch limo was parked at the curb in front of the bungalow, the car's rear door dutifully held open by Conrad's uniformed driver. Karrie was already in the driveway, wondering who owned the black Shelby Mustang. Travis, still starry-eyed from his less-than-twenty-four-hours of the luxe life, briefly imagined the muscle car was some kind of gift from the billionaire.

"Nothin' to do with you, Trav," said Gonzo, popping her son's balloon before peering back into the limo. "Connie? I'm very grateful. You're a good friend. But you understand."

"I was married once," was all Conrad cared to muster.

His reply was a dissatisfying answer to a question Gonzo hadn't asked. She left it there and turned up the short path to the bungalow. Despite the strange black car in the driveway, Gonzo felt safe enough. Parked across the street was an L.A. Sheriff's black-and-white with two armed deputies, the short-term protection on loan as a favor from the Altadena station's captain. But Gonzo's sense of security lasted for only six strides. The front door to the bungalow, though appearing shut, was unlatched, unlocked, and completely unfettered. With a cautious push of her fingertips, the door swung inward. She immediately saw the deadbolt's splintered receiver. Before she could put out an arm, Travis rushed by her in the anxious need to reconnect with his Xbox.

"Travis, no—" began Gonzo, having only just spied the blood drops in the entryway.

Then the boy screamed the poor dog's name. *Oprah!* His howl as pained as a puppy's. Gonzo rushed to her son, gathering him in her arms and turning him toward the dining room. In doing so, she'd missed Karrie, who had been on her heels until Travis's scream. Oprah lay dead across the corridor, her blood pooled and sticky. Unlike Travis, Karrie didn't react in shock or even horror. Her reaction was calm as she showed empathy for the animal by squatting next to the big mutt and laying a hand on her ribcage to see if she was breathing. But the dog was already stiffening. Despite the onset of rigor mortis, Oprah's black coat remained soft to the touch. Karrie gripped a handful of the mutt's hair as a last touch.

"Karrie?" warned Gonzo. "Step back. We don't know what happened here. Could be a crime scene."

"Lucky's alive," replied Karrie. "We know that much. What else can be wrong except for poor Oprah?"

"Goddamnit!" barked Gonzo. "Take Travis outside and let me clear the house!"

Karrie's view swung to Gonzo. A glint of afternoon sun highlighted the pistol in her hand.

"You were the one who wanted to come home," muted Karrie before rising to guide Travis back through the front door. "We shoulda listened to Lucky and stayed at Conrad's."

A phone sounded with a familiar tinny tune by R.E.M. "It's the End of the World as We Know It."

Shit, thought Gonzo. Lucky's phone. He didn't have it. He hadn't been home. That explained something. But not close to everything. Not near close.

How could things have gone so sideways so very fast? Chris Kasabian couldn't help but berate himself, every lash of his own mental whip twice as painful as the diarrhea of anger spewing from the man in the passenger seat. His father. Vartan. Vaz.

The BHA.

"I'd take you with me but this is your mess now," blamed Vaz. "Your shitferbrains brother started it. And yes. I might've made it worse trying to fix it the way I did. But you? You poured gasoline and lit a goddamn match."

Chris wanted to argue. But Lizzy. *She* brought the gun. *She* started shooting. Despite the excuse, facts were facts. In the very few hours since Chris had taken charge of the family business, a position barely ceded him by his father, he'd somehow managed to grease the pole that slid the entire family into an impossible-to-escape tub of feces. Lizzy was dead, Johnny B. was out of reach, and his mother was left inconsolable with shock and grief, while Chris was in charge of was chauffeuring his father to Van Nuys Municipal Airport. There, a rented jet was fuelling, the crew en route. Part of Chris wanted to climb aboard with his father and escape a certain and harsh investigation. Another part of him wanted to rewind the last twenty-four hours, press the reset button, and re-spawn like a computer game avatar. A third part of him wanted to grab a shotgun and pick up where Lizzy had left off. Kill them all, rescue his little brother, and return him to Glendale and his mother's loving arms.

He checked his mirrors, his speed. The car was a borrowed Nissan that smelled of cigarettes. As he signaled a change of lanes, transitioning onto the northbound 405 Freeway, he prayed to a god he didn't know, let alone believe in, that they wouldn't catch the eye of the California Highway Patrol. Speeds were within the limit, a pretend game that everything was peachy and Monday normal. As if on automatic, Chris kept the blue-gray sedan in the right-hand lane, almost autonomously exiting at the Burbank Boulevard off-ramp, as was his normal routine. The GPS program on his smartphone concurred with the decision.

The off-ramp tilted up toward the apex of the boulevard's overpass, an elevated point that provided crystalline views of the expansive horizontalism that was the San Fernando Valley. Chris set up for a left turn, half picturing his father vaulting up into that azure sky, the other half of him hazily eying the beggar of the day, cardboard sign in hand, a scribbled feel-for-me message, dirty baseball cap and shades.

There go I but for the grace . . .

As if by rote, Chris reached into his pocket and peeled the first bill from his money clip. He found the window control and heard the whine of the electric motor lowering the pane.

"What the fuck do you think you're doing?" asked Vaz. "Can't save your brother or sister but you can save this shitbag from himself? Look at him! He doesn't even look homeless!"

Obediently, Chris let his eyes follow his left hand, a twenty-dollar bill pinched between his fingers. His plane of focus shifted beyond the numerical denomination of his pull to the grateful face of his intended recipient. Chris saw lips pull back into a grin. Grateful. Only instead of relieving Chris of the paper bill, the beggar's powerful hand gripped his with a twist while his other hand pushed through the window and pressed a gun muzzle up against Chris's left eye.

"Keep your foot on the brake!" hissed Lucky. "Right hand unlocks the doors."

"GO!" panicked Vaz.

"One dead kid not enough?" clipped Lucky.

The door locks popped. Lucky swung himself into the rear seat and retrained the pistol on the back of Vaz's head.

"Green light," said Lucky, reaching over and frisking Vaz from behind. He found no weapon, but removed the mob boss' cell phone and flipped it onto the back seat. "Left turn, Chris. Keep your course for now. You carrying?"

"Under my seat," sighed Chris, following Lucky's instructions with a smooth left turn. Lucky slid behind the driver's seat, reached around, and patted down what he could of Chris, also removing the older brother's mobile phone.

"Keep both hands on the wheel and we'll be good," said Lucky. He dumped the dirty hat into the footwell. "Man. That shit smells."

"Where are we going?" asked Vaz.

"Where we going? Where were *you* going?" returned Lucky. "Wingin' it to Armenia? That's Eastern Europe, right? You know the furthest I've ever been outta the USA is a surf trip to Ensenada. Hey. You're homegrown, Chris. You ever surf?"

"No."

"Surfing's not Armo, huh?" Then Lucky instructed, "Make a right on Balboa."

"I asked you where," repeated Vaz.

"Detour," said Lucky. "Private jet's gonna have to wait. Hey. You both plannin' to blow town? Or were you gonna leave Chris behind to bury your daughter?"

Vaz stiffened and turned his chin slightly as if he were going to answer, only to shut himself off, jaw muscle setting like a pit bull's.

"Lost your sister today," Lucky aimed at Chris. "And your dad lost a daughter. Sad. Really. How about this? Let's have ourselves a wake. What do you Armos chow on when you celebrate a death?"

Lucky waited on an answer, but none came. There was a slight whistle in the car cabin as if a door or window leaked. Lucky sat back and let the silence speak, momentarily relieved that Plan A was working. If Chris hadn't made the charitable stop that Johnny B. had described so well, Lucky might have resorted to something more destructive—like a similar-styled fender bender such as the one Vaz had used as his introduction. And that would've put further damage to the old Dodge Aries he'd jimmied with a coat hanger he'd fished out of a refuse can. The only item he'd broken was the ignition lock. When all this was over—if Lucky even survived—he'd make sure to apologize and repay the owner.

"Nothin'? No answer?" broke Lucky, tired of the lack of conversation. "Right. Okay. I call Popeye's Chicken. Drive-thru coupla miles up. Hell. I'll even buy."

While the dead bodies of Lizzy, Miles, Flores, and Arkady were trucked to the city morgue in Boyle Heights and scheduled for autopsies by the Los Angeles County Medical Examiner, Sugar Freeman took it upon himself to personally visit and deliver the tragic news to Miles's wife, Stacy. It was a gutty few hours. Stacy, a sweat-stained mess from her CrossFit class, collapsed into Sugar's arms, a fetal and inconsolable lump. He stroked her hair and helped contact her scattered relatives living in the Inland Empire, all the while in the back of his mind thinking of a second, more salient duty.

Telling Amy Cho.

Since the rape, Amy had only traded a few texts with Miles, who had euphemistically called the encounter a "voyeuristic three-sie." Amy had adored Miles, trusted him, allowed him to elevate her to some thrilling sexual heights. All for them, she thought. Every ounce of it a committed twosome. Then came Saturday night and what Miles had called his "Sugar surprise." With the help of a little weed and vodka, Amy was all smiles and giggles in the aftermath. Then from the moment she had woken for her next day's work, she'd felt infected by the violation of it all. The word *rape* kept creeping into her conscious. A crime she couldn't report—at least not without giving up so much she'd worked for and earned, including Miles. Her lover had crossed a serious line from which only he could convince her that it would never, ever happen again. It was a promise she'd planned to procure at the right time and place.

When the knock came on her door, Amy hoped it was *him*. Miles. He'd usually text ahead just in case she had any of her Korean family in the apartment, though sometimes he'd admit to first scoping the scene from the street, allowing the shadows inside to inform him as to whether Amy was alone or otherwise. In those few paces from her kitchen to the door, her heart began with a flutter of apprehension. It was that word again. Stuck in the forefront of her brain.

Rape. Rape. Rape.

Perhaps because of her bewildered state, Amy didn't check the peephole. A quick look through the wide-angle door viewer was her father's rule. But she swung the door open with her left hand on the knob, her right braced on the doorjamb. The pose was meant to appear as if she might consider not letting Miles inside. When frozen shock began to form into a scream, Sugar's arms shot forward, one big mitt covering her mouth, the other pinching the back of Amy's head for leverage.

Her scream never had a chance to escape.

Sugar kicked the door shut, then pursed his lips in a release of staccato shushes. Without loosening his grip, he backed her up until the couch tripped her into a sitting position. He knelt down in front of her.

"Not gonna hurt you," calmed Sugar. "Not here neither for any of that kinky shit Miles cooked up."

Amy wanted to scream *Rape!*, utterly certain she was breaths from a second assault. Her brain was racing, heart thumping firmly against her esophagus.

"Miles is dead," said Sugar.

Miles wants me dead? is what Amy heard. That was until she stopped swerving her eyes every which way around her apartment in search of any kind of weapon she might use to strike Sugar in the head. He shook her until she looked at him straight on and could read his eyes, red and anguished.

"Miles. Is. Dead." The words were repeated, slowed down and without any room for misinterpretation.

"Miles?" she swallowed.

"Yes. Shot dead just this morning. I'm alive cuzza my vest. Look here." Sugar pulled the collar of his T-shirt, stretching it to expose his bruised sternum.

"How?" she cried. "Why?"

"Exactly why I'm here," he answered. "We're gonna do the asshole who's responsible."

"Do what?"

"Drop-kick the *fuck-nut* who got Miles dead." Sugar rose back to his feet, turned around for his bearings, and launched himself toward the kitchen. "Where is it?"

"Where's what?" Amy's words choked in her throat.

Sugar pulled open the top door of her refrigerator. The antique machine, kept running by monthly fix-it visits from Amy's father, was in need of a defrosting. A rounded edge of frozen condensation had formed across the freezer's ceiling. Below were two bottles of flavored vodkas and two clear plastic ice trays.

"Goddamnit," bitched Sugar. "I need it tonight!"

"I'm really lost," complained Amy, halfway to the kitchen door. "My Miles?"

"I need you to show me where it is," pressed Sugar, both hands on her shoulders, his eyebrows pinched into harsh punctuation. "Where do you keep the samples?"

"No," she said remotely. "Not in the fridge."

"Where?"

If she had a verbal reply, the back of her throat was so emotionally stifled it would've come out as a cough. So, Amy nodded and worked her way left, past her bedroom and bathroom doors, leading Sugar to her over-decorated magic room. The tiny space full of collectibles, books, and Magic Castle clutter had an old tanker desk pushed into a corner. Jammed into the leg space was a cube covered in blackout duvetyn. On her knees, Amy lifted the dense fabric to reveal a laboratory-sized freezer unit.

"Here," she breathed. "Everything is in here."

"Okay," said Sugar. "I need the Lucky Dey sample."

"Lucky what?"

"Lucky Dey."

"That a name? I don't have names. I just have numbers. Miles . . . He had all the whatever to correspond to the samples. It was on his phone and written down . . ."

Her words faded as she thought of her manly Miles. Dead.

"Few days back. Miles gave you some cum."

"Some what?"

"Sperm. Jizz. Ejaculate. He said he gave it to you."

"Oh. That." Amy opened the freezer and removed a three-inch-long evidence tube. "Last sample he gave me."

As Sugar reached for it, Amy withdrew.

"This is him?" she asked, sadness stuck in her throat. "This is who hurt Miles?"

"Close enough," said Sugar. "What happened today is on that son of a bitch you're holding. And we are gonna stick him like the pig he is."

"Who's we?" she braved. "I only knew Miles."

"And now you know me." Sugar nodded and held out his open palm, directing her with his other index finger exactly where to place the vial. "I'm your connect now. After today it's on me to run Miles's game. So, one way or the other, we *will* get to know each other."

34

Sunshine Canyon. 7:21 p.m.

There was no stink like landfill stink. In Lucky's opinion, it wasn't quite the worst of odors. Number two was a decomposing body—the death stench. His number one was the fetid funk of rotten eggs mixed with chicken shit, a whiff he'd only once experienced. It had been when his mother had rented a house in the North Valley burb of old San Fernando. He was twelve years old, his little brother, Tony, only eight. The boys had been hired to clean out their next-door neighbor's chicken coop, a chore long delayed. With a shovel and a wheelbarrow, Lucky was first to attack a pile of chicken droppings nearly three feet high. With his first or second thrust, a months-old egg had broken. The stink was instant and overwhelming. The brothers found themselves on their knees, puking their guts into the dirt. Tony bailed on the job, scrambling over the fence and leaving Lucky to either follow or finish. Lucky stuck it out and finished the work, figuring the five-bucks-per-man agreement would translate into him pocketing the whole ten dollars. When the nasty neighbor refused to cough up more than a five-dollar bill, Lucky dumped the last wheelbarrow load into the cheap bastard's swimming pool.

"Can't see where I'm walking," complained Vaz, his feet shuffling along the dirt, the limp almost gone.

"Jus' keep on keepin' on," instructed Lucky from behind.

Chris was shocked he was still alive. Halfway along the dirt levee that divided sections of the Sunshine Valley Landfill, he was certain that both he and his father were moments away from receiving bullets in the backs of their heads. The sky was a deep ambient blue, brightening a tick along the eastern horizon, where freeway traffic was thick, coursing north and south from the Newhall Pass. The surrounding hills were opaque silhouettes. What always looked imminently climbable from the cozy interior of a distant car appeared steep and impassible, looming over them like death itself.

Only the bullets didn't come, at least not on the levee. And any and all entreaties or negotiations for their freedom were rebuffed with the deputy interrupting with either "Shut up," or rhetorically asking "How do cops know their suspect is Armo?" When neither Vaz nor Chris could come up with a suitable punch line, Lucky would offer suggestions:

"He's thirty, drives a Mercedes, and still lives at home with mommy and daddy."

"He's got more hair on his back than his head."

"His house looks like it was decorated by Scarface."

Not expecting laughs from his prisoners, Lucky urged them onward, keeping a five-pace distance to the rear, directing them with simple instructions—*left here, down that path there, keep your feet moving.* They'd first stuck to dirt roads, driving from one bulldozed terrace to the next, eventually moving through near-complete darkness along a flat between what Chris could only surmise was a concrete culvert. Then they'd left the car and, by

Chris's guestimate, hiked a good quarter mile. He could make out only a thin strip of night sky above the top the trench some thirty or so feet above. The stench of the landfill had mostly abated. The air had turned into a thick, hanging kind of cold.

"Awright," said Lucky. "Hike's over."

Chris and Vaz stopped in place, nervous and not yet ready to die, feet scraping the dirt. A light appeared, a pinpoint bright blast from the smartphone flashlight in Lucky's hand. The father and son squinted in the brilliance, then instinctively followed the spill as Lucky swung it in the direction they were meant to go. They weren't in a culvert after all, but in a canyon of steel cargo containers, rusted and double-stacked in both directions. Lucky threw the swing-arm's bolt on the nearest container's door. It yowled with a low and hollow groan.

"Facts be," began Lucky, "I haven't decided whether to put a bullet in your pumpkins for being the scumbags you are or buy you flowers cuzza everything you lost today. So, until I figure it out . . ."

"In there?" pointed Vaz. "That's the best you can do?"

"Best I can do?" answered Lucky. "Is show you what it's like for some of the young girls you traffic. Strip. Down to your underwear."

"No!" puffed Vaz.

"Really? That's how you're gonna play it?" Lucky shifted the pistol from his right hand to his left, extended his arm, and aimed the fixed sights squarely five feet from Chris's ear. "You lost one child today, maybe even two. You wanna go for a hat trick?"

Vaz let his gaze burn holes into Lucky for a solid five count before removing his jacket. The rest of the clothes came in an organized order, each item gently left in a pile atop his Gucci loafers. Chris, ever the peacock, followed his father's cue, undressing to his Calvin Klein boxers, expertly air-folding each article with a retail store dexterity.

"What happened to you?" Lucky was pointing the pistol at Vaz's bandaged arm and leg.

"*Dzer minet shun!*" growled Vaz. *Your fucking dog.*

Father and son stepped into the container.

"Heads up. In case you get hungry . . ." Lucky tossed the takeout bag from Popeye's. Chris snatched it in the air. Lucky swung the door back shut, set the lock arm, and searched the ground until he came up with a suitable chunk of rebar. He jammed the metal rod into the locking mechanism's bolt receiver. He gave one last double rap against the container. "Make sure you don't choke on those bones."

Lucky began his trudge back to Chris's car. With half of his problem locked up in temporary suspension, his mind could focus on the other side of the coin: Judge Jim, Sugar Freeman, and whoever else they had lined up against him. Further back in his mind's eye he felt as if Gonzo were somehow watching over his every move. Arms crossed. Disapproval carved across her face. God, he loved her. In that moment he knew it as if the further he descended into darkness—the further he strayed—the better he saw her or felt the truth. Their love was real and worthy of rescue.

"I got it," whispered Lucinda from the other side of the motel room's door.

Terrified, Lee hadn't wanted to answer. In the confusion following the conflagration at the courthouse, he found himself going in reverse. Fear that a mass shooting was occurring had sent visitors and government employees into a panic, running and taking cover in all matter of directions away from the sounds of gunfire. Lee had bolted backward from the crime scene, joining the throng, retreating to the parking structure, where he was shaking with such violence he could barely insert his key into the shitmobile's ignition. The rewind inside him continued on the short drive back to his rented room, where he'd bolted shut the door in hopes that he'd finally feel safe. But the shakes refused to cease.

His body was vibrating so badly, he had jumped into a scalding hot shower thinking the warmth might put a stop to the violence coming from his core. But once inside the confines of the curtained tub, he felt that much more vulnerable, as if at any moment his bathroom door would cave in with those same deputies who'd so carelessly stomped all over him in their zeal to enter the shooting fray.

Over and over he recalled what he'd witnessed. Smelled. There had been a crackle to the air. Static-filled. As he had lain across the threshold of the courthouse's rear entrance, his body abused by deputies rushing past, he had seen her. Shia. She had her arm extended, her gun still smoking. Lee had seen that cop ease next to her and push down her gun arm while gathering her in his arms. From Lee's perspective, it may have well been a lover's embrace. It had been as if there were no longer any circumstance. No violence or aftermath. That asshole cop was comforting her. Shia was allowing *him* to comfort her. All while Lee watched. The jealousy in him twisted. Anger swilled with rejection. Lee hated him. He even hated . . .

No. Stop it, fool. Get your shit together.

Lee's twenty-two-year adventure into his personal gutter began to take on the stomach-in-mouth sensation of a free fall with no discernable bottom. His scalp tingled. His face was flush and hot and where his brain brushed up against his sinus cavity there was a constant buzzing as if a fly had been trapped inside his temporal lobe. And now he was mad for her. Mad at her. Mad and afraid of what would come next.

When the knock came on the door, it hit him like gunshots. He jumped out of his skin and considered swallowing his reply. Next came three more knocks followed by Lucinda's scratchy voice beyond the door.

"I got it! Lee? Got what you was askin' for."

For a few heartbeats, he considered she might be working for the authorities. After all, he was a witness who'd fled the scene—a stalker too close to a flame and he'd been caught.

"Lee, honey? You in there?"

"Are you alone?" he finally called out.

"Expectin' somebody else?" she sassed back.

He righted himself from the couch, crossed the five steps to the door, and cracked it open to confirm it was Lucinda and Lucinda alone. She was in her night getup: a teetering set of heels, her hair wound upward into a braided cone, thick mascara, glitter-glow eye shadow, and heavy lipstick formed into a duck-face tease.

"Not having a good day," warned Lee.

"I got what you asked," she repeated. "You want or you don't want?"

His wits returned enough for him to unhitch the door and allow his prostitute to enter. She was, as advertised, alone. Over her shoulder swung a magenta purse on a gold chain, which she pried open the moment her butt settled onto the arm of the couch. Touching the object like it was contaminated, she withdrew a Ziploc baggie, inside of which was a nickel-plated revolver, snub-nosed, five ammunition cartridges loosely arranged.

And like that, the shakes in Lee vanished.

With two hands held out, Lee accepted Lucinda's offering. He drew the gun near him, cradled it, and sat in the folding chair he used for his twice-a-day microwaved meals.

"That's two hundred you owe me," said Lucinda.

"Thought you said only a hundred?"

"Cost me one-fifty. Girl gotta make her ends, you know?"

"Close your eyes," said Lee, easing toward the kitchenette.

"Don't think I already figured out where you keep your stash?" she teased, eyes closed to reveal fake eyelashes longer than her fingernails. "Like I'd ever tell pimp-daddy your secret."

"Who'd he think you wanted the gun for?" From the cupboard, Lee pulled down a coffee can, peeled the lid, and poured out the grounds into a plastic bowl. At the bottom of the can was a metal cylinder that he unscrewed. He tapped out a roll of hundred-dollar bills. He feathered two bills into his hand, returned the cylinder to the can, and returned the coffee.

"Said it was for me 'cause I was scared of some Korean john been beatin' on girls. He hate all Koreans so we was good. Hey. Know how I know your hidey-place? I can smell the damn coffee grounds."

Lee dropped the two hundred-dollar bills into her purse, instantly swerving for the door. He held it open.

"Don't wanna know what you did with that thing," she warned.

"Haven't done anything," replied Lee.

"Not yet, you din't," she finished, dragging a soft knuckle across his cheek before sashaying her way out. "Luv my lil' Lee. Don't get your cutie self hurt."

With the door shut and latched, Lee turned about-face and fell to his knees onto the tired and stained wall-to-wall carpet. Before him lay that revolver in the baggie. Slowly, gently, Lee broke the seal, slipped a hand inside, and gripped the .38-caliber's butt. It was far heavier than he expected, a surprise considering his career as an engineer. He knew what a gun was made of and how it was designed, and could picture most of its parts in his brain. In his hands, though, it felt leaden—small but full of heft, able to withstand the forces of compression and gunpowder.

Lee felt a surge of power. Confidence. Almost impregnable. As if the world couldn't—or wouldn't—dare deny him what he desired. In a matter of moments, his pendulum had swung from impotence to ominous. He felt heady, high, and ready for what was about to come his way.

35

Sherman Oaks.

The salad bowl loaded with Halloween candy sat on an empty plant stand squarely where Shia had left it just before she'd locked the front door to her house that morning. She'd been looking forward to a quiet evening with her father, answering the doorbell for adorable trick-or-treaters and watching their little mitts splash into the colorful mélange of miniature Snickers, Kit Kat bars, and Reese's Peanut Butter Cups.

So much for planning ahead.

Instead, it was well past dark, the hordes of costumed kiddies had long since been hustled away by their mothers and fathers. That, and her crippled old man was drunk yet again. On discount Mexican beer, no less. He'd been going through twelve-ounce cans of Tecate by the case. That meant a full colostomy bag by 4:00 a.m. if Shia didn't set her alarm to change it.

"C'mon, Pop," she prodded. "Gimme one big pull."

The grab bar hanging over her father's bed looked like a trapeze. So much so that her father had woken up from nightmares where he'd been hanging from it, no bed below, only a pool full of boiling sludge. He'd also claimed to have had dreams where he'd opened his eyes and seen an old girlfriend swinging on the bar, giggling at him while wearing no apparent underwear.

"TMI, Daddy," she'd complained.

"Got nobody but the dog to share that shit with," he'd replied more than once.

Inebriated as her old man was, he elevated his arms on command, gripped the bar, and flexed. His seat lifted out of the wheelchair. Shia swung it away before assisting her dad into the hospital-style bed. As if on cue, big Hank hopped onto his post at the bottom of the mattress.

"Good ol' Hank," mumbled her father.

Shia clicked the safety gate into position, ruffled the covers until her father was covered, then pinched the urine tube before reconnecting it to the empty bag hooked to the footboard.

"Ready to go, Pops." Shia thanked God he was too drunk to see how poorly feigned her smile was. It had been an all-around shitty day. She'd recounted most of the pertinent events for a litany of investigators, over and over and over again. Tack onto that her lack of sleep and she had little reserve. Since her time at the academy, she'd become accustomed to the nightly recitations of her day. If she didn't, her father would interrogate her up to the precipice of her annoyance. She knew her work life was his entertainment. And since her assignment as Judge Sollo's bailiff, the *daddy debriefs*, as he'd refer to them, had taken on the tenor of a courtroom soap opera—easy to remember with very little of it involving her participation.

After flushing the contents of the second colostomy bag, she returned to the bed, kissed her barely cogent father on the forehead, gave Hank a quick scratch behind his nappy ear, and withdrew, making sure to fully close the door behind her. She shut her eyes, exhaled slowly, then steered herself down the thirty feet of darkened hallway to her bedroom. Unconsciousness was her destination. She even contemplated dispensing with her nighttime routine of a bath, face scrub, and moisturizer, before slipping into a T-shirt and her welcoming bed. She briefly pictured herself toppling onto the bedspread, face down, and dropping off into sleep without so much as unlacing her boots.

One glance at her bed, not slept in since two nights earlier, and she could only imagine the grime she must have been caked in. The bathroom called. By habit she left the lights off, undressing without concern for peeping neighbors. Shia began depositing her work clothes in front of her closet's sliding doors, four steps to the left of her bed. Her boots hit the carpet with a pair of dull thumps. It was after stepping out of her sheriff's green khakis that she felt the pressure—cold and metal, the slight prick of a fixed gunsight barely scraping the part between her braids.

"Don't. Move. A muscle," whispered a voice.

"*You*," she said, surprised by the familiarity of the man's tone.

"Don't talk."

"Remember. I'm a police officer—"

"The bed. On your stomach."

Shia's first inclination was to pivot and sweep. A quick move would surprise the attacker, knock the gun aside, and set her up to send a knee to the groin, or a palm-heel strike into the man's nose. Using memory to gauge his height, she cocked an elbow and twisted. Hard. Fast. But lashed at only air. She stumbled, a bit off balance. Her eyes tried to adjust, seeing little more than a shadow that had already taken three defensive steps backward into the corner. All she could make out was the gun. A shiny revolver. It wavered, not so steady, yet remained aimed in her general direction.

"Why?" she asked, her throat cutting off the word too soon.

"Bed. Face down."

"Please."

She could hear the man breathe, the air sucking into his chest, pumping out, repeating. Quick, as if he had run a mile before creeping up on her.

"Because . . ." he finally whispered. "'Cause you're his girlfriend."

Lucky ditched the Nissan in Pasadena and rode the bus up the hill into Altadena. He walked the rest of the way, exhausted, hungry, jonesing for pain pills, but mostly obsessing on getting back to his mobile phone so he could check in with Gonzo. During the afternoon, he'd tried to get ahold of her via a series of messages through contacts in both Sheriff's and LAPD. A note he'd left with the desk at Air Support Division had consisted of a short apology and an explanation that he'd temporarily lost his phone. Not that he expected it was going to soften whatever stance Gonzo might take against him. By now he was certain that she'd have heard about the gunfight at the Van Nuys courthouse. Lucky's name would surely be reported in the crime blogs. He fully expected some kind of emotional buzz saw once he was able to contact Gonzo.

The sidewalk on his street was littered with Halloween leftovers. Candy wrappers, dead safety glow sticks. On porches, carved jack-o'-lanterns flickered their last licks. He imagined the street hours earlier, filled with armies of squealing kids in costumes and vigilant parents, carefully guiding them from friendly door to friendly door. All but for the one Craftsman-era home that offered nothing to the children but darkness and nobody home. Though he didn't know the exact time—by his guess, 10:00 or 11:00 p.m.—he did think it a bit odd to see a tow truck in front of his bungalow. He marked it from a block away. A vehicle with a spinning yellow light display was putting a hook to a car parked in his driveway. Johnny B.'s Shelby Mustang. Lucky's pace quickened. He was so dehydrated, he could barely produce a sweat. Still, the air was cold and he felt a wetness at the base of his skull the closer he neared the bungalow.

"What you got there?" Lucky called to the tow driver.

"Your car?" the tow driver barked back at him. It was a rote remark, the driver far too accustomed to late-to-the-party car owners rushing up and begging him to unhook their vehicles.

"Who made the call?" asked Lucky, closing by a front-yard length.

"Lady of the house." The tow driver took the moment to remove his gloved hand from the lift lever to point at Lucky's well-lit bungalow.

In a moment of near-simultaneous recognition, Lucky marked the sheriff's black-and-white stationed across the street and did the quick math. Gonzo was no longer safely ensconced behind the walls of Conrad Ellis's estate. She had already returned home, most likely with both Travis and Karrie.

Shitballs.

At the sight of Lucky's approach, the pair of deputies in the parked radio unit popped their door locks and swung out of the car. Lucky met their move by holding forth his six-starred brass shield before turning up the path. The front door was cracked, light bleeding from the entry. He instantly marked the splintered doorjamb, the obvious remnant of a break-in—or a bad Halloween prank. When he pushed the door open, his head tilted to a large rolling suitcase and a moving box stuffed with clothes. Gonzo was hauling a third box from the back bedroom when she caught Lucky in the open doorway.

"Didn't we already do this?" were Lucky's first words.

"Can't have you here," replied Gonzo, cold, lowering the stuffed carton to the floor. "You've become way too much of a shit magnet for our comfort level."

"You took some kind of vote?"

"I'm only speaking for Travis and myself," straightened Gonzo. Casual as she looked in socks, sweats hanging low on her hips, and a pullover hoodie, her pose was hard. Erect. She appeared utterly impassable, a human bulwark. "We both know Karrie's her own girl. She's gonna go how she's gonna go."

Lucky noted a nearby wash bucket and rags bearing the telltale pink tint of blood. In the frame of the corridor he counted off three bullet strikes burrowed in the paneling.

"What happened here?" he asked.

"You tell me."

"I bugged out. Forgot my phone. After that . . ." Lucky shrugged.

"Your dog is dead," shrugged Gonzo. She was both angry and resigned. "Least she tried to defend her ground. Blood trail out the door, so I expect she got a piece of whoever kicked in our door."

With Gonzo's remark a puzzle piece fell into place. Lucky recalled the bandages on Vaz's forearm and calf. It must've been the *jefe* himself who'd busted down the door in search of Johnny B. *Respect*, thought Lucky. To Vaz for personally attempting to collect his boy—and the rescued mutt, Oprah, for her valiant defense of the family realm. Too bad one had to die.

"Where's she now?" asked Lucky.

"Said our goodbyes and put a blanket over her. Musta been a slow day for Animal Services. Already come and gone. Sorry."

The sound of a latch clicked. Soft. A light peeked from a door deep in the corridor. Lucky could see Travis's shape peering out. The teen eventually filled the doorframe but didn't dare come any nearer. Reserved. Scared, almost. Lucky could read fear, found it easy to detect. As tight as he was with Travis, the dog's death, inches from the teen's bedroom, was surely a shock to his rather delicate system.

"And Karrie?" he asked.

"Like I said. She's her own girl," reminded Gonzo. "Her car even out there? Hard to see past the muscle car that belongs to who the hell knows."

"Don't pretend like you want an explanation," played Lucky.

"I don't want anything right now other than you and your shit to get as far from us as possible—"

"I didn't start this," he defended. "But it happened so I'm handling it."

"And how's that workin' so far?" Gonzo stepped forward, an accusing finger pointed at his face. "First you have Conrad kidnap us in some lame bubble-wrap thing to protect us from God knows what. We don't hear from you for hours. Then after whatever the hell that was that broke loose in Van Nuys this morning, we come home to find a strange car in the driveway, the front door kicked in, and our dog shot to death."

"Seriously, Gonz. I'm lost," relented Lucky. "What do you want me to say?"

"Nothing. Nothing at all. Not unless you're ready to guarantee us that this shit is over."

"I'm not done yet—if that's what you want to hear."

"Then why are you even here?" she angered.

It wasn't quite long enough to be a stalemate, but the space between them took on the effect of a vacuum, with neither looking to fill the widening space. Lucky simply nodded, leaned in, placed a box under one arm and gripped the suitcase with the other, then exited. Once out the door, he hooked his way around the front of the house to the driveway and his Crown Vic. That's where he found Karrie in the front passenger seat. Her bare feet were on the cushion, chin resting on top of her knees.

"Dunno yet where I'm going," started Lucky. "But wherever that is, you can't come with."

"I know," said Karrie. "I'm stayin'. I just needed to talk some before you . . ."

"Before I what?" Lucky slid in behind the wheel.

"I dunno," she said. "Before you die?"

"Not dead yet," affirmed Lucky. "Still here."

"Yeah. But for how long?"

"Nobody knows."

"What happened today? Why we end up with a dead dog?"

"I'm in the middle of something. I was trying to keep you safe."

"What about you? You tryin' to keep yourself safe?"

"Guess that's a matter of opinion."

"So, what you're sayin' is that I should probably keep my old name. 'Cause, you know, yours might be like *pppfffttt*. Any second now. Dead. Last of the Deys."

Lucky pressed his mouth to the side but kept his gaze forward. He breathed, mulled the question, uncertain as to how he might best answer. Though he felt a glib retort rising, he stuffed it in lieu of a reply with a shade more honesty.

"Really means a lot to me—you wanting to take my name and all that," he finally said to her. "Not sure I deserve any of it. But it means a lot."

"Yeah. But does it mean enough for you to want to stay alive?"

"Means more than you can imagine."

"So?"

"So, I've got to find a place to sleep for now."

"Jus' for now, though. You *are* coming back? 'Cause this is *our* home," she pressed to confirm. "We all need you. Travis. Gonzo. We need each other, right?"

"Right," nodded Lucky.

"Gonzo's just mad, that's all."

"She makes a hell of an argument."

"But that's all it is. An argument that one day gets resolved."

"That's my hope."

"Mine too, then."

Their conversation ended with Karrie kissing the stubble on his cheek and stealing a prolonged hug. Lucky waited for her to return into the house before starting up the '99. As he backed out of the driveway, an odd notion ushered in. In a career crammed with near misses, the actual thought of his mortality had rarely been more than a fleeting notion—and then only in those pulse-raising moments when the likes of a bullet had whistled past his ear. Yet as he eased the Crown Vic backwards, his windshield filling with the family bungalow, its warmth filtering from the windows, a sadness tugged at him. Lucky asked himself if he'd ever see the house again, let alone any of its occupants. With every foot traveled in reverse down the driveway, Lucky's made-up family felt further removed, miles and miles away.

Lucky saw the sheriff's black-and-white parked across the street. He made certain to keep the cops in his every view, especially the side and rearview mirrors. He detected nary a tick from the deputies, who paid Lucky little to no mind whatsoever. Their eyes were, as he could only wish, split between sweeping the landscape and watching the bungalow. But as Lucky slowly accelerated, a second pair of headlights switched on and slipped into his wake.

Lucky marked the car behind him. Doing so at night was a bit more difficult when all he had to go on was the lights' height, shape, and color temperature, and the horizontal distance between both headlamps. The newer-model vehicles were far easier to read as each brand decorated their headlight arrays with nuanced extras like daytime running lights or yellow parking lamps, distinguishing them further without the help of streetlights or the lumen wash from an oncoming car. The most Lucky could garner from the headlights in his mirrors was that the car was economy-sized and did not utilize blue or white halogens—narrowing it down to roughly a third of all the cars in Southern Cal—all that, and the car was more than likely not even tailing him.

His mind eventually shifted to where he was going to lay his head that night. The need for sleep plagued him. And just when he thought he'd be able to circle back home for a few hours in his own bed, he was kicked out again on his proverbial ass. A left turn at the light would deliver Lucky down the hill into Pasadena. There was a section on the east end of Colorado Boulevard that sported a number of affordable motels. Despite the beckoning of a rented pillow, Lucky flipped his turn signal upward, indicating a right turn. The unknown car behind him followed suit. The vehicle remained in his rearview mirror, a safe distance behind. If it was indeed a follow-job, the driver was hardly pretending to conceal him or herself.

Lucky loped a left onto West Altadena, hoping that if the car behind him continued the stalk, the lights from the various commercial shopping centers would assist him in identifying the year or make, or even the character at the wheel. Only in the sleepy suburb most lights were extinguished after 10:00 p.m. The most Lucky was able to read in his rearview were confirmations on the vehicle's size and little more. The driver was cloaked in shadow and wise enough to keep a few car lengths of distance between his indistinguishable front end and Lucky's rear bumper.

"Fine, then," said Lucky. "You wanna dance? Let's dance."

With nothing but green lights ahead, Lucky kept his speed at no more than a lazy forty miles per hour. He eventually shifted lanes, eased right again, and climbed, the road beginning to whipsaw its way up into the San Gabriel Mountains. For a few switchback turns, the eastern basin spread out below with its usual sprawl of endless lights. Then like crawling into a gargantuan ass crack, the road sucked into the mountain and seemingly left civilization behind. Ahead of Lucky was an unfamiliar track. He wasn't much of a fan of mountains, local or otherwise. He'd grown up near the ocean and, but for working the lowdown city streets of Los Angeles, felt more comfortable navigating on a surfboard.

Behind him remained that same pair of headlights, sixty yards removed, keeping pace and leaving no mystery of intent. Because he was driving deep into unfamiliar fire country, he relied on his training. Wherever there were canyons above and around Greater Los Angeles, there were fire roads. And where there were fire roads, there were water storage tanks built onto flats. Lucky was waiting for a dirt turnoff into a bulldozed man-made plain, which would be easy to maneuver in a showdown.

He checked the sky for a covering helicopter, not entirely certain he wasn't under police surveillance. When he was convinced the sky was clean, he narrowed the suspects to one of two possibilities: an unknown member of Judge Jim's vigilante cabal or members of an Armenian revenge squad. Lucky's sub-sized SIG Sauer .45 was stuffed between his legs. He fished through the backpack behind his seat and retrieved three fully loaded magazines. For a second he was shocked back into that moment from twenty minutes earlier—the long farewell from Karrie and the odd feeling that he may never connect with his family again.

The Crown Vic's headlights swept over a cutout in the road. Beyond the eight-foot climb of chain-link topped with razor wire he saw a battleship-gray storage tank pushed up against a grove of shabby eucalyptus. Lucky aimed his right fender for the gate in expectation that the large padlock hanging from the chain wouldn't penetrate his windshield. The gate caved, sparks curled and tumbled across the hood. Lucky pounded the brakes, setting the '99 into a braking slide. During the entire skid, his eyes were switching between his rear- and side-view mirrors. At first he could only see streaks of filtered light through all the dust kicked up by his tires. As the plumes of fine sand settled, that now-familiar pair of headlights returned to view. Stalled. Just inside the shattered gate.

Then the car reversed, backing out onto the roadway.

"Oh no, you don't!" piped Lucky.

He dropped the Crown Vic into reverse and punched the gas pedal to the floor. His rear tires spun. Dirt billowed. Gripping the steering wheel, with his other arm slung over the seat, Lucky aimed for the headlights until they filled his back windshield. There was a crunch from the initial collision, a pause, then more impact. The compact car was spinning counterclockwise away from the heavier '99. Lucky kept pushing until it was finally pitched sideways in a sandy drainage ditch. No sooner had he thrown his car into park than the first bullet shattered his rearview mirror. Lucky dropped a shoulder and rolled out the door, counting the gunshots.

Two, three . . .

Using the Crown Vic as a shield, Lucky stayed in a crouch and worked left. Another *pop!* sounded. The fourth shot cut through the back window, sending marbles of safety glass onto him. Still moving, Lucky elevated himself over the lid of his car's trunk, pistol leading. He saw the compact car, brake lights in full reddened flare, half angled into the ditch, the dust almost hanging like a fog.

Then a louder *pop!* A fifth shot echoed, shattering the compact's back window. The projectile appeared directed in no particular direction—and nowhere near Lucky, who sat on his haunches, careful to keep the rear of the Crown Vic between himself and the mystery assailant.

There was a pull in Lucky to light up the compact car with a full magazine of hot stuff, a justifiable action considering the circumstances. Yet the .45 remained on safety, a mere thumb flick from ready and able to send every cartridge-load downrange. All the while the compact car lay hobbled. The only way it was getting out of the ditch was with a tow.

"WHOEVER YOU ARE!" called out Lucky, "YOU GOT FIVE SECONDS TO GET OUT BEFORE I PUNCH YOUR CAR FULLA HOLES!"

"Fuck you!" cried the voice. "You deserve to die, asshole!"

"Fine!" returned Lucky. "Here I am. All you gotta do is come out and get me."

Screw it, Lucky suddenly decided.

He flicked the pistol off of safe mode and rose with it leveled at the crippled car. He approached from the left rear, quick steps, his footfalls crunching on the mix of sand and disintegrating asphalt. He saw movement—a struggling shadow rocking in place. The driver's door cracked open. A leg appeared, shoe on the ground. A man began to stand and turn. Instead of pulling the trigger and puncturing the assailant, Lucky flattened the pistol in his hand and plowed it into the man's rather significant nose. He felt cartilage breaking as the profile of the pistol tattooed itself onto a collapsing cheekbone. The man, who at once was in motion, slumped like a boxer caught by a surprise uppercut. Whatever threat he was to Lucky was lost to momentary unconsciousness.

Lucky dropped a knee into the assailant's chest, pinching him to the dirt. While he stuck his gun muzzle into the man's chicken-thin neck, he ran his free hand over the top of his clothes, seeking evidence of secondary weapons. Moans bubbled from the man's bloody mouth, cognition returning. With his foot, Lucky hooked the man in the midsection, flipping him, lowered his knee again, and dipped into the groaning man's pockets. He discovered a tactical pen and then a black steel flip-knife.

"Who sent you?" groused Lucky.

"Fuck you," coughed Lee Chapman. "You killed her."

"Long day, pal. You're gonna have to be more specific."

"You know what you did!"

"And you stalked a cop," argued Lucky. "From my *house*, ass-wipe. Now, which side of this shit storm sent your sorry ass?"

"Jus' kill me," begged Lee. "So I can be dead with her."

"With *her*," confirmed Lucky. "Fucking Armos. So low on muscle they recruiting bean counters?"

If it was about a dead girl, Lucky knew of only two on his short list. Lizzy, the Kasabian child who'd appeared behind the courthouse like a Japanese ghost, as if from out of nowhere, armed and seeking unholy revenge. The second was the accident victim, the Barbie mom housewife from Malibu.

"Who are you?" asked Lucky.

"I'm nobody," answered Lee, lost and pathetic. "I just wanted to know her better . . . that's all . . . And not just 'cause she was black."

Black?

"What's this about?" growled Lucky.

"Bastard!" Lee cried. "You did it, you did it, you did it!"

"I. Did. What?"

The little man melted into tears and howls, convulsing in fits until he coughed up phlegm. Lucky pulled out Lee's wallet, flipped it open, and read the driver's license. Kneeling, he propped Lee against the side of the ditched Honda, slapping the man's face until he was back into something near coherence. Lucky begged him to explain.

"Phone," was all Lee could mouth.

Lucky found the man's phone. Hands shaking, Lee fumbled to operate the device, accessing the video function before handing the phone to Lucky.

"Deny *that* shit," whined Lee.

It hadn't been that hard at all for Lee to find Lucky. News reports following the courthouse shootout had revealed both victims and survivors. At first trolling every internet post on the event, Lee's primary concern was to see if the LAPD was searching for him. By the time he was satisfied that he wasn't the subject of a manhunt for having fled the scene of a crime, he'd read and reread the name of Deputy Lucas Dey enough to record it by heart. An online search uncovered the same name and a matching home address in public records involving a recent home purchase in the City of Altadena. There was a second name on the deed: Lydia Gonzalez.

By Lee's account, Lucky looked to be married. Which was how and why he found himself back at Shia's house, parked again under that massive live oak. No longer a stalker. With that just-purchased revolver in his jacket pocket, Lee had re-minted himself as Shia's guardian angel.

Deciding to record his actions in a video diary, Lee was only moments into his first monologue when a dark figure had appeared from the backyard of the house. The broad-shouldered man was in a hoodie and gloves. He gently shut the wooden drive-way gate before turning left on the sidewalk. Forgetting he was armed—as well as forgetting he was supposed to be acting as Shia's guardian angel—Lee slumped in the seat of his trusty shitmobile as the figure sauntered past. Calm. At an even pace, murmuring in a semi-gruff voice to somebody at the other end of a cell phone call. Lee eventually heard a car door shut, an engine turn over, and the sound of the vehicle pulling away.

As Lucky replayed the video, he fingered up the volume. The picture on the small screen was poor and overly pixilated from recording in such low light. But as the figure approached the car, a familiar face came into brief relief. After which the screen went practically black at the point when Lee had laid down on his seat. A muddy voice could be heard. Though the volume was peaked and distorted as it played back through the tiny speakers, the timbre and words matched perfectly.

". . . she's dead. And Lucky fuckin' Dey is the prick who done it," relayed Sugar Freeman.

Lucky pulled out his phone and dialed 911.

"Requesting an emergency welfare check at . . ." Lucky stalled, blanking on Shia's address.

"Fourteen double-oh five Califa," spat out Lee.

"One-four-zero-zero-five Califa," repeated Lucky to the 911 operator. "Charlie. Alpha. Lima. India. Foxtrot. Alpha."

"Are you a police officer?" asked the operator.

"Just send a goddamn black-and-white!" demanded Lucky. "Possible one-eight-seven. Tell me you got the address!"

"One-four-zero-zero-five Califa," read back the operator.

* * *

Nearly two hours had come and gone since he'd heard the horrific news. After stuffing Lee in the back seat of the '99 with the rear doors locked, Lucky drove back to Sherman Oaks. All the while, Lee recited back much of what he'd seen and done in a stream of confessional regurgitations. Words upon words poured out as Lee cataloged his fall from grace to his personal revelation that he'd somehow turned into Shia's stalker. He'd jealously watched Lucky arrive at Shia's house the night before. He'd witnessed the shootout behind the courthouse building. He'd run in fear of being caught. He'd illegally purchased a revolver.

As if Lucky gave a rip.

By the time Lucky and Lee landed near the Sherman Oaks address, LAPD radio units had already blocked off the street. Yellow crime-scene ribbon had been strung in a rectangular cordon, outside of which neighbors had gathered to share or gossip about their concerns.

Lucky remained inside his Crown Vic, the PD hand radio tuned to the LAPD's frequency. Between Lee's continuous chatter, Lucky picked up snippets of information. Inside the house were two homicides, one middle-aged male, one female. The deceased female was also suspected to be a victim of sexual assault. Forensic and coroner teams had been dispatched and were en route to the crime scene.

And I'm the suspected killer.

The pieces had fallen into place so quickly. From Judge Jim to Sugar to his recent sexual indiscretion with his Major Crimes colleague Zadeh Raad. The judge's tentacles were, indeed, long and deadly. No doubt, Lucky was only a matter of hours away from arrest.

"So, if you didn't do it . . ." Lee had eventually queried.

"You spend a lotta time at the courthouse, right?" returned Lucky.

"Practically every day," replied Lee. "I told you. That's where I met her. Department J."

"You know other courtrooms?"

"Most of 'em. All of 'em, I think."

"Judge Jaime Peralta?"

"Judge Jimbo? Yeah. I know him."

"Judge Jimbo." If the pain hadn't been so great, Lucky might've laughed. "Bet he likes being called that."

"Security cop called him that once. Not to his face. But I heard 'im. Same cop who calls me Mister Red Book. Cuzza my notebook. It's red."

"JPL, huh," Lucky segued. "That's NASA. Makes you a smart guy, right?"

"IQ-wise, I suppose. Guess it depends on what kinda scale you're talking about. Because I'm not feelin' that smart no more."

"Smart enough," figured Lucky.

"Smart enough for what?"

"For what happens next," finished Lucky.

Tuesday

36

There were nights when Sugar Freeman loved the long drives home. It was a way of leaving the job behind, a buffer of sorts, a transition from police work to family work. Recently, he'd turned to audiobooks to fill in the time and space between Van Nuys and distant Camarillo. Sugar would plug in his headphones and drift his way west on nonfiction word clouds read by Edward Hermann and Nelson Runger. Only after that awful Halloween, a day and evening chock-full of too many real-life scares and dirty deeds, there was no escape in well-read history tomes. With every mile, Sugar would thumb up the loudness, hoping the decibels might punish his brain into submission. Ahead of him lay a whole different kind of bother. His dear wife was understanding . . . to a point. And Halloween was that threshold. He hadn't told her about Miles. Or his involvement in the shootout. She only knew that his promise to help decorate, carve pumpkins, and safely escort their adorable little goblins on a trick-or-treat excursion around their new neighborhood had been broken—smashed into too many pieces to glue back together.

Northbound on the 101, Sugar had just crossed into Ventura County when a text banner appeared on his phone attached to a familiar number. It was Zadeh.

need 2 talk now

Barely taking his eyes off the road, Sugar replied with two simple letters:

rs

It was code for *radio silence*. Judge Jim, concerned that the ever-nosy FBI might catch on to his vigilante conspiracy, had cautioned the likes of Sugar and Zadeh to limit digital communication anywhere near and around any action. The past thirty-six hours had felt like falling dominoes leading to a nuclear meltdown. Once all the dead bodies had been connected, let alone sorted, who knew where the guilty fingers would eventually be pointed? Somebody, somehow would surely have to answer.

i have a lucky problem

rs!

can't. i think he knows bout me.

stay calm. only hrs b4 his arr

Brake lights, red and screaming, were rushing at Sugar's windshield. He stomped on the brake pedal. The Hummer's antilock brakes could only assist in slowing the more than six thousand pounds of hurtling metal before the tire rubber broke free from the asphalt's grip. What made Sugar look up from his phone screen was only a guess. The fact was he'd been distracted, wrapped up in his fevered text, and had somehow lost sense of time, space, and the road ahead. He could only hope the airbag wouldn't break his face when it deployed.

It was a chain-reaction crash, the hard-sliding Hummer crushing into the car in front, transferring the energy forward into another vehicle and then another. Five cars in all, each slowed for the California Highway Patrol cop stopping traffic to clear a mattress that had come loose from an itinerant's pickup truck. Once Sugar's airbag deflated, he glanced forward, and the elevated view from his seat revealed the pileup and the damage he'd done, including the crumpled rear end of an eighties-era Chrysler LeBaron underneath his Hummer's grille. A glance in the mirror reflected the slightest glistening of blood trickling from underneath his nose. Then, lowering his eyes back to the infernal phone, legally mounted via a cradle attached to his dashboard, he saw another text bubble of fear courtesy of Zadeh:

think he knows it wuz us

"Deputy bitch," muttered Sugar to nobody but himself, already blaming the accident on his comrade. "Can't you tell it's a fucking bad time?"

Sugar tapped out another reply:

bad timing!

After which Zadeh speedily replied:

need to see you. either i see u NOW or i gotta lawyer up.

"Jesus Christ," Sugar griped, shaking his head as if to wonder what else might go wrong in his day. Beyond the taillights and sounding car horns, Sugar spotted a Comfort Inn and Suites sign, raised high on a pole, designed to be a readable siren's call to weary travelers.

Sugar reluctantly wrote out a final text:

Comfort Inn. Thousand Oaks. 1 hr.

Sugar's professional guess was that it would take about an hour for the Highway Patrol to unravel the traffic mess. He would expedite the process with his LAPD badge, a voluntary sobriety test, and a declaration that the accident was all his fault. After concealing his cell phone in his boot, Sugar claimed he must have fallen asleep due to fatigue and the previous day's events. In no time at all, he had the attending Highway Patrolmen's complete sympathy once they were informed he'd been involved in the courthouse shootout and had lost his partner, Miles Czajkowski, to an assailant's bullet.

At least there were no major injuries as a result the freeway accident. That, and Sugar had another excuse to delay the tongue-lashing he was sure to receive from his missus—a win-win to wrap around a shoebox full of dog crap.

The Hummer was drivable. And as soon as Highway Patrol released Sugar to his own recognizance, he accelerated to the nearest exit and doubled back toward the Comfort Inn. Zadeh had already texted him that she was in a downstairs room. Number 119. Despite some relative certitude that he wasn't being followed, he circled the block both clockwise and counterclockwise before entering the parking lot and backing into a space opposite the room.

A thought came to Sugar. *Just my luck that this would be the night Zadeh needs to get laid.* Sugar wasn't sure he was interested, let alone inclined to perform. Then again, over his career he'd seen a thing or two when it came to trauma and the sexes. Something about catastrophe would often bring opposites together. By the time Sugar had crossed the pavement to the motel room's door, the mild anticipation of a quickie had manifested in a sweaty palm on the levered door handle. The timing was good. Sugar heard the deadbolt thrown and the security bar flipped the moment he pushed down on the latch. The door swung in. He saw the bathroom door was open and heard the shower was on. But it wasn't steam from the shower that hit him in the face. The hot cloud stinging his eyes was triggered from a steam iron. The flat sole plate followed, swung fast and hard against his temple.

That's when Sugar's world went from horny to black.

Zadeh was the key piece to Lucky's puzzle. His paranoia that he'd been followed all week, watched and spied upon, turned out to be right, only hampered by a sexual blind spot. After leaving Lee Chapman at a bus stop with a mission of his own, Lucky hustled downtown to the Temple Street headquarters of the Los Angeles Sheriff's Department and the Major Crimes Unit on the not so odd chance he might once again stumble into night owl Deputy Zadeh Raad. A desk sergeant easily gave up that she'd carded into the building.

"Thought that was her car," Lucky relayed over the garage intercom. "Looks like somebody did a real job on it. Tires slashed. Trunk and hood open."

Within minutes, Zadeh stormed out a garage elevator cussing an ugly streak, her voice echoing across the structure. She never noticed Lucky's '99 Crown Victoria parked in a spot conveniently out of range from the security cameras. Nor did she make it to her car. Lucky first snagged her by the ponytail and spun her into a chokehold, lowering her to the concrete while she wildly kicked and attempted to scream.

"Ssshhh," was all she heard from Lucky's lips.

Once she lost consciousness, he dragged her onto his back seat, flex-cuffed both her hands and feet, and then duct-taped a reusable Trader Joe's shopping bag over her head and mouth.

"Don't worry," he'd said to her. "The bag's breathable and environmentally safe."

After her thumbprint unlocked her iPhone, Lucky discovered

the same security app that Miles had supplied him and began to bait Sugar Freeman with a series of texts until the LAPD killer suggested meeting at the Comfort Inn near Thousand Oaks.

Lucky's captive audience of Sugar and Zadeh were both in his car, bound, bagged, and taped, stacked atop each other, feet to face, piled on the Crown Vic's back seat like cord wood. He kept to the speed limit, the sloping cascades of the San Fernando Valley's north end off of his left window. The turnoff was near, marked by an old corner cafe with a neon-lit arrow pointing at a tire-sized donut.

"We're all pretty far over the waterfall," offered Lucky in a rare show of emotion. "Bet when you woke up yesterday, you didn't figure today was the day we ourselves got smashed up on the rocks . . . Jesus. And to think all I did was say no. Well, said no to everything but the sex. And that's on me. I can live with that like the rest of it. Everything but Shia . . . I can't . . ."

He didn't finish the thought.

Lucky parked the car and unwrapped both Sugar and Zadeh's feet but kept their heads bagged and hands cuffed and attached each to the other with a two-foot bungee cord. He guided them onto the sandy path. Zadeh's legs wobbled so that she could barely stay upright, certain she was only moments from her execution. Sugar simply marched ahead. Sanguine. Worn, but ready for whatever came.

"Suppose you wanna know where you're headed. What's gonna happen next." Lucky offered, "Here's a promise. I'm not gonna kill either of you. Best I can offer is that where we're going to is a place where I can finally step off the bus."

Despite the cold and discomfort of the cargo container, Chris was eventually overcome by the need to rest. He'd become exhausted from hours arguing with his father. Vaz had lost all patience and directed his anger at his eldest son. Blame was in no short supply as father and heir apparent beat their respective eardrums into reverb submission with their barking exchanges. When Chris called it quits, he'd slid down one of the walls to the floor and lay on his side, ear to the floor, trying to tune out the shuffles of his father's pacing. Sleep followed. When he awoke with a shock it was still pitch-black, though he could locate his father by his labored breathing.

"Are you okay?" asked Chris.

"What do you care?" groaned Vaz. "I die, you're still head of the family."

"You die," replied Chris, "all I'm king of is this stupid-ass tin can."

Vaz laughed and coughed, and was laughing again when the sound of the container's lever lock squeaked and banged. A gray light entered with Lucky's silhouette keeping a defensive distance, obviously concerned about being bum-rushed by his prisoners.

"Game time," said Lucky. "Let's move."

"Move where?" complained Vaz. "Just when I'm finally comfortable?"

"Short walk," was all Lucky would say. He retreated further from the door, leaned against the opposite container, and waited, arms crossed.

Chris appeared first, discovering his clothes still piled where he had left them. A nod from Lucky, and Chris began to slowly dress. His father grudgingly followed his son's example. Once their shoes were on, Lucky gestured to his left. Chris froze for a moment, realizing that Lucky expected them to walk in the opposite direction from where they'd originally come. Vaz shrugged and moved ahead, deeper into the canyon of stacked cargo containers, Chris two steps behind. They climbed a set of steps built from railroad ties into a grassy slope. At the top was another plateau, perhaps two square acres. Dug into the flat dirt were four empty holding tanks formed from poured concrete. Uniform in size, each had a diameter of some one hundred feet and a vertical depth of twenty-five. Remnants of a long-since abandoned water treatment facility.

Lucky walked them to the edge of the nearest hole.

"Suppose introductions are in order," said Lucky. "Vartan and Chris Kasabian of the Armenian mob? Meet your enemy, LAPD Sergeant Sugar Freeman and detective Zadeh Raad of the Sheriff's Department."

Vaz and Chris looked into the holding tank to discover both Sugar and Zadeh standing at the bottom, unbound, ungagged, and seemingly trying to fabricate some way out by piling chunks of pitted concrete. The walls of the tank were graffiti-covered, painted over time and time again by new sets of teenaged taggers. There were no hand- or footholds for climbing out.

Lucky lifted an aluminum ladder and slid it down into the hole.

"Climb in," he ordered.

"Fuck that!" spat Vaz.

"Climb down or get tossed in," said Lucky. "Your choice."

"*Tstsel dzer mor krsk'er!*" *Suck your mother's dick!* belched Vaz.

Ignoring his father, Chris grabbed hold of the top of the ladder and swung himself over. He lowered himself until he was at the bottom.

"C'mon, Pop," urged Chris. "It's just another hole. I'll hold the ladder."

In the short journey from the container to the abandoned holding tank, Vaz appeared as if he'd aged ten years. Shoulders slumped, he stepped aboard the ladder and began a painstaking rung-by-rung descent. No sooner had he stepped foot on the bottom than the ladder was removed, dragged up and out by Lucky, who reappeared at the edge to address them.

"Saw this one night in Baja," Lucky began in a short speech. "Drinking game called *cuatro escorpiones en un cubo*, or some such shit. Four scorpions in a bucket. You can figure out the rest. Last scorpion breathing gets the ladder and a chance to make their case on why I should let 'em live."

Before Lucky could turn away he heard a shout—a guttural war whoop from Sugar's direction. Sugar gripped a chunk of concrete with a foot of embedded rebar. The beefy cop took no time in charging across the tank's floor at Vaz Kasabian, his caveman weapon raised, swinging it with a decided crunch.

Lucky shut his eyes, then his ears, wheeling away and walking back toward the stairs. He found a seat on the top step. The sun had just crested the horizon, sending streaks of brilliant yellow across the San Fernando Valley. He didn't attempt to imagine the blood sport unwinding in the hole some forty yards behind him. Or picture the open maws and the screams they issued. In that hole behind him were four of humanity's uncountable villains who deserved what was coming to them. If the justice system was in fact just, perhaps a courtroom and a jury would have been a wiser way to resolve his problem. Then again, the four devils he'd left in the hole had long ago discarded society's polite norms in exchange for living life by their own rules and morals. And to hell if Lucky felt the least bit sorry for any of them.

There came a squeal, high-pitched and like that of a dying pig. *Zadeh*, Lucky figured. Instead of twisting his neck he folded the shriek into the background noise of a tractor-trailer rig's distant air horn and the low-frequency rumble of freeway traffic.

He had one or two primary concerns. A helicopter flyover, kids playing hooky from school, or a spy satellite with a high-resolution camera somehow aimed at the old site. From his perch he could see all the way through the Cahuenga Pass to distant downtown. Just beyond, on the border of East Los Angeles, were Boyle Heights and the County Medical Examiner's office and the city morgue. By now, he imagined, Shia's and her father's bodies were lying on respective tables, their wounds examined and recorded. The attending examiner would be swabbing Shia for DNA and trace seminal fluid. No doubt, Lucky's semen would be discovered, though not officially identified for weeks—or even months—depending on how motivated the DA's office would be to prove what they'd probably already been informed of by an anonymous tip.

Lucky Dey was her murderer.

How long before Gonzo heard? Or Karrie or Travis? Had

they already? Or was that awful blow something still waiting to be delivered? One thing for certain, a bell was sure to be sounded that could never, ever be un-rung. Family over. Career over. Even if found not guilty—or innocent—there would be no returning from it. He'd said it already. They were too far over the waterfall to reverse what had been done. All that was left was justice.

Or injustice?

A large jet aircraft streaked overhead, banking left on final approach to Burbank's Bob Hope Airport. Lucky couldn't recall a day when the air had been so crystalline. So impossibly clear. On some days his city was achingly beautiful. But only when pictured in the macro. Its essence and ugliness were found in more acute observations. On the street. In the gutter. Or more specifically, in one of the four left-behind storage tanks to his rear.

The hollering and cries of violence had at last stopped.

"HEY, ASSHOLE!" shouted out a beleaguered voice, raspy and lost for breath. "IT'S DONE, MOTHERFUCKER . . . WHERE'S THE GODDAMN LADDER?"

37

Routine as it was, nothing about it felt so. Lee was lined up in the security queue to enter the Superior Courts building, awaiting his turn amongst the various defendants, plaintiffs, and attorneys. He wore his trademark tweed coat and porkpie hat, his red spiral notebook pressed across his chest as if he were protecting a football. In truth, though, Lee was just hanging on to himself, controlling his breathing, and carrying on with his plan. He was every bit the screenwriter he pretended. There was a movie to write. And it required the authenticity of having been there.

Lee's trip through the security gauntlet proved unremarkable. The normality of it all, he thought, belied that only twenty-four hours earlier the locality had come unglued in an avalanche of violence. The screams were gone. The panic. It was, indeed, business as usual. Lee rode the elevator up, stepped off on the sixth floor, and took up a seat in his usual spot. Only on that Tuesday he wasn't in Judge Sollo's Department J courtroom. Lee had chosen to change it up and attend Department H, an identical space, only with altogether different faces. Having already scrawled out a handwritten message—a fifth draft—Lee tore it out of the red spiral notebook, folded it neatly, then strode to the rail and offered the message to the bailiff, a big-hipped Hispanic woman in her late forties. The bailiff looked askance at the visitor, but didn't refuse. Lee returned to his seat, right and to the rear. There he waited through two hours as various attorneys argued over legal motions and scheduling conflicts. He feigned he was scribbling notations and was in all appearances attentive to the judicial machinations. His mind, though, remained dedicated to Shia. His memory of her. The shape of her body. The smell of her perfume . . .

"Mr. Chapman," Judge Jim called out from behind the bench.

"Yessir," presented Lee from his seat.

The morning lawyer-wrangling had concluded. The last pair of attorneys was packing up their case files and loading them into rolling attachés.

"You finally get bored with Judge Sollo's courtroom?" asked the judge.

"Sir?" Lee was already standing. "May I approach?"

"Come on down," waved Judge Jim with a friendly smile. "What's this special request you need?"

Lee made his way to the thigh-high swinging gate that separated the well of the court from the spectators. Judge Jim waved him closer.

"What's on your mind?" asked the judge.

"I'm writing something—" began Lee.

"We all know you're writing something," interrupted Judge Jim, teasing to the point of a joke. "And the rest of us judges have been jealous of all the attention you've lavished on Judge Sollo. What she got that we don't?"

"Not sure how to answer that, your Honor."

"This a book your writing? Movie?"

"Movie," said Lee. "Maybe a book after I write the movie. I'm still researching."

"And you've done this a lot?"

"Done what?"

"Writing."

"It's . . ." stammered Lee. "It's my last career, I think. Starting over."

"Never too late to start something new," said Judge Jim. "What was your first career, if I may ask?"

"I was a rocket scientist."

"You don't say," chuckled Judge Jim.

"Jet Propulsion Lab. NASA. I started as an engineer."

"You're not kidding."

"No, your Honor. Honest to God."

"So, what's this need for 'verisimilitude'?" Judge Jim held up Lee's note.

"Silly request. But it's about what it's like on the other side of that door."

"In chambers?" Judge Jim gestured to the door just left of the bench.

"Not what happens there," explained Lee. "What it looks like. So I can describe it accurately. Do you and the other judges share office space? Is there a community kitchen? Do the clerks have their own space?"

"No clerk space," answered Judge Jim. "Courtroom is their office. Back there's just for us jurists."

"Oh. Right. Okay."

"Wanna have a quick look-see?"

"If it's not too much to ask."

Judge Jim was just beginning to rise to his feet when he thought of another question.

"Not an unreasonable ask," said Judge Jim. "But why not ask Judge Sollo if she's your favorite?"

"Oh, that," replied Lee, appearing slightly relieved. He had his rehearsed answer at the ready. "She's a woman. Very nice woman.

I'm in court every day. Last thing I wanna do is come off as a stalker. Make her uncomfortable."

"Polite to a fault, are you?" smiled the judge.

"I'd like to hope so, your Honor."

"Two minutes. In and out. Should be enough for your verisimilitude? Good word, by the way. Haven't heard that one in decades."

The judge signaled a "no worries" motion to his bailiff and clerk, followed by one finger to explain that he'd be right back. Lee fell in behind Judge Jim. The draft created by the quick opening of the door sent the judge's flowing robe aflutter around his legs.

For Judge Jim, the quick "backstage" tour was another in a series of distractions. The past twenty-four hours had been an unmitigated nightmare, beginning with the meltdown behind the courthouse. He'd spent the rest of the day answering questions from LAPD and Sheriff's investigators, the FBI and Homeland Security, plus replying to countless entreaties from his fellow judges and other legal colleagues. Covertly, he'd had to find ways to communicate with his vigilante minions, including Sugar Freeman, to set in motion events designed to cover any potential exposure at the hands of Lucky Dey. The rest of his game was about focusing on his job and family, and appearing as if all in his life was unfolding in a normal, uneventful way. All morning, though, while hearing arguments from the litany of lawyers and appeared attentive, he'd actually been scrolling the internet in search for alerts on Lucky Dey's detainment and arrest. So far he'd clicked upon nothing. No news.

No news. *Yet,* the judge reminded himself.

"So, this is all it is," he motioned in his two-minute tour mode. "Not so sexy, is it?"

The door to the left of the judge's bench led to a nondescript corridor running the length of the floor. On one side were the doorways leading to various other courtrooms. Opposite were office doors to each judge's private chambers, men's and women's restrooms, and utility closets.

"Kitchen, such as it is, is down at that end," motioned Judge

Jim. "Fridge, microwave, coffee maker. But I make my own brew in chambers."

Judge Jim's chamber was large enough for a desk and a pair of leather couches. The windowless office was warmly lit by incandescent table lamps. Built-in shelves held law books and memorabilia and were so stuffed full of files and collectibles, it made the room feel cramped. Below a display of model Ferrari sports cars dating back to the 1950s was a five-foot-long putting green strip complete with a golf hole and automated ball return. Leaning in a corner were a variety of golf clubs—putters all—from hickory-shafted to steel.

"So, one quick question," asked the judge. "How does a fella go from a JPL engineer to hanging out in courtrooms and trying to write screenplays?"

"Long story," said Lee. "And you only gave me two minutes."

"I can make it five," said Judge Jim, seating himself behind his desk and throwing his feet up. "Longer if it's an interesting enough story."

"It's the tale of a man's descent," returned Lee.

"The screenplay? Or your life?"

"Both, I suppose," paced Lee in front of the desk.

"Legal thriller? I'll be honest. I find most of 'em pretty lame. Hardly ever get the legal stuff right."

"That's not gonna be a problem," nodded Lee. "Legal stuff I got loads of."

"Expect you do. All the time you've spent with us."

"No," said Lee. "My only problem is the ending."

"They say that's the hardest part."

"Truth is, I never really had a real ending . . ." revealed Lee. "At least not until right now."

Judge Jim had allowed himself another distraction. He was lending only half his attention to the impromptu visitor. His eyes had momentarily drifted to his laptop's screen. His right hand reached, fingers activating the cursor on his touch pad. Once again, he was instinctively, and almost unconsciously, looking for some kind of news.

Lucky Dey news.

In doing so, Judge Jaime Peralta missed seeing his guest pick up the golf club.

Lee had eased slightly to the right and gripped the first putter he could get a grip around. He lifted it with both arms, stepped forward, and struck with all the violence he could issue. Downward and with a lifetime's worth of rage. The plan in Lee's mind had been to strike the judge over and over until the room and he were coated in blood spatter. Only the club's forged metal toe was buried into the judge's bald dome. Deep. To the flange. A direct stab to the cerebrum. And there the golf club remained. Stuck. Just above Judge Jim's forever frozen and mortally final expression of abject surprise.

The deathly stare from the judge seemed permanently fixed on Lee until the former rocket scientist stumbled backward, finding the nearest sofa cutting him at the knees. Lee sat. The judge's eyes never moved or followed, fastened with a gaze aimed nowhere at all. The man was surely gone.

As the shock of the moment wore off, and while he waited to be discovered and arrested for murder, Lee Chapman felt something he hadn't in so very many years.

He felt accomplished.

Lucky slid the ladder to the edge of the abandoned storage tank, tipped it, and allowed gravity to assist. He retreated five paces, preferring to allow the surviving scorpion to carry himself out and to the surface. He filled his hand with his snub .45 and leveled the sight between the top two rails of the ladder, fully prepared to finish off the winner if he or she proved a threat.

Chris Kasabian appeared, half shirtless, scraped, and so blood-spattered that the morning sun reflected off him in hues of crimson and hot lava. In the moment he looked less like a peacock wannabe man and more like an adult. Chris stalled near the top rung once he saw the yawning muzzle of Lucky's gun.

"Gonna kill me now?" growled Chris.

"No," said Lucky, letting the gun dip downward. "Not you."

"Now what?"

"Your ol' man?"

Chris shook his head, pulled up and stepped from the hole. He let out a heavy sigh, looked up at the sky and shook his head as if to ask *why me?*

"You're a sick motherfucker," blamed Chris.

"I'm alive. And now so are you."

"What you did to my family . . ." Chris's words trailed in a guttural wallow. He was still adrenalized, pumped-up like a grizzly willing to kill anything in its path.

"Didn't do anything to your family but get out of the way."

"Fuck, fuck, fuck!"

"Grieving sucks. And you're gonna blame me until you run out of hate. But I have no doubt you'll find your way past it and see what's what in your world."

"What's what?" Chris slapped his chest.

"Your brother's gonna need you," answered Lucky.

Shaking his head as if to ask *How?*,Chris's eyes suddenly welled with equal measures of rage and tears.

"But however you do it, you can't do it from here," continued Lucky. "Somebody's gonna find the bodies. Today. Tomorrow. This'll be a crime scene. With blood work. Won't be hard for them to figure who's the missing piece."

Lucky pointed at Chris until the former peacock understood.

"So, I gotta go?" he asked.

"Wherever Armenians go," finished Lucky. "You gotta get your ass moving."

"Armenia . . ."

"Maybe the rest of your family comes to you. Or you figure something else out. At least Johnny's big brother is alive and giving a shit about him."

"Like you give a shit about him," mocked Chris. "You prick! You just used him!"

"No," Lucky shrugged. "He came to me. He wanted help. He was terrified of your father. So, I did what I could do. Can't say it was close to enough. But he's safe now. Hopefully, getting the care he needs."

"You don't know shit."

"Maybe. Maybe not," relented Lucky. "But there it is, anyway."

With nothing more to say, Lucky swiveled off his back foot in what was supposed to be his march away.

"Whoa! Wait!" charged Chris, thrusting himself three steps forward in a sudden plea. "Where you going?"

"I got my own shit to handle."

"You're gonna leave me here?"

"Like you want a ride or somethin'?" swiveled Lucky before continuing his exit. "There's murders on the both of us. And believe me. You don't wanna be anywhere near me, and vice versa. You know?"

Lucky never looked back, quickly disappearing down the steps, beating his feet in double time all the way back to his car. If there was relief for him, there was no feeling to it. A new weight was upon him, greater than the last—*what to do next?* He could motor himself downtown, take up his post in the Major Crimes Unit, and wait for his arrest. That was if he even got that far. Or he could find a barstool somewhere and sip draught beers until somebody found him, pointed him out, called 911, and reported his sighting.

Jesus, he thought, taking the seat behind the wheel. The guilt. It felt as if he'd actually killed Shia. If only he hadn't roped her into his loop and sought shelter and solace from her, she'd be alive and in her safe space in Department J at the Van Nuys courthouse.

Lucky's phone beeped, flagging him that he had a voicemail from Karrie.

"Lucky? It's me," began the recording. He couldn't precisely recall when he'd heard her voice sound so troubled. "What's happening? There were police here looking to arrest you. They wouldn't say what for but Gonzo got some calls saying you're wanted for murder? I know that can't be real. Something's gotta be really, really wrong with things for—I dunno. Where are you? Why can't you answer? We need you home. All of us. Travis is scared. Gonzo's crying. You know how she hates that but she's crying for you. What happened? What's gonna happen to us? Our family? Please, please just get back to me. We'll all figure this out together. 'Kay? All right. You're calling back the second you get this. Love you."

The voicemail ended with two seconds of static before the recording ceased. Lucky heard himself wheeze as his chest sank deeper into his emptied lungs than he could ever remember.

Call her back to say what? It's true. I'm wanted for murder. But I didn't do it.

Maybe Gonzo had been right. He *was* a shit magnet. So, he rationalized that the very last thing any of his poor family needed were his excuses, reasoned or otherwise. What they deserved from him was something concrete. Stability. A presence they could count on, lean on . . .

. . . rely upon.

No sooner had he dropped the '99 into drive than his phone rang. The incoming call carried an 818 prefix. The rest of the number on his mobile screen was unrecognizable.

Van Nuys Division, Lucky guessed. Someone from the LAPD's Homicide Unit had been given his cell number and was hoping he would answer. What was sure to follow was an appeal for him to turn himself in. Peacefully. Without incident. If Lucky didn't answer, more calls were sure to come. Most likely from cop friends, former Reapers like Flip Bledsoe or Richie Lopes. Concerned. They'd strongly recommend some kind of peaceful surrender, perhaps through a criminal lawyer.

"This is Lucky," he answered, already having chosen to yield his freedom. After all, he hadn't killed Shia or her father. But if he were convicted, it wasn't as if he didn't have plenty of other indiscretions worthy of prison time. So, there it was. A decision. Face his inevitable arrest, detainment in downtown's infamous County Jail, and then sometime prior to arraignment, when there was a process to put some faith in, finally reach out to his family. From inside, he could be their rock. Available but safely out of the way. He'd face the consequences with the old mantra.

The only way out is through.

"It's me!" spat the voice on the other end of the call. "Asshole, you broke my arm."

"Who is this?"

"You said to think about it," said the voice. "Gave me your card. So, I'm callin' to say I thought about it and here I am. Broken arm and all. Time and place, asshole. You 'n' me. I'm there."

Lucky's brain shifted into rewind. He started with leaving bloodied Chris Kasabian at the edge of the abandoned storage tank and continued backward until he landed on somebody with a broken arm.

Mr. Teardrops.

"I remember you," returned Lucky, but only the part where he'd pinched the man with his own car door and left his business card with a warning.

"Said you had a place. Where we could, you know. Get it on. Said you'd even bring a shovel. Whatever. Bring it. Don't bring it. 'Cause I'm gonna cut you to so many pieces, the coyotes are gonna feed on what's left."

"Sounds like a plan," agreed Lucky.

He gave the man directions. Interstate 15 North to Barstow. Highway 58 West past Hinkley, followed by a winding drive up Route 7 into the high desert toward Copper City. Just beyond the wind farms was a dirt road that dead-ended into a rock formation resembling a hand reaching up into the sky as if asking God for help. They would meet at high noon or thereabouts. And discuss.

Lucky's surrender to the LAPD would have to wait.

As he pointed the Crown Vic east, a scolding sun forcing him to unfold his visor, he tried to keep his thoughts ahead of him. What was behind was more than just human carnage. It was as much emotional battery as physical. If he allowed himself, he could see it all. Relive it. Feel it to his marrow. But there'd be plenty of time to do that once he was in jail.

Or dead.

What Lucky couldn't see through his mental rearview mirror was the face of a grieving mother as she was reunited with her

eighteen-year-old boy. After a horrid night in a therapeutic isolation cell, Johnny B. had concluded that all hope in his miserable
life had been abandoned at the precise moment he'd chucked that
smelly Philly cheesesteak sandwich into rush-hour traffic. Then
came the dawn, a much-needed hot breakfast, and a two-hour session with a comely psychiatrist with both an angelic disposition
and the innate ability to communicate both understanding and
forgiveness. The strain in Johnny B.'s body eased with her help
and an adjustment to his medications. This was followed by a visit
from his mother. Johnny B. met Tabitha in a windowless visiting
room. She was exhausted, sleep deprived, sad to her sinews, but
with arms open and relieved her troubled son was present, healthy-
looking, and unharmed. They ached for each other, cried together,
held on endlessly, and promised to never ever let go as they settled
into a very bittersweet future split between a half-empty home in
Glendale and twice-a-year trips to the city of Yerevan in central
Armenia.

Although the old men of the crime clan regarded him as some
kind of failure, a prince proved unfit to succeed, Chris would
find an unsettling peace in ancient Yerevan. The details of exactly
what had occurred in Los Angeles that bloody week proved murky
at best. How Vartan Kasabian ended up beaten to death in an
abandoned storage tank—along with two LAPD police officers—
appeared impossible to untangle. From a continent away, word
had filtered back to the bosses that Vaz had been concealing a
secret. His youngest, a man-child with a severe mental handicap,
had accidentally caused an innocent woman's death, toppling the
first of far too many dangerous dominoes to count. It was the view
of the old men that Vaz should have better managed the potential
complications and known how to intervene. Retard the violence.

Instead, the Armenian mob and its silent roots so deeply
sunk into the Southland had found itself temporarily exposed
and uncomfortably newsworthy. From the LAPD to the County
Sheriff's to the FBI, task forces had been assembled to partake in
some very public crackdowns. Therefore the consensus among the
bosses was to lower their profile while permanently excising Chris

Kasabian and his remaining family from all Armo business, allowing only the legitimate enterprises such as the beauty salons and asphalt business to continue under the Kasabian flag.

Add the convenience that the United States government had no extradition agreement with Armenia and young Chris would slowly discover some joy and comfort in his sudden anonymity and a life outside of organized crime. As a leg up on hurdling the language barrier, Chris eventually fell hard for his tutor, a university psychology student with a keen interest in families raising children with Autism Spectrum Disorder.

Over seven thousand miles away, the powers that be in the LAPD's Robbery-Homicide Division decided to bundle the investigation of the three bodies found in the abandoned storage tank with the mix of Armenian and cop bodies dropped behind the Van Nuys Superior Court building. This was because of some flawed thinking that they would only have to pull a single string to gather everything together neatly. As the detectives saw it, there were three disparate elements that tied all crimes scenes together: Chris Kasabian, Deputy Shia St. George . . .

. . . and Lucky Dey.

With Chris Kasabian ensconced and untouchable in Armenia and Shia St. George sadly deceased, Lucky was the lone subject who could shed light on the bloody mess. And because they had Shia's murder to shackle onto Lucky, the homicide crew expected the deputy would be more than willing to accept a reduced plea of voluntary manslaughter in exchange for some much-needed illumination. Captain Timothy J. Kleiner of the PD's homicide unit was so upbeat on the prospect of clearing all those fallen bodies from his murder board, he even had hopes Lucky would add perspective to Judge Jaime Peralta's death by clubbing by the self-admitted reprobate and confessed killer, Lee Chapman. The *Los Angeles Times* would later quote Lee's personal motive for murdering the judge:

"Seriously. What better way to accelerate my own personal descent into man's shithole than killing a goddamn above-it-all judge?" Later in the article, Lee profoundly added, "I look forward to prison life. I expect the quiet and isolation will be good for my writing. From there I will peacefully compose the screenplay of my life."

When asked under oath if he'd ever met or spoken with Lucky Dey, Lee would forever claim no recollection whatsoever.

But there was one last puzzle piece, a jagged-edged player not even imagined by Lucky or the legion of murder police and assistant prosecutors assigned to close all the cases. And that was CSI Amy Cho. The amateur collector of fringe Hollywood tales and certified magician had never forgotten one of the first rules of illusion: misdirection. And for a magical misdirection to succeed, the audience needs motive, a primary wont to be entertained. A desire that makes them ripe to be fooled.

Or fools.

When Amy had knelt at the small laboratory freezer she'd kept in the spare bedroom of her apartment, with Sugar Freeman's steamed breath at her neck, she couldn't help but be shocked back to another night—the rape Miles had amusingly referred to as her further initiation into their own private justice league. The only upside Amy could glean from the horror was that Sugar had worn a condom. After both Miles and Sugar had departed, Amy first considered flushing the disgusting prophylactic. What followed was a change of mind with implications far beyond Amy's own suffering. Donning disposable gloves, she collected Sugar's ejaculate as if it were evidence, assigned it a number, and deposited the vial in the freezer.

Then in the days that followed, Amy, still technically in shock from the rape—and the news of Miles's sudden death—was forced by Sugar to hand over the sperm sample assigned to Lucky Dey. For a moment, her hand had hovered over the correct vial. Obedient. Only the smell of Sugar, the reminder of his breath, had flipped Amy from momentary indecision to certainty. She chose the other numbered vial, handing Sugar his own tenth of an ounce—or less than a teaspoon—of incriminating semen.

After Sugar had bolted from her apartment, Amy had remained on the floor, the freezer door cooling the hurried rush of blood to her face. Within reach was another collectible, a 1970s-era waste-paper basket skinned with Lou Ferrigno as TV's Incredible Hulk. On her knees, Amy methodically emptied the freezer unit of all the cribbed DNA samples, transferred the entire contents into a Hefty garbage bag, fouled it with leftovers and expired items from her kitchen fridge, then interred it to the dumpster in the alley behind her apartment unit.

And that was that.

With Sugar's DNA tied to the double-homicide of Shia St. George and her paraplegic father, any leverage the LAPD had with Lucky Dey evaporated like mist under the hurt of morning sunshine. Only none of those revelations would unfold until well after the Thanksgiving holiday, leaving the LAPD with little motive for all the killings beyond tit for tat retaliations between the criminal Armos and a cabal of corrupt cops.

But all that was to come, as for Lucky Dey it was still only the Tuesday following Halloween, just minutes shy of that noon appointment with Mr. Teardrops. He knew nothing of the future but for a strong suspicion that his own incarceration was imminent. Lucky arrived at the dirt road's dead end. He climbed from the driver's seat, noting how the new paint on his Crown Vic was caked in a thick, filmy mix of city grime and desert dirt. He squinted at the sun, surveyed the immediate landscape for his party guest, and turned about to gaze back at the direction from which he'd come. It was midday, and the desert was already baking. To the horizon, all he could see was scrub brush and sand laid across a rocky, low-mountain topography. Then in the distance, he saw it—a rooster tail of dust kicked up from behind an approaching vehicle—an indistinguishable SUV of some sort. Mr. Teardrops, it appeared, was on his merry way to their rendezvous.

And right on time, no less.

About the Author

Doug cut his teeth writing movies like *Die Hard 2, Bad Boys,* and *Hostage* until sharp enough to pen the Lucky Dey crime thriller series. He lives in Southern California with his wife, two children, and three mutts.

You can learn more about Doug at www.dougrichardson.com and drop him a line at bydougrich@dougrichardson.com. You can also follow him at www.facebook.com/bydougrichardson, on Twitter @byDougRich, and on Instagram @bydougrich.

THE NIGHT IS NEVER BLACK

NOVEMBER

1

Copper City, California.

The shovel blade was barely penetrating. Underneath the earthy crust were eons of pressure-formed rock and continually decomposing granite that demanded force better suited from a diesel backhoe. With each downward strike, the steel edge practically bounced before it dug. But the violence generated by Lucky, unfazed in his mission-like effort to turn over yet another shovelful of dirt, would eventually evolve into a single, man-sized grave.

"Said you had a place," Mr. Teardrops had said. "Where we could, you know. Get it on. Said you'd even bring a shovel. Whatever. Bring it. Don't bring it. 'Cause I'm gonna cut you into so many pieces the coyotes are gonna feed on what's left."

"Sounds like a plan," Lucky had agreed, knowing even in the fluidity of a phone conversation that he'd reached a critical decision. A turning point from which there might be no return. Lights out. Dead and buried in a hole of his own design.

With the peaceful resignation of a condemned killer with a noose around his neck, Lucky met the hostile O.G. under a rock formation that roughly resembled a hand reaching up to God. The agreement had been for each man to come alone, but Lucky fully expected Mr. Teardrops to arrive with an arsenal of human backup. But perhaps Mr. Teardrops carried the same emotional weight as Lucky—a man so far over the edge he was either ready to take another life or meet the ultimate fate—because he had landed at the site on time and alone, armed with identical dueling knives—fixed blade, bayonet style—one for Lucky, one for himself.

"Funny," remarked Lucky. "I brought two of something as well. Shovels. Figured we'd dig the grave first. Save the survivor half the work."

Despite Mr. Teardrops's venomous protestations, Lucky began the difficult dig. He kept hacking at the earth and turning over shovelfuls of sand until his antagonist quit frothing at the mouth and joined in. A testy conversation ensued with Lucky suggesting Mr. Teardrops tell the tale—and remind him of just why the thick-necked gangster was demanding blood for blood. Until that moment, Lucky hadn't the faintest idea as to the nature of the bad guy's beef or need for recompense. He only knew there was something the man was more than willing to murder or die over. As the men tore into the earth, Mr. Teardrops admonished and complained and shed actual tears, sometimes swinging the shovel over his shoulder like an axe, pounding the dust like he imagined it was Lucky's head. Other times, Mr. Teardrops howled at the sky with the rage of a caged wolverine.

And Lucky just kept digging.

As the O.G. gangbanger's history unfolded, he told of how his younger brother had survived a gunfight with Lucky in an incident initiated with a simple traffic stop. The shooting had led to prison and been followed by a meth addiction and suicide. The assignation Mr. Teardrops placed on Lucky had culminated in the mano-a-mano showdown in the desert. It was unusual for Lucky to let himself get strung into such a willfully reckless brush, but the invite had come at a time when he'd been as close to hopeless as he'd ever felt. It had been a Halloween to forget, climaxing with more blood than even Lucky could stomach and the tragic loss of someone dear to him, for which he'd been blamed. Somehow, a noontime collision on a desolate landscape stretch of landscape near Copper City seemed deserved. And it was there where Lucky would either die or pivot into the second half of his near forty-year life.

Once the bereaved brother had been exhausted of both spit and words, Lucky leaned on his shovel and shared a story about a lost younger brother. *His own.* Murdered on a Kern County roadside and left to incinerate in a car fire. For a minute, Lucky felt like he was back in Alcoholics Anonymous, circled up in folding chairs with fellow addicts sharing the pain.

"So, what'd you do about it?" asked Mr. Teardrops. "You get who done it?"

"I got off a shot," admitted Lucky. "Hit the perp. Tried to convince myself I'd finished him off. But after all this time, I'm thinking otherwise. He's still out there."

"So you understand why it had to come to this." Mr. Teardrops had resumed an aggressive stance, hulking shoulders rounded and full of flex, his whitened knuckles around the shovel handle.

"But it don't at all," disagreed Lucky.

Lucky had already clocked the body language of his opponent—athletic pose, weight on the balls of his feet, hips locked. Only Mr. Teardrops hadn't yet readied his shovel blade to strike. So, when Lucky saw the man twist his torso and the beginning of an arm cock, he closed the distance and struck downward with his shovel's cutting edge. Before Mr. Teardrops could lower his blade, Lucky closed the distance and cracked down on the gangster's ankle. There was a cartilage-crushing *crunch*. The joint gave way. Dust plumed when Mr. Teardrops's body slapped the dirt. Next, Lucky hooked the prostrate man with the shovel's flat shoulder and pulled until Mr. Teardrops was flat-backed in the half-dug grave.

"No, no, no, no!" squealed the gangbanger, arms unconsciously up and fending off a deathblow that would never come.

"Think your little brother wanted you to die like this? I sure as shit know mine wouldn't."

"Dude!" sobbed Mr. Teardrops. "What I got left but my pain?"

Pain. Lucky was filled with it. Whatever path he was on, Lucky knew something had to change. *He* had to change.

So, in the hours that passed, Lucky sat at the edge of the shallow hole, shovel across his knees, sun drying his sweat until his skin was chapped. There both men eventually talked of everything from heartbreak to the paper-thin divide between vengeance and justice. In that lapse of time, Lucky was reflective, claiming he'd rather live in a world where Mr. Teardrops was out there, alive, breathing the same air, wrestling with the demons of right and wrong.

Finally, the men became thirsty and starved, so Lucky drove Mr. Teardrops to a high-desert Dairy Queen. The duo powered up on burgers and DQ Freezes and said their goodbyes a short hobbling distance from a Glenn County hospital trauma center. But not before one last exchange.

"Still don't get why you didn't kill me," replayed Mr. Teardrops.

"Believe in God?" asked Lucky.

"Supposed to. I'm born Catholic."

"My daughter believes," finished Lucky. "And though I'm not sure about God, I believe in her. And she believes there's a purpose to everything."

APRIL

Monday

2

Calabasas. 10:49 a.m.

"It's an awesome neighborhood," offered Austin Andrews, his salesman smile on full and rehearsed beam, capped teeth as bright as those of the Osmonds. "Close to the schools. The markets. But, hey, it's Calabasas. What's not to like?"

"What's this neighborhood called?" asked the homely woman in the back seat of the luxury car, a late model Mercedes S class.

Leased. At $799 a month, Austin couldn't technically afford the deep blue German beast. But because he continued to advertise himself as one of the West Valley's top real estate agents, he couldn't afford *not* to look the part.

"Well," paused Austin. "It's a Calabasas zip code. But I know what you're asking."

Austin knew precisely what she was asking. Calabasas, like so many Southern California burgs, was divvied up into neighborhoods with their own priceless monikers. The Oaks. Hidden Hills. The Highlands. Malibu Creek. Palatino. Las Virgenes Park. Each neighborhood implied a certain social status. But somehow the tree-lined middle-class streets of eastern Calabasas had escaped the neighborhood name game. Or worse, Austin was suffering from memory slippage. For the life of him, he couldn't recall.

"Revolution Acres," he spun, coining the neighborhood name out of thin air—inspired by a pair of nearby streets, Paul Revere Drive and Declaration Avenue.

In the front passenger seat was a matron of Eastern European extraction. She tipped out at something Austin guessed was near seventy years old, casually attired in a gold-spangled T-shirt and jeans with a yoga and cardio-maintained body that rivaled women half her age. Her forty-year-old daughter, Austin's backseat passenger, might've been best described as fleshy, a child with a late-night addiction to designer vodka and frozen bonbons rebelling against her über fit mother.

Austin guessed it was the girl's mother who was going to be shelling out the down payment on the home, thus he'd insisted the mom sit beside him, up front, with the better view of the neatly sidewalked streets. Old-growth deciduous maple and elms in spring fervor fronted the largely middle-income-sized homes, considerably marked up due to the fact that their foundations were a mere eighth to a quarter of a mile outside the subpar Los Angeles Unified School District.

"What age are your kids?" inquired Austin, eyes in his rearview mirror in search of the daughter's pie-faced expression.

"She has a sixth grader and a freshman in high school," answered the alpha mother before complaining. "LAUSD is the worst. Destroys me that my grandbabies share classrooms with so many . . ."

The mother's words trailed into silent unmentionables. Austin privately disagreed, but the salesman in him nodded his understanding. It wasn't difficult to fill in the blanks based on a cornucopia of most likely prejudices held by the mother—not that he wasn't beyond his own enmity towards others. If it had been a later hour and he had been more than a few martinis deep into his habitual day's end comedown, he might have dropped jokes about all the names used to describe Calabasas by both locals and outsiders. There was Cala-Baghdad, Cala-Bumfuck, and Cala-Badass, the latter coined for all the bad-behaving hip-hop and rap artists who'd settled into the many hilltop mansions behind guarded gates. Women from the area were often referred to as Cala-bitches or Cala-bimbos. The men were Cala-bastards, himself included, despite having left the tony township long ago.

"How many houses do we have to see in this hood?" griped the daughter.

"Two to show you today," answered Austin, buoying back with extra cheer. "First one's my own listing up around the next corner. The other is at the other end of Revere. Won't take long at all."

There was a genuine sheen to the morning. Intermittent rain showers had wet all the streets and left every leaf and blade of grass iridescent. The air smelled of chlorophyll and must, spilling into the car's interior through the back right window, which the daughter kept cracked and whistling.

Austin needed the sale like plants demanded carbon dioxide for survival. Creditors were closing in at such a nightmarish clip—blowing up his every communication link, from emails to texts—that he'd begun utilizing disposable prepaid cell phones to conduct his day-to-day business. Gossiping colleagues suspected he was dealing drugs. *If only*, he laughed to himself. Selling cocaine or meth or even prescription meds would have at least resulted in a positive cash flow. In Austin's wallet was a single ATM card, but if he'd so much as attempted to withdraw twenty dollars from his account, the transaction would have produced an insufficient funds message.

I'm broke as an aging fag joke.

Accordingly, instead of delivering buyers to multimillion-dollar listings, Austin was reduced to praying he'd split a commission on a three-bedroom mid-century property in the one section of Calabasas that didn't even rate a neighborhood name.

Revolution Acres? Ha. As if.

Austin began to worry he'd been kissing up to the mother a notch too obviously. He needed to keep the daughter engaged and feeling that, in him, she'd found a trusted advocate. He flicked the right-hand turn signal and gave another looksee into the rearview mirror, hoping to make some positive eye contact with his dreary back-seat passenger. Instead, his eyes fixed through his rear windshield and onto the sudden yawning of an oncoming truck grill. A Dodge pickup. Austin was easily able to distinguish the chromed Ram logo before he heard the thrum of the V-8's engine. His shoulder blades clinched in autonomic fear of a sudden impact. Only the jacked-up Dodge swerved a hard left, nearly kissing the leased Mercedes's rear taillight before barreling past. Metallic teal green, a pimped-out show truck. A Nissan sedan, mere feet behind and drafting the pickup's bumper, surged by. White. Arcing around the upcoming street corner, the tandem vehicles blew by the Mercedes like it was a brick with no wheels. While the Nissan hugged the asphalt, the top-heavy pickup's inside wheels appeared to practically come unglued from the pavement.

"*Oh, Gospodi!* Oh, Jesus!" chirped the mother.

"Christ, what was that?!" chimed her sullen daughter, suddenly animated.

"Teenagers," excused a breathless Austin, thinking with his tongue instead of his brain. "No matter where you go, there they are, am I right?"

"Nearly gave me a heart attack!" angered the mother. "They're gonna get somebody killed."

Austin slowed his car, easing into the same turn. He hoped to unholy hell the speedsters had vanished into the ether, leaving the street clean and idyllic. To help erase their nerves, Austin tried to refocus both women on the mission.

"Boys or girls?" asked Austin. "Your middle-schooler and ninth grader?"

"One of each—" began the daughter before her mouth stalled, her voice trailing as Austin braked quickly. Her mother sucked in a lungful of air.

The street was framed by rows of neatly kempt homes, stripes of perfect sidewalks with nary a crack, and a sky partially obstructed by green, fully foliaged trees still dripping from the rain shower. Fouling the enchanted scene were those two formerly speeding vehicles. Stopped. The pickup truck appeared to have rolled, coming to rest on its side against the trunk of a tall, thick-bodied eucalyptus. The white Nissan was angled in the middle of the street with both doors swung wide open. The sedan's driver, an ebony teen in a baggy neon sweatsuit, stood sentry at his door while his passenger, a tattooed, teacup-sized black youth in a bright orange knit cap, positioned himself in front of the pickup's peeled front windshield and aimed a pistol into the cab. With fourteen successive shots, he emptied his magazine into the upside-down, still seat-belted bodies.

The sounds of gunshots penetrated Austin's German car's heavy insulation like the popping of distant fireworks, creating an eerie disconnect from the violence only forty yards beyond the iconic Mercedes medallion. The Nissan's driver, his hair braided into knots with rubber bands that matched his togs, gripped a pistol nickeled with a heavy bore. When he took a threatening step toward Austin's Mercedes, the mother reflexively howled in staccato heaves.

"BACK UP, BACK UP!" screeched the daughter.

But Austin remained frozen, appearing like the proverbial deer caught in a poacher's spotlight. His eyes stayed fixed on the

Nissan's driver, as if telepathically sending a set of simple pleas.

I am not a threat.

I will never identify you in a lineup.

I will not cooperate with the police.

Just please, please, please let us live.

Then *thunk!* And the sound of the Nissan's passenger door slamming shut cut the cord of the stare-off. The driver cocked his head as if he'd heard "C'mon, c'mon" from his gunman passenger. With his leash clearly yanked, the driver broke off, swiveled back into the sedan and let the inertia of the car surging forward swing his own door closed. Austin heard himself breathing in with a mild, allergy-season wheeze, then felt words rising.

"Call 911!" he found himself coughing while unhitching his seat belt and leaning all his 240 pounds into the door.

"You get back in the car!" screamed the mother.

"CALL 911!" he barked back. "CALL IT NOW!"

Austin's legs felt unsteady, nearly ready to collapse under the weight of his newly acquired belly fat—a full forty-four pounds in the past two years. The gym had beckoned but he'd fallen so far behind on the payments he hadn't dared to show his pudgy face. His quadriceps ached as he pushed his fallow muscles into an awkward run, rushing toward the tipped pickup. Austin expected blood. After all, he'd consumed days of movies and cable television. But the violence that filled his eyeballs was sickening. Slashes of red were everywhere. Punctured with oozing bullet holes, both victims were black-haired, Asian, limp, and draining fluids. The passenger's jaw had partially sheered into a gaping death maw.

There was also the money.

Hundred-dollar bills were splashed between the dead driver and passenger. Some were still banded in ten-thousand-dollar-currency paper straps. Other Benjamins were simply loose and spattered in red. A small, partially unzipped gym bag held onto the rest of the cash. Bundles on top of bundles.

A hundred thousand dollars? Two hundred thousand? wondered Austin. *And what, if anything, would happen to me if I just reached in, grabbed the moneybag, and sauntered back to my car?*

Austin caught himself. Despite the horror, the instinct of his money woes was calling his subconscious. He remained staring at the duffle until he noticed the voice. Tinny. Urgent. His eyes followed the sound to the ground between himself and the pickup's displaced front windshield. In the gutter was a mobile phone with a badly cracked screen, activated and identifying the user at the other end of the line as Zipper.

"Hello?" the voice kept asking, though to Austin it sounded like a squawk. "Hello! Stop fuckin' with me, ese. What's goin' on?"

Magnetically, as if being lured to the phone, Austin crouched to pick it up. He didn't know why he did it, but would later excuse it to being in shock; that or an involuntary need to seek help for the victims.

"Jesus fucking Christ!" complained Zipper, his voice getting richer as the speaker got closer to Austin's ear. "Do we have Tung Chee's money or what? You half-assed noodle nigga better answer me!"

"Hey . . . uh . . . who's this?" stuttered Austin, his own words wavering as his body shook.

"The fuck you say?" pissed Zipper. "Who this?"

"I . . . I'm the guy at the accident," finished Austin, his eyes slashing across the landscape. Neighbors had begun to leak from front doors, but weren't venturing much further than their welcome mats.

"What accident?"

"There was . . ." confused Austin. "Men with guns. Did you call 911?"

"Did I . . . What? Who is this? Put on my cuz!"

"I'm . . . I'm Austin Anderson and I'm here," he continued to stupidly stammer. "And it's okay. I asked my clients to call 911—"

"Where's my boy, Tu'an?"

"Who?"

"The phone you're talkin' on, fool! Tell that seaweed sucker I wanna talk to him before I reach through and cut your goddamn throat."

"Don't think he can talk right now," swiveled Austin, once

again filling his eyes with the wrecked truck cab and the horror of those two dangling bodies, both dead and bled out to an obvious mortal conclusion.

"And why the fuck not?"

"'Cause I think he's dead," relayed Austin, almost robotic. "Think they're both dead."

3

Century City. 11:13 a.m.

Overkill, Lucky thought. That was most lawyers' answer to everything when it came to litigation. It was militaristic; overwhelm the enemy with swarms of legality from motions to delays to every bit of attorney trickery until the other side can only yell uncle and settle.

"Not sure I need all this," voiced Lucky, the on-the-ropes Los Angeles County sheriff's detective. He sat uncomfortably at one end of an expansive granite-topped conference table. One glass-walled suite peered into the next, giving the illusion of transparency. *What a crock*, thought Lucky. These were corporate lawyers whose prima facie occupation was concealing the sins of their masters. To Lucky's immediate right was the always crisp-suited Conrad Ellis, Lucky's sometime *consigliere* and a man wealthy beyond human reason. Next to Conrad was one member from his phalanx of attorneys—a chilly blonde best described as human vanilla—though with a vast curriculum vitae of experience negotiating against city bureaucracies.

"Best defense is a strong offense," defended the attorney, whose name Lucky could never seem to remember. Perhaps it was because upon her dry, prosecutor-like presentation he'd privately nicknamed her Ms. Vanilla. "County would like nothing more than for you to just resign. Quit. Walk the hell away."

"Purpose of outside counsel is that they're on your side," added Conrad. "And your side alone."

"Deputies' union is on my side," defended Lucky for amusement alone. He knew it was a weak argument.

"You don't believe that," said the attorney. "Otherwise, why would you be here?"

"One word why I'm here," replied Lucky. "Connie."

"As a favor to him?" she asked. "Or a favor to yourself?"

"Connie's been solid to me and my family," stated Lucky, flat and affect free. Truth was, Lucky didn't trust any lawyers, be it those working for his union reps or Conrad's battalion of business button-ups. "A real friend. So, I trust Conrad."

"And I *trust* this law firm," thumbed Conrad. "And advocates like her will fight for you and only you. On my command. That simple. So, my advice to you is to let her help."

Lucky allowed a cleansing breath, rested his gaze on the floor-to-ceiling window and the twenty-two-story view. The rainstorm had left the air unfiltered. From the Century City office tower, he could see from the Sepulveda Pass all the way to the Hollywood Sign overlooking cozy Beachwood Canyon. Cotton-ball clouds hung over the hills that divided the Basin from the San Fernando Valley. Somewhere further east, out of sight, was Altadena and the family he'd been separated from. Though it had been nearly five months, the wound from the forced detachment was still fresh enough to bleed.

"Lucky?" the lawyer asked, standing erect. Her suit was smart, light gray with tartan lines, and tailored to best flatter her plus-sized frame. "The question is, what do you want? What's the outcome that you most desire?"

Outcome?

Lucky's number-one desire was to be reunited with his family. Though he'd never married Gonzo nor legally given his name to her son Travis, he had a genuine bond with them, not to mention his adopted daughter Karrie. And their absence from his life had proven more crushing than he could have imagined. But that wasn't the subject at hand. After a career publicly decried as "dubiously dangerous" by newly named County Sheriff Paul McGill—as well as a much-publicized recent domino effect of tragedy and death from which Lucky was eventually exonerated, but darkly tainted—the sixteen-year veteran was considered too hot to handle; a veritable catalyst for violence. The Sheriff's Department wanted to quietly retire Lucky. But he wanted to continue serving in some form of frontline duty.

"Don't wanna take a desk," answered Lucky. "Not just to keep my pension. Me on forced admin duty? Certified shit show."

"Understood," said Ms. Vanilla. "But what kind of leverage do we have if they refuse to return you to a position you approve?"

Zero. Zip. Nada. Lucky knew it like he knew the meaning of *Miranda.*

"Would you ever think of returning to Kern County?" asked Conrad.

"Too far away . . ." Lucky was shaking his head. Conrad understood. Plus, there were no actual gutters to patrol in shit-kicker Kern. Just illegal weed farms and miles of backyard meth labs.

"In the last letter from the County it's pretty clear what they'd like is for you to step away from the job," said the attorney. "And in my one off-the-record conversation with a county lawyer, you were twice referred to as a 'shit magnet.'"

Lucky didn't nod his agreement, though he had heard the phrase more than once before. The last utterance was from Gonzo right before she'd kicked him out of the house.

"County seems to believe," she continued, "that the only unknown is what you're willing to accept in the way of a settlement. Pension at X. Benefits vested up to Y."

"Union already argued the same," said Lucky.

"Fine. So, you want to know what does Vignam, Brent, and Herschowitz bring to the party?" she asked rhetorically, dropping the firm's name like a thousand-pound block of marble.

"No. I want to know what *you* bring to the party," finished Lucky.

"What we bring . . . what *I* bring . . ." chuckled the attorney, "is some serious push. Conrad's a valued client. The senior partners here have relationships in all levels of the local power structures. A whisper here and there? And when the County recognizes that we are your sole counsel in the dispute? Maybe they discover some extra wiggle room in their offer and the final outcome is your returning to the kind of duty you desire."

Lucky leaned forward, sifting through the open file between them until he came up with a Xeroxed letter. He spun it toward the attorney.

"Says I'm unfit for duty," said Lucky. "Their statement of fact."

"Statement of fact or just the first salvo of a negotiation?"

"Yeah," said Lucky, "but how do you know I'm not?"

"You're not what? Fit to be a cop?"

Lucky raised his eyebrows. A challenge.

"I'm not supposed to know," she replied. "I'm supposed to be your lawyer. Your advocate and your advocate only."

That much Lucky knew. She didn't know him beyond the man who sat cross-legged in the high-backed executive chair. For that matter, neither did Conrad, really. At least not well. It was the oft-repeated complaint about Lucky. He wasn't good at letting people in—even Gonzo and Travis. But Karrie? She might be the exception. Lucky wasn't her birth father. That man was deceased. But Karrie, who was legally emancipated and only weeks away from turning eighteen, had taken Lucky's last name nearly a year earlier. During his months of paid suspension, she had introduced him to her Muay Thai workouts, the Brazilian martial art she'd become addicted to. In turn, Lucky was teaching Karrie how to surf.

"It's a process," reminded the attorney. "And nothing happens overnight."

"Like sucking cement through a straw," added Conrad.

"In the meantime," continued the lawyer, "for the sake of your case you must keep a seriously low profile. No trouble of any kind. Nothing that would give the County a stronger case that you *are* a shit magnet."

"Some things easier said than done," smirked Lucky.

Ms. Vanilla put her hands on top of the table and leaned in.

"Harsh question," she parried. "Did you ever once think it was just that kind of *fuck you* attitude that got you into this pickle?"

Lucky knew all too well why he was in the lawyer's office. He was who he was. No apologies. It had always been a matter of time as to when the bureaucracy would drop a ton of bricks on him. His life, though, would remain all about what he could get done before someone eventually found a way to put a stop to his beating heart. Between old enemies and those yet to be identified, Lucky knew he wasn't over his catalytic behavior.

Join Doug's mailing list
for sneak previews, exclusive content, and
news on the release of the latest Lucky Dey Thriller.

Visit www.dougrichardson.com

www.ingramcontent.com/pod-product-compliance
Lightning Source LLC
Chambersburg PA
CBHW030656120726
47905CB00001B/229